EVERYMAN'S LIBRARY

962

FICTION

Everyman, I will go with thee, and be thy guide,
In thy most need to go by thy side

THOMAS MANN, born at Lübeck 6th June 1875, son of Johann Heinrich Mann, went to school there and completed his education in Munich and Rome. Achieved European reputation as a writer in the early 1900's. Married 1905. Nobel Prize for literature 1929. Voluntarily exiled from Germany before the Nazi regime, first to Zürich, then to the U.S.A. Returned to Europe in 1953 and settled in Switzerland.

THOMAS MANN'S
STORIES AND EPISODES

INTRODUCTION BY
ERICH HELLER
Professor of German, University College, Swansea

LONDON J. M. DENT & SONS LTD

INTRODUCTION

IT IS a commonplace of literary judgment that modern German literature is, on its highest elevations, too problematical and speculative, and, on its more easily accessible levels, too provincially mediocre ever to gain as secure a place in the world of letters as that indisputably held by English, French, and Russian writers. There is, it is true, the monumental reputation of Goethe; but his work is more a landmark of the educated European mind than part of its familiar equipment, more a weighty document of humanity than frequently chosen reading matter. There is Hölderlin, hardly translatable, whose name is evoked, and often in vain, as marking the root of modern poetic rootlessness and the grand mystical home of the homelessness of the spirit. There is, of course, Rilke, Orpheus of the voiceless inner life and lyrical redeemer of the waste land of reality. And there is, finally, Kafka, worshipper in the god-deserted church of Europe, narrator of a common agony and land surveyor of the land without hope. Monumental classicism, spiritual uprootedness, lyrical mysticism, and the superb prose exploration of a pathological predicament—this, it seems, is all that the literary world, within its present scope of interest and general information, is prepared to acknowledge as the German contribution. It can hardly be regarded as the acknowledgment of a sound body of national literature.

Yet this national literature, beset by all manner of problems, and unsteadied by a stormy and altogether anomalous historical situation, does exist, and if, after all, something of its spirit has reached the contemporary world

outside Germany, this is due to the work of Thomas
Mann.   He is, as novelist and teller of stories in the
grand manner, the late heir of the central tradition of
modern German literature.   It may seem arbitrary to
look upon the nineteenth-century German novel and
Novelle as 'central,' and to say that, if there is a centre at
all, it is to be found in the *Bildungsroman*, the narrative
unfolding of the formation of characters, in such works as
Goethe's *Wilhelm Meister*, Gottfried Keller's *Der grüne
Heinrich*, and Stifter's *Nachsommer*, or in those shorter
works, enacted in what we have come to call a 'realistic
setting' and dominated by atmosphere, social conflict,
abrupt adventures of soul and mind or dramatic moral
decisions, works associated with the names of Jean Paul,
C. F. Meyer, Jeremias Gotthelf, Wilhelm Raabe, Storm,
and Fontane.   This arbitrary choice, however, can be
excused with the blatant absence of any central and
common dedication in the more spectacular employments
of German literary genius by poets and writers such as
Novalis, Kleist, E. T. A. Hoffmann, or Büchner.   If,
in addition, we agree that the period in question was the
age of the bourgeois, then we may be doubly justified in
regarding as central the literature of the *Bürger*—the
German word for bourgeois, which is yet so different in
its connotations from the more political and sociological
meaning of the French term.

Thomas Mann was born in 1875 at Lübeck.   In this
old and secluded city of the Hanseatic League the traditional forms and attitudes of bourgeois existence survived
with a higher degree of self-assurance and conservatism
than in many of the German or European metropolitan
centres.   Moreover, Thomas Mann's family belonged to
the merchant-patrician aristocracy of that city of medieval
gothic, commercial urbanity, sea-bound trade, Baltic
equanimity, inbred snobbery, and provincial crankiness.

The decay of this burgher community, and his own estrangement from it (partly ascribed to the blood inheritance from a southern exotic mother) were Thomas Mann's first inspiration. Lübeck was for him what Dublin was for James Joyce. Yet while Joyce soon acknowledged, through his very passion for literary experimentation, the end of a certain tradition, Thomas Mann remained even artistically a burgher. He too experimented, but his experiment consisted in the audacious attempt to remain a conservative artist in a revolutionary age, and to present in the *traditional* forms of novel and *Novelle* the dissolution of all established patterns of living. Where other writers pursued newly discovered complications of life with equally complicated mechanisms of style and form, especially constructed for the purpose, Thomas Mann simply knotted more tightly the old net of the story-teller. Compared, say, to Proust or James Joyce, his presentation of highly problematical matters presents hardly any literary problems.

This is in itself a highly ironical situation, and it is indeed irony that pervades the whole work of Thomas Mann. When in 1901 the very long novel *Buddenbrooks* appeared, its author was twenty-six. It was a time when a young writer was expected to join the *avant-garde*. Revolutionary literary manifestoes poured forth from the pages of the fashionable journals; everywhere new gestures of style and expression were rehearsed, campaigns were arranged for ultimate conquests of mind, soul, and 'reality,' agonies and triumphs were celebrated with cosmic, if somewhat breathless, trumpets. In the midst of this naturalist, symbolist, and expressionist turmoil there appeared a novel that showed the unmistakable imprint of a master in the peaceful art of literary manufacture from a period before the machines of the industrial revolution in literature had come into their own. Nobody would have guessed that it was written by a young man. Its epic detachment, steady tone of irony, unmilitant conciliatory psychology—*tout comprendre*, while the rebellious mood of the day was *ne rien pardonner*—and, above all, the fact that its writer obviously had the time and patience to produce a piece of exquisitely elaborate craftsmanship, seemed to point to a surprisingly vigorous survival from a past epoch. Yet after an initial resistance of the reading public the book was read, read indeed to the point of becoming, on this level of literary distinction, a unique and persistent best-seller, appealing alike to the sophisticated and the naïve. When she had finished reading the book, a woman artist from Munich said to Thomas Mann: 'I was not bored when I read your book, and with every page I read I was astonished that I was not bored.'

Why did she expect to be bored? Because *Buddenbrooks* seemed an old-fashioned book, the story, indeed the history, of a family of Lübeck merchants, of their rise, prosperity, and decay. Who cared? One knew the bourgeoisie was doomed, and its doom had long since ceased to be 'fascinating'; and as for Lübeck in its remote Baltic corner—'Where or what is Aberystwyth?' as Bernard Shaw is reported to have replied to an invitation of a students' debating society in the University College of Wales. And why was she, after all, not bored? Because Thomas Mann had succeeded in blending the apparently honest brew with the subtler intoxicants of *fin de siècle*. The Lübeck burgher world came to life in a literary medium that, in all its bourgeois realism, was conditioned by exceedingly modern ingredients. It was built according to a design of ideas provided by Schopenhauer's metaphysical pessimism, indeed the novel was fitted into it with such consummate skill that no trace of the abstract fabric was left uncovered. Wagner's music

too had obviously been assimilated into the writer's
artistry. He had learned from the composer-dramatist
not only the use of the *leit-motif*, but showed, by the very
inflexion of his sentences and the architecture of his
narrative, that he was steeped in a music in which psychological cunning, leisurely story-telling, and theatrical show-
manship combined in a singularly potent irritant affecting
the region between the nervous system and the soul.
Also Nietzsche's voice was discernible, the influence, not
of his apocalyptic prophecy, but of his ruthless psychology
exploding cherished bourgeois beliefs and illusions.

The contours of these radical minds, however, were
softened and mellowed in a mood of humour and contemplative melancholy that took the sadness of things and
the ridiculousness of human self-deception for granted
without ever sacrificing a pittance at least of charity and
affection to the grim grandeur of ultimate intellectual
consistency. Thomas Mann remained a burgher in his
determination to build a solid house on a metaphysically
condemned site, and to act as a moderator of the extremes
of knowledge. He was to play this role all his life,
sometimes incongruously to the point of intellectual embarrassment, but always with moving generosity.
'Dostoevsky—with Moderation' is the title of one of
his essays. In the course of his long career as *homme de
lettres*, he might have affixed this word to many more
names and things with whom he concerned himself:
not only to Schopenhauer, Wagner, and Nietzsche,
but also to Frederick the Great, Marx, Freud, German
nationalism, Western liberalism, and Eastern socialism,
indeed to Life, Spirit, and Art itself. With the one
exception which, to the lasting honour of German
literature, taught him absolute hatred—Hitler's dominion
—he has, amidst the discords of the European mind,
almost always played the part of the Lübeck merchant

* 962

senator, weighing arguments, testing qualities, and announcing the spirit's readiness to assimilate, moderate, and humanely negotiate.   There has always been, in the heat and dust of warring opposites, the immaculately white edge of the ironical handkerchief showing from the well-cut burgher jacket.

Buddenbrooks is a masterpiece of ironical realism, in its quiet epic way already foreshadowing the daring literary device of *Doctor Faustus*, published forty-eight years later (1949), where the last burgher in a Germany, then in the grips of the Apocalypse, is the bewildered, helplessly uncomprehending and yet strangely competent recorder of the most un-burgher-like occurrences on an extreme frontier, an uncanny meeting-place of Art, Thought, Politics, and Hell.   The same technique is employed in *The Holy Sinner* (1951), the short-story epilogue, in a humorous key, to *Doctor Faustus*, in which an Irish monk, apparently naïve and uninitiated, is the narrator of a story of sensual outrage, inscrutable doom, and complicated blessing.

Irony, with Thomas Mann, is not only an attitude of mind conveyed through ironical diction; it extends, decisively modifying it, into his chosen literary form. The fascination of his works is partly due to a fundamental incongruity, which is yet artistically mastered, between the story told and the manner of telling it.   From *Budden-brooks* to *Doctor Faustus* Thomas Mann has again and again excelled in wearing an outworn literary fashion with the persuasive assurance of one who seems sincerely convinced that it was modelled for the very need and taste of the hour.   If the result is parody, it is parody of rare distinction and significance.   It is at once creation and critique, high entertainment, and intellectual exploration —something like an attempt to realize the German Romantic expectation of *Universalpoesie*.   And it is, in

addition, the moral protest of the burgher, declared through
the preserved form itself, against those forces of life and
life experience that threaten with extinction the accustomed ways of living and literary pleasure: the moral
protest of *Tonio Kröger* (1903) against the artist's new
freedom sadly won from a society in which he lives as an
exile, a freedom that so easily deteriorates into *libertinage*,
cynicism, and irresponsible playfulness, or—as was to be
revealed later by the Adrian Leverkühn of *Doctor Faustus*
—to an alliance with the very powers of evil.

Perhaps it is *Death in Venice* (1911) that is Thomas
Mann's most successful experiment in incongruity and
in a mode of irony realized through the ironical juxta-
position of form and substance. These are, as it were,
at premeditated loggerheads. The author himself once
referred to this story as parody. In *Death in Venice* a
composition of great subtlety and classical order is used
to tell a most unclassical tale of disorder and decomposition.
And what irony—and here it is the irony of the moralist
—that conjures up, by means even of occasional Greek
hexameters and German lyricisms, the very religious
centres of the worship of beauty: classical antiquity and
the Venice of Romanticism, of Platen, of Richard
Wagner, in order to set against such memories the story
of an artist who falls a victim to the fatal ambiguity of the
Beautiful, dying a *Liebestod* before the backcloth of a sea
as blue as that of the Archipelago, but in the vicinity of a
plague-ridden city. Thomas Mann has produced greater
works than *Death in Venice*; but neither before nor after
has he achieved so complete a success with such economy,
and declared his artistic and moral purpose through an
example so perfectly executed and accomplished.

If Tonio Kröger, in the moralizing egotism of the
young artist, knew and deplored only his own separation
from 'Life,' and if *Death in Venice*, with still greater

intensity, points to the moral dubiousness of the artist's dedication to Form and Beauty, Thomas Mann soon realized the dangers that 'Life' incurred through its emancipation from a 'Spirit' that, with all its inclination towards adventure and disorderliness, remains at heart the spirit of order and humane sympathy. In *Buddenbrooks*, *Tonio Kröger*, and *Death in Venice* it was Art that was suspect, and placed under clinical observation by the artist-moralist, who felt almost like protecting Life in its innocent simplicity from the corroding artistic refinements. In the great novel *The Magic Mountain* (1924), Life itself, the body and mind of Europe, is seen to be diseased. This book, an outstanding achievement of modern European literature, is the ironical consummation of the genre *Bildungsroman*. While Goethe's Wilhelm and Keller's Heinrich set out on their life-journey as highly problematical natures, travelling through many a crisis towards increasing steadiness of character and acceptance of their place in a humane community, the hero of *The Magic Mountain* enters the story as an unproblematical, adequately 'adjusted' young man, and receives his unsteadying education at the hands of a society representative of the moral and intellectual chaos of modern Europe. He, too, in an exalted moment of his story, has a vision of the good life, but the vision remains a dream dreamt at the threshold of death in a mountain-desert of snow and ice, a dream without hope of ever coming true either amidst the eccentricities of his alpine 'pedagogical province' or down in the 'flatland' of bourgeois triviality. He, too, like the good hero of every *Bildungsroman*, finally accepts life again, but life is death on a battle-field of Flanders.

Mario and the Magician (1929) can now be seen as an essay in a mode of writing that was to be developed on the grandest scale in *Doctor Faustus*. Although it is, of course, a story in its own right, it is also political allegory, the highly individualized, indeed grotesque representation of a social cataclysm: of the subjugation of individual wills within an amorphous, hysterically abandoned society, 'on holiday' from its disciplined commitments, by the theatrically displayed vulgar will of a hypnotic *duce* and leader, and of the late, all too late and therefore inevitably catastrophic, rebellion of violated human dignity.

In *Doctor Faustus*, finally, Thomas Mann's persistently hostile protagonists, Life and Spirit, Society and Art, have come together at last—not, however, in the harmony of a good life, but in the unison of Hell. Both are doomed. In this extraordinary work—a work of old age, but ironically distinguished among Thomas Mann's productions by a youthful luxuriance of invention and composition that would normally suggest the storm and stress period of a writer—a musical Tonio Kröger, powerfully enhanced in stature and destiny, is no longer confronted by 'Life' in its lovable innocence, but by a life that, tired of its own blue-eyed banality, has 'spiritualized' itself and entered, like the artist himself, into an alliance with the demons of 'the deep that lieth under.'

Thomas Mann's most despairing book was, however, preceded by his most serene achievements: the *Joseph* tetralogy (1934–45) and the Goethe novel *Lotte in Weimar* (1940), products of an amazing combination of encyclopaedic knowledge, enduring inspiration, and eminent literary skill. In *Joseph*, moreover, Thomas Mann has succeeded in poetically realizing that hope of which *Doctor Faustus* despairs: the hope of a life that is no stranger to the spirit, and of a spirit that is no deserter from life. This biblical story of the dreamer and interpreter of dreams who, estranged from his crudely wakeful brothers, is reunited with them in their need as the provider of bread, has been re-told and vastly enlarged by

Thomas Mann with a poetic intelligence and graceful irony that, rainbow-like, spans the gulf between myth and psychology, between divine and human comedy. It is with his *Joseph*, above all, that Thomas Mann has risen to the rank of those writers whom Stendhal praises as the most excellent for 'kindling that delicious smile which is a sign of intellectual pleasure.'

ERICH HELLER

1954

BIBLIOGRAPHICAL NOTE

The following is a list of the principal works of Thomas Mann which are available in English translations. Unless otherwise stated, the translator is Mrs H. T. Lowe-Porter. The English publishers of Thomas Mann's works are Messrs Martin Secker and Warburg, London. The dates given in the Introduction refer to the German originals, those listed below to the time of English publication.

NOVELS AND LONGER STORIES

Royal Highness, trans. by A. Cecil Curtis, 1916, 1940; *Buddenbrooks*, 1924; *The Magic Mountain*, 1927; *Early Sorrow and Mario and the Magician*, 1934; *The Tales of Jacob*, 1934; *Young Joseph*, 1935; *Joseph in Egypt*, 1938; *Joseph the Provider*, 1945; *Lotte in Weimar*, 1940; *The Transposed Heads*, 1941; *Doctor Faustus*, 1949; *The Holy Sinner*, 1952; *The Black Swan* (trans. by Willard R. Trask), 1954.

COLLECTIONS OF STORIES

Children and Fools, trans. by H. G. Scheffauer, 1928.
Stories of Three Decades, 1936:
    Contents:
        Little Herr Friedemann (1897)
        Disillusionment (1896)

The Dilettante (1897)
Tobias Mindernickel (1897)
Little Lizzy (1897)
The Wardrobe (1899)
The Way to the Churchyard (1901)
Tonio Kröger (1903)
Tristan (1902)
The Hungry (1902)
The Infant Prodigy (1903)
Gladius Dei (1902)
Fiorenza (1904)
A Gleam (1904)
At the Prophet's (1904)
A Weary Hour (1905)
The Blood of the Walsungs (1905)
Railway Accident (1907)
The Fight between Jappe and Do Escobar (1911)
Felix Krull (1911)
Death in Venice (1911)
A Man and His Dog (1918)
Disorder and Early Sorrow (1925)
Mario and the Magician (1929)

COLLECTIONS OF ESSAYS

Three Essays, 1932 (containing 'Goethe and Tolstoi,' 'Frederick the Great,' 'An Experience in the Occult'); *Past Masters and Other Papers,* 1933; *Order of the Day,* 1942, trans. by H. T. Lowe-Porter, Eric Sutton, and Agnes E. Meyer.

Essays of Three Decades, 1947:
    Contents:
        Goethe's *Faust* (1938)
        Goethe's Career as a Man of Letters (1932)
        Goethe as Representative of the Bourgeois Age (1932)
        Anna Karenina (1939)
        Lessing (1929)
        Kleist's *Amphitryon* (1926)
        Chamisso (1911)
        Platen (1930)

Theodor Storm (1930)
The Old Fontane (1910)
Sufferings and Greatness of Richard Wagner (1933)
Richard Wagner and the *Ring* (1937)
Schopenhauer (1938)
Freud and the Future (1936)
Voyage with Don Quixote (1934)

See J. Cleugh: *Thomas Mann. A Study*, 1933; J. G. Brennan: *Thomas Mann's World*, 1942; F. Lion: *Thomas Mann*, 1946.

CONTENTS

This volume is published through the courtesy of the author and Martin Secker and Warburg

TONIO KRÖGER

The winter sun, poor ghost of itself, hung milky and wan behind layers of cloud above the huddled roofs of the town. In the gabled streets it was wet and windy, and there came in gusts a sort of soft hail, not ice, not snow.

School was out. The hosts of the released streamed over the paved court and out at the wrought-iron gate, where they broke up and hastened off right and left. Elder pupils held their books in a strap high on the left shoulder and rowed, right arm against the wind, towards dinner. Small people trotted gaily off, splashing the slush with their feet, the tools of learning rattling amain in their walrus-skin satchels. But one and all pulled off their caps and cast down their eyes in awe before the Olympian hat and ambrosial beard of a master moving homewards with measured stride. . . .

'Ah, there you are at last, Hans,' said Tonio Kröger. He had been waiting a long time in the street and went up with a smile to the friend he saw coming out of the gate in talk with other boys and about to go off with them. . . . 'What?' said Hans, and looked at Tonio. 'Right-oh! We'll take a little walk, then.'

Tonio said nothing and his eyes were clouded. Did Hans forget, had he only just remembered that they were to take a walk together to-day? And he himself had looked forward to it with almost incessant joy.

'Well, good-bye, fellows,' said Hans Hansen to his comrades. 'I'm taking a walk with Kröger.' And the two turned to their left, while the others sauntered off in the opposite direction.

Hans and Tonio had time to take a walk after school because in neither of their families was dinner served before four o'clock. Their fathers were prominent business men, who held public office and were of consequence in the town. Hans's people had owned for some generations the big wood yards down by the river, where powerful machine saws hissed and spat and cut up timber; while Tonio was the son of Consul Kröger, whose grain sacks with the firm name in great black letters you might see any day driven through the streets; his large, old ancestral home was the finest house in all the town. The two friends had to keep taking off their hats to their many acquaintances; some folk did not even wait for the fourteen-year-old lads to speak first, as by rights they should.

Both of them carried their satchels across their shoulders and both were well and warmly dressed: Hans in a short sailor jacket, with the wide blue collar of his sailor suit turned out over shoulders and back, and Tonio in a belted grey overcoat. Hans wore a Danish sailor cap with black ribbons, beneath which streamed a shock of straw-coloured hair. He was uncommonly handsome and well built, broad in the shoulders and narrow in the hips, with keen, far-apart, steel-blue eyes; while beneath Tonio's round fur cap was a brunette face with the finely chiselled features of the south; the dark eyes, with delicate shadows and too heavy lids, looked dreamily and a little timorously on the world. Tonio's walk was idle and uneven, whereas the other's slim legs in their black stockings moved with an elastic, rhythmic tread.

Tonio did not speak. He suffered. His rather oblique brows were drawn together in a frown, his lips were rounded to whistle, he gazed into space with his head on one side. Posture and manner were habitual.

Suddenly Hans shoved his arm into Tonio's, with a sideways look—he knew very well what the trouble was.

And Tonio, though he was silent for the next few steps, felt his heart soften.

'I hadn't forgotten, you see, Tonio,' Hans said, gazing at the pavement, 'I only thought it wouldn't come off to-day because it was so wet and windy. But I don't mind that at all, and it's jolly of you to have waited. I thought you had gone home, and I was cross. . . .'

Everything in Tonio leaped and jumped for joy at the words.

'All right; let's go over the wall,' he said with a quaver in his voice. 'Over the Mill Wall and the Holsten Wall, and I'll go as far as your house with you, Hans. Then I'll have to walk back alone, but that doesn't matter; next time you can go round my way.'

At bottom he was not really convinced by what Hans said; he quite knew the other attached less importance to this walk than he did himself. Yet he saw Hans was sorry for his remissness and willing to be put in a position to ask pardon, a pardon that Tonio was far indeed from withholding.

The truth was, Tonio loved Hans Hansen, and had already suffered much on his account. He who loves the more is the inferior and must suffer; in this hard and simple fact his fourteen-year-old soul had already been instructed by life; and he was so organized that he received such experiences consciously, wrote them down as it were inwardly, and even, in a certain way, took pleasure in them, though without ever letting them mould his conduct, indeed, or drawing any practical advantage from them. Being what he was, he found this know-ledge far more important and far more interesting than the sort they made him learn in school; yes, during his lesson hours in the vaulted Gothic classrooms he was mainly occupied in feeling his way about among these intuitions of his and penetrating them. The process

gave him the same kind of satisfaction as that he felt
when he moved about in his room with his violin—for
he played the violin—and made the tones, brought out
as softly as ever he knew how, mingle with the plashing
of the fountain that leaped and danced down there in the
garden beneath the branches of the old walnut-tree.

The fountain, the old walnut-tree, his fiddle, and away
in the distance the North Sea, within sound of whose
summer murmurings he spent his holidays—these were
the things he loved, within these he enfolded his spirit,
among these things his inner life took its course. And
they were all things whose names were effective in verse
and occurred pretty frequently in the lines Tonio Kröger
sometimes wrote.

The fact that he had a note-book full of such things,
written by himself, leaked out through his own carelessness and injured him no little with the masters as well as
among his fellows. On the one hand, Consul Kröger's
son found their attitude both cheap and silly, and despised
his schoolmates and his masters as well, and in his turn
(with extraordinary penetration) saw through and disliked
their personal weaknesses and bad breeding. But then,
on the other hand, he himself felt his verse-making extravagant and out of place and to a certain extent agreed
with those who considered it an unpleasing occupation.
But that did not enable him to leave off.

As he wasted his time at home, was slow and absent-
minded at school, and always had bad marks from the
masters, he was in the habit of bringing home pitifully
poor reports, which troubled and angered his father, a
tall, fastidiously dressed man, with thoughtful blue eyes,
and always a wild flower in his buttonhole. But for his
mother, she cared nothing about the reports—Tonio's
beautiful black-haired mother, whose name was Consuelo,
and who was so absolutely different from the other ladies

in the town, because father had brought her long ago from some place far down on the map.

Tonio loved his dark, fiery mother, who played the piano and mandolin so wonderfully, and he was glad his doubtful standing among men did not distress her. Though at the same time he found his father's annoyance a more dignified and respectable attitude, and despite his scoldings understood him very well, whereas his mother's blithe indifference always seemed just a little wanton. His thoughts at times would run something like this: 'It is true enough that I am what I am and will not and cannot alter: heedless, self-willed, with my mind on things nobody else thinks of. And so it is right they should scold and punish me and not smother things all up with kisses and music. After all, we are not gipsies living in a green wagon; we're respectable people, the family of Consul Kröger.' And not seldom he would think: 'Why is it I am different, why do I fight everything, why am I at odds with the masters and like a stranger among the other boys? The good scholars, and the solid majority—they don't find the masters funny, they don't write verses, their thoughts are all about things that people do think about and can talk about out loud. How regular and comfortable they must feel, knowing that everybody knows just where they stand! It must be nice! But what is the matter with me, and what will be the end of it all?'

These thoughts about himself and his relation to life played an important part in Tonio's love for Hans Hansen. He loved him in the first place because he was handsome; but in the next because he was in every respect his own opposite and foil. Hans Hansen was a capital scholar, and a jolly chap to boot, who was head at drill, rode and swam to perfection, and lived in the sunshine of popularity. The masters were almost tender with him, they called

him Hans and were partial to him in every way; the other
pupils curried favour with him; even grown people stopped
him on the street, twitched the shock of hair beneath his
Danish sailor cap, and said: 'Ah, here you are, Hans
Hansen, with your pretty blond hair! Still head of the
school? Remember me to your father and mother,
that's a fine lad!'

Such was Hans Hansen; and ever since Tonio Kröger
had known him, from the very minute he set eyes on him,
he had burned inwardly with a heavy, envious longing.
'Who else has blue eyes like yours, or lives in such
friendliness and harmony with all the world? You are
always spending your time in some right and proper
occupation. When you have done your prep. you take
your riding lesson, or make things with a fret-saw; even
in the holidays, at the seashore, you row and sail and
swim all the time, while I wander off somewhere and lie
down in the sand and stare at the strange and mysterious
changes that whisk over the face of the sea. And all that
is why your eyes are so clear. To be like you . . .'

He made no attempt to be like Hans Hansen, and
perhaps hardly even seriously wanted to. What he did
ardently, painfully want was that just as he was, Hans
Hansen should love him; and he wooed Hans Hansen in
his own way, deeply, lingeringly, devotedly, with a melancholy that gnawed and burned more terribly than all the
sudden passion one might have expected from his exotic
looks.

And he wooed not in vain. Hans respected Tonio's
superior power of putting certain difficult matters into
words; moreover, he felt the lively presence of an uncommonly strong and tender feeling for himself; he was
grateful for it, and his response gave Tonio much happiness—though also many pangs of jealousy and disillusion
over his futile efforts to establish a communion of spirit

between them.   For the queer thing was that Tonio, who after all envied Hans Hansen for being what he was, still kept on trying to draw him over to his own side; though of course he could succeed in this at most only at moments and superficially. . . .

'I have just been reading something so wonderful and splendid . . .' he said.   They were walking and eating together out of a bag of fruit toffees they had bought at Iverson's sweet shop in Mill Street for ten pfennigs. 'You must read it, Hans, it is Schiller's *Don Carlos*. . . . I 'll lend it to you if you like. . . .'

'Oh, no,' said Hans Hansen, 'you needn't, Tonio, that 's not anything for me.   I 'll stick to my horse books. There are wonderful cuts in them, let me tell you.   I 'll show them to you when you come to see me.   They are instantaneous photography—the horse in motion; you can see him trot and canter and jump, in all positions, that you never can get to see in real life, because they happen so fast. . . .'

'In all positions?' asked Tonio politely.   'Yes, that must be great.   But about *Don Carlos*—it is beyond anything you could possibly dream of.   There are places in it that are so lovely they make you jump . . . as though it were an explosion——'

'An explosion?' asked Hans Hansen.   'What sort of an explosion?'

'For instance, the place where the king has been crying because the marquis betrayed him . . . but the marquis did it only out of love for the prince, you see, he sacrifices himself for his sake.   And the word comes out of the cabinet into the antechamber that the king has been weeping.   "Weeping?   The king been weeping?"   All the courtiers are fearfully upset, it goes through and through you, for the king has always been so frightfully stiff and stern.   But it is so easy to understand why he cried, and I feel sorrier for him than for the prince and the marquis put together. He is always so alone, nobody loves him, and then he thinks he has found one man, and then *he* betrays him. . . .'

Hans Hansen looked sideways into Tonio's face, and something in it must have won him to the subject, for suddenly he shoved his arm once more into Tonio's, and said:

'How had he betrayed him, Tonio?'

Tonio went on.

'Well,' he said, 'you see, all the letters for Brabant and Flanders——'

'There comes Irwin Immerthal,' said Hans.

Tonio stopped talking. If only the earth would open and swallow Immerthal up! 'Why does he have to come disturbing us? If he only doesn't go with us all the way and talk about the riding lessons!' For Irwin Immerthal had riding lessons too. He was the son of the bank president and lived close by, outside the city wall. He had already been home and left his bag, and now he walked towards them through the avenue. His legs were crooked and his eyes like slits.

"Lo, Immerthal,' said Hans. 'I 'm taking a little walk with Kröger. . . .'

'I have to go into town on an errand,' said Immerthal. 'But I 'll walk a little way with you. Are those fruit toffees you 've got? Thanks, I 'll have a couple. To-morrow we have our next lesson, Hans.' He meant the riding lessons.

'What larks!' said Hans. 'I 'm going to get the leather gaiters for a present, because I was top lately in our papers.'

'You don't take riding lessons, I suppose, Kröger?' asked Immerthal, and his eyes were only two gleaming cracks.

'No . . .' answered Tonio, uncertainly.

'You ought to ask your father,' Hans Hansen remarked, 'so you could have lessons too, Kröger.'

'Yes . . .' said Tonio. He spoke hastily and without interest; his throat had suddenly contracted, because Hans had called him by his last name. Hans seemed conscious of it too, for he said by way of explanation: 'I call you Kröger because your first name is so crazy. Don't mind my saying so, I can't do with it all. Tonio—why, what sort of name is that? Though of course I know it's not your fault in the least.'

'No, they probably called you that because it sounds so foreign and sort of something special,' said Immerthal, obviously with intent to say just the right thing.

Tonio's mouth twitched. He pulled himself together and said:

'Yes, it's a silly name—Lord knows I'd rather be called Heinrich or Wilhelm. It's all because I'm named after my mother's brother Antonio. She comes from down there, you know . . .'

There he stopped and let the others have their say about horses and saddles. Hans had taken Immerthal's arm; he talked with a fluency that *Don Carlos* could never have roused in him. . . . Tonio felt a mounting desire to weep pricking his nose from time to time; he had hard work to control the trembling of his lips.

Hans could not stand his name—what was to be done? He himself was called Hans, and Immerthal was called Irwin; two good, sound, familiar names, offensive to nobody. And Tonio was foreign and queer. Yes, there was always something queer about him, whether he would or no, and he was alone, the regular and usual would none of him; although after all he was no gipsy in a green wagon, but the son of Consul Kröger, a member of the Kröger family. But why did Hans call him Tonio as long as they were alone and then feel ashamed as soon as anybody else was by? Just now he had won him over, they had been close together, he was sure. 'How had he betrayed him, Tonio?' Hans asked, and took his arm. But he had breathed easier directly Immerthal came up, he had dropped him like a shot, even gratuitously taunted him with his outlandish name. How it hurt to have to see through all this! . . . Hans Hansen did like him a little, when they were alone, that he knew. But let a third person come, he was ashamed, and offered up his friend. And again he was alone. He thought of King Philip. The king had wept. . . .

'Goodness, I have to go,' said Irwin Immerthal. 'Good-bye, and thanks for the toffee.' He jumped upon a bench that stood by the way, ran along it with his crooked legs, jumped down, and trotted off.

'I like Immerthal,' said Hans, with emphasis. He had a spoilt and arbitrary way of announcing his likes and dislikes, as though graciously pleased to confer them like an order on this person and that. . . . He went on talking about the riding lessons where he had left off. Anyhow, it was not very much farther to his house; the walk over the walls was not a long one. They held their caps and bent their heads before the strong, damp wind that rattled and groaned in the leafless trees. And Hans Hansen went on talking, Tonio throwing in a forced yes or no from time to time. Hans talked eagerly, had taken his arm again; but the contact gave Tonio no pleasure. The nearness was only apparent, not real; it meant nothing. . . .

They struck away from the walls close to the station, where they saw a train puff busily past, idly counted the coaches, and waved to the man who was perched on top of the last one bundled in a leather coat. They stopped in front of the Hansen villa on the Lindenplatz, and Hans

went into detail about what fun it was to stand on the
bottom rail of the garden gate and let it swing on its creaking hinges.   After that they said good-bye.

'I must go in now,' said Hans.   'Good-bye, Tonio.
Next time I 'll take you home, see if I don't.'

'Good-bye, Hans,' said Tonio.   'It was a nice walk.'

They put out their hands, all wet and rusty from the
garden gate.   But as Hans looked into Tonio's eyes, he
bethought himself, a look of remorse came over his
charming face.

'And I 'll read *Don Carlos* pretty soon, too,' he said
quickly.   'That bit about the king in his cabinet must
be nuts.'   Then he took his bag under his arm and ran
off through the front garden.   Before he disappeared he
turned and nodded once more.

And Tonio went off as though on wings.   The wind
was at his back; but it was not the wind alone that bore
him along so lightly.

Hans would read *Don Carlos*, and then they would have
something to talk about, and neither Irwin Immerthal nor
another could join in.   How well they understood each
other!   Perhaps—who knew?—some day he might even
get Hans to write poetry! . . . No, no, that he did not
ask.   Hans must not become like Tonio, he must stop
just as he was, so strong and bright, everybody loved him
as he was, and Tonio most of all.   But it would do him
no harm to read *Don Carlos*. . . . Tonio passed under
the squat old city gate, along by the harbour, and up the
steep, wet, windy, gabled street to his parents' house.
His heart beat richly: longing was awake in it, and a
gentle envy; a faint contempt, and no little innocent bliss.

Ingeborg Holm, blonde little Inge, the daughter of
Dr Holm, who lived on Market Square opposite the
tall old Gothic fountain with its manifold spires—she

it was Tonio Kröger loved when he was sixteen years old.

Strange how things come about! He had seen her a thousand times; then one evening he saw her again; saw her in a certain light, talking with a friend in a certain saucy way, laughing and tossing her head; saw her lift her arm and smooth her back hair with her schoolgirl hand, that was by no means particularly fine or slender, in such a way that the thin white sleeve slipped down from her elbow; heard her speak a word or two, a quite indifferent phrase, but with a certain intonation, with a warm ring in her voice; and his heart throbbed with ecstasy, far stronger than that he had once felt when he looked at Hans Hansen long ago, when he was still a little, stupid boy.

That evening he carried away her picture in his eyes: the thick blond plait, the longish, laughing blue eyes, the saddle of pale freckles across the nose. He could not go to sleep for hearing that ring in her voice; he tried in a whisper to imitate the tone in which she had uttered the commonplace phrase, and felt a shiver run through and through him. He knew by experience that this was love. And he was accurately aware that love would surely bring him much pain, affliction, and sadness, that it would certainly destroy his peace, filling his heart to overflowing with melodies which would be no good to him because he would never have the time or tranquillity to give them permanent form. Yet he received this love with joy, surrendered himself to it, and cherished it with all the strength of his being; for he knew that love made one vital and rich, and he longed to be vital and rich, far more than he did to work tranquilly on anything to give it permanent form.

Tonio Kröger fell in love with merry Ingeborg Holm in Frau Consul Hustede's drawing-room on the evening

when it was emptied of furniture for the weekly dancing
class.   It was a private class, attended only by members of
the first families; it met by turns in the various parental
houses to receive instruction from Knaak, the dancing-
master, who came from Hamburg expressly for the
purpose.

François Knaak was his name, and what a man he was!
'J'ai l'honneur de me vous représenter,' he would say, 'mon
nom est Knaak. . . . This is not said during the bowing,
but after you have finished and are standing up straight
again.   In a low voice, but distinctly.   Of course one
does not need to introduce oneself in French every day
in the week, but if you can do it correctly and faultlessly
in French you are not likely to make a mistake when you
do it in German.'   How marvellously the silky black
frock coat fitted his chubby hips!   His trouser legs fell down
in soft folds upon his patent leather pumps with their
wide satin bows, and his brown eyes glanced about him
with languid pleasure in their own beauty.

All this excess of self-confidence and good form was
positively overpowering.   He went trippingly—and nobody tripped like him, so elastically, so weavingly, rock-
ingly, royally—up to the mistress of the house, made a
bow, waited for a hand to be put forth.   This vouchsafed,
he gave murmurous voice to his gratitude, stepped buoy-
antly back, turned on his left foot, swiftly drawing the
right one backwards on its toe-tip, and moved away,
with his hips shaking.

When you took leave of company you must go backwards out at the door; when you fetched a chair, you
were not to shove it along the floor or clutch it by one
leg; but gently, by the back, and set it down without a
sound.   When you stood, you were not to fold your hands
on your tummy or seek with your tongue the corners of
your mouth.   If you did, Herr Knaak had a way of

showing you how it looked that filled you with disgust for that particular gesture all the rest of your life.

This was deportment. As for dancing, Herr Knaak was, if possible, even more of a master at that. The salon was emptied of furniture and lighted by a gas chandelier in the middle of the ceiling and candles on the mantelshelf. The floor was strewn with talc, and the pupils stood about in a dumb semicircle. But in the next room, behind the portières, mothers and aunts sat on plush-upholstered chairs and watched Herr Knaak through their lorgnettes, as in little springs and hops, curtsying slightly, the hem of his frock coat held up on each side by two fingers, he demonstrated the single steps of the mazurka. When he wanted to dazzle his audience completely he would suddenly and unexpectedly spring from the ground, whirling his two legs about each other with bewildering swiftness in the air, as it were trilling with them, and then, with a subdued bump, which nevertheless shook everything within him to its depths, returned to earth.

'What an unmentionable monkey!' thought Tonio Kröger to himself. But he saw the absorbed smile on jolly little Inge's face as she followed Herr Knaak's movements; and that, though not that alone, roused in him something like admiration of all this wonderfully controlled corporeality. How tranquil, how imperturbable was Herr Knaak's gaze! His eyes did not plumb the depth of things to the place where life becomes complex and melancholy; they knew nothing save that they were beautiful brown eyes. But that was just why his bearing was so proud. To be able to walk like that, one must be stupid; then one was loved, then one was lovable. He could so well understand how it was that Inge, blonde, sweet little Inge, looked at Herr Knaak as she did. But would a girl never look at him like that?

Oh, yes, there would, and did. For instance, Magdalena Vermehren, Attorney Vermehren's daughter, with the gentle mouth and the great, dark, brilliant eyes, so serious and adoring. She often fell down in the dance; but when it was 'ladies' choice' she came up to him; she knew he wrote verses and twice she had asked him to show them to her. She often sat at a distance, with drooping head, and gazed at him. He did not care. It was Inge he loved, blonde, jolly Inge, who most assuredly despised him for his poetic effusions . . . he looked at her, looked at her narrow blue eyes full of fun and mockery, and felt an envious longing; to be shut away from her like this, to be for ever strange—he felt it in his breast, like a heavy, burning weight.

'First couple *en avant*,' said Herr Knaak; and no words can tell how marvellously he pronounced the nasal. They were to practise the quadrille, and to Tonio Kröger's profound alarm he found himself in the same set with Inge Holm. He avoided her where he could, yet somehow was for ever near her; kept his eyes away from her person and yet found his gaze ever on her. There she came, tripping up hand in hand with red-headed Ferdinand Matthiessen; she flung back her braid, drew a deep breath, and took her place opposite Tonio. Herr Heinzelmann, at the piano, laid bony hands upon the keys, Herr Knaak waved his arm, the quadrille began.

She moved to and fro before his eyes, forwards and back, pacing and swinging; he seemed to catch a fragrance from her hair or the folds of her thin white frock, and his eyes grew sadder and sadder. 'I love you, dear, sweet Inge,' he said to himself, and put into his words all the pain he felt to see her so intent upon the dance with not a thought of him. Some lines of an exquisite poem by Storm came into his mind; 'I would sleep, but thou must dance.' It seemed against all sense, and most

depressing, that he must be dancing when he was in
love. . . .

'First couple *en avant*,' said Herr Knaak; it was the
next figure. '*Compliment! Moulinet des dames! Tour
de main!*' and he swallowed the silent *e* in the '*de*,' with
quite indescribable ease and grace.

'Second couple *en avant!*' This was Tonio Kröger
and his partner. '*Compliment!*' And Tonio Kröger
bowed. '*Moulinet des dames!*' And Tonio Kröger
with bent head and gloomy brows, laid his hand on those
of the four ladies, on Ingeborg Holm's hand, and danced
the *moulinet*.

Round about rose a tittering and laughing. Herr
Knaak took a ballet pose conventionally expressive of
horror. 'Oh, dear! Oh, dear!' he cried. 'Stop!
Stop! Kröger among the ladies! *En arrière*, Fräulein
Kröger, step back, *fi donc!* Everybody else understood
it but you. Shoo! Get out! Get away!' He drew
out his yellow silk handkerchief and flapped Tonio
Kröger back to his place.

Every one laughed, the girls and the boys and the
ladies beyond the portières; Herr Knaak had made something too utterly funny out of the little episode, it was as
amusing as a play. But Herr Heinzelmann at the piano
sat and waited, with a dry, business-like air, for a sign to
go on; he was hardened against Herr Knaak's effects.

Then the quadrille went on. And the intermission
followed. The parlourmaid came clinking in with a
tray of wine-jelly glasses, the cook followed in her wake
with a load of plum cake. But Tonio Kröger stole
away. He stole out into the corridor and stood there,
his hands behind his back, in front of a window with the
blind down. He never thought that one could not see
through the blind and that it was absurd to stand there as
though one were looking out.

For he was looking within, into himself, the theatre of so much pain and longing. Why, why was he here? Why was he not sitting by the window in his own room, reading Storm's *Immensee* and lifting his eyes to the twilight garden outside, where the old walnut-tree moaned? That was the place for him! Others might dance, others bend their fresh and lively minds upon the pleasure in hand! . . . But no, no, after all, his place was here, where he could feel near Inge, even although he stood lonely and aloof, seeking to distinguish the warm notes of her voice amid the buzzing, clattering, and laughter within. Oh, lovely Inge, blonde Inge of the narrow, laughing blue eyes! So lovely and laughing as you are one can only be if one does not read *Immensee* and never tries to write things like it. And that was just the tragedy!

Ah, she *must* come! She *must* notice where he had gone, must feel how he suffered! She must slip out to him, even pity must bring her, to lay her hand on his shoulder and say: 'Do come back to us, ah, don't be sad—I love you, Tonio.' He listened behind him and waited in frantic suspense. But she came not at all. Such things did not happen on this earth.

Had she laughed at him too, like all the others? Yes, she had, however gladly he would have denied it for both their sakes. And yet it was only because he had been so taken up with her that he had danced the *moulinet des dames*. Suppose he had—what did that matter? Had not a magazine accepted a poem of his a little while ago—even though the magazine had failed before his poem could be printed? The day was coming when he would be famous, when they would print everything he wrote; and *then* he would see if that made any impression on Inge Holm! No, it would make no impression at all; that was just it. Magdalena Vermehren, who was always falling down in the dances, yes, she would be impressed. But never Ingeborg Holm, never blue-eyed, laughing Inge. So what was the good of it?

Tonio Kröger's heart contracted painfully at the thought. To feel stirring within you the wonderful and melancholy play of strange forces and to be aware that those others you yearn for are blithely inaccessible to all that moves you—what a pain is this! And yet! He stood there aloof and alone, staring hopelessly at a drawn blind and making, in his distraction, as though he could look out. But yet he was happy. For he lived. His heart was full; hotly and sadly it beat for thee, Ingeborg Holm, and his soul embraced thy blonde, simple, pert, commonplace little personality in blissful self-abnegation.

Often after that he stood thus, with burning cheeks, in lonely corners, whither the sound of the music, the tinkling of glasses and fragrance of flowers came but faintly, and tried to distinguish the ringing tones of thy voice amid the distant happy din; stood suffering for thee—and still was happy! Often it angered him to think that he might talk with Magdalena Vermehren, who always fell down in the dance. She understood him, she laughed or was serious in the right places; while Inge the fair, let him sit never so near her, seemed remote and estranged, his speech not being her speech. And still—he was happy. For happiness, he told himself, is not in being loved—which is a satisfaction of the vanity and mingled with disgust. Happiness is in loving, and perhaps in snatching fugitive little approaches to the beloved object. And he took inward note of this thought, wrote it down in his mind; followed out all its implications and felt it to the depths of his soul.

'Faithfulness,' thought Tonio Kröger. 'Yes, I will be faithful, I will love thee, Ingeborg, as long as I live!'

He said this in the honesty of his intentions. And yet a still, small voice whispered misgivings in his ear: after all, he had forgotten Hans Hansen utterly, even though he saw him every day! And the hateful, the pitiable fact was that this still, small, rather spiteful voice was right: time passed and the day came when Tonio Kröger was no longer so unconditionally ready as once he had been to die for the lively Inge, because he felt in himself desires and powers to accomplish in his own way a host of wonderful things in this world.

And he circled with watchful eye the sacrificial altar, where flickered the pure, chaste flame of his love; knelt before it and tended and cherished it in every way, because he so wanted to be faithful. And in a little while, unobservedly, without sensation or stir, it went out after all.

But Tonio Kröger still stood before the cold altar, full of regret and dismay at the fact that faithfulness was impossible upon this earth. Then he shrugged his shoulders and went his way.

He went the way that go he must, a little idly, a little irregularly, whistling to himself, gazing into space with his head on one side; and if he went wrong it was because for some people there is no such thing as a right way. Asked what in the world he meant to become, he gave various answers, for he was used to say (and had even already written it) that he bore within himself the possibility of a thousand ways of life, together with the private conviction that they were all sheer impossibilities.

Even before he left the narrow streets of his native city, the threads that bound him to it had gently loosened. The old Kröger family gradually declined, and some people quite rightly considered Tonio Kröger's own existence and way of life as one of the signs of decay. His father's mother, the head of the family, had died, and not long after his own father followed, the tall,

thoughtful, carefully dressed gentleman with the field
flower in his buttonhole. The great Kröger house,
with all its stately tradition, came up for sale, and the
firm was dissolved. Tonio's mother, his beautiful, fiery
mother, who played the piano and mandolin so wonderfully and to whom nothing mattered at all, she married
again after a year's time; married a musician, moreover, a
virtuoso with an Italian name, and went away with him
into remote blue distances. Tonio Kröger found this
a little irregular, but who was he to call her to order,
who wrote poetry himself and could not even give an
answer when asked what he meant to do in life?

And so he left his native town and its tortuous, gabled
streets with the damp wind whistling through them; left
the fountain in the garden and the ancient walnut-tree,
familiar friends of his youth; left the sea too, that he loved
so much, and felt no pain to go. For he was grown up
and sensible and had come to realize how things stood
with him; he looked down on the lowly and vulgar life
he had led so long in these surroundings.

He surrendered utterly to the power that to him
seemed the highest on earth, to whose service he felt called,
which promised him elevation and honours; the power
of intellect, the power of the Word, that lords it with a
smile over the unconscious and inarticulate. To this
power he surrendered with all the passion of youth, and
it rewarded him with all it had to give, taking from him
inexorably, in return, all that it is wont to take.

It sharpened his eyes and made him see through the
large words which puff out the bosoms of mankind; it
opened for him men's souls and his own, made him clair-
voyant, showed him the inwardness of the world and
the ultimate behind men's words and deeds. And all
that he saw could be put in two words: the comedy and
the tragedy of life.

And then, with knowledge, its torment and its arrogance, came solitude; because he could not endure the blithe and innocent with their darkened understanding, while they in turn were troubled by the sign on his brow. But his love of the word kept growing sweeter and sweeter, and his love of form; for he used to say (and had already said it in writing) that knowledge of the soul would unfailingly make us melancholy if the pleasures of expression did not keep us alert and of good cheer.

He lived in large cities and in the south, promising himself a luxuriant ripening of his art by southern suns; perhaps it was the blood of his mother's race that drew him thither. But his heart being dead and loveless, he fell into adventures of the flesh, descended into the depths of lust and searing sin, and suffered unspeakably thereby. It might have been his father in him, that tall, thoughtful, fastidiously dressed man with the wild flower in his button-hole, that made him suffer so down there in the south; now and again he would feel a faint, yearning memory of a certain joy that was of the soul; once it had been his own, but now, in all his joys, he could not find it again.

Then he would be seized with disgust and hatred of the senses; pant after purity and seemly peace, while still he breathed the air of art, the tepid, sweet air of permanent spring, heavy with fragrance where it breeds and brews and burgeons in the mysterious bliss of creation. So for all result he was flung to and fro for ever between two crass extremes: between icy intellect and scorching sense, and what with his pangs of conscience led an exhausting life, rare, extraordinary, excessive, which at bottom he, Tonio Kröger, despised. 'What a labyrinth!' he sometimes thought. 'How could I possibly have got into all these fantastic adventures? As though I had a wagonful of travelling gipsies for my ancestors!'

But as his health suffered from these excesses, so his

artistry was sharpened; it grew fastidious, precious, *raffiné*, morbidly sensitive in questions of tact and taste, rasped by the banal.   His first appearance in print elicited much applause; there was joy among the elect, for it was a good and workmanlike performance, full of humour and acquaintance with pain.   In no long time his name— the same by which his masters had reproached him, the same he had signed to his earliest verses on the walnut-tree and the fountain and the sea, those syllables compact of the north and the south, that good middle-class name with the exotic twist to it—became a synonym for excellence; for the painful thoroughness of the experiences he had gone through, combined with a tenacious ambition and a persistent industry, joined battle with the irritable fastidiousness of his taste and under grinding torments issued in work of a quality quite uncommon.

He worked, not like a man who works that he may live; but as one who is bent on doing nothing but work; having no regard for himself as a human being but only as a creator; moving about grey and unobtrusive among his fellows like an actor without his make-up, who counts for nothing as soon as he stops representing something else.   He worked withdrawn out of sight and sound of the small fry, for whom he felt nothing but contempt, because to them a talent was a social asset like another; who, whether they were poor or not, went about ostentatiously shabby or else flaunted startling cravats, all the time taking jolly good care to amuse themselves, to be artistic and charming without the smallest notion of the fact that good work only comes out under pressure of a bad life; that he who lives does not work; that one must die to life in order to be utterly a creator.

'Shall I disturb you?' asked Tonio Kröger on the threshold of the atelier.   He held his hat in his hand and bowed with some ceremony, although Lisabeta Ivanovna was a good friend of his, to whom he told all his troubles.

'Mercy on you, Tonio Kröger! Don't be so formal!' answered she, with her lilting intonation. 'Everybody knows you were taught good manners in your nursery.' She transferred her brush to her left hand, that held the palette, reached him her right, and looked him in the face, smiling and shaking her head.

'Yes, but you are working,' he said. 'Let's see. Oh, you've been getting on,' and he looked at the colour sketches leaning against chairs at both sides of the easel and from them to the large canvas covered with a square linen mesh, where the first patches of colour were beginning to appear among the confused and schematic lines of the charcoal sketch.

This was in Munich, in a back building in Schelling-strasse, several stories up. Beyond the wide window facing the north were blue sky, sunshine, birds twittering; the young sweet breath of spring streaming through an open pane mingled with the smells of paint and fixative. The afternoon light, bright golden, flooded the spacious emptiness of the atelier; it made no secret of the bad flooring or the rough table under the window, covered with little bottles, tubes, and brushes; it illumined the unframed studies on the unpapered walls, the torn silk screen that shut off a charmingly furnished little living corner near the door; it shone upon the inchoate work on the easel, upon the artist and the poet there before it.

She was about the same age as himself—slightly past thirty. She sat there on a low stool, in her dark-blue apron, and leant her chin in her hand. Her brown hair, compactly dressed, already a little grey at the sides, was parted in the middle and waved over the temples, framing a sensitive, sympathetic, dark-skinned face, which was Slavic in its facial structure, with flat nose, strongly accentuated cheek bones, and little bright black eyes. She sat there measuring her work with her head on one side and her eyes screwed up; her features were drawn with a look of misgiving, almost of vexation.

He stood beside her, his right hand on his hip, with the other furiously twirling his brown moustache. His dress, reserved in cut and a soothing shade of grey, was punctilious and dignified to the last degree. He was whistling softly to himself, in the way he had, and his slanting brows were gathered in a frown. The dark-brown hair was parted with severe correctness, but the laboured forehead beneath showed a nervous twitching, and the chiselled southern features were sharpened as though they had been gone over again with a graver's tool. And yet the mouth—how gently curved it was, the chin how softly formed! . . . After a little he drew his hand across his brow and eyes and turned away.

'I ought not to have come,' he said.

'And why not, Tonio Kröger?'

'I 've just got up from my desk, Lisabeta, and inside my head it looks just the way it does on this canvas. A scaffolding, a faint first draft smeared with corrections and a few splotches of colour; yes, and I come up here and see the same thing. And the same conflict and contradiction in the air,' he went on, sniffing, 'that has been torturing me at home. It 's extraordinary. If you are possessed by an idea, you find it expressed everywhere, you even *smell* it. Fixative and the breath of spring; art and—what? Don't say nature, Lisabeta, "nature" isn't exhausting. Ah, no, I ought to have gone for a walk, though it 's doubtful if it would have made me feel better. Five minutes ago, not far from here, I met a man I know, Adalbert, the novelist. "God damn the spring!" says he, in the aggressive way he has. "It is and always has been the most ghastly time of the year.

Can you get hold of a single sensible idea, Kröger? Can you sit still and work out even the smallest effect, when your blood tickles till it 's positively indecent and you are teased by a whole host of irrelevant sensations that when you look at them turn out to be unworkable trash? For my part, I am going to a café. A café is neutral territory, the change of the seasons doesn't affect it; it represents, so to speak, the detached and elevated sphere of the literary man, in which one is only capable of refined ideas." And he went into the café . . . and perhaps I ought to have gone with him.'

Lisabeta was highly entertained.

'I like that, Tonio Kröger. That part about the indecent tickling is good. And he is right too, in a way, for spring is really not very conducive to work. But now listen. Spring or no spring, I will just finish this little place—work out this little effect, as your friend Adalbert would say. Then we 'll go into the salon and have tea, and you can talk yourself out, for I can perfectly well see you are too full for utterance. Will you just compose yourself somewhere—on that chest, for instance, if you are not afraid for your aristocratic garments——'

'Oh, leave my clothes alone, Lisabeta Ivanovna! Do you want me to go about in a ragged velveteen jacket or a red waistcoat? Every artist is as bohemian as the deuce, inside! Let him at least wear proper clothes and behave outwardly like a respectable being. No, I am not too full for utterance,' he said as he watched her mixing her paints. 'I 've told you, it is only that I have a problem and a conflict, that sticks in my mind and disturbs me at my work. . . . Yes, what was it we were just saying? We were talking about Adalbert, the novelist, that stout and forthright man. "Spring is the most ghastly time of the year," says he, and goes into a café. A man has to know what he needs, eh? Well, you see he's not the only one; the spring makes me nervous, too; I get dazed with the triflingness and sacredness of the memories and feelings it evokes; only that I don't succeed in looking down on it; for the truth is it makes me ashamed; I quail before its sheer naturalness and triumphant youth. And I don't know whether I should envy Adalbert or despise him for his ignorance. . . .

'Yes, it is true; spring is a bad time for work; and why? Because we are feeling too much. Nobody but a beginner imagines that he who creates must feel. Every real and genuine artist smiles at such naïve blunders as that. A melancholy enough smile, perhaps, but still a smile. For what an artist talks about is never the main point; it is the raw material, in and for itself indifferent, out of which, with bland and serene mastery, he creates the work of art. If you care too much about what you have to say, if your heart is too much in it, you can be pretty sure of making a mess. You get pathetic, you wax sentimental; something dull and doddering, without roots or outlines, with no sense of humour—something tiresome and banal grows under your hand, and you get nothing out of it but apathy in your audience and disappointment and misery in yourself. For so it is, Lisabeta; feeling, warm, heartfelt feeling, is always banal and futile; only the irritations and icy ecstasies of the artist's corrupted nervous system are artistic. The artist must be unhuman, extra-human; he must stand in a queer aloof relationship to our humanity; only so is he in a position, I ought to say only so would he be tempted, to represent it, to present it, to portray it to good effect. The very gift of style, of form and expression, is nothing else than this cool and fastidious attitude towards humanity; you might say there has to be this impoverishment and devastation as a preliminary condition. For sound natural feeling, say what you like, has no taste. It is all up with the artist as soon as he becomes a man and begins to feel. Adalbert knows that; that's why he betook himself to the café, the neutral territory—God help him!'

'Yes, God help him, *batushka*,' said Lisabeta, as she washed her hands in a tin basin. 'You don't need to follow his example.'

'No, Lisabeta, I am not going to; and the only reason is that I am now and again in a position to feel a little ashamed of the springtime of my art. You see, sometimes I get letters from strangers, full of praise and thanks and admiration from people whose feelings I have touched. I read them and feel touched myself at these warm if ungainly emotions I have called up; a sort of pity steals over me at this naïve enthusiasm; and I positively blush at the thought of how these good people would freeze up if they were to get a look behind the scenes. What they, in their innocence, cannot comprehend is that a properly constituted, healthy, decent man never writes, acts, or composes—all of which does not hinder me from using his admiration for my genius to goad myself on; nor from taking it in deadly earnest and aping the airs of a great man. Oh, don't talk to me, Lisabeta. I tell you I am sick to death of depicting humanity without having any part or lot in it. . . . Is an artist a male, anyhow? Ask the females! It seems to me we artists are all of us something like those unsexed papal singers . . . we sing like angels; but——'

'Shame on you, Tonio Kröger. But come to tea. The water is just on the boil, and here are some *papyros*. You were talking about singing soprano, do go on. But really you ought to be ashamed of yourself. If I did not know your passionate devotion to your calling and how proud you are of it——'

'Don't talk about "calling," Lisabeta Ivanovna.

Literature is not a calling, it is a curse, believe me! When does one begin to feel the curse? Early, horribly early. At a time when one ought by rights still to be living in peace and harmony with God and the world. It begins by your feeling yourself set apart, in a curious sort of opposition to the nice, regular people; there is a gulf of ironic sensibility, of knowledge, scepticism, disagreement, between you and the others; it grows deeper and deeper, you realize that you are alone; and from then on any *rapprochement* is simply hopeless! What a fate! That is, if you still have enough heart, enough warmth of affections, to feel how frightful it is! . . . Your self-consciousness is kindled, because you among thousands feel the sign on your brow and know that every one else sees it. I once knew an actor, a man of genius, who had to struggle with a morbid self-consciousness and instability. When he had no role to play, nothing to represent, this man, consummate artist but impoverished human being, was overcome by an exaggerated consciousness of his ego. A genuine artist—not one who has taken up art as a profession like another, but artist foreordained and damned —you can pick out, without boasting very sharp perceptions, from a group of men. The sense of being set apart and not belonging, of being known and observed, something both regal and incongruous shows in his face. You might see something of the same sort on the features of a prince walking through a crowd in ordinary clothes. But no civilian clothes are any good here, Lisabeta. You can disguise yourself, you can dress up like an attaché or a lieutenant of the guard on leave; you hardly need to give a glance or speak a word before every one knows you are not a human being, but something else: something queer, different, inimical.

'But what is it, to be an artist? Nothing shows up the general human dislike of thinking, and man's innate

craving to be comfortable, better than his attitude to this
question. When these worthy people are affected by a
work of art, they say humbly that that sort of thing is a
"gift." And because in their innocence they assume
that beautiful and uplifting results must have beautiful
and uplifting causes, they never dream that the "gift" in
question is a very dubious affair and rests upon extremely
sinister foundations. Everybody knows that artists are
"sensitive" and easily wounded; just as everybody knows
that ordinary people, with a normal bump of self-confidence, are not. Now you see, Lisabeta, I cherish at
the bottom of my soul all the scorn and suspicion of the
artist gentry—translated into terms of the intellectual—
that my upright old forbears there on the Baltic would
have felt for any juggler or mountebank that entered their
houses. Listen to this. I know a banker, a grey-haired
business man, who has a gift for writing stories. He
employs this gift in his idle hours, and some of his stories
are of the first rank. But despite—I say despite—this
excellent gift his withers are by no means unwrung:
on the contrary, he has had to serve a prison sentence, on
anything but trifling grounds. Yes, it was actually first
in prison that he became conscious of his gift, and his
experiences as a convict are the main theme in all his
works. One might be rash enough to conclude that a man
has to be at home in some kind of jail in order to become
a poet. But can you escape the suspicion that the source
and essence of his being an artist had less to do with his
life in prison than they had with the reasons that *brought
him there*? A banker who writes—that is a rarity, isn't
it? But a banker who isn't a criminal, who is irreproach-
ably respectable, and yet writes—he doesn't exist. Yes,
you are laughing, and yet I am more than half serious.
No problem, none in the world, is more tormenting
than this of the artist and his human aspect. Take the

most miraculous case of all, take the most typical and therefore the most powerful of artists, take such a morbid and profoundly equivocal work as *Tristan and Isolde*, and look at the effect it has on a healthy young man of thoroughly normal feelings. Exaltation, encouragement, warm, downright enthusiasm, perhaps incitement to "artistic" creation of his own. Poor young dilettante! In us artists it looks fundamentally different from what he wots of, with his "warm heart" and "honest enthusiasm." I 've seen women and youths go mad over artists . . . and I *knew* about them . . .! The origin, the accompanying phenomena, and the conditions of the artist life—good Lord, what haven't I observed about them, over and over!'

'Observed, Tonio Kröger? If I may ask, only "observed"?'

He was silent, knitting his oblique brown brows and whistling softly to himself.

'Let me have your cup, Tonio. The tea is weak. And take another cigarette. Now, you perfectly know that you are looking at things as they do not necessarily have to be looked at. . . .'

'That is Horatio's answer, dear Lisabeta. "'Twere to consider too curiously, to consider so."'

'I mean, Tonio Kröger, that one can consider them just exactly as well from another side. I am only a silly painting female, and if I can contradict you at all, if I can defend your own profession a little against you, it is not by saying anything new, but simply by reminding you of some things you very well know yourself: of the purifying and healing influence of letters, the subduing of the passions by knowledge and eloquence; literature as the guide to understanding, forgiveness, and love, the redeeming power of the word, literary art as the noblest manifestation of the human mind, the poet as the most highly developed

of human beings, the poet as saint. Is it to consider
things not curiously enough, to consider them so?'

'You may talk like that, Lisabeta Ivanovna, you have
a perfect right. And with reference to Russian literature,
and the works of your poets, one can really worship
them; they really come close to being that elevated literature you are talking about. But I am not ignoring your
objections, they are part of the things I have in my mind
to-day. . . . Look at me, Lisabeta. I don't look any
too cheerful, do I? A little old and tired and pinched,
eh? Well, now to come back to the "knowledge."
Can't you imagine a man, born orthodox, mild-mannered,
well-meaning, a bit sentimental, just simply over-stimu-
lated by his psychological clairvoyance, and going to the
dogs? Not to let the sadness of the world unman you;
to read, mark, learn, and to put to account even the most
torturing things and to be of perpetual good cheer, in
the sublime consciousness of moral superiority over the
horrible invention of existence—yes, thank you! But
despite all the joys of expression once in a while the thing
gets on your nerves. "Tout comprendre c'est tout pardonner." I don't know about that. There is something
I call being sick of knowledge, Lisabeta: when it is
enough for you to see through a thing in order to be sick
to death of it, and not in the least in a forgiving mood.
Such was the case of Hamlet the Dane, that typical
literary man. He knew what it meant to be called to
knowledge without being born to it. To see things
clear, if even through your tears, to recognize, notice,
observe—and have to put it all down with a smile, at the
very moment when hands are clinging, and lips meeting,
and the human gaze is blinded with feeling—it is infamous,
Lisabeta, it is indecent, outrageous—but what good does
it do to be outraged?

'Then another and no less charming side of the thing,

of course, is your ennui, your indifferent and ironic attitude towards truth. It is a fact that there is no society in the world so dumb and hopeless as a circle of literary people who are hounded to death as it is. All knowledge is old and tedious to them. Utter some truth that it gave you considerable youthful joy to conquer and possess—and they will all chortle at you for your *naïveté*. Oh, yes, Lisabeta, literature is a wearing job. In human society, I do assure you, a reserved and sceptical man can be taken for stupid, whereas he is really only arrogant and perhaps lacks courage. So much for "knowledge." Now for the "Word." It isn't so much a matter of the "redeeming power" as it is of putting your emotions on ice and serving them up chilled! Honestly, don't you think there's a good deal of cool cheek in the prompt and superficial way a writer can get rid of his feelings by turning them into literature? If your heart is too full, if you are overpowered with the emotions of some sweet or exalted moment—nothing simpler! Go to the literary man, he will put it all straight for you instanter. He will analyse and formulate your affair, label it and express it and discuss it and polish it off and make you indifferent to it for time and eternity —and not charge you a farthing. You will go home quite relieved, cooled off, enlightened; and wonder what it was all about and why you were so mightily moved. And will you seriously enter the lists in behalf of this vain and frigid charlatan? What is uttered, so runs this *credo*, is finished and done with. If the whole world could be expressed, it would be saved, finished and done. . . . Well and good. But I am not a nihilist——'

'You are not a——' said Lisabeta. . . . She was lifting a teaspoonful of tea to her mouth and paused in the act to stare at him.

'Come, come, Lisabeta, what's the matter? I say

I am not a nihilist, with respect, that is, to lively feeling. You see, the literary man does not understand that life may go on living, unashamed, even after it has been expressed and therewith finished. No matter how much it has been redeemed by becoming literature, it keeps right on sinning—for all action is sin in the mind's eye——

'I'm nearly done, Lisabeta. Please listen. I love life—this is an admission. I present it to you, you may have it. I have never made it to any one else. People say—people have even written and printed—that I hate life, or fear or despise or abominate it. I liked to hear this, it has always flattered me; but that does not make it true. I love life. You smile; and I know why, Lisabeta. But I implore you not to take what I am saying for literature. Don't think of Caesar Borgia or any drunken philosophy that has him for a standard bearer. He is nothing to me, your Caesar Borgia. I have no opinion of him, and I shall never comprehend how one can honour the extraordinary and daemonic as an ideal. No, life as the eternal antinomy of mind and art does not represent itself to us as a vision of savage greatness and ruthless beauty; we who are set apart and different do not conceive it as, like us, unusual; it is the normal, respectable, and admirable that is the kingdom of our longing; life, in all its seductive banality! That man is very far from being an artist, my dear, whose last and deepest enthusiasm is the *raffiné*, the eccentric and satanic; who does not know a longing for the innocent, the simple, and the living, for a little friendship, devotion, familiar human happiness— the gnawing, surreptitious hankering, Lisabeta, for the bliss of the commonplace. . . .

'A genuine human friend. Believe me, I should be proud and happy to possess a friend among men. But up to now all the friends I have had have been daemons, kobolds, impious monsters, and spectres dumb with excess of knowledge—that is to say, literary men.

'I may be standing upon some platform, in some hall in front of people who have come to listen to me. And I find myself looking round among my hearers, I catch myself secretly peering about the auditorium, and all the while I am thinking who it is that has come here to listen to me, whose grateful applause is in my ears, with whom my art is making me one. . . . I do not find what I seek, Lisabeta, I find the herd. The same old community, the same old gathering of early Christians, so to speak: people with fine souls in uncouth bodies, people who are always falling down in the dance, if you know what I mean; the kind to whom poetry serves as a sort of mild revenge on life. Always and only the poor and suffering, never any of the others, the blue-eyed ones, Lisabeta— they do not need mind. . . .

'And, after all, would it not be a lamentable lack of logic to want it otherwise? It is against all sense to love life and yet bend all the powers you have to draw it over to your own side, to the side of finesse and melancholy and the whole sickly aristocracy of letters. The kingdom of art increases and that of health and innocence declines on this earth. What there is left of it ought to be carefully preserved; one ought not to tempt people to read poetry who would much rather read books about the instantaneous photography of horses.

'For, after all, what more pitiable sight is there than life led astray by art? We artists have a consummate contempt for the dilettante, the man who is leading a living life and yet thinks he can be an artist too if he gets the chance. I am speaking from personal experience, I do assure you. Suppose I am in a company in a good house, with eating and drinking going on, and plenty of conversation and good feeling; I am glad and grateful

to be able to lose myself among good regular people for a
while. Then all of a sudden—I am thinking of something that actually happened—an officer gets up, a
lieutenant, a stout, good-looking chap, whom I could
never have believed guilty of any conduct unbecoming
his uniform, and actually in good set terms asks the
company's permission to read some verses of his own
composition. Everybody looks disconcerted, they laugh,
and tell him to go on, and he takes them at their word
and reads from a sheet of paper he has up to now been
hiding in his coat-tail pocket—something about love and
music, as deeply felt as it is inept. But I ask you: a
lieutenant! A man of the world! He surely did not
need to . . . Well, the inevitable result is long faces,
silence, a little artificial applause, everybody thoroughly
uncomfortable. The first sensation I am conscious of
is guilt—I feel partly responsible for the disturbance this
rash youth has brought upon the company; and no wonder,
for I, as a member of the same guild, am a target for some
of the unfriendly glances. But next minute I realize
something else: this man for whom just now I felt the
greatest respect has suddenly sunk in my eyes. I feel a
benevolent pity. Along with some other brave and
good-natured gentlemen I go up and speak to him.
"Congratulations, Herr Lieutenant," I say, "that is a
very pretty talent you have. It was charming." And I
am within an ace of clapping him on the shoulder. But
is that the way one is supposed to feel towards a lieutenant
—benevolent? . . . It was his own fault. There he
stood, suffering embarrassment for the mistake of thinking
that one may pluck a single leaf from the laurel-tree of art
without paying for it with his life. No, there I go with
my colleague, the convict banker—but don't you find,
Lisabeta, that I have quite a Hamlet-like flow of oratory
to-day?'

'Are you done, Tonio Kröger?'

'No. but there won't be any more.'

'And quite enough too. Are you expecting a reply?'

'Have you one ready?'

'I should say so. I have listened to you faithfully, Tonio, from beginning to end, and I will give you the answer to everything you have said this afternoon and the solution of the problem that has been upsetting you. Now: the solution is that you, as you sit there, are, quite simply, a bourgeois.'

'Am I?' he asked, a little crestfallen.

'Yes; that hits you hard, it must. So I will soften the judgment just a little. You are a bourgeois on the wrong path, a bourgeois *manqué*.'

Silence. Then he got up resolutely and took his hat and stick.

'Thank you, Lisabeta Ivanovna; now I can go home in peace. I am expressed.'

Towards autumn Tonio Kröger said to Lisabeta Ivanovna:

'Well, Lisabeta, I think I 'll be off. I need a change of air. I must get away, out into the open.'

'Well, well, well, little father! Does it please your Highness to go down to Italy again?'

'Oh, get along with your Italy, Lisabeta. I 'm fed up with Italy, I spew it out of my mouth. It 's a long time since I imagined I could belong down there. Art, eh? Blue-velvet sky, ardent wine, the sweets of sensuality. In short, I don't want it—I decline with thanks. The whole *bellezza* business makes me nervous. All those frightfully animated people down there with their black animal-like eyes; I don't like them either. These Romance peoples have no soul in their eyes. No, I 'm going to take a trip to Denmark.'

'To Denmark?'

'Yes. I 'm quite sanguine of the results. I happen never to have been there, though I lived all my youth so close to it. Still, I have always known and loved the country. I suppose I must have this northern tendency from my father, for my mother was really more for the *bellezza*, in so far, that is, as she cared very much one way or the other. But just take the books that are written up there, that clean, meaty, whimsical Scandinavian literature, Lisabeta, there 's nothing like it, I love it. Or take the Scandinavian meals, those incomparable meals, which can only be digested in strong sea air (I don't know whether I can digest them in any sort of air); I know them from my home, too, because we ate that way up there. Take even the names, the given names that people rejoice in up north; we have a good many of them in my part of the country too: Ingeborg, for instance, isn't it the purest poetry—like a harp-tone? And then the sea—up there it 's the Baltic! . . . In a word, I am going, Lisabeta. I want to see the Baltic again and read the books and hear the names on their native heath; I want to stand on the terrace at Kronberg, where the ghost appeared to Hamlet, bringing despair and death to that poor, noble-souled youth. . . .'

'How are you going, Tonio, if I may ask? What route are you taking?'

'The usual one,' he said, shrugging his shoulders, and blushed perceptibly. 'Yes, I shall touch my—my point of departure, Lisabeta, after thirteen years, and that may turn out rather funny.'

She smiled.

'That is what I wanted to hear, Tonio Kröger. Well, be off, then, in God's name. Be sure to write to me, do

you hear? I shall expect a letter full of your experiences
in—Denmark.'

And Tonio Kröger travelled north. He travelled in
comfort (for he was wont to say that any one who suffered
inwardly more than other people had a right to a little
outward ease); and he did not stay until the towers of the
little town he had left rose up in the grey air. Among
them he made a short and singular stay.

The dreary afternoon was merging into evening when
the train pulled into the narrow, reeking shed, so marvellously familiar. The volumes of thick smoke rolled
up to the dirty glass roof and wreathed to and fro there
in long tatters, just as they had, long ago, on the day
when Tonio Kröger, with nothing but derision in his
heart, had left his native town. He arranged to have
his luggage sent to his hotel, and walked out of the
station.

There were the cabs, those enormously high, enormously wide black cabs drawn by two horses, standing in
a rank. He did not take one, he only looked at them, as
he looked at everything: the narrow gables, and the
pointed towers peering over the roofs close at hand; the
plump, fair, easy-going populace, with their broad yet
rapid speech. And a nervous laugh mounted in him,
mysteriously akin to a sob. He walked on, slowly, with
the damp wind constantly in his face, across the bridge,
with the mythological statues on the railings, and some
distance along the harbour.

Good Lord, how tiny and close it all seemed! The
comical little gabled streets were climbing up just as of
yore from the port to the town! And on the ruffled
waters the smoke stacks and masts of the ships dipped
gently in the wind and twilight. Should he go up that
next street, leading, he knew, to a certain house? No,

to-morrow. He was too sleepy. His head was heavy from the journey, and slow, vague trains of thought passed through his mind.

Sometimes in the past thirteen years, when he was suffering from indigestion, he had dreamed of being back home in the echoing old house in the steep, narrow street. His father had been there too, and reproached him bitterly for his dissolute manner of life, and this, each time, he had found quite as it should be. And now the present refused to distinguish itself in any way from one of those tantalizing dream fabrications in which the dreamer asks himself if this be delusion or reality and is driven to decide for the latter, only to wake up after all in the end. . . . He paced through the half-empty streets with his head inclined against the wind, moving as though in his sleep in the direction of the hotel, the first hotel in the town, where he meant to sleep. A bow-legged man, with a pole at the end of which burned a tiny fire, walked before him with a rolling, seafaring gait and lighted the gas lamps.

What was at the bottom of this? What was it burning darkly beneath the ashes of his fatigue, refusing to burst out into a clear blaze? Hush, hush, only no talk. Only don't make words! He would have liked to go on so, for a long time, in the wind, through the dusky, dreamily familiar streets—but everything was so little and close together here. You reached your goal at once.

In the upper town there were arc lamps, just lighted. There was the hotel with the two black lions in front of it; he had been afraid of them as a child. And there they were, still looking at each other as though they were about to sneeze; only they seemed to have grown much smaller. Tonio Kröger passed between them into the hotel.

As he came on foot, he was received with no great

ceremony.   There was a porter, and a lordly gentleman
dressed in black, to do the honours; the latter, shoving
back his cuffs with his little fingers, measured him from
the crown of his head to the soles of his boots, obviously
with intent to place him, to assign him to his proper
category socially and hierarchically speaking and then
mete out the suitable degree of courtesy.   He seemed
not to come to any clear decision and compromised on a
moderate display of politeness.   A mild-mannered waiter
with yellow-white side whiskers, in a dress suit shiny
with age, and rosettes on his soundless shoes, led him up
two flights into a clean old room furnished in patriarchal
style.   Its windows gave on a twilit view of courts and
gables, very medieval and picturesque, with the fantastic
bulk of the old church close by.   Tonio Kröger stood
awhile before this window; then he sat down on the wide
sofa, crossed his arms, drew down his brows, and whistled
to himself.

Lights were brought and his luggage came up.   The
mild-mannered waiter laid the hotel register on the table,
and Tonio Kröger, his head on one side, scrawled something on it that might be taken for a name, a station, and
a place of origin.   Then he ordered supper and went
on gazing into space from his sofa corner.   When it
stood before him he let it wait long untouched, then took
a few bites and walked up and down an hour in his room,
stopping from time to time and closing his eyes.   Then
he very slowly undressed and went to bed.   He slept
long and had curiously confused and ardent dreams.

It was broad day when he woke.   Hastily he recalled
where he was and got up to draw the curtains; the pale-
blue sky, already with a hint of autumn, was streaked
with frayed and tattered cloud; still, above his native city
the sun was shining.

He spent more care than usual upon his toilette, washed

and shaved and made himself fresh and immaculate as
though about to call upon some smart family where a
well-dressed and flawless appearance was *de rigueur*; and
while occupied in this wise he listened to the anxious
beating of his heart.

How bright it was outside! He would have liked
better a twilight air like yesterday's, instead of passing
through the streets in the broad sunlight, under everybody's eye. Would he meet people he knew, be stopped
and questioned and have to submit to be asked how he
had spent the last thirteen years? No, thank goodness,
he was known to nobody here; even if anybody remembered him, it was unlikely he would be recognized—for
certainly he had changed in the meantime! He sur-
veyed himself in the glass and felt a sudden sense of
security behind his mask, behind his work-worn face,
that was older than his years. . . . He sent for breakfast,
and after that he went out; he passed under the disdainful
eye of the porter and the gentleman in black, through the
vestibule and between the two lions, and so into the
street.

Where was he going? He scarcely knew. It was
the same as yesterday. Hardly was he in the midst of
this long-familiar scene, this stately conglomeration of
gables, turrets, arcades, and fountains, hardly did he feel
once more the wind in his face, that strong current
wafting a faint and pungent aroma from far-off dreams,
than the same mistiness laid itself like a veil about his
senses. . . . The muscles of his face relaxed, and he
looked at men and things with a look grown suddenly
calm. Perhaps right there, on that street corner, he
might wake up after all. . . .

Where was he going? It seemed to him the direction
he took had a connection with his sad and strangely rueful
dreams of the night. . . . He went to Market Square,

under the vaulted arches of the Rathaus, where the butchers were weighing out their wares red-handed, where the tall old Gothic fountain stood with its manifold spires. He paused in front of a house, a plain narrow building, like many another, with a fretted baroque gable; stood there lost in contemplation. He read the plate on the door, his eyes rested a little while on each of the windows. Then slowly he turned away.

Where did he go? Towards home. But he took a roundabout way outside the walls—for he had plenty of time. He went over the Mill Wall and over the Holsten Wall, clutching his hat, for the wind was rushing and moaning through the trees. He left the wall near the station, where he saw a train puffing busily past, idly counted the coaches, and looked after the man who sat perched upon the last. In the Lindenplatz he stopped at one of the pretty villas, peered long into the garden and up at the windows, lastly conceived the idea of swinging the gate to and fro upon its hinges till it creaked. Then he looked awhile at his moist, rust-stained hand and went on, went through the squat old gate, along the harbour, and up the steep, windy street to his parents' house.

It stood aloof from its neighbours, its gable towering above them; grey and sombre, as it had stood there these three hundred years; and Tonio Kröger read the pious, half-illegible motto above the entrance. Then he drew a long breath and went in.

His heart gave a throb of fear, lest his father might come out of one of the doors on the ground floor, in his office coat, with the pen behind his ear, and take him to task for his excesses. He would have found the reproach quite in order; but he got past unchidden. The inner door was ajar, which appeared to him reprehensible, though at the same time he felt as one does in certain broken dreams, where obstacles melt away of themselves, and one presses onward in marvellous favour with fortune. The wide entry, paved with great square flags, echoed to his tread. Opposite the silent kitchen was the curious projecting structure, of rough boards, but cleanly varnished, that had been the servants' quarters. It was quite high up and could only be reached by a sort of ladder from the entry. But the great cupboards and carven presses were gone. The son of the house climbed the majestic staircase, with his hand on the white-enamelled, fretwork balustrade. At each step he lifted his hand, and put it down again with the next as though testing whether he could call back his ancient familiarity with the stout old railing. . . . But at the landing of the *entresol* he stopped. For on the entrance door was a white plate; and on it in black letters he read: 'Public Library.'

'Public Library?' thought Tonio Kröger. What were either literature or the public doing here? He knocked . . . heard a 'Come in,' and obeying it with gloomy suspense gazed upon a scene of most unhappy alteration.

The story was three rooms deep, and all the doors stood open. The walls were covered nearly all the way up with long rows of books in uniform bindings, standing in dark-coloured book-cases. In each room a poor creature of a man sat writing behind a sort of counter. The farthest two just turned their heads, but the nearest one got up in haste and, leaning with both hands on the table, stuck out his head, pursed his lips, lifted his brows, and looked at the visitor with eagerly blinking eyes.

'I beg your pardon,' said Tonio Kröger, without turning his eyes from the book-shelves. 'I am a stranger here, seeing the sights. So this is your Public Library? May I examine your collection a little?'

'Certainly, with pleasure,' said the official, blinking still more violently. 'It is open to everybody. . . . Pray look about you. Would you care for a catalogue?'

'No, thanks,' answered Tonio Kröger, 'I shall soon find my way about.' And he began to move slowly along the walls, with the appearance of studying the rows of books. After a while he took down a volume, opened it, and posted himself at the window.

This was the breakfast room. They had eaten here in the morning instead of in the big dining-room upstairs, with its white statues of gods and goddesses standing out against the blue walls. . . . Beyond there had been a bedroom, where his father's mother had died—only after a long struggle, old as she was, for she had been of a plea-sure-loving nature and clung to life. And his father too, had drawn his last breath in the same room: that tall, correct, slightly melancholy and pensive gentleman with the wild flower in his button hole. . . . Tonio had sat at the foot of his death bed, quite given over to unutterable feelings of love and grief. His mother had knelt at the bedside, his lovely, fiery mother, dissolved in hot tears; and after that she had withdrawn with her artist into the far blue south. . . . And beyond still, the small third room, likewise full of books and presided over by a shabby man—that had been for years on end his own. Thither he had come after school and a walk—like to-day's; against that wall his table had stood with the drawer where he had kept his first clumsy, heartfelt attempts at verse. . . . The walnut-tree . . . a pang went through him. He gave a sidewise glance out at the window. The garden lay desolate, but there stood the old walnut-tree where it used to stand, groaning and creaking heavily in the wind. And Tonio Kröger let his gaze fall upon the book he had in his hands, an excellent piece of work, and very familiar. He followed the black lines of print, the paragraphs, the flow of words that flowed with so much art, mounting in the ardour of creation to a certain climax and effect, and then as artfully breaking off. . . .

'Yes, that was well done,' he said; put back the book and turned away. Then he saw that the functionary still stood bolt upright, blinking with a mingled expression of zeal and misgiving.

'A capital collection, I see,' said Tonio Kröger. 'I have already quite a good idea of it. Much obliged to you. Good-bye.' He went out; but it was a poor exit, and he felt sure the official would stand there perturbed and blinking for several minutes.

He felt no desire for further researches. He had been home. Strangers were living upstairs in the large rooms behind the pillared hall; the top of the stairs was shut off by a glass door which used not to be there, and on the door was a plate. He went away, down the steps, across the echoing corridor, and left his parental home. He sought a restaurant, sat down in a corner, and brooded over a heavy, greasy meal. Then he returned to his hotel.

'I am leaving,' he said to the fine gentleman in black. 'This afternoon.' And he asked for his bill, and for a carriage to take him down to the harbour where he should take the boat for Copenhagen. Then he went up to his room and sat there stiff and still, with his cheek on his hand, looking down on the table before him with absent eyes. Later he paid his bill and packed his things. At the appointed hour the carriage was announced and Tonio Kröger went down in travel array.

At the foot of the stairs the gentleman in black was waiting.

'Beg pardon,' he said, shoving back his cuffs with his little fingers. . . . 'Beg pardon, but we must detain you just a moment. Herr Seehaase, the proprietor, would like to exchange two words with you. A matter of form. . . . He is back there. . . . If you will have the goodness to step this way. . . . It is *only* Herr Seehaase, the proprietor.'

And he ushered Tonio Kröger into the background of the vestibule. . . . There, in fact, stood Herr Seehaase. Tonio Kröger recognized him from old time. He was small, fat, and bow-legged. His shaven side-whisker was white, but he wore the same old low-cut dress coat and little velvet cap embroidered in green. He was not alone. Beside him, at a little high desk fastened into the wall, stood a policeman in a helmet, his gloved right hand resting on a document in coloured inks; he turned towards Tonio Kröger with his honest, soldierly face as though he expected Tonio to sink into the earth at his glance.

Tonio Kröger looked at the two and confined himself to waiting.

'You came from Munich?' the policeman asked at length in a heavy, good-natured voice.

Tonio Kröger said he had.

'You are going to Copenhagen?'

'Yes, I am on the way to a Danish seaside resort.'

'Seaside resort? Well, you must produce your papers,' said the policeman. He uttered the last word with great satisfaction.

'Papers . . .?' He had no papers. He drew out his pocket-book and looked into it; but aside from notes there was nothing there but some proof sheets of a story which he had taken along to finish reading. He hated relations with officials and had never got himself a passport.

'I am sorry,' he said, 'but I don't travel with papers.'

'Ah!' said the policeman. 'And what might be your name?'

Tonio replied.

'Is that a fact?' asked the policeman, suddenly erect, and expanding his nostrils as wide as he could. . . .

'Yes, that is a fact,' answered Tonio Kröger.

'And what are you, anyhow?'

Tonio Kröger gulped and gave the name of his trade in a firm voice. Herr Seehaase lifted his head and looked him curiously in the face.

'H'm,' said the policeman. 'And you give out that you are not identical with an individdle named'—he said 'individdle' and then, referring to his document in coloured inks, spelled out an involved, fantastic name which mingled all the sounds of all the races—Tonio Kröger forgot it next minute—'of unknown parentage and unspecified means,' he went on, 'wanted by the Munich police for various shady transactions, and probably in flight towards Denmark?'

'Yes, I give out all that, and more,' said Tonio Kröger, wriggling his shoulders. The gesture made a certain impression.

'What? Oh, yes, of course,' said the policeman. 'You say you can't show any papers——'

Herr Seehaase threw himself into the breach.

'It is only a formality,' he said pacifically, 'nothing else. You must bear in mind the official is only doing his duty. If you could only identify yourself somehow— some document . . .'

They were all silent. Should he make an end of the business, by revealing to Herr Seehaase that he was no swindler without specified means, no gipsy in a green wagon, but the son of the late Consul Kröger, a member of the Kröger family? No, he felt no desire to do that. After all, were not these guardians of civic order within their right? He even agreed with them —up to a point. He shrugged his shoulders and kept quiet.

'What have you got, then?' asked the policeman, 'In your portfoly, I mean?'

'Here? Nothing. Just a proof sheet,' answered Tonio Kröger.

'Proof sheet? What's that? Let's see it.'

And Tonio Kröger handed over his work. The policeman spread it out on the shelf and began reading. Herr Seehaase drew up and shared it with him. Tonio Kröger looked over their shoulders to see what they read. It was a good moment, a little effect he had worked out to perfection. He had a sense of self-satisfaction.

'You see,' he said, 'there is my name. I wrote it, and it is going to be published, you understand.'

'All right, that will answer,' said Herr Seehaase with decision, gathered up the sheets and gave them back. 'That will have to answer, Petersen,' he repeated crisply, shutting his eyes and shaking his head as though to see and hear no more. 'We must not keep the gentleman any longer. The carriage is waiting. I implore you to pardon the little inconvenience, sir. The officer has only done his duty, but I told him at once he was on the wrong track. . . .'

'Indeed!' thought Tonio Kröger.

The officer seemed still to have his doubts; he muttered something else about individdle and document. But Herr Seehaase, overflowing with regrets, led his guest through the vestibule, accompanied him past the two lions to the carriage, and himself, with many respectful bows, closed the door upon him. And then the funny, high, wide old cab rolled and rattled and bumped down the steep, narrow street to the quay.

And such was the manner of Tonio Kröger's visit to his ancestral home.

Night fell and the moon swam up with silver gleam as Tonio Kröger's boat reached the open sea. He stood at the prow wrapped in his cloak against a mounting wind,

and looked beneath into the dark going and coming of the
waves as they hovered and swayed and came on, to meet
with a clap and shoot erratically away in a bright gush of
foam.

He was lulled in a mood of still enchantment. The
episode at the hotel, their wanting to arrest him for a
swindler in his own home, had cast him down a little,
even although he found it quite in order—in a certain
way. But after he came on board he had watched, as
he used to do as a boy with his father, the lading of goods
into the deep bowels of the boat, amid shouts of mingled
Danish and Plattdeutsch; not only boxes and bales, but
also a Bengal tiger and a polar bear were lowered in cages
with stout iron bars. They had probably come from
Hamburg and were destined for a Danish menagerie.
He had enjoyed these distractions. And as the boat
glided along between flat river banks he quite forgot
Officer Petersen's inquisition; while all the rest—his
sweet, sad, rueful dreams of the night before, the walk
he had taken, the walnut-tree—had welled up again in
his soul. The sea opened out and he saw in the distance
the beach where he as a lad had been let to listen to the
ocean's summer dreams; saw the flashing of the lighthouse
tower and the lights of the Kurhaus where he and his
parents had lived. . . . The Baltic! He bent his head
to the strong salt wind; it came sweeping on, it enfolded
him, made him faintly giddy and a little deaf; and in that
mild confusion of the senses all memory of evil, of anguish
and error, effort and exertion of the will, sank away into
joyous oblivion and were gone. The roaring, foaming,
flapping, and slapping all about him came to his ears like
the groan and rustle of an old walnut-tree, the creaking of
a garden gate. . . . More and more the darkness came on.

'The stars! Oh, my Lord, look at the stars!' a voice
suddenly said, with a heavy sing-song accent that seemed

to come out of the inside of a tun.   He recognized it.
It belonged to a young man with red-blond hair who had
been Tonio Kröger's neighbour at dinner in the salon.
His dress was very simple, his eyes were red, and he had
the moist and chilly look of a person who has just bathed.
With nervous and self-conscious movements he had
taken unto himself an astonishing quantity of lobster
omelet.   Now he leaned on the rail beside Tonio
Kröger and looked up at the skies, holding his chin
between thumb and forefinger.   Beyond a doubt he was
in one of those rare and festal and edifying moods that
cause the barriers between man and man to fall; when
the heart opens even to the stranger, and the mouth
utters that which otherwise it would blush to speak. . . .

'Look, by dear sir, just look at the stars.   There they
stahd and glitter; by goodness, the whole sky is full of
theb!   And I ask you, when you stahd and look up at
theb, and realize that bany of theb are a huddred tibes
larger thad the earth, how does it bake you feel?   Yes,
we have idvehted the telegraph and the telephode and
all the triuphs of our bodern tibes.   But whed we look
up there, after all we have to recogdize and understad
that we are worbs, biserable worbs, and dothing else.
Ab I right, sir, or ab I wrog?   Yes, we are worbs,' he
answered himself, and nodded meekly and abjectly in the
direction of the firmament.

'Ah, he has no literature in his belly,' thought Tonio
Kröger.   And he recalled something he had lately read,
an essay by a famous French writer on cosmological and
psychological philosophies, a very delightful *causerie*.

He made some sort of reply to the young man's feeling
remarks, and they went on talking, leaning over the rail,
and looking into the night with its movement and fitful
lights.   The young man, it seemed, was a Hamburg
merchant on his holiday.

'Y' ought to travel to Copedhagen on the boat, thigks I, and so here I ab, and so far it's been fide. But they shouldn't have given us the lobster obelet, sir, for it's going to be storby—the captain said so hibself—and that's do joke with indigestible food like that in your stobach. . . .'

Tonio Kröger listened to all this engaging artlessness and was privately drawn to it.

'Yes,' he said, 'all the food up here is too heavy. It makes one lazy and melancholy.'

'Belancholy?' repeated the young man, and looked at him, taken aback. Then he asked, suddenly: 'You are a stradger up here, sir?'

'Yes, I have come from a long way off,' answered Tonio Kröger vaguely, waving his arm.

'But you're right,' said the youth; 'Lord knows you are right about the belancholy. I am dearly always belancholy, but specially on evedings like this when there are stars in the sky.' And he supported his chin again with thumb and forefinger.

'Surely this man writes verses,' thought Tonio Kröger; 'business man's verses, full of deep feeling and single-mindedness.'

Evening drew on. The wind had grown so violent as to prevent them from talking. So they thought they would sleep a bit, and wished each other good night.

Tonio Kröger stretched himself out on the narrow cabin bed, but he found no repose. The strong wind with its sharp tang had power to rouse him; he was strangely restless with sweet anticipations. Also he was violently sick with the motion of the ship as she glided down a steep mountain of wave and her screw vibrated as in agony, free of the water. He put on all his clothes again and went up to the deck.

Clouds raced across the moon. The sea danced. It

did not come on in full-bodied, regular waves; but far
out in the pale and flickering light the water was lashed,
torn, and tumbled; leaped upward like great licking
flames; hung in jagged and fantastic shapes above dizzy
abysses, where the foam seemed to be tossed by the playful
strength of colossal arms and flung upward in all directions.
The ship had a heavy passage; she lurched and stamped
and groaned through the welter; and far down in her
bowels the tiger and the polar bear voiced their acute
discomfort.   A man in an oilskin, with the hood drawn
over his head and a lantern strapped to his chest, went
straddling painfully up and down the deck.   And at the
stern, leaning far out, stood the young man from Hamburg, suffering the worst.   'Lord!' he said, in a hollow,
quavering voice, when he saw Tonio Kröger.   'Look
at the uproar of the elebents, sir!'   But he could say no
more—he was obliged to turn hastily away.

Tonio Kröger clutched at a taut rope and looked
abroad into the arrogance of the elements.   His exultation outvied storm and wave; within himself he chanted
a song to the sea, instinct with love of her: 'O thou wild
friend of my youth, Once more I behold thee——' But
it got no farther, he did not finish it.   It was not fated
to receive a final form nor in tranquillity to be welded
to a perfect whole.   For his heart was too full. . . .

Long he stood; then stretched himself out on a bench
by the pilot house and looked up at the sky, where stars
were flickering.   He even slept a little.   And when the
cold foam splashed his face it seemed in his half-dreams
like a caress.

Perpendicular chalk cliffs, ghostly in the moonlight,
came in sight.   They were nearing the island of Möen.
Then sleep came again, broken by salty showers of spray
that bit into his face and made it stiff. . . . When he
really roused, it was broad day, fresh and palest grey, and

the sea had gone down. At breakfast he saw the young man from Hamburg again, who blushed rosy-red for shame of the poetic indiscretions he had been betrayed into by the dark, ruffled up his little red-blond moustache with all five fingers, and called out a brisk and soldierly good morning—after that he studiously avoided him.

And Tonio Kröger landed in Denmark. He arrived in Copenhagen, gave tips to everybody who laid claim to them, took a room at an hotel, and roamed the city for three days with an open guide-book and the air of an intelligent foreigner bent on improving his mind. He looked at the King's New Market and the Horse in the middle of it, gazed respectfully up the columns of the Frauenkirch, stood long before Thorwaldsen's noble and beautiful statuary, climbed the round tower, visited castles, and spent two lively evenings in the Tivoli. But all this was not exactly what he saw.

The doors of the houses—so like those of his native town, with open-work gables of baroque shape—bore names known to him of old; names that had a tender and precious quality, and withal in their syllables an accent of plaintive reproach, of repining after the lost and gone. He walked, he gazed, drawing deep, lingering draughts of moist sea air; and everywhere he saw eyes as blue, hair as blond, faces as familiar, as those that had visited his rueful dreams the night he had spent in his native town. There in the open street it befell him that a glance, a ringing word, a sudden laugh would pierce him to his marrow.

He could not stand the bustling city for long. A restlessness, half memory and half hope, half foolish and half sweet, possessed him; he was moved to drop this role of ardently inquiring tourist and lie somewhere, quite quietly, on a beach. So he took ship once more and travelled under a cloudy sky, over a black water, northwards along the coast of Zealand towards Helsingör. Thence he drove, at once, by carriage, for three-quarters of an hour, along and above the sea, reaching at length his ultimate goal, the little white 'bath hotel' with green blinds. It stood surrounded by a settlement of cottages, and its shingled turret tower looked out on the beach and the Swedish coast. Here he left the carriage, took possession of the light room they had ready for him, filled shelves and presses with his kit, and prepared to stop a while.

It was well on in September; not many guests were left in Aalsgaard. Meals were served on the ground floor, in the great beamed dining-room, whose lofty windows led out upon the veranda and the sea. The landlady presided, an elderly spinster with white hair and faded eyes, a faint colour in her cheek and a feeble twittering voice. She was for ever arranging her red hands to look well upon the table cloth. There was a short-necked old gentleman, quite blue in the face, with a grey sailor beard; a fish dealer he was, from the capital, and strong at the German. He seemed entirely congested and inclined to apoplexy; breathed in short gasps, kept putting his beringed first finger to one nostril, and snorting violently to get a passage of air through the other. Notwithstanding, he addressed himself constantly to the whisky bottle, which stood at his place at luncheon and dinner, and breakfast as well. Besides him the company consisted only of three tall American youths with their governor or tutor, who kept adjusting his glasses in unbroken silence. All day long he played football with his charges, who had narrow, taciturn faces and reddish-yellow hair parted in the middle. 'Please pass the *wurst*,' said one. 'That 's not *wurst*, it 's *schinken*,' said the other, and this was the extent of their conversation, as the rest of the time they sat there dumb, drinking hot water.

Tonio Kröger could have wished himself no better table companions. He revelled in the peace and quiet, listened to the Danish palatals, the clear and the clouded vowels in which the fish dealer and the landlady desultorily conversed; modestly exchanged views with the fish dealer on the state of the barometer, and then left the table to go through the veranda and on to the beach once more, where he had already spent long, long morning hours.

Sometimes it was still and summery there. The sea lay idle and smooth, in stripes of blue and russet and bottle-green, played all across with glittering silvery lights. the seaweed shrivelled in the sun and the jelly-fish lay steaming. There was a faintly stagnant smell and a whiff of tar from the fishing boat against which Tonio Kröger leaned, so standing that he had before his eyes not the Swedish coast but the open horizon, and in his face the pure, fresh breath of the softly breathing sea.

Then grey, stormy days would come. The waves lowered their heads like bulls and charged against the beach; they ran and ramped high up the sands and left them strewn with shining wet sea grass, driftwood, and mussels. All abroad beneath an overcast sky extended ranges of billows, and between them foaming valleys palely green; but above the spot there the sun hung behind the cloud a patch like white velvet lay on the sea.

Tonio Kröger stood wrapped in wind and tumult, sunk in the continual dull, drowsy uproar that he loved. When he turned away it seemed suddenly warm and silent all about him. But he was never unconscious of the sea at his back; it called, it lured, it beckoned him. And he smiled.

He went landward, by lonely meadow paths, and was

swallowed up in the beech groves that clothed the rolling landscape near and far. Here he sat down on the moss, against a tree, and gazed at the strip of water he could see between the trunks. Sometimes the sound of surf came on the wind—a noise like boards collapsing at a distance. And from the tree tops over his head a cawing—hoarse, desolate, forlorn. He held a book on his knee, but did not read a line. He enjoyed profound forgetfulness, hovered disembodied above space and time; only now and again his heart would contract with a fugitive pain, a stab of longing and regret, into whose origin he was too lazy to inquire.

Thus passed some days. He could not have said how many and had no desire to know. But then came one on which something happened; happened while the sun stood in the sky and people were about; and Tonio Kröger, even, felt no vast surprise.

The very opening of the day had been rare and festal. Tonio Kröger woke early and suddenly from his sleep, with a vague and exquisite alarm; he seemed to be looking at a miracle, a magic illumination. His room had a glass door and balcony facing the sound; a thin white gauze curtain divided it into living and sleeping quarters, both hung with delicately tinted paper and furnished with an airy good taste that gave them a sunny and friendly look. But now to his sleep-drunken eyes it lay bathed in a serene and roseate light, an unearthly brightness that gilded walls and furniture and turned the gauze curtain to radiant pink cloud. Tonio Kröger did not at once understand. Not until he stood at the glass door and looked out did he realize that this was the sunrise.

For several days there had been clouds and rain; but now the sky was like a piece of pale-blue silk, spanned shimmering above sea and land, and shot with light from red and golden clouds. The sun's disk rose in splendour from a crisply glittering sea that seemed to quiver and burn beneath it. So began the day. In a joyous daze Tonio Kröger flung on his clothes, and breakfasting in the veranda before everybody else, swam from the little wooden bath house some distance out into the sound, then walked for an hour along the beach. When he came back, several omnibuses were before the door, and from the dining-room he could see people in the parlour next door where the piano was, in the veranda, and on the terrace in front; quantities of people sitting at little tables enjoying beer and sandwiches amid lively discourse. There were whole families, there were old and young, there were even a few children.

At second breakfast—the table was heavily laden with cold viands, roast, pickled, and smoked—Tonio Kröger inquired what was going on.

'Guests,' said the fish-dealer. 'Tourists and ball guests from Helsingör. Lord help us, we shall get no sleep this night! There will be dancing and music, and I fear me it will keep up till late. It is a family reunion, a sort of celebration and excursion combined; they all subscribe to it and take advantage of the good weather. They came by boat and bus and they are having breakfast. After that they go on with their drive, but at night they will all come back for a dance here in the hall. Yes, damn it, you 'll see we shan't get a wink of sleep.'

'Oh, it will be a pleasant change,' said Tonio Kröger.

After that there was nothing more said for some time. The landlady arranged her red fingers on the cloth, the fish dealer blew through his nostril, the Americans drank hot water and made long faces.

Then all at once a thing came to pass: *Hans Hansen and Ingeborg Holm walked through the room.*

Tonio Kröger, pleasantly fatigued after his swim and rapid walk, was leaning back in his chair and eating smoked salmon on toast; he sat facing the veranda and the ocean. All at once the door opened and the two entered hand in hand—calmly and unhurried. Ingeborg, blonde Inge, was dressed just as she used to be at Herr Knaak's dancing class. The light flowered frock reached down to her ankles and it had a tulle fichu draped with a pointed opening that left her soft throat free. Her hat hung by its ribbons over her arm. She, perhaps, was a little more grown up than she used to be, and her wonderful plait of hair was wound round her head; but Hans Hansen was the same as ever. He wore his sailor overcoat with gilt buttons, and his wide blue sailor collar lay across his shoulders and back; the sailor cap with its short ribbons he was dangling carelessly in his hand. Ingeborg's narrow eyes were turned away; perhaps she felt shy before the company at table. But Hans Hansen turned his head straight towards them, and measured one after another defiantly with his steel-blue eyes; challengingly, with a sort of contempt. He even dropped Ingeborg's hand and swung his cap harder than ever, to show what manner of man he was. Thus the two, against the silent, blue-dyed sea, measured the length of the room and passed through the opposite door into the parlour.

This was at half-past eleven in the morning. While the guests of the house were still at table the company in the veranda broke up and went away by the side door. No one else came into the dining-room. The guests could hear them laughing and joking as they got into the omnibuses, which rumbled away one by one. . . . 'So they are coming back?' asked Tonio Kröger.

'That they are,' said the fish dealer. 'More's the pity. They have ordered music, let me tell you—and my room is right above the dining-room.'

'Oh, well, it's a pleasant change,' repeated Tonio Kröger. Then he got up and went away.

That day he spent as he had the others, on the beach and in the wood, holding a book on his knee and blinking in the sun. He had but one thought; they were coming back to have a dance in the hall, the fish dealer had promised they would; and he did nothing but be glad of this, with a sweet and timorous gladness such as he had not felt through all these long dead years. Once he happened, by some chance association, to think of his friend Adalbert, the novelist, the man who had known what he wanted and betaken himself to the café to get away from the spring. Tonio Kröger shrugged his shoulders at the thought of him.

Luncheon was served earlier than usual, also supper, which they ate in the parlour because the dining-room was being got ready for the ball, and the whole house flung in disorder for the occasion. It grew dark; Tonio Kröger, sitting in his room, heard on the road and in the house the sounds of approaching festivity. The picnickers were coming back; from Helsingör, by bicycle and carriage, new guests were arriving; a fiddle and a nasal clarinet might be heard practising down in the dining-room. Everything promised a brilliant ball. . . .

Now the little orchestra struck up a march; he could hear the notes, faint but lively. The dancing opened with a polonaise. Tonio Kröger sat for a while and listened. But when he heard the march-time go over into a waltz he got up and slipped noiselessly out of his room.

From his corridor it was possible to go by the side stairs to the side entrance of the hotel and thence to the veranda without passing through a room. He took this route, softly and stealthily as though on forbidden paths, feeling along through the dark, relentlessly drawn by this stupid jigging music, that now came up to him loud and clear.

The veranda was empty and dim, but the glass door stood open into the hall, where shone two large oil lamps, furnished with bright reflectors. Thither he stole on soft feet; and his skin prickled with the thievish pleasure of standing unseen in the dark and spying on the dancers there in the brightly lighted room. Quickly and eagerly he glanced about for the two whom he sought. . . .

Even though the ball was only half an hour old, the merriment seemed in full swing; however, the guests had come hither already warm and merry, after a whole day of carefree, happy companionship. By bending forward a little, Tonio Kröger could see into the parlour from where he was. Several old gentlemen sat there smoking, drinking, and playing cards; others were with their wives on the plush-upholstered chairs in the foreground watching the dance. They sat with their knees apart and their hands resting on them, puffing out their cheeks with a prosperous air; the mothers, with bonnets perched on their parted hair, with their hands folded over their stomachs and their heads on one side, gazed into the whirl of dancers. A platform had been erected on the long side of the hall, and on it the musicians were doing their utmost. There was even a trumpet, that blew with a certain caution, as though afraid of its own voice, and yet after all kept breaking and cracking. Couples were dipping and circling about, others walked arm in arm up and down the room. No one wore ballroom clothes; they were dressed as for an outing in the summer time: the men in countrified suits which were obviously their Sunday wear; the girls in light-coloured frocks with bunches of field flowers in their bodices. Even a few children were there, dancing with each other in their own way, even after the music stopped. There was a long-legged man in a coat with a little swallow-tail, a provincial lion with an eye-glass and frizzed hair, a post office clerk or some such thing; he was like a comic figure stepped bodily out of a Danish novel; and he seemed to be the leader and manager of the ball.   He was everywhere at once, bustling, perspiring, officious, utterly absorbed; setting down his feet, in shiny, pointed, military half-boots, in a very artificial and involved manner, toes first; waving his arms to issue an order, clapping his hands for the music to begin; here, there, and everywhere, and glancing over his shoulder in pride at his great bow of office, the streamers of which fluttered grandly in his rear.

Yes, there they were, those two, who had gone by Tonio Kröger in the broad light of day; he saw them again—with a joyful start he recognized them almost at the same moment.   Here was Hans Hansen by the door, quite close; his legs apart, a little bent over, he was eating with circumspection a large piece of sponge cake, holding his hand cupwise under his chin to catch the crumbs. And there by the wall sat Ingeborg Holm, Inge the fair; the post office clerk was just mincing up to her with an exaggerated bow and asking her to dance.   He laid one hand on his back and gracefully shoved the other into his bosom.   But she was shaking her head in token that she was a little out of breath and must rest awhile, whereat the post office clerk sat down by her side.

Tonio Kröger looked at them both, these two for whom he had in time past suffered love—Hans and Ingeborg.   They were Hans and Ingeborg not so much by virtue of individual traits and similarity of costume as by similarity of race and type.   This was the blond, fair-haired breed of the steel-blue eyes, which stood to him for the pure, the blithe, the untroubled in life; for a virginal aloofness that was at once both simple and full of pride. . . .   He looked at them.   Hans Hansen was standing there in his sailor suit, lively and well built as

ever, broad in the shoulders and narrow in the hips;
Ingeborg was laughing and tossing her head in a certain
high-spirited way she had; she carried her hand, a schoolgirl hand, not at all slender, not at all particularly aristocratic, to the back of her head in a certain manner so that
the thin sleeve fell away from her elbow—and suddenly
such a pang of home-sickness shook his breast that involuntarily he drew farther back into the darkness lest
someone should see his features twitch.

'Had I forgotten you?' he asked. 'No, never. Not
thee, Hans, not thee, Inge the fair! It was always you
I worked for; when I heard applause I always stole a look
to see if you were there. . . . Did you read *Don Carlos*,
Hans Hansen, as you promised me at the garden gate?
No, don't read it! I do not ask it any more. What
have you to do with a king who weeps for loneliness?
You must not cloud your clear eyes or make them dreamy
and dim by peering into melancholy poetry. . . . To be
like you! To begin again, to grow up like you, regular
like you, simple and normal and cheerful, in conformity
and understanding with God and man, beloved of the
innocent and happy. To take you, Ingeborg Holm,
to wife, and have a son like you, Hans Hansen—to live
free from the curse of knowledge and the torment of
creation, live and praise God in blessed mediocrity!
Begin again? But it would do no good. It would turn
out the same—everything would turn out the same as it
did before. For some go of necessity astray, because for
them there is no such thing as a right path.'

The music ceased; there was a pause in which refreshments were handed round. The post office assistant
tripped about in person with a trayful of herring salad
and served the ladies; but before Ingeborg Holm he even
went down on one knee as he passed her the dish, and she
blushed for pleasure.

But now those within began to be aware of a spectator behind the glass door; some of the flushed and pretty faces turned to measure him with hostile glances; but he stood his ground. Ingeborg and Hans looked at him too, at almost the same time, both with that utter indifference in their eyes that looks so like contempt. And he was conscious too of a gaze resting on him from a different quarter; turned his head and met with his own the eyes that had sought him out. A girl stood not far off, with a fine, pale little face—he had already noticed her. She had not danced much, she had few partners, and he had seen her sitting there against the wall, her lips closed in a bitter line. She was standing alone now too; her dress was a thin light stuff, like the others, but beneath the transparent frock her shoulders showed angular and poor, and the thin neck was thrust down so deep between those meagre shoulders that as she stood there motionless she might almost be thought a little deformed. She was holding her hands in their thin mitts across her flat breast, with the finger-tips touching; her head was drooped, yet she was looking up at Tonio Kröger with black swimming eyes. He turned away. . . .

Here, quite close to him, were Ingeborg and Hans. He had sat down beside her—she was perhaps his sister—and they ate and drank together surrounded by other rosy-cheeked folk; they chattered and made merry, called to each other in ringing voices, and laughed aloud. Why could he not go up and speak to them? Make some trivial remark to him or her, to which they might at least answer with a smile? It would make him happy—he longed to do it; he would go back more satisfied to his room if he might feel he had established a little contact with them. He thought out what he might say; but he had not the courage to say it. Yes, this too was just as it had been: they would not understand him, they would listen like strangers to anything he was able to say. For their speech was not his speech.

It seemed the dance was about to begin again. The leader developed a comprehensive activity. He dashed hither and thither, adjuring everybody to get partners; helped the waiters to push chairs and glasses out of the way, gave orders to the musicians, even took some awkward people by the shoulders and shoved them aside. . . . What was coming? They formed squares of four couples each. . . . A frightful memory brought the colour to Tonio Kröger's cheeks. They were forming for a quadrille.

The music struck up, the couples bowed and crossed over. The leader gave his orders—heaven save us— in French! And pronounced the nasals with great distinction. Ingeborg Holm danced close by, in the set nearest the glass door. She moved to and fro before him, forwards and back, pacing and turning; he caught a waft from her hair or the thin stuff of her frock, and it made him close his eyes with the old, familiar feeling, the fragrance and bitter-sweet enchantment he had faintly felt in all these days, that now filled him utterly with irresistible sweetness. And what was the feeling? Longing, tenderness? Envy? Self-contempt? . . . *Moulinet des dames!* 'Did you laugh, Ingeborg the blonde, did you laugh at me when I disgraced myself by dancing the *moulinet*? And would you still laugh to-day even after I have become something like a famous man? Yes, that you would, and you would be right to laugh. Even if I in my own person had written the nine sym-phonies and *The World as Will and Idea* and painted the 'Last Judgment,' you would still be eternally right to laugh. . . .' As he looked at her he thought of a line of verse once so familiar to him, now long forgotten: 'I would sleep, but thou must dance.' How well he knew it, that melancholy northern mood it evoked—its heavy inarticulateness. To sleep. . . . to long to be allowed to live the life of simple feeling, to rest sweetly and passively in feeling alone, without compulsion to act and achieve—and yet to be forced to dance, dance the cruel and perilous sword-dance of art; without even being allowed to forget the melancholy conflict within oneself; to be forced to dance, the while one loved. . . .

A sudden wild extravagance had come over the scene. The sets had broken up, the quadrille was being succeeded by a galop, and all the couples were leaping and gliding about. They flew past Tonio Kröger to a maddeningly quick tempo, crossing, advancing, retreating, with quick, breathless laughter. A couple came rushing and circling towards Tonio Kröger; the girl had a pale, refined face and lean, high shoulders. Suddenly, directly in front of him, they tripped and slipped and stumbled. . . . The pale girl fell, so hard and violently it almost looked dangerous; and her partner with her. He must have hurt himself badly, for he quite forgot her, and, half rising, began to rub his knee and grimace; while she, quite dazed, it seemed, still lay on the floor. Then Tonio Kröger came forward, took her gently by the arms, and lifted her up. She looked dazed, bewildered, wretched; then suddenly her delicate face flushed pink.

'*Tak, O, mange tak!*' she said, and gazed up at him with dark, swimming eyes.

'You should not dance any more, Fräulein,' he said gently. Once more he looked round at *them*, at Ingeborg and Hans, and then he went out, left the ball and the veranda and returned to his own room.

He was exhausted with jealousy, worn out with the gaiety in which he had had no part. Just the same, just the same as it had always been. Always with burning cheeks he had stood in his dark corner and suffered for you, you blond, you living, you happy ones! And then quite simply gone away. Somebody *must* come now! Ingeborg *must* notice he had gone, must slip after him, lay a hand·on his shoulder and say: 'Come back and be happy. I love you!' But she came not at all. No, such things did not happen. Yes, all was as it had been, and he too was happy, just as he had been. For his heart was alive. But between that past and this present what had happened to make him become that which he now was? Icy desolation, solitude; mind, and art, forsooth!

He undressed, lay down, put out the light. Two names he whispered into his pillow, the few chaste northern syllables that meant for him his true and native way of love, of longing and happiness; that meant to him life and home, meant simple and heartfelt feeling. He looked back on the years that had passed. He thought of the dreamy adventures of the senses, nerves, and mind in which he had been involved; saw himself eaten up with intellect and introspection, ravaged and paralysed by insight, half worn out by the fevers and frosts of creation, helpless and in anguish of conscience between two extremes, flung to and fro between austerity and lust; *raffiné*, impoverished, exhausted by frigid and artificially heightened ecstasies; erring, forsaken, martyred, and ill— and sobbed with nostalgia and remorse.

Here in his room it was still and dark. But from below life's lulling, trivial waltz rhythm came faintly to his ears.

Tonio Kröger sat up in the north, composing his promised letter to his friend Lisabeta Ivanovna.

'Dear Lisabeta, down there in Arcady, whither I shall shortly return,' he wrote, 'here is something like a letter, but it will probably disappoint you, for I mean to keep it rather general. Not that I have nothing to tell; for indeed, in my way, I have had experiences; for instance, in my native town they were even going to arrest me . . . but of that by word of mouth. Sometimes now I have days when I would rather state things in general terms than go on telling stories.

'You probably still remember, Lisabeta, that you called me a bourgeois, a bourgeois *manqué*? You called me that in an hour when, led on by other confessions I had previously let slip, I confessed to you my love of life, or what I call life. I ask myself if you were aware how very close you came to the truth, how much my love of "life" is one and the same thing as my being a bourgeois. This journey of mine has given me much occasion to ponder the subject.

'My father, you know, had the temperament of the north: solid, reflective, puritanically correct, with a tendency to melancholia. My mother, of indeterminate foreign blood, was beautiful, sensuous, naïve, passionate, and careless at once, and, I think, irregular by instinct. The mixture was no doubt extraordinary and bore with it extraordinary dangers. The issue of it, a bourgeois who strayed off into art, a Bohemian who feels nostalgic yearnings for respectability, an artist with a bad conscience. For surely it is my bourgeois conscience makes me see in the artist life, in all irregularity and all genius, something profoundly suspect, profoundly disreputable; that fills me with this lovelorn *faiblesse* for the simple and good, the comfortably normal, the average unendowed respectable human being.

'I stand between two worlds. I am at home in neither, and I suffer in consequence. You artists call me a bourgeois, and the bourgeois try to arrest me. . . . I don't know which makes me feel worse. The bourgeois are stupid; but you adorers of the beautiful, who call me phlegmatic and without aspirations, you ought to realize that there is a way of being an artist that goes so deep and is so much a matter of origins and destinies that no longing seems to it sweeter and more worth knowing than longing after the bliss of the commonplace.

'I admire those proud, cold beings who adventure upon the paths of great and daemonic beauty and despise 'mankind'; but I do not envy them. For if anything is capable of making a poet of a literary man, it is my bourgeois love of the human, the living and usual. It is the source of all warmth, goodness, and humour; I even almost think it is itself that love of which it is written that one may speak with the tongues of men and of angels and yet having it not is as a sounding brass and a tinkling cymbal.

'The work I have so far done is nothing or not much —as good as nothing. I will do better, Lisabeta—this is a promise. As I write, the sea whispers to me and I close my eyes. I am looking into a world unborn and formless, that needs to be ordered and shaped; I see into a whirl of shadows of human figures who beckon to me to weave spells to redeem them: tragic and laughable figures, and some that are both together—and to these I am drawn. But my deepest and most secret love belongs to the blonde and blue-eyed, the fair and living, the happy, lovely, and commonplace.

'Do not chide this love, Lisabeta; it is good and fruitful. There is longing in it, and a gentle envy; a touch of contempt and no little innocent bliss.'

DEATH IN VENICE

GUSTAV ASCHENBACH—or von Aschenbach, as he had been known officially since his fiftieth birthday—had set out alone from his house in Prince Regent Street, Munich, for a long walk. It was a spring afternoon in that year of grace 19—, when Europe looked in such imminent danger for long months. Aschenbach was overwrought by a morning of hard, nerve-taxing work, work which had not ceased to exact his uttermost in the way of sustained concentration, conscientiousness, and tact; and after the noon meal found himself powerless to check the onward sweep of the productive mechanism within him, that *motus animi continuus* in which, according to Cicero, eloquence resides. He had sought but not found relaxation in sleep—though the wear and tear upon his system had come to make a daily nap more and more imperative—and now had sought the open soon after tea, in the hope that air and exercise might send him back refreshed to a good evening's work.

May had begun, and after weeks of cold and wet a mock summer had set in. The English Gardens, though in tenderest leaf, felt as sultry as in August and were full of vehicles and pedestrians near the city. But towards Aumeister the paths were solitary and still, and Aschenbach strolled thither, stopping awhile to watch the lively crowds in the restaurant garden with its fringe of carriages and cabs. Thence he took his homeward way outside the park and across the sunset fields. By the time he reached the North Cemetery, however, he felt tired, and a storm was brewing above Föhring; so he waited

69

at the stopping place for a tram to carry him back
to the city.

He found the neighbourhood quite empty. Not a
wagon in sight, either on the paved Ungererstrasse, with
its gleaming tramlines stretching off towards Schwabing,
nor on the Föhring highway. Nothing stirred behind
the hedge in the stone mason's yard, where crosses,
monuments, and commemorative tablets made a supernumerary and untenanted graveyard opposite the real
one. The mortuary chapel, a structure in Byzantine
style, stood facing it, silent in the gleam of the ebbing
day. Its façade was adorned with Greek crosses and
tinted hieratic designs, and displayed a symmetrically
arranged selection of scriptural texts in gilded letters, all
of them with a bearing upon the future life, such as:
'They are entering into the House of the Lord' and
'May the Light Everlasting shine upon them.' Aschenbach beguiled some minutes of his waiting with reading
these formulas and letting his mind's eye lose itself in
their mystical meaning. He was brought back to reality
by the sight of a man standing in the portico, above the
two apocalyptic beasts that guarded the staircase, and
something not quite usual in this man's appearance gave
his thoughts a fresh turn.

Whether he had come out of the hall through the
bronze doors or mounted unnoticed from outside, it was
impossible to tell. Aschenbach casually inclined to the
first idea. He was of medium height, thin, beardless,
and strikingly snub-nosed; he belonged to the red-haired
type and possessed its milky, freckled skin. He was
obviously not Bavarian; and the broad, straight-brimmed
straw hat he had on even made him look distinctly exotic.
True, he had the indigenous rucksack buckled on his
back, wore a belted suit of yellowish woollen stuff,
apparently frieze, and carried a grey mackintosh cape

across his left forearm, which was propped against his waist. In his right hand, slantwise to the ground, he held an iron-shod stick, and braced himself against its crook, with his legs crossed. His chin was up, so that the Adam's apple looked very bald in the lean neck rising from the loose shirt; and he stood there sharply peering up into space out of colourless, red-lashed eyes, while two pronounced perpendicular furrows showed on his forehead in curious contrast to his little turned-up nose. Perhaps his heightened and heightening position helped out the impression Aschenbach received. At any rate, standing there as though at survey, the man had a bold and domineering, even a ruthless, air, and his lips completed the picture by seeming to curl back, either by reason of some deformity or else because he grimaced, being blinded by the sun in his face; they laid bare the long, white, glistening teeth to the gums.

Aschenbach's gaze, though unawares, had very likely been inquisitive and tactless; for he became suddenly conscious that the stranger was returning it, and indeed so directly, with such hostility, such plain intent to force the withdrawal of the other's eyes, that Aschenbach felt an unpleasant twinge and, turning his back, began to walk along the hedge, hastily resolving to give the man no further heed. He had forgotten him the next minute. Yet whether the pilgrim air the stranger wore kindled his fantasy or whether some other physical or psychical influence came into play, he could not tell; but he felt the most surprising consciousness of a widening of inward barriers, a kind of vaulting unrest, a youthfully ardent thirst for distant scenes—a feeling so lively and so new, or at least so long ago outgrown and forgot, that he stood there rooted to the spot, his eyes on the ground and his hands clasped behind him, exploring these sentiments of his, their bearing and scope.

True, what he felt was no more than a longing to
travel; yet coming upon him with such suddenness and
passion as to resemble a seizure, almost a hallucination.
Desire projected itself visually: his fancy, not quite yet
lulled since morning, imaged the marvels and terrors of the
manifold earth. He saw. He beheld a landscape, a
tropical marshland, beneath a reeking sky, steaming,
monstrous, rank—a kind of primeval wilderness world
of islands, morasses, and alluvial channels. Hairy palm-
trunks rose near and far out of lush brakes of fern, out of
bottoms of crass vegetation, fat, swollen, thick with
incredible bloom. There were trees, misshapen as a
dream, that dropped their naked roots straight through
the air into the ground or into water that was stagnant
and shadowy and glassy-green, where mammoth milk-
white blossoms floated, and strange high-shouldered birds
with curious bills stood gazing sideways without sound or
stir. Among the knotted joints of a bamboo thicket the
eyes of a crouching tiger gleamed—and he felt his heart
throb with terror, yet with a longing inexplicable. Then
the vision vanished. Aschenbach, shaking his head, took
up his march once more along the hedge of the stone
mason's yard.

He had, at least ever since he commanded means to
get about the world at will, regarded travel as a necessary
evil, to be endured now and again willy-nilly for the sake
of one's health. Too busy with the tasks imposed upon
him by his own ego and the European soul, too laden
with the care and duty to create, too preoccupied to be
an amateur of the gay outer world, he had been content
to know as much of the earth's surface as he could without
stirring far outside his own sphere—had, indeed, never
even been tempted to leave Europe. Now more than
ever, since his life was on the wane, since he could
no longer brush aside as fanciful his artist fear of not

having done, of not being finished before the works
ran down, he had confined himself to close range, had
hardly stepped outside the charming city which he
had made his home and the rude country house he had
built in the mountains, whither he went to spend the
rainy summers.

And so the new impulse which thus late and suddenly
swept over him was speedily made to conform to the
pattern of self-discipline he had followed from his youth
up. He had meant to bring his work, for which he lived,
to a certain point before leaving for the country, and the
thought of a leisurely ramble across the globe, which should
take him away from his desk for months, was too fantastic
and upsetting to be seriously entertained. Yet the
source of the unexpected contagion was known to him
only too well. This yearning for new and distant scenes,
this craving for freedom, release, forgetfulness—they
were, he admitted to himself, an impulse towards flight,
flight from the spot which was the daily theatre of a rigid,
cold, and passionate service. That service he loved, had
even almost come to love the enervating daily struggle
between a proud, tenacious, well-tried will and this
growing fatigue, which no one must suspect, nor the
finished product betray by any faintest sign that his
inspiration could ever flag or miss fire. On the other
hand, it seemed the part of common sense not to bend
the bow too far, not to suppress summarily a need that so
unequivocally asserted itself. He thought of his work,
and the place where yesterday and again to-day he had
been forced to lay it down, since it would not yield either
to patient effort or a swift *coup de main*. Again and again
he had tried to break or untie the knot—only to retire
at last from the attack with a shiver of repugnance. Yet
the difficulty was actually not a great one; what sapped his
strength was distaste for the task, betrayed by a fastidiousness

he could no longer satisfy.   In his youth, indeed, the
nature and inmost essence of the literary gift had been, to
him, this very scrupulosity; for it he had bridled and
tempered his sensibilities, knowing full well that feeling
is prone to be content with easy gains and blithe half
perfection.   So now, perhaps, feeling, thus tyrannized,
avenged itself by leaving him, refusing from now on to
carry and wing his art and taking away with it all the
ecstasy he had known in form and expression.   Not that
he was doing bad work.   So much, at least, the years had
brought him, that at any moment he might feel tranquilly
assured of mastery.   But he got no joy out of it—not
though a nation paid it homage.   To him it seemed his
work had ceased to be marked by that fiery play of fancy
which is the product of joy, and more, and more potently,
than any intrinsic content, forms in turn the joy of the
receiving world.   He dreaded the summer in the country,
alone with the maid who prepared his food and the man
who served him; dreaded to see the familiar mountain
peaks and walls that would shut him up again with his
heavy discontent.   What he needed was a break, an
interim existence, a means of passing time, other air and
a new stock of blood, to make the summer tolerable
and productive.   Good, then, he would go a journey.
Not far—not all the way to the tigers.   A night in
a *wagon-lit*, three or four weeks of lotus-eating at
some one of the gay world's playgrounds in the lovely
south. . . .

So ran his thoughts, while the clang of the electric
tram drew nearer down the Ungererstrasse; and as he
mounted the platform he decided to devote the evening
to a study of maps and railway guides.   Once in, he
bethought him to look back after the man in the straw
hat, the companion of this brief interval which had after
all been so fruitful.   But he was not in his former place,

nor in the tram itself, nor yet at the next stop; in short, his whereabouts remained a mystery.

Gustav Aschenbach was born at L——, a country town in the province of Silesia. He was the son of an upper official in the judicature, and his forbears had all been officers, judges, departmental functionaries—men who lived their strict, decent, sparing lives in the service of king and State. Only once before had a livelier mentality—in the person of a clergyman—turned up among them; but swifter, more perceptive blood had in the generation before the poet's flowed into the stock from the mother's side, she being the daughter of a Bohemian musical conductor. It was from her he had the foreign traits that betrayed themselves in his appearance. The union of dry, conscientious officialdom and ardent, obscure impulse produced an artist—and this particular artist: author of the lucid and vigorous prose epic on the life of Frederick the Great; careful, tireless weaver of the richly patterned tapestry entitled *Maia*, a novel that gathers up the threads of many human destinies in the warp of a single idea; creator of that powerful narrative *The Abject*, which taught a whole grateful generation that a man can still be capable of moral resolution even after he has plumbed the depths of knowledge; and lastly —to complete the tale of works of his mature period— the writer of that impassioned discourse on the theme of Mind and Art whose ordered force and antithetic eloquence led serious critics to rank it with Schiller's *Simple and Sentimental Poetry*.

Aschenbach's whole soul, from the very beginning, was bent on fame—and thus, while not precisely precocious, yet thanks to the unmistakable trenchancy of his personal accent he was early ripe and ready for a career. Almost before he was out of high school he had a name.

Ten years later he had learned to sit at his desk and sustain
and live up to his growing reputation, to write gracious
and pregnant phrases in letters that must needs be brief,
for many claims press upon the solid and successful man.
At forty, worn down by the strains and stresses of his
actual task, he had to deal with a daily post heavy with
tributes from his own and foreign countries.

Remote on one hand from the banal, on the other from
the eccentric, his genius was calculated to win at once the
adhesion of the general public and the admiration, both
sympathetic and stimulating, of the connoisseur. From
childhood up he was pushed on every side to achievement,
and achievement of no ordinary kind; and so his young
days never knew the sweet idleness and blithe *laissez-aller*
that belong to youth. A nice observer once said of him
in company—it was at the time when he fell ill in Vienna
in his thirty-fifth year: 'You see, Aschenbach has always
lived like this'—here the speaker closed the fingers of his
left hand to a fist—'never like this'—and he let his open
hand hang relaxed from the back of his chair. It was apt.
And this attitude was the more morally valiant in that
Aschenbach was not by nature robust—he was only called
to the constant tension of his career, not actually born to it.

By medical advice he had been kept from school and
educated at home. He had grown up solitary, without
comradeship; yet had early been driven to see that he
belonged to those whose talent is not so much out of the
common as is the physical basis on which talent relies
for its fulfilment. It is a seed that gives early of its fruit,
whose powers seldom reach a ripe old age. But his
favourite motto was 'Hold fast'; indeed, in his novel on
the life of Frederick the Great he envisaged nothing else
than the apotheosis of the old hero's word of command,
'Durchhalten,' which seemed to him the epitome of fortitude under suffering. Besides, he deeply desired to live

to a good old age, for it was his conviction that only the artist to whom it has been granted to be fruitful on all stages of our human scene can be truly great, or universal, or worthy of honour.

Bearing the burden of his genius, then, upon such slender shoulders and resolved to go so far, he had the more need of discipline—and discipline, fortunately, was his native inheritance from the father's side. At forty, at fifty, he was still living as he had begun to live in the years when others are prone to waste and revel, dream high thoughts, and postpone fulfilment. He began his day with a cold shower over chest and back; then, setting a pair of tall wax candles in silver holders at the head of his manuscript, he sacrificed to art, in two or three hours of almost religious fervour, the powers he had assembled in sleep. Outsiders might be pardoned for believing that his *Maia* world and the epic amplitude revealed by the life of Frederick were a manifestation of great power working under high pressure, that they came forth, as it were, all in one breath. It was the greater triumph for his morale; for the truth was that they were heaped up to greatness in layer after layer, in long days of work, out of hundreds and hundreds of single inspirations; they owed their excellence, both of mass and detail, to one thing and one alone: that their creator could hold out for years under the strain of the same piece of work, with an endurance and a tenacity of purpose like that which had conquered his native province of Silesia, devoting to actual composition none but his best and freshest hours.

For an intellectual product of any value to exert an immediate influence which shall also be deep and lasting, it must rest on an inner harmony, yes, an affinity, between the personal destiny of its author and that of his contemporaries in general. Men do not know why they award fame to one work of art rather than another. Without being in the faintest degree connoisseurs, they think to justify the warmth of their commendations by discovering in it a hundred virtues, whereas the real ground of their applause is inexplicable—it is sympathy. Aschenbach had once given direct expression—though in an unobtrusive place—to the idea that almost everything conspicuously great is great in despite: has come into being in defiance of affliction and pain, poverty, destitution, bodily weakness, vice, passion, and a thousand other obstructions. And that was more than observation—it was the fruit of experience, it was precisely the formula of his life and fame, it was the key to his work. What wonder, then, if it was also the fixed character, the outward gesture, of his most individual figures?

The new type of hero favoured by Aschenbach, and recurring many times in his works, had early been analysed by a shrewd critic: 'The conception of an intellectual and virginal manliness, which clenches its teeth and stands in modest defiance of the swords and spears that pierce its side.' That was beautiful, it was *spirituel*, it was exact, despite the suggestion of too great passivity it held. Fortitude in the face of fate, beauty constant under torture, are not merely passive. They are a positive achievement, an explicit triumph; and the figure of Sebastian is the most beautiful symbol, if not of art as a whole, yet certainly of the art we speak of here. Within that world of Aschenbach's creation were exhibited many phases of this theme: there was the aristocratic self-command that can conceal to the last moment its inner undermining and its biologic decline from the eyes of the world; the sere and ugly outside, hiding the embers of smouldering fire—and having power to fan them to so pure a flame as to challenge supremacy in the domain of beauty itself; the pallid languors of the flesh, contrasted with the fiery

ardours of the spirit within, which can fling a whole
proud people down at the foot of the Cross, at the feet of
its own sheer self-abnegation; the gracious bearing
preserved in the stern, stark service of form; the
unreal, precarious existence of the born intrigant
with its swiftly enervating alternation of schemes and
desires—all these human fates and many more of their
like one read in Aschenbach's pages, and reading them
might doubt the existence of any other kind of heroism
than the heroism born of weakness. And, after all, what
kind could be truer to the spirit of the times? Gustav
Aschenbach was the poet spokesman of all those who
labour at the edge of exhaustion; of the overburdened,
of those who are already worn out but still hold themselves
upright; of all our modern moralizers of accomplishment,
with stunted growth and scanty resources, who yet
contrive by skilful husbanding and prodigious spasms of
will to produce, at least for a while, the effect of greatness.
There are many such, they are the heroes of the age.
And in Aschenbach's pages they saw themselves; he
justified, he exalted them, he sang their praise—and they,
they were grateful, they heralded his fame.

He had been young and crude with the times and by
them badly counselled. He had taken false steps, blun-
dered, exposed himself, offended in speech and writing
against tact and good sense. But he had attained to
honour, and honour, he used to say, is the natural goal
towards which every considerable talent presses with
whip and spur. Yes, one might put it that his whole
career had been one conscious and overweening ascent
to honour, which left in the rear all the misgivings or
self-derogation which might have hampered him.

What pleases the public is lively and vivid delineation
which makes no demands on the intellect; but passionate
and absolutist youth can only be enthralled by a problem.

And Aschenbach was as absolute, as problematist, as any
youth of them all. He had done homage to intellect,
had overworked the soil of knowledge and ground up
her seed corn; had turned his back on the 'mysteries,'
called genius itself in question, held art up to scorn—yes,
even while his faithful following revelled in the characters
he created, he, the young artist, was taking away the
breath of the twenty-year-olds with his cynical utterances
on the nature of art and the artist life.

But it seems that a noble and active mind blunts itself
against nothing so quickly as the sharp and bitter irritant
of knowledge. And certain it is that the youth's constancy of purpose, no matter how painfully conscientious,
was shallow beside the mature resolution of the master
of his craft, who made a right-about-face, turned his
back on the realm of knowledge, and passed it by with
averted face, lest it should lame his will or power of action,
paralyse his feelings or his passions, deprive any of these
of their conviction or utility. How else interpret the
oft-cited story of *The Abject* than as a rebuke to the excesses
of a psychology-ridden age, embodied in the delineation
of the weak and silly fool who manages to lead fate by
the nose; driving his wife, out of sheer innate pusillanimity,
into the arms of a beardless youth, and making this disaster
an excuse for trifling away the rest of his life?

With rage the author here rejects the rejected, casts
out the outcast—and the measure of his fury is the measure
of his condemnation of all moral shilly-shallying. Explicitly he renounces sympathy with the abyss, explicitly
he refutes the flabby humanitarianism of the phrase:
'Tout comprendre c'est tout pardonner.' What was
here unfolding, or rather was already in full bloom,
was the 'miracle of regained detachment,' which a little
later became the theme of one of the author's dialogues,
dwelt upon not without a certain oracular emphasis.

Strange sequence of thought! Was it perhaps an intellectual consequence of this rebirth, this new austerity, that from now on his style showed an almost exaggerated sense of beauty, a lofty purity, symmetry, and simplicity, which gave his productions a stamp of the classic, of conscious and deliberate mastery? And yet: this moral fibre, surviving the hampering and disintegrating effect of knowledge, does it not result in its turn in a dangerous simplification, in a tendency to equate the world and the human soul, and thus to strengthen the hold of the evil, the forbidden, and the ethically impossible? And has not form two aspects? Is it not moral and immoral at once: moral in so far as it is the expression and result of discipline, immoral—yes, actually hostile to morality—in that of its very essence it is indifferent to good and evil, and deliberately concerned to make the moral world stoop beneath its proud and undivided sceptre?

Be that as it may. Development is destiny; and why should a career attended by the applause and adulation of the masses necessarily take the same course as one which does not share the glamour and the obligations of fame? Only the incorrigible Bohemian smiles or scoffs when a man of transcendent gifts outgrows his carefree prentice stage, recognizes his own worth, and forces the world to recognize it too and pay it homage, though he puts on a courtly bearing to hide his bitter struggles and his loneliness. Again, the play of a developing talent must give its possessor joy, if of a wilful, defiant kind. With time, an official note, something almost expository, crept into Gustav Aschenbach's method. His later style gave up the old sheer audacities, the fresh and subtle nuances—it became fixed and exemplary, conservative, formal, even formulated. Like Louis XIV—or as tradition has it of him—Aschenbach, as he went on in years, banished from his style every common word. It was at this time that the school authorities adopted selections from his works into their text-books.   And he found it only fitting—and had no thought but to accept— when a German prince signalized his accession to the throne by conferring upon the poet-author of the life of Frederick the Great on his fiftieth birthday the letters patent of nobility.

He had roved about for a few years, trying this town and that as a place of residence, before choosing, as he soon did, the city of Munich for his permanent home.   And there he lived, enjoying among his fellow citizens the honour which is in rare cases the reward of intellectual eminence.   He married young, the daughter of a university family; but after a brief term of wedded happiness his wife had died.   A daughter, already married, remained to him.   A son he never had.

Gustav von Aschenbach was somewhat below middle height, dark and smooth-shaven, with a head that looked rather too large for his almost delicate figure.   He wore his hair brushed back; it was thin at the parting, bushy and grey on the temples, framing a lofty, rugged, knotty brow—if one may so characterize it.   The nose piece of his rimless gold spectacles cut into the base of his thick, aristocratically hooked nose.   The mouth was large, often lax, often suddenly narrow and tense; the cheeks lean and furrowed, the pronounced chin slightly cleft. The vicissitudes of fate, it seemed, must have passed over this head, for he held it, plaintively, rather on one side; yet it was art, not the stern discipline of an active career, that had taken over the office of modelling these features. Behind this brow were born the flashing thrust and parry of the dialogue between Frederick and Voltaire on the theme of war; these eyes, weary and sunken, gazing through their glasses, had beheld the blood-stained inferno of the hospitals in the Seven Years War.   Yes, personally speaking too, art heightens life. She gives deeper joy, she consumes more swiftly. She engraves adventures of the spirit and the mind on the faces of her votaries; let them lead outwardly a life of the most cloistered calm, she will in the end produce in them a fastidiousness, and over-refinement, a nervous fever and exhaustion such as a career of extravagant passions and pleasures can hardly show.

Eager though he was to be off, Aschenbach was kept in Munich by affairs both literary and practical for some two weeks after that walk of his. But at length he ordered his country home to be put ready against his return within the next few weeks, and on a day between the middle and the end of May took the evening train for Trieste, where he stopped only twenty-four hours, embarking for Pola the next morning but one.

What he sought was a fresh scene, without associations, which should yet be not too out of the way; and accordingly he chose an island in the Adriatic, not far off the Istrian coast. It had been well known some years, for its splendidly rugged cliff formations on the side next the open sea, and its population, clad in a bright flutter of rags and speaking an outlandish tongue. But there was rain and heavy air; the society at the hotel was provincial Austrian, and limited; besides, it annoyed him not to be able to get at the sea—he missed the close and soothing contact which only a gentle sandy slope affords. He could not feel this was the place he sought; an inner impulse made him wretched, urging him on he knew not whither; he racked his brains, he looked up boats, then all at once his goal stood plain before his eyes. But of course! When one wanted to arrive overnight at the incomparable, the fabulous, the like-nothing-else-in-the-world, where was it one went? Why, obviously; he had

intended to go there, what ever was he doing here? A
blunder. He made all haste to correct it, announcing
his departure at once. Ten days after his arrival on the
island a swift motor boat bore him and his luggage in the
misty dawning back across the water to the naval station,
where he landed only to pass over the landing stage and
on to the wet decks of a ship lying there with steam up
for the passage to Venice.

It was an ancient hulk belonging to an Italian line,
obsolete, dingy, grimed with soot. A dirty hunchbacked
sailor, smirkingly polite, conducted him at once below
to a cavernous, lamplit cabin. There behind a table
sat a man with a beard like a goat's; he had his hat
on the back of his head, a cigar stump in the corner of
his mouth; he reminded Aschenbach of an old-fashioned
circus director. This person put the usual questions and
wrote out a ticket to Venice, which he issued to the
traveller with many commercial flourishes.

'A ticket for Venice,' repeated he, stretching out his
arm to dip the pen into the thick ink in a tilted inkstand.
'One first class to Venice! Here you are, *signore mio*.'
He made some scrawls on the paper, strewed bluish sand
on it out of a box, thereafter letting the sand run off into
an earthen vessel, folded the paper with bony yellow
fingers, and wrote on the outside. 'An excellent choice,'
he rattled on. 'Ah, Venice! What a glorious city!
Irresistibly attractive to the cultured man for her past
history as well as her present charm.' His copious
gesturings and empty phrases gave the odd impression
that he feared the traveller might alter his mind. He
changed Aschenbach's note, laying the money on the
spotted table cover with the glibness of a croupier. 'A
pleasant visit to you, signore,' he said, with a melodramatic
bow. 'Delighted to serve you.' Then he beckoned
and called out: 'Next,' as though a stream of passengers

stood waiting to be served, though in point of fact there was not one. Aschenbach returned to the upper deck.

He leaned an arm on the railing and looked at the idlers lounging along the quay to watch the boat go out. Then he turned his attention to his fellow passengers. Those of the second class, both men and women, were squatted on their bundles of luggage on the forward deck. The first cabin consisted of a group of lively youths, clerks from Pola, evidently, who had made up a pleasure excursion to Italy and were not a little thrilled at the prospect, bustling about and laughing with satisfaction at the stir they made. They leaned over the railings and shouted, with a glib command of epithet, derisory remarks at such of their fellow clerks as they saw going to business along the quay; and these in turn shook their sticks and shouted as good back again. One of the party, in a dandified buff suit, a rakish panama with a coloured scarf, and a red cravat, was loudest of the loud; he outcrowed all the rest. Aschenbach's eye dwelt on him, and he was shocked to see that the apparent youth was no youth at all. He was an old man, beyond a doubt, with wrinkles and crow's-feet round eyes and mouth; the dull carmine of the cheeks was rouge, the brown hair a wig. His neck was shrunken and sinewy, his turned-up moustaches and small imperial were dyed, and the unbroken double row of yellow teeth he showed when he laughed were but too obviously a cheapish false set. He wore a seal ring on each forefinger, but the hands were those of an old man. Aschenbach was moved to shudder as he watched the creature and his association with the rest of the group. Could they not see he was old, that he had no right to wear the clothes they wore or pretend to be one of them? But they were used to him, it seemed; they suffered him among them, they paid back his jokes in kind and the playful pokes in the ribs he gave them. How could they?

Aschenbach put his hand to his brow, and covered his eyes, for he had slept little, and they smarted. He felt not quite normal, as though the world were suffering a dream-like distortion of perspective which he might arrest by shutting it all out for a few minutes and then looking at it afresh. At this instant he felt a floating sensation, and opened his eyes with unreasoning alarm to find that the ship's dark sluggish bulk was slowly leaving the jetty. Inch by inch, with the to-and-fro motion of her machinery, the strip of iridescent dirty water widened, the boat manœuvred clumsily and turned her bow to the open sea. Aschenbach moved over to the starboard side, where the hunchbacked sailor had set up a deck chair for him, and a steward in a greasy dress coat asked for orders.

The sky was grey, the wind humid. Harbour and island dropped behind, all sight of land soon vanished in mist. Flakes of sodden, clammy soot fell upon the still undried deck. Before the boat was an hour out a canvas had to be spread as a shelter from the rain.

Wrapped in his cloak, a book in his lap, our traveller rested; the hours slipped by unawares. It stopped raining, the canvas was taken down. The horizon was visible right round: beneath the sombre dome of the sky stretched the vast plain of empty sea. But immeasurable unarticulated space weakens our power to measure time as well; the time sense falters and grows dim. Strange, shadowy figures—the elderly coxcomb, the goat-bearded man from the bowels of the ship—passed and repassed with vague gesturings and mutterings through the traveller's mind as he lay. He fell asleep.

At midday he was summoned to luncheon in a corridor-like saloon with the sleeping cabins giving off it. He ate at the head of the long table; the party of clerks, including the old man, sat with the jolly captain at the other end, where they had been carousing since ten o'clock. The meal was wretched, and soon done. Aschenbach was driven to seek the open and look at the sky—perhaps it would lighten presently above Venice.

He had not dreamed it could be otherwise, for the city had ever given him a brilliant welcome. But sky and sea remained leaden, with spurts of fine, mistlike rain; he reconciled himself to the idea of seeing a different Venice from that he had always approached on the landward side. He stood by the foremast, his gaze on the distance, alert for the first glimpse of the coast. And he thought of the melancholy and susceptible poet who had once seen the towers and turrets of his dreams rise out of these waves; repeated the rhythms born of his awe, his mingled emotions of joy and suffering—and easily susceptible to a prescience already shaped within him, he asked his own sober, weary heart if a new enthusiasm, a new preoccupation, some late adventure of the feelings could still be in store for the idle traveller.

The flat coast showed on the right, the sea was soon populous with fishing boats. The Lido appeared and was left behind as the ship glided at half speed through the narrow harbour of the same name, coming to a full stop on the lagoon in sight of garish, badly built houses. Here it waited for the boat bringing the sanitary inspector.

An hour passed. One had arrived—and yet not. There was no conceivable haste—yet one felt harried. The youths from Pola were on deck, drawn there by the martial sound of horns coming across the water from the direction of the public gardens. They had drunk a good deal of Asti and were moved to shout and hurrah at the drilling *bersaglieri*. But the young-old man was a truly repulsive sight in the condition to which his company with youth had brought him. He could not carry his wine like them: he was pitiably drunk. He swayed as he stood—watery-eyed, a cigarette between his shaking

*D 962

fingers, keeping upright with difficulty. He could not have taken a step without falling and knew better than to stir, but his spirits were deplorably high. He button-holed any one who came within reach, he stuttered, he giggled, he leered, he fatuously shook his beringed old forefinger; his tongue kept seeking the corner of his mouth in a suggestive motion ugly to behold. Aschenbach's brow darkened as he looked, and there came over him once more a dazed sense, as though things about him were just slightly losing their ordinary perspective, beginning to show a distortion that might merge into the grotesque. He was prevented from dwelling on the feeling, for now the machinery began to thud again, and the ship took up its passage through the Canale di San Marco which had been interrupted so near the goal.

He saw it once more, that landing place that takes the breath away, that amazing group of incredible structures the republic set up to meet the awestruck eye of the approaching seafarer: the airy splendour of the palace and Bridge of Sighs, the columns of lion and saint on the shore, the glory of the projecting flank of the fairy temple, the vista of gateway and clock. Looking, he thought that to come to Venice by the station is like entering a palace by the back door. No one should approach, save by the high seas as he was doing now, this most improbable of cities.

The engines stopped. Gondolas pressed alongside, the landing stairs were let down, customs officials came on board and did their office, people began to go ashore. Aschenbach ordered a gondola. He meant to take up his abode by the sea and needed to be conveyed with his luggage to the landing stage of the little steamers that ply between the city and the Lido. They called down his order to the surface of the water where the gondoliers were quarrelling in dialect. Then came another delay while his trunk was worried down the ladder-like stairs. Thus he was forced to endure the importunities of the ghastly young-old man, whose drunken state obscurely urged him to pay the stranger the honour of a formal farewell. 'We wish you a very pleasant sojourn,' he babbled, bowing and scraping. 'Pray keep us in mind. *Au revoir, excusez et bonjour, votre Excellence.*' He drooled, he blinked, he licked the corner of his mouth, the little imperial bristled on his elderly chin. He put the tips of two fingers to his mouth and said thickly: 'Give her our love, will you, the p-pretty little dear'— here his upper plate came away and fell down on the lower one. . . . Aschenbach escaped. 'Little sweety-sweety-sweetheart,' he heard behind him, gurgled and stuttered, as he climbed down the rope stair into the boat.

Is there any one but must repress a secret thrill, on arriving in Venice for the first time—or returning thither after long absence—and stepping into a Venetian gondola? That singular conveyance, come down unchanged from ballad times, black as nothing else on earth except a coffin —what pictures it calls up of lawless, silent adventures in the plashing night; or even more, what visions of death itself, the bier and solemn rites and last soundless voyage! And has any one remarked that the seat in such a bark, the arm-chair lacquered in coffin-black and dully black-upholstered, is the softest, most luxurious, most relaxing seat in the world? Aschenbach realized it when he had let himself down at the gondolier's feet, opposite his luggage, which lay neatly composed on the vessel's beak. The rowers still gestured fiercely; he heard their harsh, incoherent tones. But the strange stillness of the water city seemed to take up their voices gently, to disembody and scatter them over the sea. It was warm here in the harbour. The lukewarm air of the sirocco breathed upon him, he leaned back among his cushions and gave himself to the yielding element, closing his eyes for very pleasure in an indolence as unaccustomed as sweet. 'The trip will be short,' he thought, and wished it might last for ever. They gently swayed away from the boat with its bustle and clamour of voices.

It grew still and stiller all about. No sound but the splash of the oars, the hollow slap of the wave against the steep, black, halbert-shaped beak of the vessel, and one sound more—a muttering by fits and starts, squeezed out as it were by the motion of his arms, from the lips of the gondolier. He was talking to himself, between his teeth. Aschenbach glanced up and saw with surprise that the lagoon was widening, his vessel was headed for the open sea. Evidently it would not do to give himself up to the *dolce far niente*; he must see his wishes carried out.

'You are to take me to the steamboat landing, you know,' he said, half turning round towards it. The muttering stopped. There was no reply.

'Take me to the steamboat landing,' he repeated, and this time turned quite round and looked up into the face of the gondolier as he stood there on his little elevated deck, high against the pale grey sky. The man had an unpleasing, even brutish face, and wore blue clothes like a sailor's, with a yellow sash; a shapeless straw hat with the braid torn at the brim perched rakishly on his head. His facial structure, as well as the curling blond moustache under the short snub nose, showed him to be of non-Italian stock. Physically rather undersized, so that one would not have expected him to be very muscular, he pulled vigorously at the oar, putting all his body weight behind each stroke. Now and then the effort he made curled back his lips and bared his white teeth to the gums. He spoke in a decided, almost curt voice, looking out to sea over his fare's head: 'The signore is going to the Lido.'

Aschenbach answered: 'Yes, I am. But I only took the gondola to cross over to San Marco. I am using the *vaporetto* from there.'

'But the signore cannot use the *vaporetto*.'

'And why not?'

'Because the *vaporetto* does not take luggage.'

It was true. Aschenbach remembered it. He made no answer. But the man's gruff, overbearing manner, so unlike the usual courtesy of his countrymen towards the stranger, was intolerable. Aschenbach spoke again: 'That is my own affair. I may want to deposit my luggage. You will turn round.'

No answer. The oar splashed, the wave struck dull against the prow. And the muttering began anew, the gondolier talked to himself, between his teeth.

What should the traveller do? Alone on the water with this tongue-tied, obstinate, uncanny man, he saw no way of enforcing his will. And if only he did not excite himself, how pleasantly he might rest! Had he not wished the voyage might last for ever? The wisest thing—and how much the pleasantest!—was to let matters take their own course. A spell of indolence was upon him; it came from the chair he sat in—this low, black-upholstered arm-chair, so gently rocked at the hands of the despotic boatman in his rear. The thought passed dreamily through Aschenbach's brain that perhaps he had fallen into the clutches of a criminal; it had not the power to rouse him to action. More annoying was the simpler explanation: that the man was only trying to extort money. A sense of duty, a recollection, as it were, that this ought to be prevented, made him collect himself to say:

'How much do you ask for the trip?'

And the gondolier, gazing out over his head, replied: 'The signore will pay.'

There was an established reply to this; Aschenbach made it, mechanically:

'I will pay nothing whatever if you do not take me where I want to go.'

'The signore wants to go to the Lido.'

'But not with you.'

'I am a good rower, signore.   I will row you well.'

'So much is true,' thought Aschenbach, and again he relaxed.   'That is true, you row me well.   Even if you mean to rob me, even if you hit me in the back with your oar and send me down into the kingdom of Hades, even then you will have rowed me well.'

But nothing of the sort happened.   Instead, they fell in with company: a boat came alongside and waylaid them, full of men and women singing to guitar and mandolin.   They rowed persistently alongside with the gondola and filled the silence that had rested on the waters with their lyric love of gain.   Aschenbach tossed money into the hat they held out.   The music stopped at once, they rowed away.   And once more the gondolier's mutter became audible as he talked to himself in fits and snatches.

Thus they rowed on, rocked by the wash of a steamer returning citywards.   At the landing two municipal officials were walking up and down with their hands behind their backs and their faces turned towards the lagoon.   Aschenbach was helped on shore by the old man with a boat-hook who is the permanent feature of every landing stage in Venice; and having no small change to pay the boatman, crossed over into the hotel opposite.   His wants were supplied in the lobby; but when he came back his possessions were already on a hand cart on the quay, and gondola and gondolier were gone.

'He ran away, signore,' said the old boatman.   'A bad

lot, a man without a licence.   He is the only gondolier
without one.   The others telephoned over, and he knew
we were on the look-out, so he made off.'

Aschenbach shrugged.

'The signore has had a ride for nothing,' said the old
man, and held out his hat.   Aschenbach dropped some
coins.   He directed that his luggage should be taken to the
Hôtel des Bains and followed the hand cart through the
avenue, that white - blossoming avenue with taverns,
booths, and pensions on either side of it, which runs across
the island diagonally to the beach.

He entered the hotel from the garden terrace at the
back and passed through the vestibule and hall into the
office.   His arrival was expected, and he was served
with courtesy and dispatch.   The manager, a small, soft,
dapper man with a black moustache and a caressing way
with him, wearing a French frock coat, himself took him
up in the lift and showed him his room.   It was a pleasant
chamber, furnished in cherry wood, with lofty windows
looking out to sea.   It was decorated with strong-
scented flowers.   Aschenbach, as soon as he was alone,
and while they brought in his trunk and bags and disposed
them in the room, went up to one of the windows and
stood looking out upon the beach in its afternoon emptiness,
and at the sunless sea, now at the flood-tide and sending
long, low waves with rhythmic beat upon the sand.

A solitary, unused to speaking of what he sees and feels,
has mental experiences which are at once more intense
and less articulate than those of a gregarious man.   They
are sluggish, yet more wayward, and never without a
melancholy tinge.   Sights and impressions which others
brush aside with a glance, a light comment, a smile,
occupy him more than their due; they sink silently in,
they take on meaning, they become experience, emotion,
adventure.   Solitude gives birth to the original in us,

to beauty unfamiliar and perilous—to poetry. But also, it gives birth to the opposite: to the perverse, the illicit, the absurd. Thus the traveller's mind still dwelt with disquiet on the episodes of his journey hither; on the horrible old fop with his drivel about a mistress, on the outlaw boatman and his lost tip. They did not offend his reason, they hardly afforded food for thought; yet they seemed by their very nature fundamentally strange, and thereby vaguely disquieting. Yet here was the sea; even in the midst of such thoughts he saluted it with his eyes, exulting that Venice was near and accessible. At length he turned round, disposed his personal belongings and made certain arrangements with the chambermaid for his comfort, washed, and was conveyed to the ground floor by the green-uniformed Swiss who ran the lift.

He took tea on the terrace facing the sea, and afterwards went down and walked some distance along the shore promenade in the direction of the Hôtel Excelsior. When he came back it seemed to be time to change for dinner. He did so, slowly and methodically as his way was, for he was accustomed to work while he dressed; but even so found himself a little early when he entered the hall, where a large number of guests had collected—strangers to each other and affecting mutual indifference, yet united in expectancy of the meal. He picked up a paper, sat down in a leather arm-chair, and took stock of the company, which compared most favourably with that he had just left.

This was a broad and tolerant atmosphere, of wide horizons. Subdued voices were speaking most of the principal European tongues. That uniform of civilization, the conventional evening dress, gave outward conformity to the varied types. There were long, dry Americans, large-familied Russians, English ladies, German children with French *bonnes*. The Slavic element predominated, it seemed. In Aschenbach's neighbourhood Polish was being spoken.

Round a wicker table next him was gathered a group of young folk in charge of a governess or companion— three young girls, perhaps fifteen to seventeen years old, and a long-haired boy of about fourteen. Aschenbach noticed with astonishment the lad's perfect beauty. His face recalled the noblest moment of Greek sculpture— pale, with a sweet reserve, with clustering honey-coloured ringlets, the brow and nose descending in one line, the winning mouth, the expression of pure and godlike serenity. Yet with all this chaste perfection of form it was of such unique personal charm that the observer thought he had never seen, either in nature or art, anything so utterly happy and consummate. What struck him further was the strange contrast the group afforded, a difference in educational method, so to speak, shown in the way the brother and sisters were clothed and treated. The girls, the eldest of whom was practically grown up, were dressed with an almost disfiguring austerity. All three wore half-length slate-coloured frocks of cloister-like plainness, arbitrarily unbecoming in cut, with white turn-over collars as their only adornment. Every grace of outline was wilfully suppressed; their hair lay smoothly plastered to their heads, giving them a vacant expression, like a nun's. All this could only be by the mother's orders; but there was no trace of the same pedagogic severity in the case of the boy. Tenderness and softness, it was plain, conditioned his existence. No scissors had been put to the lovely hair that (like the Spinario's) curled about his brows, above his ears, longer still in the neck. He wore an English sailor suit, with puffed sleeves that narrowed round the delicate wrists of his long and slender though still childish hands. And this

suit, with its breast-knot, lacings, and embroideries, lent
the slight figure something 'rich and strange,' a spoilt,
exquisite air. The observer saw him in half profile,
with one foot in its black patent leather advanced, one
elbow resting on the arm of his basket chair, the cheek
nestled into the closed hand in a pose of easy grace, quite
unlike the stiff subservient mien which was evidently
habitual to his sisters. Was he delicate? His facial
tint was ivory-white against the golden darkness of his
clustering locks. Or was he simply a pampered darling,
the object of a self-willed and partial love? Aschenbach
inclined to think the latter. For in almost every artist
nature is inborn a wanton and treacherous proneness to
side with the beauty that breaks hearts, to single out
aristocratic pretensions and pay them homage.

A waiter announced, in English, that dinner was served.
Gradually the company dispersed through the glass doors
into the dining-room. Late comers entered from the
vestibule or the lifts. Inside, dinner was being served;
but the young Poles still sat and waited about their wicker
table. Aschenbach felt comfortable in his deep arm-
chair, he enjoyed the beauty before his eyes, he waited
with them.

The governess, a short, stout, red-faced person, at
length gave the signal. With lifted brows she pushed
back her chair and made a bow to the tall woman, dressed
in palest grey, who now entered the hall. This lady's
abundant jewels were pearls, her manner was cool and
measured; the fashion of her gown and the arrangement
of her lightly powdered hair had the simplicity prescribed
in certain circles whose piety and aristocracy are equally
marked. She might have been, in Germany, the wife
of some high official. But there was something faintly
fabulous, after all, in her appearance, though lent it solely
by the pearls she wore: they were well-nigh priceless, and

consisted of ear-rings and a three-stranded necklace, very long, with gems the size of cherries.

The brother and sisters had risen briskly. They bowed over their mother's hand to kiss it, she turning away from them, with a slight smile on her face, which was carefully preserved but rather sharp-nosed and worn. She addressed a few words in French to the governess, then moved towards the glass door. The children followed, the girls in order of age, then the governess, and last the boy. He chanced to turn before he crossed the threshold, and as there was no one else in the room, his strange, twilight grey eyes met Aschenbach's, as our traveller sat there with the paper on his knee, absorbed in looking after the group.

There was nothing singular, of course, in what he had seen. They had not gone in to dinner before their mother, they had waited, given her a respectful salute, and but observed the right and proper forms on entering the room. Yet they had done all this so expressly, with such self-respecting dignity, discipline, and sense of duty, that Aschenbach was impressed. He lingered still a few minutes, then he, too, went into the dining-room, where he was shown a table a long way from the Polish family, as he noted at once, with a stirring of regret.

Tired, yet mentally alert, he beguiled the long, tedious meal with abstract, even with transcendent matters: pondered the mysterious harmony that must come to subsist between the individual human being and the universal law, in order that human beauty may result; passed on to general problems of form and art, and came at length to the conclusion that what seemed to him fresh and happy thoughts were like the flattering inventions of a dream, which the waking sense proves worthless and insubstantial. He spent the evening in the park, that was sweet with the odours of evening—sitting, smoking, wandering about; went to bed betimes, and passed the night in deep, unbroken sleep, visited, however, by varied and lively dreams.

The weather next day was no more promising. A land breeze blew. Beneath a colourless, overcast sky the sea lay sluggish, and as it were shrunken, so far withdrawn as to leave bare several rows of long sand banks. The horizon looked close and prosaic. When Aschenbach opened his window he thought he smelt the stagnant odour of the lagoons.

He felt suddenly out of sorts and already began to think of leaving. Once, years before, after weeks of bright spring weather, this wind had found him out; it had been so bad as to force him to flee from the city like a fugitive. And now it seemed beginning again—the same feverish distaste, the pressure on his temples, the heavy eyelids. It would be a nuisance to change again; but if the wind did not turn, this was no place for him. To be on the safe side, he did not entirely unpack. At nine o'clock he went down to the buffet, which lay between the hall and the dining-room and served as breakfast-room.

A solemn stillness reigned here, such as it is the ambition of all large hotels to achieve. The waiters moved on noiseless feet. A rattling of tea things, a whispered word —and no other sounds. In a corner diagonally to the door, two tables off his own, Aschenbach saw the Polish girls with their governess. They sat there very straight, in their stiff blue linen frocks with little turn-over collars and cuffs, their ash-blond hair newly brushed flat, their eyelids red from sleep; and handed each other the marmalade. They had nearly finished their meal. The boy was not there.

Aschenbach smiled. 'Aha, little Phaex,' he thought. 'It seems you are privileged to sleep yourself out.' With sudden gaiety he quoted:

'Oft veränderten Schmuck und warme Bäder und Ruhe.'

He took a leisurely breakfast. The porter came up with his braided cap in his hand, to deliver some letters that had been sent on. Aschenbach lighted a cigarette and opened a few letters and thus was still seated to witness the arrival of the sluggard.

He entered through the glass doors and passed diagonally across the room to his sisters at their table. He walked with extraordinary grace—the carriage of the body, the action of the knee, the way he set down his foot in its white shoe—it was all so light, it was at once dainty and proud, it wore an added charm in childish shyness which made him twice turn his head as he crossed the room, made him give a quick glance and then drop his eyes. He took his seat, with a smile and a murmured word in his soft and blurry tongue; and Aschenbach, sitting so that he could see him in profile, was astonished anew, yes, startled, at the godlike beauty of the human being. The lad had on a light sailor suit of blue-and-white striped cotton, with a red silk breast knot and a simple white standing collar round the neck—a not very elegant effect—yet above this collar the head was poised like a flower, in incomparable loveliness. It was the head of Eros, with the yellowish bloom of Parian marble, with fine serious brows, and dusky clustering ringlets standing out in soft plenteousness over temples and ears.

'Good, oh, very good indeed!' thought Aschenbach, assuming the patronizing air of the connoisseur to hide, as artists will, their ravishment over a masterpiece. 'Yes,' he went on to himself, 'if it were not that sea and beach were waiting for me, I should sit here as long as you do.' But he went out on that, passing through the hall, beneath the watchful eye of the functionaries, down the steps and directly across the board walk to the section of the beach reserved for the guests of the hotel. The bathing attendant, a barefoot old man in linen

trousers and sailor blouse, with a straw hat, showed him
the cabin that had been rented for him, and Aschenbach
got him to set up table and chair on the sandy platform
before it.   Then he dragged the reclining chair through
the pale yellow sand, closer to the sea, sat down, and
composed himself.

He delighted, as always, in the scene on the beach, the
sight of sophisticated society giving itself over to a simple
life at the edge of the element.   The shallow grey sea
was already gay with children wading, with swimmers,
with figures in bright colours lying on the sand banks
with arms behind their heads.   Some were rowing in
little keelless boats painted red and blue, and laughing
when they capsized.   A long row of *capanne* ran down
the beach, with platforms, where people sat as on verandas,
and there was social life, with bustle and with indolent
repose; visits were paid, amid much chatter, punctilious
morning toilets hob - nobbed with comfortable and
privileged dishabille.   On the hard wet sand close to the
sea figures in white bath robes or loose wrappings in
garish colours strolled up and down.   A mammoth sand-
hill had been built up on Aschenbach's right, the work
of children, who had stuck it full of tiny flags.   Vendors
of sea shells, fruit, and cakes knelt beside their wares
spread out on the sand.   A row of cabins on the left stood
obliquely to the others and to the sea, thus forming the
boundary of the enclosure on this side; and on the little
veranda in front of one of these a Russian family was
encamped; bearded men with strong white teeth, ripe,
indolent women, a Fräulein from the Baltic provinces,
who sat at an easel painting the sea and tearing her hair
in despair; two ugly but good-natured children and an
old maidservant in a head cloth, with the caressing,
servile manner of the born dependent.   There they sat
together in grateful enjoyment of their blessings: con-

stantly shouting at their romping children, who paid not
the slightest heed; making jokes in broken Italian to the
funny old man who sold them sweetmeats, kissing each
other on the cheeks—no jot concerned that their domes-
ticity was overlooked.

'I 'll stop,' thought Aschenbach. 'Where could it be
better than here?' With his hands clasped in his lap he
let his eyes swim in the wideness of the sea, his gaze lose
focus, blur, and grow vague in the misty immensity of
space. His love of the ocean had profound sources; the
hard-worked artist's longing for rest, his yearning to seek
refuge from the thronging manifold shapes of his fancy
in the bosom of the simple and the vast; and another yearning, opposed to his art and perhaps for that very reason a
lure, for the unorganized, the immeasurable, the eternal—
in short, for nothingness. He whose preoccupation is
with excellence longs fervently to find rest in perfection;
and is not nothingness a form of perfection? As he sat
there dreaming thus, deep, deep into the void, suddenly
the margin line of the shore was cut by a human form.
He gathered up his gaze and withdrew it from the illimit-
able, and lo, it was the lovely boy who crossed his vision
coming from the left along the sand. He was barefoot,
ready for wading, the slender legs uncovered above the
knee, and he moved slowly, yet with such a proud, light
tread as to make it seem he had never worn shoes. He
looked towards the diagonal row of cabins; and the sight
of the Russian family, leading their lives there in joyous
simplicity, distorted his features in a spasm of angry disgust. His brow darkened, his lips curled, one corner of
the mouth was drawn down in a harsh line that marred
the curve of the cheek, his frown was so heavy that
the eyes seemed to sink in and to speak the black
and vicious language of hate. He looked down, looked
threateningly back once more; then giving it up with a

violent and contemptuous shoulder shrug, he left his enemies in the rear.

A feeling of delicacy, a qualm, almost like a sense of shame, made Aschenbach turn away as though he had not seen; he felt unwilling to take advantage of having been, by chance, privy to this passionate reaction. But he was in truth both moved and exhilarated—that is to say, he was delighted. This childish exhibition of fanaticism, directed against the best-natured simplicity in the world—it gave to the godlike and inexpressive the final human touch. The figure of the half-grown lad, a masterpiece from nature's own hand, had been significant enough when it gratified the eye alone; and now it evoked sympathy as well—the little episode had set it off, lent it a dignity in the onlooker's eyes that was beyond its years.

Aschenbach listened with still averted head to the boy's voice announcing his coming to his companions at the sand heap. The voice was clear, though a little weak, but they answered, shouting his name—or his nickname —again and again. Aschenbach was not without curiosity to learn it, but could make out nothing more exact than two musical syllables, something like Adgio—or, oftener still, Adjiu, with a long-drawn-out *u* at the end. He liked the melodious sound, and found it fitting; said it over to himself a few times and turned back with satisfaction to his papers.

Holding his travelling pad on his knees, he took his fountain pen and began to answer various items of his correspondence. But presently he felt it too great a pity to turn his back, and the eyes of his mind, for the sake of mere commonplace correspondence, to this scene which was, after all, the most rewarding one he knew. He put aside his papers and swung round to the sea; in no long time, beguiled by the voices of the children at play, he had turned his head and sat resting it against the chair back, while he gave himself up to contemplating the activities of the exquisite Adgio.

His eye found him out at once, the red breast knot was unmistakable. With some nine or ten companions, boys and girls of his own age and younger, he was busy putting in place an old plank to serve as a bridge across the ditches between the sand piles. He directed the work by shouting and motioning with his head, and they were all chattering in many tongues—French, Polish, and even some of the Balkan languages. But his was the name oftenest on their lips, he was plainly sought after, wooed, admired. One lad in particular, a Pole like himself, with a name that sounded something like Jaschiu, a sturdy lad with brilliantined black hair, in a belted linen suit, was his particular liegeman and friend. Operations at the sand pile being ended for the time, they two walked away along the beach, with their arms round each other's waists, and once the lad Jaschiu gave Adgio a kiss.

Aschenbach felt like shaking a finger at him. 'But you, Critobulus,' he thought with a smile, 'you I advise to take a year's leave. That long, at least, you will need for complete recovery.' A vendor came by with straw-berries, and Aschenbach made his second breakfast of the great, luscious, dead-ripe fruit. It had grown very warm, although the sun had not availed to pierce the heavy layer of mist. His mind felt relaxed, his senses revelled in this vast and soothing communion with the silence of the sea. The grave and serious man found sufficient occupation in speculating what name it could be that sounded like Adgio. And with the help of a few Polish memories he at length fixed on Tadzio, a shortened form of Thaddeus, which sounded, when called, like Tadziu or Adziu.

Tadzio was bathing. Aschenbach had lost sight of

him for a moment, then descried him far out in the water,
which was shallow a very long way—saw his head, and
his arm striking out like an oar.   But his watchful
family were already on the alert; the mother and governess called from the veranda in front of their bathing-
cabin, until the lad's name, with its softened consonants
and long-drawn *u*-sound, seemed to possess the beach
like a rallying cry; the cadence had something sweet
and wild: 'Tadziu! Tadziu!'   He turned and ran back
against the water, churning the waves to a foam, his head
flung high.   The sight of this living figure, virginally
pure and austere, with dripping locks, beautiful as a tender
young god, emerging from the depths of sea and sky, out-
running the element—it conjured up mythologies, it was
like a primeval legend, handed down from the beginning
of time, of the birth of form, of the origin of the gods.
With closed lids Aschenbach listened to this poesy hymn-
ing itself silently within him, and anon he thought it was
good to be here and that he would stop awhile.

Afterwards Tadzio lay on the sand and rested from his
bathe, wrapped in his white sheet, which he wore drawn
underneath the right shoulder, so that his head was
cradled on his bare right arm.   And even when Aschenbach read, without looking up, he was conscious that the
lad was there; that it would cost him but the slightest
turn of the head to have the rewarding vision once more
in his purview.   Indeed, it was almost as though he sat
there to guard the youth's repose; occupied, of course,
with his own affairs, yet alive to the presence of that noble
human creature close at hand.   And his heart was stirred,
it felt a father's kindness: such an emotion as the possessor
of beauty can inspire in one who has offered himself up in
spirit to create beauty.

At midday he left the beach, returned to the hotel, and
was carried up in the lift to his room.   There he lingered

a little time before the glass and looked at his own grey hair, his keen and weary face. And he thought of his fame, and how people gazed respectfully at him in the streets, on account of his unerring gift of words and their power to charm. He called up all the worldly successes his genius had reaped, all he could remember, even his patent of nobility. Then went to luncheon down in the dining-room, sat at his little table and ate. Afterwards he mounted again in the lift, and a group of young folk, Tadzio among them, pressed with him into the little compartment. It was the first time Aschenbach had seen him close at hand, not merely in perspective, and could see and take account of the details of his humanity. Someone spoke to the lad, and he, answering, with indescribably lovely smile, stepped out again, as they had come to the first floor, backwards, with his eyes cast down. 'Beauty makes people self-conscious,' Aschenbach thought, and considered within himself imperatively why this should be. He had noted, further, that Tadzio's teeth were imperfect, rather jagged and bluish, without a healthy glaze, and of that peculiar brittle transparency which the teeth of chlorotic people often show. 'He is delicate, he is sickly,' Aschenbach thought. 'He will most likely not live to grow old.' He did not try to account for the pleasure the idea gave him.

In the afternoon he spent two hours in his room, then took the *vaporetto* to Venice, across the foul-smelling lagoon. He got out at San Marco, had his tea in the Piazza, and then, as his custom was, took a walk through the streets. But this walk of his brought about nothing less than a revolution in his mood and an entire change in all his plans.

There was a hateful sultriness in the narrow streets. The air was so heavy that all the manifold smells wafted out of the houses, shops, and cook shops—smells of oil, perfumery, and so forth—hung low, like exhalations, not dissipating. Cigarette smoke seemed to stand in the air, it drifted so slowly away. To-day the crowd in these narrow lanes oppressed the stroller instead of diverting him. The longer he walked, the more was he in tortures under that state which is the product of the sea air and the sirocco and which excites and enervates at once. He perspired painfully. His eyes rebelled, his chest was heavy, he felt feverish, the blood throbbed in his temples. He fled from the huddled, narrow streets of the commercial city, crossed many bridges, and came into the poor quarter of Venice. Beggars waylaid him, the canals sickened him with their evil exhalations. He reached a quiet square, one of those that exist at the city's heart, forsaken of God and man; there he rested awhile on the margin of a fountain, wiped his brow, and admitted to himself that he must be gone.

For the second time, and now quite definitely, the city proved that in certain weathers it could be directly inimical to his health. Nothing but sheer unreasoning obstinacy would linger on, hoping for an unprophesiable change in the wind. A quick decision was called for. He could not go home at this stage, neither summer nor winter quarters would be ready. But Venice had not a monopoly of sea and shore: there were other spots where these were to be had without the evil concomitants of lagoon and fever-breeding vapours. He remembered a little bathing place not far from Trieste of which he had had a good report. Why not go thither? At once, of course, in order that this second change might be worth the making. He resolved, he rose to his feet and sought the nearest gondola landing, where he took a boat and was conveyed to San Marco through the gloomy windings of many canals, beneath balconies of delicate marble traceries flanked by carven lions; round slippery corners of wall, past melancholy façades with ancient business shields reflected in the rocking water. It was not too easy to arrive at his destination, for his gondolier, being in league with various lace-makers and glass-blowers, did his best to persuade his fare to pause, look, and be tempted to buy. Thus the charm of this bizarre passage through the heart of Venice, even while it played upon his spirit, yet was sensibly cooled by the predatory commercial spirit of the fallen queen of the seas.

Once back in his hotel, he announced at the office, even before dinner, that unforeseen circumstances obliged him to leave early next morning. The management expressed its regret, it changed his money and receipted his bill. He dined, and spent the lukewarm evening in a rocking chair on the rear terrace, reading the newspapers. Before he went to bed, he made his luggage ready against the morning.

His sleep was not of the best, for the prospect of another journey made him restless. When he opened his window next morning, the sky was still overcast, but the air seemed fresher—and there and then his regret began. Had he not given notice too soon? Had he not let himself be swayed by a slight and momentary indisposition? If he had only been patient, not lost heart so quickly, tried to adapt himself to the climate, or even waited for a change in the weather before deciding! Then, instead of the hurry and flurry of departure, he would have before him now a morning like yesterday's on the beach. Too late! He must go on wanting what he had wanted yesterday. He dressed and at eight o'clock went down to breakfast.

When he entered the breakfast room it was empty. Guests came in while he sat waiting for his order to be filled. As he sipped his tea he saw the Polish girls enter with their governess, chaste and morning-fresh, with

sleep-reddened eyelids. They crossed the room and
sat down at their table in the window. Behind them
came the porter, cap in hand, to announce that it was time
for him to go. The car was waiting to convey him and
other travellers to the Hôtel Excelsior, whence they would
go by motor boat through the company's private canal
to the station. Time pressed. But Aschenbach found
it did nothing of the sort. There still lacked more than
an hour of train time. He felt irritated at the hotel habit
of getting the guests out of the house earlier than necessary; and requested the porter to let him breakfast in
peace. The man hesitated and withdrew, only to come
back again five minutes later. The car could wait no
longer. Good, then it might go, and take his trunk
with it, Aschenbach answered with some heat. He
would use the public conveyance, in his own time; he
begged them to leave the choice of it to him. The
functionary bowed. Aschenbach, pleased to be rid of
him, made a leisurely meal, and even had a newspaper
of the waiter. When at length he rose, the time was
grown very short. And it so happened that at that
moment Tadzio came through the glass doors into the
room.

To reach his own table he crossed the traveller's path,
and modestly cast down his eyes before the grey-haired
man of the lofty brows—only to lift them again in that
sweet way he had and direct his full soft gaze upon
Aschenbach's face. Then he was past. 'For the last
time, Tadzio,' thought the elder man. 'It was all too
brief!' Quite unusually for him, he shaped a farewell
with his lips, he actually uttered it, and added: 'May
God bless you!' Then he went out, distributed tips,
exchanged farewells with the mild little manager in the
frock coat, and, followed by the porter with his hand
luggage, left the hotel. On foot as he had come, he

passed through the white-blossoming avenue, diagonally across the island to the boat landing. He went on board at once—but the tale of his journey across the lagoon was a tale of woe, a passage through the very valley of regrets.

It was the well-known route: through the lagoon, past San Marco, up the Grand Canal. Aschenbach sat on the circular bench in the bows, with his elbow on the railing, one hand shading his eyes. They passed the public gardens, once more the princely charm of the Piazzetta rose up before him and then dropped behind, next came the great row of palaces, the canal curved, and the splendid marble arches of the Rialto came in sight. The traveller gazed—and his bosom was torn. The atmosphere of the city, the faintly rotten scent of swamp and sea, which had driven him to leave—in what deep, tender, almost painful draughts he breathed it in! How was it he had not known, had not thought, how much his heart was set upon it all! What this morning had been slight regret, some little doubt of his own wisdom, turned now to grief, to actual wretchedness, a mental agony so sharp that it repeatedly brought tears to his eyes, while he questioned himself how he could have foreseen it. The hardest part, the part that more than once it seemed he could not bear, was the thought that he should nevermore see Venice again. Since now for the second time the place had made him ill, since for the second time he had had to flee for his life, he must henceforth regard it as a forbidden spot, to be for ever shunned; senseless to try it again, after he had proved himself unfit. Yes, if he fled it now, he felt that wounded pride must prevent his return to this spot where twice he had made actual bodily surrender. And this conflict between inclination and capacity all at once assumed, in this middle-aged man's mind, immense weight and importance; the physical defeat seemed a shameful thing, to be avoided at whatever cost; and he stood amazed at the ease with which on the day before he had yielded to it.

Meanwhile the steamer neared the station landing; his anguish of irresolution amounted almost to panic. To leave seemed to the sufferer impossible, to remain not less so. Torn thus between two alternatives, he entered the station. It was very late, he had not a moment to lose. Time pressed, it scourged him onward. He hastened to buy his ticket and looked round in the crowd to find the hotel porter. The man appeared and said that the trunk had already gone off. 'Gone already?' 'Yes, it has gone to Como.' 'To Como?' A hasty exchange of words—angry questions from Aschenbach, and puzzled replies from the porter—at length made it clear that the trunk had been put with the wrong luggage even before leaving the hotel, and in company with other trunks was now well on its way in precisely the wrong direction.

Aschenbach found it hard to wear the right expression as he heard this news. A reckless joy, a deep incredible mirthfulness shook him almost as with a spasm. The porter dashed off after the lost trunk, returning very soon, of course, to announce that his efforts were unavailing. Aschenbach said he would not travel without his luggage; that he would go back and wait at the Hôtel des Bains until it turned up. Was the company's motor boat still outside? The man said yes, it was at the door. With his native eloquence he prevailed upon the ticket agent to take back the ticket already purchased; he swore that he would wire, that no pains should be spared, that the trunk would be restored in the twinkling of an eye. And the unbelievable thing came to pass: the traveller, twenty minutes after he had reached the station, found himself once more on the Grand Canal on his way back to the Lido.

What a strange adventure indeed, this right-about-face of destiny—incredible, humiliating, whimsical as any dream! To be passing again, within the hour, these scenes from which in profoundest grief he had but now taken leave for ever! The little swift-moving vessel, a furrow of foam at its prow, tacking with droll agility between steamboats and gondolas, went like a shot to its goal; and he, its sole passenger, sat hiding the panic and thrills of a truant schoolboy beneath a mask of forced resignation. His breast still heaved from time to time with a burst of laughter over the *contretemps*. Things could not, he told himself, have fallen out more luckily. There would be the necessary explanations, a few astonished faces—then all would be well once more, a mischance prevented, a grievous error set right; and all he had thought to have left for ever was his own once more, his for as long as he liked. . . . And did the boat's swift motion deceive him, or was the wind now coming from the sea?

The waves struck against the tiled sides of the narrow canal. At the Hôtel Excelsior the motor omnibus awaited the returned traveller and bore him along by the crisping waves back to the Hôtel des Bains. The little mustachioed manager in the frock coat came down the steps to greet him.

In dulcet tones he deplored the mistake, said how painful it was to the management and himself; applauded Aschenbach's resolve to stop on until the errant trunk came back; his former room, alas, was already taken, but another as good awaited his approval. 'Pas de chance, monsieur,' said the Swiss lift porter, with a smile, as he conveyed him upstairs. And the fugitive was soon quartered in another room which in situation and furnishings almost precisely resembled the first.

He laid out the contents of his hand-bag in their wonted

places; then, tired out, dazed by the whirl of the extraordinary forenoon, subsided into the arm-chair by the
open window. The sea wore a pale-green cast, the air
felt thinner and purer, the beach with its cabins and boats
had more colour, notwithstanding the sky was still grey.
Aschenbach, his hands folded in his lap, looked out. He
felt rejoiced to be back, yet displeased with his vacillating
moods, his ignorance of his own real desires. Thus for
nearly an hour he sat, dreaming, resting, barely thinking.
At midday he saw Tadzio, in his striped sailor suit with
red breast knot, coming up from the sea, across the barrier
and along the board walk to the hotel. Aschenbach
recognized him, even at this height, knew it was he before
he actually saw him, had it in mind to say to himself: 'Well,
Tadzio, so here you are again too!' But the casual
greeting died away before it reached his lips, slain by the
truth in his heart. He felt the rapture of his blood, the
poignant pleasure, and realized that it was for Tadzio's
sake the leave taking had been so hard.

He sat quite still, unseen at his high post, and looked
within himself. His features were lively, he lifted his
brows; a smile, alert, inquiring, vivid, widened the mouth.
Then he raised his head, and with both hands, hanging
limp over the chair arms, he described a slow motion,
palms outward, a lifting and turning movement, as
though to indicate a wide embrace. It was a gesture
of welcome, a calm and deliberate acceptance of what
might come.

Now daily the naked god with cheeks aflame drove his
four fire-breathing steeds through heaven's spaces; and
with him streamed the strong east wind that fluttered his
yellow locks. A sheen, like white satin, lay over all the
idly rolling sea's expanse. The sand was burning hot.
Awnings of rust-coloured canvas were spanned before

the bathing-huts, under the ether's quivering silver-blue; one spent the morning hours within the small, sharp square of shadow they purveyed. But evening too was rarely lovely: balsamic with the breath of flowers and shrubs from the nearby park, while overhead the constellations circled in their spheres, and the murmuring of the night-girt sea swelled softly up and whispered to the soul. Such nights as these contained the joyful promise of a sunlit morrow, brim-full of sweetly ordered idleness, studded thick with countless precious possibilities.

The guest detained here by so happy a mischance was far from finding the return of his luggage a ground for setting out anew. For two days he had suffered slight inconvenience and had to dine in the large salon in his travelling clothes. Then the lost trunk was set down in his room, and he hastened to unpack, filling presses and drawers with his possessions. He meant to stay on—and on; he rejoiced in the prospect of wearing a silk suit for the hot morning hours on the beach and appearing in acceptable evening dress at dinner.

He was quick to fall in with the pleasing monotony of this manner of life, readily enchanted by its mild soft brilliance and ease. And what a spot it is, indeed!—uniting the charms of a luxurious bathing resort by a southern sea with the immediate nearness of a unique and marvellous city. Aschenbach was not pleasure-loving. Always, wherever and whenever it was the order of the day to be merry, to refrain from labour and make glad the heart, he would soon be conscious of the imperative summons—and especially was this so in his youth—back to the high fatigues, the sacred and fasting service that consumed his days. This spot and this alone had power to beguile him, to relax his resolution, to make him glad. At times—of a forenoon perhaps, as he lay in the shadow of his awning, gazing out dreamily over the blue of the southern sea, or in the mildness of the night, beneath the wide starry sky, ensconced among the cushions of the gondola that bore him Lido-wards after an evening on the Piazza, while the gay lights faded and the melting music of the serenades died away on his ear—he would think of his mountain home, the theatre of his summer labours. There clouds hung low and trailed through the garden, violent storms extinguished the lights of the house at night, and the ravens he fed swung in the tops of the fir-trees. And he would feel transported to Elysium, to the ends of the earth, to a spot most carefree for the sons of men, where no snow is, and no winter, no storms or downpours of rain; where Oceanus sends a mild and cooling breath, and days flow on in blissful idleness, without effort or struggle, entirely dedicate to the sun and the feasts of the sun.

Aschenbach saw the boy Tadzio almost constantly. The narrow confines of their world of hotel and beach, the daily round followed by all alike, brought him in close, almost uninterrupted touch with the beautiful lad. He encountered him everywhere—in the salons of the hotel, on the cooling rides to the city and back, among the splendours of the Piazza, and besides all this in many another going and coming as chance vouchsafed. But it was the regular morning hours on the beach which gave him the happiest opportunity to study and admire the lovely apparition. Yes, this immediate happiness, this daily recurring boon at the hand of circumstance, this it was that filled him with content, with joy in life, enriched his stay, and lengthened out the succession of sunny days that fell into place so pleasantly one behind the other.

He rose early—as early as though he had a battering press of work—and was among the first on the beach, when the sun was still benign and the sea lay dazzling white in its morning slumber. He gave the watchman a friendly good morning and chatted with the barefoot, white-haired old man who prepared his place, spread the awning, trundled out the chair and table on to the little platform. Then he settled down; he had three or four hours before the sun reached its height and the fearful climax of its power; three or four hours while the sea went deeper and deeper blue; three or four hours in which to watch Tadzio.

He would see him come up, on the left, along the margin of the sea; or from behind, between the cabins; or, with a start of joyful surprise, would discover that he himself was late, and Tadzio already down, in the blue-and-white bathing suit that was now his only wear on the beach; there and engrossed with his usual activities in the sand, beneath the sun. It was a sweetly idle, trifling, fitful life, of play and rest, of strolling, wading, digging, fishing, swimming, lying on the sand. Often the women sitting on the platform would call out to him in their high voices: 'Tadziu! Tadziu!' and he would come running and waving his arms, eager to tell them what he had done, show them what he had found, what caught—shells, sea horses, jelly-fish, and sidewards-running crabs. Aschenbach understood not a word he said; it might be the sheerest commonplace, in his ear it became mingled harmonies. Thus the lad's foreign birth raised his speech to music; a wanton sun showered splendour on him, and the noble distances of the sea formed the background which set off his figure.

Soon the observer knew every line and pose of this form that limned itself so freely against sea and sky; its every loveliness, though conned by heart, yet thrilled him each day afresh; his admiration knew no bounds, the delight of his eye was unending. Once the lad was summoned to speak to a guest who was waiting for his mother at their cabin. He ran up, ran dripping wet out of the sea, tossing his curls, and put out his hand, standing with his weight on one leg, resting the other foot on the toes; as he stood there in a posture of suspense the turn of his body was enchanting, while his features wore a look half shamefaced, half conscious of the duty breeding laid upon him to please.   Or he would lie at full length, with his bath robe around him, one slender young arm resting on the sand, his chin in the hollow of his hand; the lad they called Jaschiu squatting beside him, paying him court. There could be nothing lovelier on earth than the smile and look with which the playmate thus singled out rewarded his humble friend and vassal.   Again, he might be at the water's edge, alone, removed from his family, quite close to Aschenbach; standing erect, his hands clasped at the back of his neck, rocking slowly on the balls of his feet, day-dreaming away into blue space, while little waves ran up and bathed his toes.   The ringlets of honey-coloured hair clung to his temples and neck, the fine down along the upper vertebrae was yellow in the sun-light; the thin envelope of flesh covering the torso be-trayed the delicate outlines of the ribs and the symmetry of the breast structure.   His armpits were still as smooth as a statue's, smooth the glistening hollows behind the knees, where the blue network of veins suggested that the body was formed of some stuff more transparent than mere flesh.   What discipline, what precision of thought were expressed by the tense youthful perfection of this form!   And yet the pure, strong will which had laboured in darkness and succeeded in bringing this godlike work of art to the light of day—was it not known and familiar to him, the artist?   Was not the same force at work in himself when he strove in cold fury to liberate from the marble mass of language the slender forms of his art which he saw with the eye of his mind and would body forth to men as the mirror and image of spiritual beauty?

Mirror and image! His eyes took in the proud bearing of that figure there at the blue water's edge; with an outburst of rapture he told himself that what he saw was beauty's very essence; form as divine thought, the single and pure perfection which resides in the mind, of which an image and likeness, rare and holy, was here raised up for adoration. This was very frenzy—and without a scruple, nay, eagerly, the ageing artist bade it come. His mind was in travail, his whole mental background in a state of flux. Memory flung up in him the primitive thoughts which are youth's inheritance, but which with him had remained latent, never leaping up into a blaze. Has it not been written that the sun beguiles our attention from things of the intellect to fix it on things of the sense? The sun, they say, dazzles; so bewitching reason and memory that the soul for very pleasure forgets its actual state, to cling with doting on the loveliest of all the objects she shines on. Yes, and then it is only through the medium of some corporeal being that it can raise itself again to contemplation of higher things. Amor, in sooth, is like the mathematician who in order to give children a knowledge of pure form must do so in the language of pictures; so, too, the god, in order to make visible the spirit, avails himself of the forms and colours of human youth, gilding it with all imaginable beauty that it may serve memory as a tool, the very sight of which then sets us afire with pain and longing.

Such were the devotee's thoughts, such the power of his emotions. And the sea, so bright with glancing sunbeams, wove in his mind a spell and summoned up a lovely picture: there was the ancient plane-tree outside the walls of Athens, a hallowed, shady spot, fragrant with willow blossom and adorned with images and votive offerings in honour of the nymphs and Achelous. Clear ran the smooth-pebbled stream at the foot of the spreading tree.

Crickets were fiddling. But on the gentle grassy slope, where one could lie yet hold the head erect, and shelter from the scorching heat, two men reclined, an elder with a younger, ugliness paired with beauty and wisdom with grace. Here Socrates held forth to youthful Phaedrus upon the nature of virtue and desire, wooing him with insinuating wit and charming turns of phrase. He told him of the shuddering and unwonted heat that come upon him whose heart is open, when his eye beholds an image of eternal beauty; spoke of the impious and corrupt, who cannot conceive beauty though they see its image, and are incapable of awe; and of the fear and reverence felt by the noble soul when he beholds a godlike face or a form which is an image of beauty: how as he gazes he worships the beautiful one and scarcely dares to look upon him, but would offer sacrifice as to an idol or a god, did he not fear to be thought stark mad. 'For beauty, my Phaedrus, beauty alone, is lovely and visible at once. For, mark you, it is the whole aspect of the spiritual which we can perceive through our senses, or bear so to perceive. Else what would become of us, if the divine, if reason and virtue and truth, were to speak to us through the senses? Should we not perish and be consumed by love, as Semele aforetime was by Zeus? So beauty, then, is the beauty-lover's way to the spirit—but only the way, only the means, my little Phaedrus.' . . . And then, sly arch-lover that he was, he said the subtlest thing of all: that the lover was nearer the divine than the beloved; for the god was in the one but not in the other—perhaps the tenderest, most mocking thought that ever was thought, and source of all the guile and secret bliss the lover knows.

Thought that can emerge wholly into feeling, feeling that can emerge wholly into thought—these are the artist's highest joy. And our solitary felt in himself at this moment power to command and wield a thought

that thrilled with emotion, an emotion as precise and
concentrated as thought; namely, that nature herself
shivers with ecstasy when the mind bows down in homage
before beauty. He felt a sudden desire to write. Eros,
indeed, we are told, loves idleness, and for idle hours alone
was he created. But in this crisis the violence of our
sufferer's seizure was directed almost wholly towards
production, its occasion almost a matter of indifference.
News had reached him on his travels that a certain problem
had been raised, the intellectual world challenged for its
opinion on a great and burning question of art and taste.
By nature and experience the theme was his own; and he
could not resist the temptation to set it off in the glistering
foil of his words. He would write, and moreover he
would write in Tadzio's presence. This lad should be
in a sense his model, his style should follow the lines of
this figure that seemed to him divine; he would snatch
up this beauty into the realms of the mind, as once the
eagle bore the Trojan shepherd aloft. Never had the
pride of the word been so sweet to him, never had he
known so well that Eros is in the word, as in those perilous
and precious hours when he sat at his rude table, within
the shade of his awning, his idol full in his view and the
music of his voice in his ears, and fashioned his little essay
after the model Tadzio's beauty set: that page and a half
of choicest prose, so chaste, so lofty, so poignant with
feeling, which would shortly be the wonder and admiration
of the multitude. Verily it is well for the world that it
sees only the beauty of the completed work and not its
origins nor the conditions whence it sprang; since knowledge of the artist's inspiration might often but confuse
and alarm and so prevent the full effect of its excellence.
Strange hours, indeed, these were, and strangely un-
nerving the labour that filled them! Strangely fruitful
intercourse this, between one body and another mind!

When Aschenbach put aside his work and left the beach he felt exhausted, he felt broken—conscience reproached him, as it were after a debauch.

Next morning on leaving the hotel he stood at the top of the stairs leading down from the terrace and saw Tadzio in front of him on his way to the beach. The lad had just reached the gate in the railings, and he was alone. Aschenbach felt, quite simply, a wish to overtake him, to address him and have the pleasure of his reply and answering look; to put upon a blithe and friendly footing his relation with this being who all unconsciously had so greatly heightened and quickened his emotions. The lovely youth moved at a loitering pace—he might easily be overtaken; and Aschenbach hastened his own step. He reached him on the board walk that ran behind the bathing cabins, and all but put out his hand to lay it on shoulder or head, while his lips parted to utter a friendly salutation in French. But — perhaps from the swift pace of his last few steps—he found his heart throbbing unpleasantly fast, while his breath came in such quick pants that he could only have gasped had he tried to speak. He hesitated, sought after self-control, was suddenly panic-stricken lest the boy notice him hanging there behind him and look round. Then he gave up, abandoned his plan, and passed him with bent head and hurried step.

'Too late! Too late!' he thought as he went by. But was it too late? This step he had delayed to take might so easily have put everything in a lighter key, have led to a sane recovery from his folly. But the truth may have been that the ageing man did not want to be cured, that his illusion was far too dear to him. Who shall unriddle the puzzle of the artist nature? Who understands that mingling of discipline and licence in which it stands so deeply rooted? For not to be able to want sobriety is licentious folly. Aschenbach was no longer disposed to self-analysis. He had no taste for it; his self-esteem, the attitude of mind proper to his years, his maturity and single-mindedness, disinclined him to look within himself and decide whether it was constraint or puerile sensuality that had prevented him from carrying out his project. He felt confused, he was afraid some-one, if only the watchman, might have been observing his behaviour and final surrender—very much he feared being ridiculous. And all the time he was laughing at himself for his serio-comic seizure. 'Quite crestfallen,' he thought. 'I was like the gamecock that lets his wings droop in the battle. That must be the love-god himself, who makes us hang our heads at sight of beauty and weighs our proud spirits low as the ground.' Thus he played with the idea—he embroidered upon it, and was too arrogant to admit fear of an emotion.

The term he had set for his holiday passed by unheeded; he had no thought of going home. Ample funds had been sent him. His sole concern was that the Polish family might leave, and a chance question put to the hotel barber elicited the information that they had come only very shortly before himself. The sun browned his face and hands, the invigorating salty air heightened his emotional energies. Heretofore he had been wont to give out at once, in some new effort, the powers accumu-lated by sleep or food or outdoor air; but now the strength that flowed in upon him with each day of sun and sea and idleness he spent in one extravagant gush of emotional intoxication.

His sleep was fitful; the priceless, equable days were divided one from the next by brief nights filled with happy unrest. He went, indeed, early to bed, for at nine o'clock, with the departure of Tadzio from the scene, the day was over for him. But in the faint greyness of

the morning a tender pang would go through him as his
heart was minded of its adventure; he could no longer
bear his pillow and, rising, would wrap himself against
the early chill and sit down by the window to await the
sunrise.   Awe of the miracle filled his soul new-risen
from its sleep.   Heaven, earth, and its waters yet lay
enfolded in the ghostly, glassy pallor of dawn; one paling
star still swam in the shadowy vast.   But there came a
breath, a winged word from far and inaccessible abodes,
that Eos was rising from the side of her spouse; and there
was that first sweet reddening of the farthest strip of sea
and sky that manifests creation to man's sense.   She neared,
the goddess, ravisher of youth, who stole away Clitus
and Cephalus and, defying all the envious Olympians,
tasted beautiful Orion's love.   At the world's edge began
a strewing of roses, a shining and a blooming ineffably
pure; baby cloudlets hung illumined, like attendant
amoretti, in the blue and blushful haze; purple effulgence
fell upon the sea, that seemed to heave it forward on its
welling waves; from horizon to zenith went great quivering thrusts like golden lances, the gleam became a glare;
without a sound, with godlike violence, glow and glare
and rolling flames streamed upwards, and with flying hoof-
beats the steeds of the sun-god mounted the sky.   The
lonely watcher sat, the splendour of the god shone on him,
he closed his eyes and let the glory kiss his lids.   Forgotten
feelings, precious pangs of his youth, quenched long since
by the stern service that had been his life and now returned
so strangely metamorphosed—he recognized them with a
puzzled, wondering smile.   He mused, he dreamed, his
lips slowly shaped a name; still smiling, his face turned
seawards and his hands lying folded in his lap, he fell
asleep once more as he sat.

But that day, which began so fierily and festally,
was not like other days; it was transmuted and gilded

with mythical significance. For whence could come the breath, so mild and meaningful, like a whisper from higher spheres, that played about temple and ear? Troops of small feathery white clouds ranged over the sky, like grazing herds of the gods. A stronger wind arose, and Poseidon's horses ran up, arching their manes, among them too the steers of him with the purpled locks, who lowered their horns and bellowed as they came on; while like prancing goats the waves on the farther strand leaped among the craggy rocks. It was a world possessed, peopled by Pan, that closed round the spell-bound man, and his doting heart conceived the most delicate fancies. When the sun was going down behind Venice, he would sometimes sit on a bench in the park and watch Tadzio, white-clad, with gay-coloured sash, at play there on the rolled gravel with his ball; and at such times it was not Tadzio whom he saw, but Hyacinthus, doomed to die because two gods were rivals for his love. Ah, yes, he tasted the envious pangs that Zephyr knew when his rival, bow and cithara, oracle and all forgot, played with the beauteous youth; he watched the discus, guided by tor-turing jealousy, strike the beloved head; paled as he received the broken body in his arms, and saw the flower spring up, watered by that sweet blood and signed for evermore with his lament.

There can be no relation more strange, more critical, than that between two beings who know each other only with their eyes, who meet daily, yes, even hourly, eye each other with a fixed regard, and yet by some whim or freak of convention feel constrained to act like strangers. Uneasiness rules between them, unslaked curiosity, a hysterical desire to give rein to their suppressed impulse to recognize and address each other; even, actually, a sort of strained but mutual regard. For one human being instinctively feels respect and love for another human being so long as he does not know him well enough to judge him; and that he does not, the craving he feels is evidence.

Some sort of relation and acquaintanceship was perforce set up between Aschenbach and the youthful Tadzio; it was with a thrill of joy the older man perceived that the lad was not entirely unresponsive to all the tender notice lavished on him. For instance, what should move the lovely youth, nowadays when he descended to the beach, always to avoid the board walk behind the bathing huts and saunter along the sand, passing Aschenbach's tent in front, sometimes so unnecessarily close as almost to graze his table or chair? Could the power of an emotion so beyond his own draw or fascinate its innocent object? Daily Aschenbach would wait for Tadzio. Then sometimes, on his approach, he would pretend to be preoccupied and let the charmer pass unregarded by. But sometimes he looked up, and their glances met; when that happened both were profoundly serious. The elder's dignified and cultured mien let nothing appear of his inward state; but in Tadzio's eyes a question lay—he faltered in his step, gazed on the ground, then up again with that ineffably sweet look he had; and when he was past, something in his bearing seemed to say that only good breeding hindered him from turning round.

But once, one evening, it fell out differently. The Polish brother and sisters, with their governess, had missed the evening meal, and Aschenbach had noted the fact with concern. He was restive over their absence, and after dinner walked up and down in front of the hotel, in evening dress and a straw hat; when suddenly he saw the nunlike sisters with their companion appear in the light of the arc lamps, and four paces behind them Tadzio. Evidently they came from the steamer landing, having dined for some reason in Venice. It had been chilly on the lagoon, for Tadzio wore a dark blue reefer jacket with gilt buttons, and a cap to match. Sun and sea air could not burn his skin, it was the same creamy marble hue as at first—though he did look a little pale, either from the cold or in the bluish moonlight of the arc lamps. The shapely brows were so delicately drawn, the eyes so deeply dark—lovelier he was than words could say, and as often the thought visited Aschenbach, and brought its own pang, that language could but extol, not reproduce, the beauties of the sense.

The sight of that dear form was unexpected, it had appeared unhoped-for, without giving him time to compose his features. Joy, surprise, and admiration might have painted themselves quite openly upon his face— and just at this second it happened that Tadzio smiled. Smiled at Aschenbach, unabashed and friendly, a speaking, winning, captivating smile, with slowly parting lips. With such a smile it might be that Narcissus bent over the mirroring pool, a smile profound, infatuated, lingering, as he put out his arms to the reflection of his own beauty; the lips just slightly pursed, perhaps half realizing his own folly in trying to kiss the cold lips of his shadow— with a mingling of coquetry and curiosity and a faint unease, enthralling and enthralled.

Aschenbach received that smile and turned away with it as though entrusted with a fatal gift. So shaken was he that he had to flee from the lighted terrace and front gardens and seek out with hurried steps the darkness of the park at the rear. Reproaches strangely mixed, in- dignant and tender, burst from him: 'How dare you smile like that! No one is allowed to smile like that!' He flung himself on a bench, his composure gone to the winds, and breathed in the nocturnal fragrance of the garden. He leaned back, with hanging arms, quivering from head to foot, and quite unmanned he whispered the hackneyed phrase of love and longing—impossible in these circumstances, absurd, abject, ridiculous enough, yet sacred too, and not unworthy of honour even here: 'I love you!'

In the fourth week of his stay on the Lido, Gustav von Aschenbach made certain singular observations touching the world about him. He noticed, in the first place, that though the season was approaching its height, yet the number of guests declined and, in particular, that the German tongue had suffered a rout, being scarcely or never heard in the land. At table and on the beach he caught nothing but foreign words. One day at the barber's—where he was now a frequent visitor—he heard something rather startling. The barber mentioned a German family who had just left the Lido after a brief stay, and rattled on in his obsequious way: 'The signore is not leaving—he has no fear of the sickness, has he?' Aschenbach looked at him. 'The sickness?' he repeated. Whereat the prattler fell silent, became very busy all at once, affected not to hear. When Aschenbach persisted he said he really knew nothing at all about it, and tried in a fresh burst of eloquence to drown the embarrassing subject.

That was one forenoon. After luncheon Aschenbach had himself ferried across to Venice, in a dead calm, under a burning sun; driven by his mania, he was following the Polish young folk, whom he had seen with their companion, taking the way to the landing stage. He did not find his idol on the Piazza. But as he sat there at tea, at a little round table on the shady side, suddenly he noticed a peculiar odour, which, it seemed to him now, had been in the air for days without his being aware: a sweetish, medicinal smell, associated with wounds and disease and doubtful cleanliness. He sniffed and pondered and at length recognized it; finished his tea and left the square at the end facing the cathedral. In the narrow space the stench grew stronger. At the street corners placards were stuck up, in which the city authorities warned the population against the danger of certain infections of the gastric system, prevalent during the hot season; advising them not to eat oysters or other shell fish and not to use the canal waters. The ordinance showed every sign of minimizing an existing situation. Little groups of people stood about silently in the squares and on the bridges; the traveller moved among them, watched and listened and thought.

He spoke to a shopkeeper lounging at his door among dangling coral necklaces and trinkets of artificial amethyst, and asked him about the disagreeable odour. The man looked at him, heavy-eyed, and hastily pulled himself together. 'Just a formal precaution, signore,' he said, with a gesture. 'A police regulation we have to put up with. The air is sultry—the sirocco is not wholesome, as the signore knows. Just a precautionary measure, you understand—probably unnecessary. . . .' Aschenbach thanked him and passed on. And on the boat that bore him back to the Lido he smelt the germicide again.

On reaching his hotel he sought the table in the lobby and buried himself in the newspapers. The foreign-language sheets had nothing. But in the German papers certain rumours were mentioned, statistics given, then officially denied, then the good faith of the denials called in question. The departure of the German and Austrian contingent was thus made plain. As for other nationals, they knew or suspected nothing—they were still undisturbed. Aschenbach tossed the newspapers back on the table. 'It ought to be kept quiet,' he thought, aroused. 'It should not be talked about.' And he felt in his heart a curious elation at these events impending in the world

about him.   Passion is like crime: it does not thrive on
the established order and the common round; it welcomes
every blow dealt the bourgeois structure, every weaken-
ing of the social fabric, because therein it feels a sure hope
of its own advantage.   These things that were going on
in the unclean alleys of Venice, under cover of an official
hushing-up policy—they gave Aschenbach a dark satisfaction.   The city's evil secret mingled with the one in
the depths of his heart—and he would have staked all he
possessed to keep it, since in his infatuation he cared for
nothing but to keep Tadzio here, and owned to himself,
not without horror, that he could not exist were the lad
to pass from his sight.

He was no longer satisfied to owe his communion with
his charmer to chance and the routine of hotel life; he
had begun to follow and waylay him.   On Sundays, for
example, the Polish family never appeared on the beach.
Aschenbach guessed they went to mass at San Marco
and pursued them thither.   He passed from the glare
of the Piazza into the golden twilight of the holy place
and found him he sought bowed in worship over a
prie-dieu.   He kept in the background, standing on the
fissured mosaic pavement among the devout populace,
that knelt and muttered and made the sign of the cross;
and the crowded splendour of the oriental temple weighed
voluptuously on his sense.   A heavily ornate priest
intoned and gesticulated before the altar, where little
candle flames flickered helplessly in the reek of incense-
breathing smoke; and with that cloying sacrificial smell
another seemed to mingle—the odour of the sickened
city.   But through all the glamour and glitter Aschenbach saw the exquisite creature there in front turn his
head, seek out and meet his lover's eye.

The crowd streamed out through the portals into the
brilliant square thick with fluttering doves, and the fond

fool stood aside in the vestibule on the watch. He saw
the Polish family leave the church. The children took
ceremonial leave of their mother, and she turned towards
the Piazzetta on her way home, while his charmer and
the cloistered sisters, with their governess, passed beneath
the clock tower into the Merceria. When they were a
few paces on, he followed—he stole behind them on their
walk through the city. When they paused, he did so
too; when they turned round, he fled into inns and court-
yards to let them pass. Once he lost them from view,
hunted feverishly over bridges and in filthy culs-de-sac,
only to confront them suddenly in a narrow passage
whence there was no escape, and experience a moment of
panic fear. Yet it would be untrue to say he suffered.
Mind and heart were drunk with passion, his footsteps
guided by the daemonic power whose pastime it is to
trample on human reason and dignity.

Tadzio and his sisters at length took a gondola. Aschenbach hid behind a portico or fountain while they embarked,
and directly they pushed off did the same. In a furtive
whisper he told the boatman he would tip him well to
follow at a little distance the other gondola, just rounding
a corner, and fairly sickened at the man's quick, sly grasp
and ready acceptance of the go-between's role.

Leaning back among soft, black cushions he swayed
gently in the wake of the other black-snouted bark, to
which the strength of his passion chained him. Sometimes it passed from his view, and then he was assailed
by an anguish of unrest. But his guide appeared to have
long practice in affairs like these; always, by dint of short
cuts or deft manœuvres, he contrived to overtake the
coveted sight. The air was heavy and foul, the sun
burnt down through a slate coloured haze. Water
slapped gurgling against wood and stone. The gondolier's
cry, half warning, half salute, was answered with singular

accord from far within the silence of the labyrinth. They passed little gardens, high up the crumbling wall, hung with clustering white and purple flowers that sent down an odour of almonds. Moorish lattices showed shadowy in the gloom. The marble steps of a church descended into the canal, and on them a beggar squatted, displaying his misery to view, showing the whites of his eyes, holding out his hat for alms. Farther on a dealer in antiquities cringed before his lair, inviting the passer by to enter and be duped. Yes, this was Venice, this the fair frailty that fawned and that betrayed, half fairy tale, half snare; the city in whose stagnating air the art of painting once put forth so lusty a growth, and where musicians were moved to accords so weirdly lulling and lascivious. Our adventurer felt his senses wooed by this voluptuousness of sight and sound, tasted his secret knowledge that the city sickened and hid its sickness for love of gain, and bent an ever more unbridled leer on the gondola that glided on before him.

It came at last to this—that his frenzy left him capacity for nothing else but to pursue his flame; to dream of him absent, to lavish, loverlike, endearing terms on his mere shadow. He was alone, he was a foreigner, he was sunk deep in this belated bliss of his—all which enabled him to pass unblushing through experiences wellnigh unbelievable. One night, returning late from Venice, he paused by his beloved's chamber door in the second story, leaned his head against the panel, and remained there long, in utter drunkenness, powerless to tear himself away, blind to the danger of being caught in so mad an attitude.

And yet there were not wholly lacking moments when he paused and reflected, when in consternation he asked himself what path was this on which he had set his foot. Like most other men of parts and attainments, he had an aristocratic interest in his forbears, and when he achieved a success he liked to think he had gratified them, compelled their admiration and regard. He thought of them now, involved as he was in this illicit adventure, in the grip of these exotic excesses of feeling; thought of their stern self-command and decent manliness, and gave a melancholy smile. What would they have said? What, indeed, would they have said to his entire life, that varied to the point of degeneracy from theirs? This life in the bonds of art, had not he himself, in the days of his youth and in the very spirit of those bourgeois forefathers, pronounced mocking judgment upon it? And yet, at bottom, it had been so like their own! It had been a service, and he a soldier, like some of them; and art was war—a grilling, exhausting struggle that nowadays wore one out before one could grow old. It had been a life of self-conquest, a life against odds, dour, steadfast, abstinent; he had made it symbolical of the kind of overstrained heroism the time admired, and he was entitled to call it manly, even courageous. He wondered if such a life might not be somehow specially pleasing in the eyes of the god who had him in his power. For Eros had received most countenance among the most valiant nations—yes, were we not told that in their cities prowess made him flourish exceedingly? And many heroes of olden time had willingly borne his yoke, not counting any humiliation such if it happened by the god's decree; vows, prostrations, self-abasements, these were no source of shame to the lover; rather they reaped him praise and honour.

Thus did the fond man's folly condition his thoughts; thus did he seek to hold his dignity upright in his own eyes. And all the while he kept doggedly on the traces of the disreputable secret the city kept hidden at its heart, just as he kept his own—and all that he learned fed his passion with vague, lawless hopes. He turned over newspapers at cafés, bent on finding a report on the progress of the disease; and in the German sheets, which had ceased to appear on the hotel table, he found a series of contradictory statements. The deaths, it was variously asserted, ran to twenty, to forty, to a hundred or more; yet in the next day's issue the existence of the pestilence was, if not roundly denied, reported as a matter of a few sporadic cases such as might be brought into a seaport town. After that the warnings would break out again, and the protests against the unscrupulous game the authorities were playing. No definite information was to be had.

And yet our solitary felt he had a sort of first claim on a share in the unwholesome secret; he took a fantastic satisfaction in putting leading questions to such persons as were interested in concealing, and forcing them to explicit untruths by way of denial. One day he attacked the manager, that small, soft-stepping man in the French frock coat, who was moving about among the guests at luncheon, supervising the service and making himself socially agreeable. He paused at Aschenbach's table to exchange a greeting, and the guest put a question, with a negligent, casual air: 'Why in the world are they for ever disinfecting the city of Venice?' 'A police regulation,' the adroit one replied; 'a precautionary measure, intended to protect the health of the public during this unseasonably warm and sultry weather.' 'Very praiseworthy of the police,' Aschenbach gravely responded. After a further exchange of meteorological commonplaces the manager passed on.

It happened that a band of street musicians came to perform in the hotel gardens that evening after dinner. They grouped themselves beneath an iron stanchion supporting an arc light, two women and two men, and turned their faces, that shone white in the glare, up

towards the guests who sat on the hotel terrace enjoying
this popular entertainment along with their coffee and
iced drinks. The hotel lift boys, waiters, and office
staff stood in the doorway and listened; the Russian
family displayed the usual Russian absorption in their
enjoyment—they had their chairs put down into the
garden to be nearer the singers and sat there in a half-
circle with gratitude painted on their features, the old
serf in her turban erect behind their chairs.

These strolling players were adepts at mandolin,
guitar, harmonica, even compassing a reedy violin.
Vocal numbers alternated with instrumental, the younger
woman, who had a high shrill voice, joining in a love
duet with the sweetly falsettoing tenor. The actual
head of the company, however, and incontestably its
most gifted member, was the other man, who played the
guitar. He was a sort of baritone *buffo*; with no voice to
speak of, but possessed of a pantomimic gift and remarkable
burlesque *élan*. Often he stepped out of the group and
advanced towards the terrace, guitar in hand, and his
audience rewarded his sallies with bursts of laughter.
The Russians in their parterre seats were beside themselves
with delight over this display of southern vivacity; their
shouts and screams of applause encouraged him to bolder
and bolder flights.

Aschenbach sat near the balustrade, a glass of pomegranate juice and soda water sparkling ruby-red before
him, with which he now and then moistened his lips.
His nerves drank in thirstily the unlovely sounds, the
vulgar and sentimental tunes, for passion paralyses good
taste and makes its victim accept with rapture what
a man in his senses would either laugh at or turn from
with disgust. Idly he sat and watched the antics of the
buffoon with his face set in a fixed and painful smile,
while inwardly his whole being was rigid with the intensity

of the regard he bent on Tadzio, leaning over the railings six paces off.

He lounged there, in the white belted suit he some-times wore at dinner, in all his innate, inevitable grace, with his left arm on the balustrade, his legs crossed, the right hand on the supporting hip; and looked down on the strolling singers with an expression that was hardly a smile, but rather a distant curiosity and polite toleration. Now and then he straightened himself and with a charm-ing movement of both arms drew down his white blouse through his leather belt, throwing out his chest. And sometimes—Aschenbach saw it with triumph, with horror, and a sense that his reason was tottering—the lad would cast a glance, that might be slow and cautious, or might be sudden and swift, as though to take him by surprise, to the place where his lover sat. Aschenbach did not meet the glance. An ignoble caution made him keep his eyes in leash. For in the rear of the terrace sat Tadzio's mother and governess; and matters had gone so far that he feared to make himself conspicuous. Several times, on the beach, in the hotel lobby, on the Piazza, he had seen, with a stealing numbness, that they called Tadzio away from his neighbourhood. And his pride revolted at the affront, even while conscience told him it was deserved.

The performer below presently began a solo, with guitar accompaniment, a street song in several stanzas, just then the rage all over Italy. He delivered it in a striking and dramatic recitative, and his company joined in the refrain. He was a man of slight build, with a thin, undernourished face; his shabby felt hat rested on the back of his neck, a great mop of red hair sticking out in front; and he stood there on the gravel in advance of his troupe, in an impudent, swaggering posture, twanging the strings of his instrument and flinging a witty and rollicking recitative up to the terrace, while the veins on his forehead swelled with the violence of his effort. He was scarcely a Venetian type, belonging rather to the race of Neapolitan jesters, half bully, half comedian, brutal, blustering, an unpleasant customer, and entertaining to the last degree. The words of his song were trivial and silly, but on his lips, accompanied with gestures of head, hands, arms, and body, with leers and winks and the loose play of the tongue in the corner of his mouth, they took on meaning; an equivocal meaning, yet vaguely offensive. He wore a white sports shirt with a suit of ordinary clothes, and a strikingly large and naked-looking Adam's apple rose out of the open collar. From that pale, snub-nosed face it was hard to judge of his age; vice sat on it, it was furrowed with grimacing, and two deep wrinkles of defiance and self-will, almost of desperation, stood oddly between the red brows, above the grinning, mobile mouth. But what more than all drew upon him the profound scrutiny of our solitary watcher was that this suspicious figure seemed to carry with it its own suspicious odour. For whenever the refrain occurred and the singer, with waving arms and antic gestures, passed in his grotesque march immediately beneath Aschenbach's seat, a strong smell of carbolic was wafted up to the terrace.

After the song he began to take up money, beginning with the Russian family, who gave liberally, and then mounting the steps to the terrace. But here he became as cringing as he had before been forward. He glided between the tables, bowing and scraping, showing his strong white teeth in a servile smile, though the two deep furrows on the brow were still very marked. His audience looked at the strange creature as he went about collecting his livelihood, and their curiosity was not unmixed with disfavour. They tossed coins with their

finger tips into his hat and took care not to touch it.
Let the enjoyment be never so great, a sort of embarrassment always comes when the comedian oversteps the
physical distance between himself and respectable people.
This man felt it and sought to make his peace by fawning.
He came along the railing to Aschenbach, and with him
came that smell no one else seemed to notice.

'Listen!' said the solitary, in a low voice, almost
mechanically; 'they are disinfecting Venice—why?'
The mountebank answered hoarsely: 'Because of the
police. Orders, signore. On account of the heat and
the sirocco. The sirocco is oppressive. Not good for
the health.' He spoke as though surprised that any one
could ask, and with the flat of his hand he demonstrated
how oppressive the sirocco was. 'So there is no plague
in Venice?' Aschenbach asked the question between his
teeth, very low. The man's expressive face fell, he put
on a look of comical innocence. 'A plague? What
sort of plague? Is the sirocco a plague? Or perhaps
our police are a plague! You are making fun of us,
signore! A plague! Why should there be? The
police make regulations on account of the heat and the
weather. . . .' He gestured. 'Quite,' said Aschenbach once more, soft and low; and dropping an unduly
large coin into the man's hat dismissed him with a sign.
He bowed very low and left. But he had not reached
the steps when two of the hotel servants flung themselves
on him and began to whisper, their faces close to his.
He shrugged, seemed to be giving assurances, to be swear-
ing he had said nothing. It was not hard to guess the
import of his words. They let him go at last and he
went back into the garden, where he conferred briefly
with his troupe and then stepped forward for a farewell
song.

It was one Aschenbach had never to his knowledge

heard before, a rowdy air, with words in impossible dialect. It had a laughing refrain in which the other three artistes joined at the top of their lungs. The refrain had neither words nor accompaniment, it was nothing but rhythmical, modulated, natural laughter, which the soloist in particular knew how to render with most deceptive realism. Now that he was farther off his audience, his self-assurance had come back, and this laughter of his rang with a mocking note. He would be overtaken before he reached the end of the last line of each stanza; he would catch his breath, lay his hand over his mouth, his voice would quaver and his shoulders shake, he would lose power to contain himself longer. Just at the right moment each time, it came whooping, bawling, crashing out of him, with a verisimilitude that never failed to set his audience off in profuse and unpremeditated mirth that seemed to add gusto to his own. He bent his knees, he clapped his thigh, he held his sides, he looked ripe for bursting. He no longer laughed, but yelled, pointing his finger at the company there above as though there could be in all the world nothing so comic as they; until at last they laughed in hotel, terrace, and garden, down to the waiters, lift boys, and servants— laughed as though possessed.

Aschenbach could no longer rest in his chair, he sat poised for flight. But the combined effect of the laughing, the hospital odour in his nostrils, and the nearness of the beloved was to hold him in a spell; he felt unable to stir. Under cover of the general commotion he looked across at Tadzio and saw that the lovely boy returned his gaze with a seriousness that seemed the copy of his own; the general hilarity, it seemed to say, had no power over him, he kept aloof. The grey-haired man was overpowered, disarmed by this docile, childlike deference, with difficulty he refrained from hiding his face in his hands. Tadzio's habit, too, of drawing himself up and taking a deep sighing breath struck him as being due to an oppression of the chest. 'He is sickly, he will never live to grow up,' he thought once again, with that dispassionate vision to which his madness of desire sometimes so strangely gave way. And compassion struggled with the reckless exultation of his heart.

The players, meanwhile, had finished and gone; their leader bowing and scraping, kissing his hands and adorning his leave-taking with antics that grew madder with the applause they evoked. After all the others were outside, he pretended to run backwards full tilt against a lamp post and slunk to the gate apparently doubled over with pain. But there he threw off his buffoon's mask, stood erect, with an elastic straightening of his whole figure, ran out his tongue impudently at the guests on the terrace, and vanished in the night. The company dispersed. Tadzio had long since left the balustrade. But he, the lonely man, sat for long, to the waiters' great annoyance, before the dregs of pomegranate juice in his glass. Time passed, the night went on. Long ago, in his parental home, he had watched the sand filter through an hour-glass—he could still see, as though it stood before him, the fragile, symbolic little toy. Soundless and fine the rust-red streamlet ran through the narrow neck, and made, as it declined in the upper cavity, an exquisite little vortex.

The very next afternoon the solitary took another step in pursuit of his fixed policy of baiting the outer world. This time he had all possible success. He went, that is, into the English travel bureau in the Piazza, changed some money at the desk, and posing as the suspicious foreigner, put his fateful question. The clerk was a tweed-clad young Britisher, with his eyes set close together, his hair parted in the middle, and radiating that steady reliability which makes his like so strange a pheno-

menon in the *gamin*, agile-witted south. He began:
'No ground for alarm, sir. A mere formality. Quite
regular in view of the unhealthy climatic conditions.'
But then, looking up, he chanced to meet with his own
blue eyes the stranger's weary, melancholy gaze, fixed
on his face. The Englishman coloured. He continued
in a lower voice, rather confused: 'At least, that is the
official explanation, which they see fit to stick to. I may
tell you there's a bit more to it than that.' And then,
in his good, straightforward way, he told the truth.

For several years past Asiatic cholera had shown a
strong tendency to spread. Its source was the hot, moist
swamps of the delta of the Ganges, where it bred in the
mephitic air of that primeval island jungle, among whose
bamboo thickets the tiger crouches, where life of every
sort flourishes in rankest abundance, and only man
avoids the spot. Thence the pestilence had spread
throughout Hindustan, raging with great violence;
moved eastwards to China, westwards to Afghanistan and
Persia; following the great caravan routes, it brought
terror to Astrakhan, terror to Moscow. Even while
Europe trembled lest the spectre should be seen striding
westward across country, it was carried by sea from Syrian
ports and appeared simultaneously at several points on the
Mediterranean littoral: raised its head in Toulon and
Malaga, Palermo and Naples, and soon got a firm hold
in Calabria and Apulia. Northern Italy had been
spared—so far. But in May the horrible vibrions were
found on the same day in two bodies: the emaciated,
blackened corpses of a bargee and a woman who kept a
greengrocer's shop. Both cases were hushed up. But
in a week there were ten more—twenty, thirty in different quarters of the town. An Austrian provincial,
having come to Venice on a few days' pleasure trip, went
home and died with all the symptoms of the plague.

Thus was explained the fact that the German-language papers were the first to print the news of the Venetian outbreak. The Venetian authorities published in reply a statement to the effect that the state of the city's health had never been better; at the same time instituting the most necessary precautions. But by that time the food supplies—milk, meat, or vegetables—had probably been contaminated, for death unseen and unacknowledged was devouring and laying waste in the narrow streets, while a brooding, unseasonable heat warmed the waters of the canals and encouraged the spread of the pestilence. Yes, the disease seemed to flourish and wax strong, to redouble its generative powers. Recoveries were rare. Eighty out of every hundred died, and horribly, for the onslaught was of the extremest violence, and not infrequently of the 'dry' type, the most malignant form of the contagion. In this form the victim's body loses power to expel the water secreted by the blood-vessels, it shrivels up, he passes with hoarse cries from convulsion to convulsion, his blood grows thick like pitch, and he suffocates in a few hours. He is fortunate indeed, if, as sometimes happens, the disease, after a slight malaise, takes the form of a profound unconsciousness, from which the sufferer seldom or never rouses. By the beginning of June the quarantine buildings of the *ospedale civico* had quietly filled up, the two orphan asylums were entirely occupied, and there was a hideously brisk traffic between the *Nuovo Fondamento* and the island of San Michele, where the cemetery was. But the city was not swayed by high-minded motives or regard for international agreements. The authorities were more actuated by fear of being out of pocket, by regard for the new exhibition of paintings just opened in the public gardens, or by apprehension of the large losses the hotels and shops that catered to foreigners would suffer in case of panic and blockade. And the fears of the people supported the persistent official policy of silence and denial. The city's first medical officer, an honest and competent man, had indignantly resigned his office and been privily replaced by a more compliant person. The fact was known; and this corruption in high places played its part, together with the suspense as to where the walking terror might strike next, to demoralize the baser elements in the city and encourage those anti-social forces which shun the light of day. There was intemperance, indecency, increase of crime. In the evenings one saw many drunken people, which was unusual. Gangs of men in surly mood made the streets unsafe, theft and assault were said to be frequent, even murder; for in two cases persons supposedly victims of the plague were proved to have been poisoned by their own families. And professional vice was rampant, displaying excesses heretofore unknown and only at home much farther south and in the east.

Such was the substance of the Englishman's tale. 'You would do well,' he concluded, 'to leave to-day instead of to-morrow. The blockade cannot be more than a few days off.'

'Thank you,' said Aschenbach, and left the office.

The Piazza lay in sweltering sunshine. Innocent foreigners sat before the cafés or stood in front of the cathedral, the centre of clouds of doves that, with fluttering wings, tried to shoulder each other away and pick the kernels of maize from the extended hand. Aschenbach strode up and down the spacious flags, feverishly excited, triumphant in possession of the truth at last, but with a sickening taste in his mouth and a fantastic horror at his heart. One decent, expiatory course lay open to him; he considered it. To-night, after dinner, he might approach the lady of the pearls and address her in words which he precisely formulated in his mind: 'Madame,

will you permit an entire stranger to serve you with a
word of advice and warning which self-interest prevents
others from uttering?   Go away.   Leave here at once,
without delay, with Tadzio and your daughters.   Venice
is in the grip of pestilence.'   Then might he lay his
hand in farewell upon the head of that instrument of a
mocking deity; and thereafter himself flee that accursed
morass.   But he knew that he was far indeed from any
serious desire to take such a step.   It would restore
him, would give him back himself once more; but he
who is beside himself revolts at the idea of self-possession.
There crossed his mind the vision of a white building
with inscriptions on it, glittering in the sinking sun—he
recalled how his mind had dreamed away into their
transparent   mysticism;   recalled   the   strange   pilgrim
apparition that had wakened in the ageing man a lust for
strange countries and fresh sights.   And these memories,
again, brought in their train the thought of returning
home,   returning to reason, self-mastery, an ordered
existence, to the old life of effort.   Alas! the bare thought
made him wince with a revulsion that was like physical
nausea.   'It must be kept quiet,' he whispered fiercely.
'I will not speak!'   The knowledge that he shared the
city's secret, the city's guilt—it put him beside himself,
intoxicated him as a small quantity of wine will a man
suffering from brain fag.   His thoughts dwelt upon the
image of the desolate and calamitous city, and he was
giddy with fugitive, mad, unreasoning hopes and visions
of a monstrous sweetness.   That tender sentiment he
had a moment ago evoked, what was it compared with
such images as these?   His art, his moral sense, what
were they in the balance beside the boons that chaos might
confer?   He kept silence, he stopped on.

That night he had a fearful dream—if dream be the
right word for a mental and physical experience which

did indeed befall him in deep sleep, as a thing quite apart and real to his senses, yet without seeing himself as present in it. Rather its theatre seemed to be his own soul, and the events burst in from outside, violently overcoming the profound resistance of his spirit; passed through him and left him, left the whole cultural structure of a life-time trampled on, ravaged, and destroyed.

The beginning was fear; fear and desire, with a shud-dering curiosity. Night reigned, and his senses were on the alert; he heard loud, confused noises from far away, clamour and hubbub. There was a rattling, a crashing, a low dull thunder; shrill halloos and a kind of howl with a long-drawn *u*-sound at the end. And with all these, dominating them all, flute notes of the cruellest sweetness, deep and cooing, keeping shamelessly on until the listener felt his very entrails bewitched. He heard a voice, naming, though darkly, that which was to come: 'The stranger god!' A glow lighted up the surrounding mist and by it he recognized a mountain scene like that about his country home. From the wooded heights, from among the tree trunks and crumbling moss-covered rocks, a troop came tumbling and raging down, a whirling rout of men and animals, and overflowed the hillside with flames and human forms, with clamour and the reeling dance. The females stumbled over the long, hairy pelts that dangled from their girdles; with heads flung back they uttered loud hoarse cries and shook their tambourines high in air; brandished naked daggers or torches vomiting trails of sparks. They shrieked, holding their breasts in both hands; coiling snakes with quivering tongues they clutched about their waists. Horned and hairy males, girt about the loins with hides, drooped heads and lifted arms and thighs in unison, as they beat on brazen vessels that gave out droning thunder, or thumped madly on drums. There were troops of beardless youths armed

F 962

with garlanded staves; these ran after goats and thrust their staves against the creatures' flanks, then clung to the plunging horns and let themselves be borne off with triumphant shouts. And one and all the mad rout yelled that cry, composed of soft consonants with a long-drawn *u*-sound at the end, so sweet and wild it was together, and like nothing ever heard before! It would ring through the air like the bellow of a challenging stag, and be given back many-tongued; or they would use it to goad each other on to dance with wild excess of tossing limbs—they never let it die. But the deep, beguiling notes of the flute wove in and out and over all. Beguiling too it was to him who struggled in the grip of these sights and sounds, shamelessly awaiting the coming feast and the uttermost surrender. He trembled, he shrank, his will was steadfast to preserve and uphold his own god against this stranger who was sworn enemy to dignity and self-control. But the mountain wall took up the noise and howling and gave it back manifold; it rose high, swelled to a madness that carried him away. His senses reeled in the steam of panting bodies, the acrid stench from the goats, the odour as of stagnant waters—and another, too familiar smell—of wounds, uncleanness, and disease. His heart throbbed to the drums, his brain reeled, a blind rage seized him, a whirling lust, he craved with all his soul to join the ring that formed about the obscene symbol of the godhead, which they were unveiling and elevating monstrous and wooden, while from full throats they yelled their rallying cry. Foam dripped from their lips, they drove each other on with lewd gesturings and beckoning hands. They laughed, they howled, they thrust their pointed staves into each other's flesh and licked the blood as it ran down. But now the dreamer was in and of them, the stranger god was his own. Yes, it was he who was flinging himself upon the animals, who

bit and tore and swallowed smoking gobbets of flesh—
while on the trampled moss there now began the rites in
honour of the god, an orgy of promiscuous embraces—
and in his very soul he tasted the bestial degradation of
his fall.

The unhappy man woke from this dream shattered,
unhinged, powerless in the demon's grip. He no longer
avoided men's eyes nor cared whether he exposed himself
to suspicion. And anyhow, people were leaving; many
of the bathing cabins stood empty, there were many
vacant places in the dining-room, scarcely any foreigners
were seen in the streets. The truth seemed to have
leaked out; despite all efforts to the contrary, panic was
in the air. But the lady of the pearls stopped on with her
family; whether because the rumours had not reached
her or because she was too proud and fearless to heed them.
Tadzio remained; and it seemed at times to Aschenbach,
in his obsessed state, that death and fear together might
clear the island of all other souls and leave him there
alone with him he coveted. In the long mornings on
the beach his heavy gaze would rest, a fixed and reckless
stare, upon the lad; towards nightfall, lost to shame, he
would follow him through the city's narrow streets where
horrid death stalked too, and at such time it seemed to
him as though the moral law were fallen in ruins and
only the monstrous and perverse held out a hope.

Like any lover, he desired to please; suffered agonies
at the thought of failure, and brightened his dress with
smart ties and handkerchiefs and other youthful touches.
He added jewellery and perfumes and spent hours each
day over his toilet, appearing at dinner elaborately arrayed
and tensely excited. The presence of the youthful
beauty that had bewitched him filled him with disgust at
his own ageing body; the sight of his own sharp features
and grey hair plunged him in hopeless mortification; he

made desperate efforts to recover the appearance and freshness of his youth and began paying frequent visits to the hotel barber. Enveloped in the white sheet, beneath the hands of that garrulous personage, he would lean back in the chair and look at himself in the glass with misgiving.

'Grey,' he said, with a grimace.

'Slightly,' answered the man. 'Entirely due to neglect, to a lack of regard for appearances. Very natural, of course, in men of affairs, but, after all, not very sensible, for it is just such people who ought to be above vulgar prejudice in matters like these. Some folk have very strict ideas about the use of cosmetics; but they never extend them to the teeth, as they logically should. And very disgusted other people would be if they did. No, we are all as old as we feel, but no older, and grey hair can misrepresent a man worse than dyed. You, for instance, signore, have a right to your natural colour. Surely you will permit me to restore what belongs to you?'

'How?' asked Aschenbach.

For answer the oily one washed his client's hair in two waters, one clear and one dark, and lo, it was as black as in the days of his youth. He waved it with the tongs in wide, flat undulations, and stepped back to admire the effect.

'Now if we were just to freshen up the skin a little,' he said.

And with that he went on from one thing to another, his enthusiasm waxing with each new idea. Aschenbach sat there comfortably; he was incapable of objecting to the process—rather as it went forward it roused his hopes. He watched it in the mirror and saw his eyebrows grow more even and arching, the eyes gain in size and brilliance, by dint of a little application below the lids. A delicate carmine glowed on his cheeks where the skin had been so brown and leathery. The dry, anaemic lips grew full, they turned the colour of ripe strawberries, the lines round eyes and mouth were treated with a facial cream and gave place to youthful bloom. It was a young man who looked back at him from the glass—Aschenbach's heart leaped at the sight. The artist in cosmetic at last professed himself satisfied; after the manner of such people, he thanked his client profusely for what he had done himself. 'The merest trifle, the merest, signore,' he said as he added the final touches. 'Now the signore can fall in love as soon as he likes.' Aschenbach went off as in a dream, dazed between joy and fear, in his red neck-tie and broad straw hat with its gay striped band.

A lukewarm storm wind had come up. It rained a little now and then, the air was heavy and turbid and smelt of decay. Aschenbach, with fevered cheeks beneath the rouge, seemed to hear rushing and flapping sounds in his ears, as though storm spirits were abroad— unhallowed ocean harpies who follow those devoted to destruction, snatch away and defile their viands. For the heat took away his appetite and thus he was haunted with the idea that his food was infected.

One afternoon he pursued his charmer deep into the stricken city's huddled heart. The labyrinthine little streets, squares, canals, and bridges, each one so like the next, at length quite made him lose his bearings. He did not even know the points of the compass; all his care was not to lose sight of the figure after which his eyes thirsted. He slunk under walls, he lurked behind buildings or people's backs; and the sustained tension of his senses and emotions exhausted him more and more, though for a long time he was unconscious of fatigue. Tadzio walked behind the others, he let them pass ahead in the narrow alleys, and as he sauntered slowly after, he would turn his head and assure himself with a glance of his

strange, twilit grey eyes that his lover was still following.
He saw him—and he did not betray him. The knowledge enraptured Aschenbach. Lured by those eyes,
led on the leading-string of his own passion and folly,
utterly lovesick, he stole upon the footsteps of his un-
seemly hope—and at the end found himself cheated.
The Polish family crossed a small vaulted bridge, the
height of whose archway hid them from his sight, and
when he climbed it himself they were nowhere to be seen.
He hunted in three directions—straight ahead and on
both sides the narrow, dirty quay—in vain. Worn
quite out and unnerved, he had to give over the search.

His head burned, his body was wet with clammy
sweat, he was plagued by intolerable thirst. He looked
about for refreshment, of whatever sort, and found a little
fruit shop where he bought some strawberries. They
were overripe and soft; he ate them as he went. The
street he was on opened out into a little square, one of
those charmed, forsaken spots he liked; he recognized it
as the very one where he had sat weeks ago and conceived
his abortive plan of flight. He sank down on the steps
of the well and leaned his head against its stone rim.
It was quiet here. Grass grew between the stones, and
rubbish lay about. Tall, weather-beaten houses bor-
dered the square, one of them palatial, with vaulted
windows, gaping now, and little lion balconies. In the
ground floor of another was an apothecary's shop. A
waft of carbolic acid was borne on a warm gust of wind.

There he sat, the master: this was he who had found
a way to reconcile art and honours; who had written
The Abject, and in a style of classic purity renounced
bohemianism and all its works, all sympathy with the
abyss and the troubled depths of the outcast human soul.
This was he who had put knowledge underfoot to
climb so high; who had outgrown the ironic pose and

adjusted himself to the burdens and obligations of fame; whose renown had been officially recognized and his name ennobled, whose style was set for a model in the schools. There he sat. His eyelids were closed, there was only a swift, sidelong glint of the eyeballs now and again, something between a question and a leer; while the rouged and flabby mouth uttered single words of the sentences shaped in his disordered brain by the fantastic logic that governs our dreams.

'For mark you, Phaedrus, beauty alone is both divine and visible; and so it is the sense way, the artist's way, little Phaedrus, to the spirit. But, now tell me, my dear boy, do you believe that such a man can ever attain wisdom and true manly worth, for whom the path to the spirit must lead through the senses? Or do you rather think—for I leave the point to you—that it is a path of perilous sweetness, a way of transgression, and must surely lead him who walks in it astray? For you know that we poets cannot walk the way of beauty without Eros as our companion and guide. We may be heroic after our fashion, disciplined warriors of our craft, yet are we all like women, for we exult in passion, and love is still our desire—our craving and our shame. And from this you will perceive that we poets can be neither wise nor worthy citizens. We must needs be wanton, must needs rove at large in the realm of feeling. Our magisterial style is all folly and pretence, our honourable repute a farce, the crowd's belief in us is merely laughable. And to teach youth, or the populace, by means of art is a dangerous practice and ought to be forbidden. For what good can an artist be as a teacher, when from his birth up he is headed direct for the pit? We may want to shun it and attain to honour in the world; but however we turn, it draws us still. So, then, since knowledge might destroy us, we will have none of it. For knowledge,

Phaedrus, does not make him who possesses it dignified
or austere. Knowledge is all-knowing, understanding,
forgiving; it takes up no position, sets no store by form.
It has compassion on the abyss—it *is* the abyss. So we
reject it, firmly, and henceforward our concern shall be
with beauty only. And by beauty we mean simplicity,
largeness, and renewed severity of discipline; we mean a
return to detachment and to form. But detachment,
Phaedrus, and preoccupation with form lead to intoxication and desire, they may lead the noblest among us to
frightful emotional excesses, which his own stern cult of
the beautiful would make him the first to condemn.
So they too, they too, lead to the bottomless pit. Yes,
they lead us thither, I say, us who are poets—who by
our natures are prone not to excellence but to excess.
And now, Phaedrus, I will go. Remain here; and only
when you can no longer see me, then do you depart also.'

A few days later Gustave Aschenbach left his hotel
rather later than usual in the morning. He was not
feeling well and had to struggle against spells of giddiness
only half physical in their nature, accompanied by a
swiftly mounting dread, a sense of futility and hopelessness
—but whether this referred to himself or to the outer
world he could not tell. In the lobby he saw a quantity
of luggage lying strapped and ready; asked the porter
whose it was, and received in answer the name he already
knew he should hear—that of the Polish family. The
expression of his ravaged features did not change; he only
gave that quick lift of the head with which we sometimes
receive the uninteresting answer to a casual query. But
he put another: 'When?' 'After luncheon,' the man
replied. He nodded, and went down to the beach.

It was an unfriendly scene. Little crisping shivers
ran all across the wide stretch of shallow water between
the shore and the first sand bank. The whole beach,

once so full of colour and life, looked now autumnal, out of season; it was nearly deserted and not even very clean. A camera on a tripod stood at the edge of the water, apparently abandoned; its black cloth snapped in the freshening wind.

Tadzio was there, in front of his cabin, with the three or four playfellows still left him. Aschenbach set up his chair some half-way between the cabins and the water, spread a rug over his knees, and sat looking on. The game this time was unsupervised, the elders being probably busy with their packing, and it looked rather lawless and out of hand. Jaschiu, the sturdy lad in the belted suit, with the black, brilliantined hair, became angry at a handful of sand thrown in his eyes; he challenged Tadzio to a fight, which quickly ended in the downfall of the weaker. And perhaps the coarser nature saw here a chance to avenge himself at last, by one cruel act, for his long weeks of subserviency: the victor would not let the vanquished get up, but remained kneeling on Tadzio's back, pressing Tadzio's face into the sand—for so long a time that it seemed the exhausted lad might even suffocate. He made spasmodic efforts to shake the other off, lay still, and then began a feeble twitching. Just as Aschenbach was about to spring indignantly to the rescue, Jaschiu let his victim go. Tadzio, very pale, half sat up, and remained so, leaning on one arm, for several minutes, with darkening eyes and rumpled hair. Then he rose and walked slowly away. The others called him, at first gaily, then imploringly; he would not hear. Jaschiu was evidently overtaken by swift remorse; he followed his friend and tried to make his peace, but Tadzio motioned him back with a jerk of one shoulder and went down to the water's edge. He was barefoot and wore his striped linen suit with the red breast knot.

There he stayed a little, with bent head, tracing figures

in the wet sand with one toe; then stepped into the shallow water, which at its deepest did not wet his knees; waded idly through it and reached the sand bar. Now he paused again, with his face turned seaward; and next began to move slowly leftwards along the narrow strip of sand the sea left bare. He paced there, divided by an expanse of water from the shore, from his mates by his moody pride; a remote and isolated figure, with floating locks, out there in sea and wind, against the misty inane. Once more he paused to look: with a sudden recollection, or by an impulse, he turned from the waist up, in an exquisite movement, one hand resting on his hip, and looked over his shoulder at the shore. The watcher sat just as he had sat that time in the lobby of the hotel when first the twilit grey eyes had met his own. He rested his head against the chair back and followed the movements of the figure out there, then lifted it, as it were in answer to Tadzio's gaze. It sank on his breast, the eyes looked out beneath their lids, while his whole face took on the relaxed and brooding expression of deep slumber. It seemed to him the pale and lovely Summoner out there smiled and beckoned; as though, with the hand he lifted from his hip, he pointed outward as he hovered on before into an immensity of richest expectation.

Some minutes passed before any one hastened to the aid of the elderly man sitting there collapsed in his chair. They bore him to his room. And before nightfall a shocked and respectful world received the news of his decease.

THERMOMETER

HANS CASTORP'S week here[1] ran from Tuesday to Tuesday, for on a Tuesday he had arrived. Two or three days before, he had gone down to the office and paid his second weekly bill, a modest account of a round one hundred and sixty francs, modest and cheap enough, even without taking into consideration the nature of some of the advantages of a stay up here—advantages priceless in themselves, though for that very reason they could not be included in the bill—and even without counting extras like the fortnightly concert and Dr Krokowski's lectures, which might conceivably have been included. The sum of one hundred and sixty francs represented simply and solely the actual hospitality extended by the Berghof to Hans Castorp: his comfortable accommodation and his five stupendous meals.

'It isn't much, it is rather cheap than otherwise,' remarked the guest to the old inhabitant. 'You cannot complain of being overcharged up here. You need a round six hundred and fifty francs a month for board and lodging, treatment included. Let us assume that you spend another thirty francs for tips, if you are decent and like to have friendly faces about you. That makes six hundred and eighty. Good. Of course I know there are fixed fees and other sorts of small expenses: toilet articles, tobacco, drives, and excursions, now and then a bill for shoes or clothing. Very good. But all that won't bring it up to a thousand francs, say what you like. Not eight hundred even. That isn't ten thousand francs a year. Certainly not more. That is what it costs you.'

[1] The sanatorium in Davos, which is the scene of the story of *The Magic Mountain*.

'Mental arithmetic very fair,' Joachim said. 'I never knew you were such a shot at doing sums in your head. And how broad-minded of you to calculate it by the year like that! You 've learned something since you 've been up here. But your figure is too high. I don't smoke, and I certainly don't expect to buy any suits while I am here, thank you.'

'Then it would be lower still,' Hans Castorp answered, rather confused. Why, indeed, he should have included tobacco and a new wardrobe in his calculation of Joachim's expenses is a puzzle. But for the rest, his brilliant display of arithmetic had simply been so much dust thrown in his cousin's eyes; for here, as elsewhere, his mental processes were rather slow than fast, and the truth is that a previous calculation with pencil and paper underlay his present facility. One night on his balcony (for he even took the evening cure out of doors now, like the rest) a sudden thought had struck him and he had got out of his comfortable chair to fetch pencil and paper. As the result of some simple figuring, he concluded that his cousin— or, speaking generally, a patient at the Berghof—would need twelve thousand francs a year to cover the sum total of his expenses. Thus he amused himself by establishing the fact that he, Hans Castorp, could amply afford to live up here, if he chose, being a man of eighteen or nine-teen thousand francs yearly income.

He had, as we have said, paid his second weekly bill three days before, and accordingly found himself in the middle of the third and last week of his appointed stay. The coming Sunday, as he remarked to himself and his cousin, would see the performance of another of the fort-nightly concerts, and the Monday another lecture by Dr Krokowski; then, on Tuesday or Wednesday, he would be off, and Joachim would be left up here alone— poor Joachim, for whom Rhadamanthus would prescribe

God knew how many more months! Already there came a shade over his gentle black eyes whenever Hans Castorp's swiftly approaching departure was spoken of. Where, in heaven's name, had the holiday gone? It had rushed past, it had flown—and left one wondering how. For, after all, three weeks, twenty-one days, is a considerable stretch of time, too long, at least, for one to see the end from the beginning. And now, on a sudden, there remained of it no more than a miserable three or four days, nothing worth mentioning. They would, it was true, comprehend the lecture and the concert, those two recurrent variations in the weekly programme, and, thus weighted, might move a little more slowly. But on the other hand, they would be taken up with packing and leave-taking. Three weeks up here was as good as nothing at all; they had all told him so in the beginning. The smallest unit of time was the month, Settembrini had said; and as Hans Castorp's stay was less than that, it amounted to nothing; it was a 'week-end visit,' as Hofrat Behrens put it. Had the swift flight of time up here anything to do with the uniformly accelerated rate of organic combustion? At any rate, here was a consoling thought for Joachim during his five remaining months—in case he really got off with five. But Hans Castorp felt that during these three weeks they ought to have paid more attention, to have kept better watch, as Joachim did in his daily measurings, during which the seven minutes seemed like a quite considerable stretch of time. Hans Castorp grieved for his cousin, reading in his eyes his pain at the approaching parting. He felt the strongest possible sympathy at the thought of the poor chap's having to stop on up here when he himself was down in the flat land, helping to bring the nations together through the development of commerce and communications. His own regret was at times so lively as to burn in his breast and cause him to doubt whether he would have the heart, when the time came, to leave Joachim alone; and this vicarious suffering was probably the reason why he himself referred less and less to his impending departure. It was Joachim who came back to it; for Hans Castorp, moved by native tact and delicacy, seemed to wish to forget it up to the last moment.

'At least,' Joachim said more than once in these days, 'let us hope it has done you good to be up here, and that you will feel the benefit when you are at home again.'

'I 'll remember you to everybody,' Hans Castorp responded, 'and say you are coming back in five months at the outside. Done me good? If it has done me good to be up here? I should like to think so; some improvement must surely have taken place, even in this short time. I have received a great many new impressions, new in every sense of the word; very stimulating, but a good deal of strain too, physically and mentally. I have not at all the feeling of having really got acclimatized —which would certainly be the first necessary step towards improvement. Maria, thank goodness, is her old self; for several days now, I have been able to get the aroma. But my handkerchief still becomes red from time to time when I use it—and this damned heat in my face, and these idiotic palpitations, I shall apparently have them up to the last minute. No, it seems I can't talk about being acclimatized—how could I, either, in so short a time? It would take longer than this to overcome the change of atmosphere and adjust oneself perfectly to the unusual conditions, so that a real recovery could begin and I should commence to put on flesh. It is too bad. It was certainly a mistake not to have given myself more time—for of course I could have had it. I have the feeling that once I am at home again I shall need to sleep three weeks on end to get rested from the rest I 've had! That shows you how tired I sometimes feel. And now, to cap the climax, I get this catarrh——'

It looked, in fact, as though Hans Castorp would return home in possession of a first-class cold. He had caught it, probably, in the rest cure, and, again probably, in the evening rest cure—which for almost a week now he had been taking in the balcony, despite the long spell of cold, wet weather. He was aware that weather of this kind was not recognized as bad; such a conception hardly existed up here, where the most inclement conceivable went unheeded and had no terrors for any one. With the easy adaptability of youth, which suits itself to any environment, Hans Castorp had begun to imitate this indifference. It might rain in bucketfuls, but the air was not supposed to be the more damp for that—nor was it, in all probability, for the dry heat in the face persisted, as though after drinking wine, or sitting in an overheated room. And however cold it got, the radiators were never heated unless it snowed, so it was of no avail to take refuge in one's chamber, since it was quite as comfortable on the balcony, when one lay in one's excellent chair, wrapped in a paletot and two good camel's-hair rugs put on according to the ritual. As comfortable? It was incomparably more so. It was, in Hans Castorp's reasoned judgment, a state of life which appealed to him more than any in all his previous experience, so far as he could remember. He did not propose to be shaken in this view for any *carbonaro* or quill-driver in existence, no matter how many malicious and equivocal jokes he made on the subject of the 'horizontal.' Especially he liked it in the evening, when with his little lamp on the stand before him and his long-lost and now restored Maria alight between his lips he enjoyed the ineffable excellencies of his reclining-chair. True, his nose felt frozen, and the hands that held his book—he was still reading

Ocean Steamships—were red and cramped from the cold. He looked through the arch of his loggia over the darkening valley, jewelled with clustered or scattered lights, and listened to the music that drifted up nearly every evening for almost an hour. There was a concert below, and he could hear, pleasantly subdued by the distance, familiar operatic selections, snatches from *Carmen*, *Il Trovatore*, *Freischütz*; or well-built, facile waltzes, marches so spirited that he could not help keeping time with his head, and gay mazurkas. Mazurka? No, Marusja was her name, Marusja of the little ruby. And in the next loggia, behind the thick wall of milky glass, lay Joachim, with whom Hans Castorp exchanged a word now and then, low-toned, out of consideration for the other horizontallers. Joachim was as well off in his loggia as Hans Castorp in his, though, being entirely unmusical, he could not take the same pleasure in the concerts. Too bad! He was probably studying his Russian primer instead. But Hans Castorp let *Ocean Steamships* fall on the coverlet and gave himself up to the music; he contemplated with such inward gratification the translucent depth of a musical invention full of individuality and charm that he thought with nothing but hostility of Settembrini and the irritating things he had said about music—that it was politically suspect was the worst, and little better than the remark of Grandfather Giuseppe about the July Revolution and the six days of creation.

Joachim, though he could not partake of Hans Castorp's pleasure in the music, nor the pungent gratification purveyed by Maria, lay as snugly ensconced as his cousin. The day was at an end. For the time everything was at an end; there would be no more emotional alarums, no more strain on the heart muscles. But equally there was the assurance that to-morrow it would begin all over

again, all the favouring probabilities afforded by pro-
pinquity and the household regimen. And this pleasing
combination of snugness and confident hope, together with
the music and the restored charms of Maria, made the
evening cure a state almost amounting to beatification
for young Hans Castorp.

All of which had not prevented the guest and novice
from catching a magnificent cold, either in the evening
rest cure or elsewhere. He felt the onset of catarrh,
with oppression in the frontal sinus, and inflamed uvula;
he could not breathe easily through the passage provided
by nature; the air struck cold and painfully as it struggled
through, and caused constant coughing. His voice took
on overnight the tonal quality of a hollow bass the
worse for strong drink. According to him, he had not
closed an eye, his parched throat making him start up
every five minutes from his pillow.

'Very vexatious,' Joachim said, 'and most unfortunate.
Colds, you know, are not the thing at all, up here; they
are not *reçus*. The authorities don't admit their existence;
the official attitude is that the dryness of the air entirely
prevents them. If you were a patient, you would
certainly fall foul of Behrens, if you went to him and said
you had a cold. But it is a little different with a guest—
you have a right to have a cold if you want to. It would
be good if we could check the catarrh. There are things
to do, down below, but here—I doubt if any one would
take enough interest in it. It is not advisable to fall
ill up here; you aren't taken any notice of. It's an
old story—but you will come to hear it in the end. When
I was new up here, there was a lady who complained
of her ear for a whole week and told everybody how
she suffered. Behrens finally looked at it: "Make
yourself quite easy, madame," he said; "it is not tuber-
cular." That was the end of the matter! Well, we

must see what can be done. I will speak to the bath
attendant early to-morrow morning, when he comes to
my room. Then it will go through the regular channels,
and perhaps something will come of it.'

Thus Joachim; and the regular channels proved
reliable. On Friday, after Hans Castorp returned from
the morning round, there was a knock at his door, and he
was vouchsafed the pleasure of personal acquaintance
with Fräulein von Mylendonk—Frau Director, as she
was called. Up to now he had seen this over-occupied
person only from a distance, crossing the corridor from
one patient's room to another, or when she had popped
up for a moment in the dining-room and he had been aware
of her raucous voice. But now he himself was the object
of her visit. His catarrh had fetched her. She knocked
a short, bony knock, entered almost before he had said
'Come in,' and then, upon the threshold, bent round to
make sure of the number of the room.

'Thirty-four,' she croaked briskly. 'Right. Well,
young 'un, on me dit que vous avez pris faoid. Wy,
kaschetsja, prostudilisj, Lei è raffreddato, I hear you have
caught a cold. What language do you speak? Oh, I see,
you are young Ziemssen's guest. I am due in the operat-
ing-room. Somebody there to be chloroformed, and he
has just been eating bean salad. I have to have my
eyes everywhere. Well, young 'un, so you have a cold?'

Hans Castorp was taken aback by this mode of address,
in the mouth of a dame of ancient lineage. In her rapid
speech she slurred over her words, all the time restlessly
moving her head about with a circular action, the nose
sniffingly in the air—the motion of a caged beast of prey.
Her freckled right hand, loosely closed with the thumb
uppermost, she held in front of her and waved it to and
fro on the wrist, as though to say: 'Come, make haste,
don't attend to what I say, but say what you have to and let

me be off!' She was in the forties, of stunted growth, without form or comeliness, clad in a belted pinaforeish garment of clinical white, with a garnet cross on her breast. Sparse, reddish hair showed beneath the white coif of her profession; her eyes were a watery blue, with inflamed lids, and one of them, as a finishing touch, had a sty in a well-advanced stage of development in the corner. Their glance was unsteady and flickering. Her nose was turned up, her mouth like a frog's, and furnished to boot with a wry and protruding lower lip, which she used like a shovel to get her words out. Hans Castorp looked at her, and all the modest and confiding friendliness native to him spoke in his eyes.

'What sort of cold is it, eh?' repeated the directress. She seemed to try to concentrate her gaze and make it penetrate; but it slipped aside. 'We don't care for such colds. Are you subject to them? Your cousin has been too, hasn't he? How old are you? Twenty-four? Yes, it's the age. And so you come up here and get a cold? There ought not to be any talk about colds up here; that sort of tommy-rot belongs down below.' It was fearsome to see how she shovelled out this word with her lower lip. 'You have a beautiful bronchial catarrh, that is plain.' Again she made that curious effort to pierce him with her gaze, and again she could not hold it steady. 'But catarrhs are not caused by cold; they come from an infection, which one takes from being in a receptive state. So the question is, are we dealing with a harmless infection or with something more serious? Everything else is tommy-rot. It is possible that your receptivity inclines to the harmless kind,' she went on, and looked at him with her over-ripe sty, he knew not how. 'Here, I will give you a simple antiseptic—it may do you good,' and she took a small packet out of the leather bag that hung from her girdle. It was formamint.

'But you look flushed—as though you had fever.' She never stopped trying to fix him with her gaze, and always the eyes glided off to one side. 'Have you "measured"?'

He answered in the negative.

'Why not?' she asked, and her protruding lower lip hung in the air after she spoke.

He made no answer. The poor youth was still young; he had never got over his schoolboy shyness. He sat, so to speak, on his bench, did not know the answer and took refuge in dumbness.

'Perhaps you never do take your temperature?'

'Oh, yes, Frau Director, when I have fever.'

'My dear chap, one takes it in the first instance to see whether one has fever. According to you, you have none now?'

'I can't tell, Frau Director. I cannot really tell the difference. Ever since I came up here, I have been a little hot and shivery.'

'Aha! And where is your thermometer?'

'I haven't one with me, Frau Director. Why should I? I am not ill; I am only up here on a visit.'

'Tommy-rot! Did you send for me because you weren't ill?'

'No,' he laughed politely, 'it was because I caught a little——'

'Cold. We 've often seen such colds. Here, young 'un,' she said, and rummaged again in her bag. She brought out two longish leather cases, one red and one black, and put them on the table. 'This one is three francs fifty, the other five. The five-franc one is better, of course. It will last you a lifetime if you take care of it.'

Smilingly he took up the red case and opened it. The glass instrument lay like a jewel within, fitted neatly into its red velvet groove. The degrees were marked by red strokes, the tenths by black ones; the figures were in red and the tapering end was full of glittering quicksilver. The column stood below blood-heat.

Hans Castorp knew what was due to himself and his upbringing. 'I will take this one,' he said, not even looking at the other. 'The one at five francs. May I——'

'Then that's settled,' croaked the directress. 'I see you don't niggle over important purchases. No hurry, it will come on the bill. Give him to me. We'll drive him right down.' She took the thermometer out of his hand and waved it several times through the air, until the mercury stood below 95°. 'He'll soon climb up again!' she said. 'Here is your new acquisition. You know how we do it up here? Straight under the tongue, seven minutes, four times a day, and shut the lips well over it. Well, young 'un, I must get on. Good luck!' And she was out at the door.

Hans Castorp bowed her out, then stood by the table, staring from the door through which she had disappeared to the instrument she had left behind. 'So that,' he thought, 'was Directress von Mylendonk. Settembrini doesn't care for her, and certainly she has her unpleasant side. The sty isn't pretty — but of course she does not have it all the time. But why does she call me 'young 'un,' like that? Rather rough and familiar, seems to me. So she has sold me a thermometer—I suppose she always has one or two in her pocket. They are to be had everywhere here, Joachim said, even in shops where you would least expect it. But I didn't need to take the trouble to buy it; it just fell into my lap.' He took the article out of its case, looked at it, and walked restlessly up and down the room. His heart beat strong and rapidly. He looked towards the open balcony door, and considered seeking counsel of Joachim, but thought better of it and paused again by the table.   He cleared his throat by way of testing his voice; then he coughed.

'Yes,' he said.   'I must see if I have the fever that goes with the cold.'   Quickly he put the thermometer in his mouth, the mercury beneath the tongue, so that the instrument stuck slantingly upwards from his lips. He closed them firmly, that no air might get in.   Then he looked at his wrist watch.   It was six minutes after the half-hour.   And he began to wait for the seven minutes to pass.

'Not a second too long,' he thought, 'and not one too short.   They can depend on me, in both directions. They needn't give me a "silent sister," like that Ottilie Kneifer Settembrini told us of.'   He walked about, pressing down the thermometer with his tongue.

The time crept on; the term seemed unending.   When he looked at his watch, two and a half minutes had passed —and he had feared the seven minutes were already more than up.   He did a thousand things: picked up objects about the room and set them down again, walked out on the balcony—taking care that his cousin should not notice his presence—and looked at the landscape of this high valley, now so familiar to him in all its phases; with its horns, its crests and walls, with the projecting wing of the 'Brembühl,' the ridge of which sloped steeply down to the valley, its flanks covered with rugged under-growth, with its formations on the right side of the valley, whose names were no less familiar than the others, and the Alteinwand, which from this point appeared to close in the valley on the south.   He looked down on the garden beds and paths, the grotto and the silver fir; he listened to the murmur that rose from the rest hall; and he returned to his room, settling the thermometer under his tongue. Then, with a motion of the arm which drew away the sleeve from his wrist, he brought the forearm before his eyes and found that by dint of pushing and shoving, pulling and hauling, he had managed to get rid of full six minutes. The last one he spent standing in the middle of the room—but then, unfortunately, he let his thoughts wander and fell into a 'doze,' so that the sixty seconds flew by on the wings of the wind; and, when he looked again, the eighth minute was already past its first quarter. 'It doesn't really matter, so far as the result is concerned,' he thought, and tearing the instrument out of his mouth, he stared at it in confusion.

He was not immediately the wiser. The gleam of the quicksilver blended with the reflection of the glass tube where the light struck it, and he could not tell whether the mercury had ascended the whole length of the column, or whether it was not there at all. He brought the instrument close to his eyes, turned it hither and thither —all to no purpose. But at last a lucky turn gave him a clearer view; he hastily arrested his hand and brought his intelligence to bear. Mercurius, in fact, had climbed up again, just as the Frau Director said. The column was perceptibly lengthened; it stood several of the black strokes above normal. Hans Castorp had 99·6°.

Ninety-nine and six-tenths degrees in broad daylight, between ten and half-past in the morning. That was too much; it was 'temperature.' It was fever consequent on an infection, for which his system had been eager. The question was now, what kind of infection? 99·6° —why, Joachim had no more, nor any one else up here, except the moribund and bedridden. Not Fräulein Kleefeld with her pneumothorax, nor—nor Madame Chauchat. Naturally, in his case it was not the same kind, certainly not; he had what would have been called at home a feverish cold. But the distinction was not such a simple one to make. Hans Castorp doubted whether the fever had only come on when the cold did, and he regretted not having consulted a thermometer at the outset, when the Hofrat suggested it.   He could see now that this had been very reasonable advice; Settembrini had been wrong to sneer at it as he had—Settembrini, with his republic and his *bello stile*.   Hans Castorp loathed and contemned the republic and the *bello stile* as he stood there consulting his thermometer; he kept on losing the mark and turning the instrument this way and that to find it again.   Yes, it registered 99·6°—and this in the early part of the day!

He was thoroughly upset.   He walked the length of the room twice or thrice, the thermometer held horizontally in his hand, so as not to jiggle it and make it read differently.   Then he carefully deposited it on the washhand stand, and went with his overcoat and rugs into the balcony.   Sitting down, he threw the covers about him, with practised hand, first from one side, then from the other, and lay still, waiting until it should be time for Joachim to fetch him for second breakfast.   Now and then he smiled—it was precisely as though he smiled *at* somebody.   And now and then his breast heaved as he caught his breath and was seized with his bronchial cough.

Joachim found him still lying when he entered at eleven o'clock, at the sound of the gong for second breakfast.

'Well?' he asked in surprise, coming up to his cousin's chair.

Hans Castorp sat awhile without answering, looking in front of him.   Then he said: 'Well, the latest is that I have some fever.'

'What do you mean?' Joachim asked.   'Do you feel feverish?'

Again Hans Castorp let him wait a little for the answer, then delivered himself airily as follows: 'Feverish, my dear fellow, I have felt for a long time—all the time I have been up here, in fact. But at the moment it is not a matter of subjective emotion, but of fact. I have taken my temperature.'

'You 've taken your temperature? What with?' Joachim cried, startled.

'With a thermometer, naturally,' answered Hans Castorp, not without a caustic tinge to his voice. 'Frau Director sold me one. Why she should call me young 'un I can't imagine. It is distinctly not *comme il faut*. But she lost no time in selling me an excellent thermometer; if you would like to convince yourself, you can; it is there on the wash-hand stand. It is only slight fever.'

Joachim turned on his heel and went into the bedroom. When he came back, he said hesitatingly: 'Yes, it is $99 \cdot 5\frac{1}{2}°$.'

'Then it has gone down a little,' his cousin responded hastily. 'It was six.'

'But you can't call that slight fever,' Joachim said. 'Certainly not for the forenoon. This is a pretty how-d'ye-do!' And he stood by his cousin's side as one stands before a how-d'ye-do, arms akimbo and head dropped. 'You 'll have to go to bed.'

Hans Castorp had his answer ready. 'I can't see,' he remarked, 'why I should go to bed with a temperature of $99 \cdot 6°$ when the rest of you, who haven't any less, can run about as you like.'

'But that is different,' Joachim said. 'Your fever is acute and harmless, the result of a cold.'

'In the first place,' said Hans Castorp, speaking with dignity and dividing his remarks into categories, 'I cannot comprehend why, with a harmless fever—assuming for the moment, that there is such a thing—one must keep one's bed, while with one that is not harmless you needn't. And secondly, I tell you the fever has not made me hotter than I was before. My position is that 99·6° is 99·6°. If you can run about with it, so can I.'

'But I had to lie for four weeks when I first came,' objected Joachim, 'and they only let me get up when it was clear that the fever persisted even after I had lain in bed.'

Hans Castorp smiled. 'Well, and———?' he asked. 'I thought it was different with you. It seems to me you are contradicting yourself; first you say our cases are different; then you say they are alike. That seems utter tommy-rot to me.'

Joachim made a right-about turn. When he turned round again, his sun-tanned visage showed an even darker shade.

'No,' he said, 'I am not saying they are alike; you 're getting muddled. I only mean that you 've a very nasty cold. I can hear it in your voice, and you ought to go to bed, to cut it short, if you mean to go home next week. But if you don't want to—I mean go to bed—why, don't. I am not prescribing for you. Anyhow, let 's go to breakfast. Make haste, we are late already.'

'Right-oh!' said Hans Castorp, and flung off his covers. He went into his room to run the brush over his hair, and Joachim looked again at the thermometer on the wash-hand stand. Hans Castorp watched him. They went down, silently, and took their places in the dining-room, which, as always at this hour, shimmered white with milk.

The dwarf waitress brought Hans Castorp his Kulmbacher beer, as usual, but he pulled a long face and waved it away. He would drink no beer to-day; he would drink nothing at all, or at most a swallow of water. The attention of his table mates was attracted; they wanted to know the cause of his caprice. Hans Castorp said carelessly that he had a little fever—really minimal: 99·6°.

Then how altogether ludicrous it was to see them! They shook their fingers at him, they winked maliciously, they put their heads on one side, crooked their forefingers beside their ears and waggled them in a pantomime suggestive of their delight at having found him out, who had played the innocent so long.

'Aha,' said the schoolmistress, the flush mounting in her ancient cheek, 'what sort of scandal is this?'

And 'Aha, aha!' went Frau Stöhr too, holding her stumpy finger next her stumpy nose. 'So our respected guest has some temperament too! Foxy-loxy is in the same boat with the rest of us after all!'

Even the great-aunt, when the news travelled up to her end of the table, gave him a meaningful glance and smile; pretty Marusja, who had barely looked at him up to now, leaned over and stared, with her round brown eyes, her handkerchief to her lips—and shook her finger too. Frau Stöhr whispered the news to Dr Blumenkohl, who could hardly do otherwise than join in the game, though without looking at Hans Castorp. Only Miss Robinson sat as she always did and took no share in what was going on. Joachim kept his eyes on the table cloth.

It flattered Hans Castorp's vanity to be taken so much notice of; but he felt that modesty required him to disclaim their attentions. 'No, no,' he said. 'You are all mistaken, my fever is the most harmless thing in the world; I simply have a cold, my eyes run, and my chest is stopped up. I have coughed half the night; it is thoroughly unpleasant of course.' But they would not listen; they laughed and flapped their hands at him.

'Yes, of course, we know all about it—we know these colds; they are all gammon—you can't fool us!' and with one accord they challenged Hans Castorp to an examination on the spot. The news excited them. Throughout

the meal their table was the liveliest among the seven.
Frau Stöhr became almost hysterical. Her peevish face
looked scarlet above her neck ruche, and tiny purple
veins showed in the cheeks. She began to talk about
how fascinating it was to cough. It was a solid satis-
tion, when you felt a tickling come in your chest, deep
down, and grow and grow, to reach down after it, and
get at it, so to say. Sneezing was much the same thing.
You kept on wanting to sneeze until you simply couldn't
stand it any longer; you looked as if you were tipsy;
you drew a couple of breaths; then out it came, and you
forgot everything else in the bliss of the sensation. Sometimes the explosion repeated itself two or three times.
That was the sort of pleasure life gave you free of charge.
Another one was the joy of scratching your chilblains
in the spring, when they itched so gorgeously; you took a
furious pleasure in scratching till the blood came; and if
you happened to look in the glass you would be astonished
to see the ghastly face you made.

The coarse creature regaled the table with these repulsive details throughout the brief but hearty meal.
When it was over, the cousins walked down to the
Platz; Joachim seemed preoccupied; Hans Castorp was
in an agony of snuffles and cleared his rasping throat
continually.

On the way home Joachim said: 'I 'll make you a suggestion. To-morrow, after the midday meal, I have my
regular monthly examination. It is not the general one;
Behrens just auscultates a little and has Krokowski make
some notes. You might come along and ask them to
listen to you a bit. It is too absurd—if you were at
home, you would send for Heidekind, and up here, with
two specialists in the house, you run about and don't
know where you are, nor how serious it is, and if it would
not be better for you to go to bed.'

'Very good,' said Hans Castorp. 'It's as you say, of course. I can do that. And it will be interesting to see an examination.'

Thus it was settled between them, and it fell out that as they arrived before the sanatorium, they met the Hofrat himself, and took the occasion to put their request at once.

Behrens came out of the vestibule, tall and stooping, a bowler hat on the back of his head, a cigar in his mouth; purple-cheeked, watery-eyed, in the full flow of his professional activities. He had just come from the operating room, so he said, and was on his way to private practice in the village.

"Morning, gentlemen, 'morning,' he said. 'Always on the jump, eh? How's everything in the big world? I've just come from an unequal duel with saw and scalpel —great thing, you know, resection of ribs. Fifty per cent of the cases used to be left on the table. Nowadays we do better than that; but even so it's a good plan to get the *mortis causa* fixed up beforehand. The chap to-day knew how to take the joke—put up a good fight for a minute or so. Crazy thing, a human thorax that's all gone; pulpy, you know, nothing to catch hold of —slight confusion of ideas, so to speak. Well, well— and how are your constitutionalities? Sanctified metabolisms functioning O.K., doing their duty in the sight of the Lord? The walks go better in company, Ziemssen, old fellow, what? Hallo, what are you crying about, Mr Tripper?' He suddenly turned on Hans Castorp. 'It's against the rules to cry in public—they might all start doing it!'

'It's only my cold, Herr Hofrat,' answered Hans Castorp. 'I don't know how I managed it, but I've a simply priceless catarrh. It's right down on my chest, and I cough a good deal too.'

'Indeed!' Behrens remarked. 'You ought to consult a reliable physician.'

Both cousins laughed, and Joachim answered, heels together: 'We were just going to, Herr Hofrat. I have my examination to-morrow, and we wanted to ask if you would be so kind as to look my cousin over as well. The question is whether he will be well enough to travel on Tuesday.'

'A. Y. S.,' said Behrens. 'At your service. With all the pleasure in life. Ought to have done it long ago. Once you are up here, why not? But one doesn't like to seem forthcoming. Very good then, to-morrow at two —directly after grub.'

'I have a little fever too,' Hans Castorp further observed.

'You don't say!' Behrens cried out. 'I suppose you think you are telling me news? Do you think I've no eyes in my head?' He pointed with his great index finger to his goggling, bloodshot, watery eyes. 'Well, and how much?'

Hans Castorp modestly mentioned the figure.

'Forenoon, eh? H'm, that's not so bad. Not bad at all, for a beginner—shows talent. Very good then, the two of you, to-morrow at two. Very much honoured. Well, so long—enjoy yourselves!' He paddled away downhill, his knees bent, leaving a long streamer of cigar smoke behind him.

'Well, that came out just as you wanted it to,' Hans Castorp said. 'We couldn't have struck it luckier, and now I am in for it. He won't be able to do much, of course—he may prescribe some sort of pectoral syrup or some cough lozenges. However, it is good to have a little encouragement when you feel the way I do. But for heaven's sake what makes him rattle on so? It struck me as funny at first, but in the long run I can't say I like it. "Sanctified metabolism"—what sort of gibberish is that? If I understand what he means by metabolism, it is nothing but physiology, and to talk about its being sanctified—irreverent, I call it. I don't enjoy seeing him smoke, either; it distresses me, because I know it is not good for him and gives him melancholia. Settembrini said his joviality is forced, and one must admit that Settembrini has his own views and knows whereof he speaks. I probably ought to have more opinions of my own, as he says, and not take everything as it comes, the way I do. But sometimes one starts out with having an opinion and feeling righteous indignation and all that, and then something comes up that has nothing to do with judgments and criticism, and then it is all up with your severity, and you feel disgusted with the republic and the *bello stile . . .*'

He rambled on incoherently, not clear himself as to what he wanted to say. His cousin merely gave him a side glance, and then turned away with an *au revoir*, and each betook himself to his own balcony.

'How much?' asked Joachim softly, after a while—as though he had seen Hans Castorp consult his thermometer.

And the latter answered indifferently: 'Nothing new.'

He had in fact, directly he entered, taken up his new acquisition from the wash-hand stand and waved it repeatedly through the air, to obliterate the morning's record. Then he went into the balcony with the glass cigar in his mouth, like an old hand. But, contrary to some rather exaggerated expectations, Mercurius climbed no farther than before—though Hans Castorp kept the instrument under his tongue eight minutes for good measure. But, after all, 99·6° was unquestionably fever, even though no higher than the earlier record. In the afternoon the gleaming column mounted up as far as 99·7°, but declined to 99·5° by evening, when the patient

was weary with the excitement of the day. Next
morning it showed 99·6°, climbing during the morning
to the same level as before.   And so arrived the hour for
the main meal of the day, bringing the examination in its
wake.

Hans Castorp later recalled that Madame Chauchat
was wearing that day a golden-yellow sweater, with large
buttons and embroidered pockets.   It was a new sweater,
at least new to Hans Castorp, and when she made her
entrance, tardily as usual, she had paused an instant and,
in a way he knew so well, presented herself to the room.
Then she had glided to her place at the table, slipped softly
into it, and begun to eat and chatter to her table mates.
All this was as it happened every day, five times a day;
Hans Castorp observed it as usual, or perhaps even more
poignantly than usual, looking over at the 'good' Russian
table past Settembrini's back, as he sat at the cross-
wise table between.   He saw the turn of her head in
conversation, the rounded neck, the stooping back.   Frau
Chauchat, for her part, never once turned round during
the whole meal.   But when the sweet had been handed,
and the great clock on the wall above the 'bad' Russian
table struck two, it actually happened, to Hans Castorp's
amazement and mystification, that precisely as the hour
struck, one, two, the fair patient turned her head and
twisted her body a little and looked over her shoulder quite
openly and pointedly at Hans Castorp's table.   And not
only at his table.   No, she looked at himself, unmistakably and personally, with a smile about the closed lips and
the narrow, Pribislav eyes, as though to say: 'Well, it is
time: are you going?'   And the eyes said 'thou,' for that
is the language of the eyes, even when the tongue uses a
more formal address.   This episode shook and bewildered
Hans Castorp to the depths of his being.   He hardly
trusted his senses, and at first gazed enraptured in Frau

Chauchat's face, then, lifting his eyes, stared into vacancy over the top of her head. Was it possible she knew he was to be examined at two o'clock? It looked like it; but that was as impossible as that she should be aware of the thought that had visited his mind in the last minute, namely, that he might as well send word to the Hofrat, through Joachim, that his cold was better, and he considered an examination superfluous. This idea had presented itself to him in an advantageous light, but now withered away under that searching smile, transmuted into a hideous sense of futility. The second after, Joachim had laid his rolled-up serviette beside his plate, signalled to his cousin by raising his eyebrows, and, with a low bow to the company, risen from the table. Whereat Hans Castorp, inwardly reeling, though outwardly firm in step and bearing, rose too, and feeling that look and smile upon his back, followed Cousin Joachim out of the room.

Since the previous morning they had not spoken of what lay before them, and silently now they moved down the corridor together. Joachim hastened his steps, for it was already past the appointed hour, and Hofrat Behrens laid stress on punctuality. They passed the door of the office and went down the clean, linoleum-covered stairs to the 'basement.' Joachim knocked at the door facing them; it bore a porcelain shield with the word *Consulting Room.*

'Come in,' called Behrens, stressing the first word. He was standing in the middle of the room, in his white smock, holding the black stethoscope in his hand and tapping his thigh with it.

'Tempo, tempo,' said he, directing his goggling gaze to the clock on the wall. 'Un poco più presto, signori! We are not here simply and solely for the honourable gentlemen's convenience.'

Dr Krokowski was sitting at the double-barrelled writing table by the window. He wore his usual black alpaca shirt, setting off the pallor of his face; his elbows rested on the table, in one hand a pen, the other fingering his beard; while before him lay various papers, probably the documents in reference to the patients to be examined. He looked at the cousins as they entered, but it was with the idle glance of a person who is present only in an auxiliary capacity.

'Well, give us your report card,' the Hofrat answered to Joachim's apologies, and took the fever chart out of his hand. He looked it over, while the patient made haste to remove his upper garments down to the waist and hang them on the rack by the door. No one troubled about Hans Castorp. He looked on awhile standing, then let himself down in a little old-fashioned easy chair with bob tassels on the arms, beside a small table with a carafe on it. Bookcases lined the walls, full of pamphlets and broad-backed medical works. Other furniture there was none, except an adjustable chaise-longue covered with oilcloth. It had a paper serviette spread over the pillow.

'Point seven, point nine, point eight,' Behrens said, running through the weekly card, whereon were entered the results of Joachim's five daily 'measurings.' 'Still a little too much lighted up, my dear Ziemssen. Can't exactly say you 've got more robust just lately'—by lately he meant during the past four weeks. 'Not free from infection,' he said. 'Well, that doesn't happen between one day and the next; we 're not magicians.'

Joachim nodded and shrugged his bare shoulders. He refrained from saying that he had been up here since a good deal longer than yesterday.

'How about the stitches in the right hilum, where it always sounded so sharp? Better, eh? Well, come

along, let me thump you about a bit.' And the auscultation began.

The Hofrat stood leaning backwards, feet wide apart,
his stethoscope under his arm, and tapped from the wrist,
using the powerful middle finger of his right hand as a
hammer, and the left as a support. He tapped first high
up on Joachim's shoulder blade at the side of the back,
above and below—the well-trained Joachim lifting his arm
to let himself be tapped under the arm-pit. Then the
process was repeated on the left side; then the Hofrat
commanded: 'Turn!' and began tapping the chest;
first next the collar bone, then above and below the breast,
right and left. When he had tapped to his satisfaction,
he began to listen, setting his stethoscope on Joachim's
chest and back, and putting his ear to the ear piece.
Then Joachim had to breathe deeply and cough—which
seemed to strain him, for he got out of breath, and tears
came into his eyes. And everything that the Hofrat
heard he announced in curt, technical phrases to his
assistant over at the writing table, in such a way that
Hans Castorp was forcibly reminded of the proceedings
at the tailor's, when a very correctly groomed gentleman
measures you for a suit, laying the tape about your trunk
and limbs and calling off the figures in the order hallowed
by tradition for the assistant to take them down in his
book. 'Faint,' 'diminished,' dictated Hofrat Behrens.
'Vesicular,' and then again 'vesicular' (that was good,
apparently). 'Rough,' he said, and made a face. 'Very
rough.' 'Rhonchi.' And Dr Krokowski entered it all
in his book, just like the tailor's assistant.

Hans Castorp followed the proceedings with his head
on one side, absorbed in contemplation of his cousin's
torso. The ribs—thank heaven, he had them all!—
rose under the taut skin as he took deep inhalations,
and the stomach fell away. Hans Castorp studied that

youthful figure, slender, yellowish-bronze, with a black
fell along the breastbone and the powerful arms.   On
one wrist Joachim wore a gold chain bracelet.   'Those
are the arms of an athlete,' thought Hans Castorp.   'I
never made much of gymnastics, but he always liked
them, and that is partly the reason why he wanted to be a
soldier.   He has always been more inclined than I to the
things of the body—or inclined in a different way.   I 've
always been a civilian and cared more about warm baths
and good eating and drinking, whereas he has gone in for
manly exertion.   And now his body has come into the
foreground in another sense and made itself important
and independent of the rest of him—namely, through
illness.   He is all "lit up" within and can't get rid of the
infection and become healthy, poor Joachim, no matter
how much he wants to get down to the valley and be a
soldier.   And yet look how he is developed, like a picture
in a book, a regular Apollo Belvedere, except for the hair.
But the disease makes him ailing within and fevered
without; disease makes men more physical, it leaves them
nothing but body'—his own thought startled him, and
he looked quickly at Joachim with a questioning glance,
that travelled from the bared body up to the large, gentle
black eyes.   Tears stood out in them, from the effort of
the forced breathing and coughing, and they gazed into
space with a pathetic expression as the examination went on.

But at last Hofrat Behrens had come to an end.   'Very
good, Ziemssen,' he said.   'Everything in order, so far
as possible.   Next time' (that would be in four weeks)
'it is bound to show further improvement.'

'And, Herr Hofrat, how much longer do you think——

'So you are going to pester me again?   How do you
expect to give your lads the devil down below, in the lit-
up state you are in?   I told you the other day to call it
half a year; you can reckon from then if you like, but

you must regard it as minimal. Have a little ordinary
politeness! It's a decent enough life up here, after all;
it's not a convict prison, nor a Siberian penal settlement!
Or perhaps you think it is? Very good, Ziemssen, be
off with you! Next! Step lively!' He stretched out
his arm and handed the stethoscope to Dr Krokowski,
who got up and began some supernumerary tapping on
Joachim's person.

Hans Castorp had sprung up. With his eyes fixed
on the Hofrat, standing there with his legs apart and his
mouth open, lost in thought, the young man began in all
haste to make ready, with the result that he defeated his
own purpose and fumbled in getting out of his shirt.
But finally he stood there, blond, white-skinned, and
narrow-chested, before Hofrat Behrens. Compared with
Joachim, he looked distinctly the civilian type.

The Hofrat, still lost in thought, let him stand. Dr
Krokowski had finished and sat down, and Joachim was
dressing before Behrens finally decided to take notice.

'Oho!' he said, 'so it's you, is it?' He gripped Hans
Castorp on the upper arm with his mighty hand, pushed
him away, and looked at him sharply—not in the face,
as one man looks at another, but at his body; turned him
round, as one would turn an inanimate object, and looked
at his back. 'H'm,' he said. 'Well, we shall see.' And
began tapping as before.

He tapped all over, as he had with Joachim, and several
times went back and tapped again. For some while, for
purposes of comparison, he tapped by turns on the left-
hand side near the collar bone, and then somewhat lower
down.

'Hear that?' he asked Dr Krokowski. And the
other, sitting at the table five paces off, nodded to signify
that he did. He sunk his head on his chest with a serious
mien, and the points of his whiskers stuck out.

'Breathe deep! Cough!' commanded the Hofrat, who had taken up the stethoscope again; and Hans Castorp worked hard for eight or ten minutes, while the Hofrat listened. He uttered no word, simply set the instrument here or there and listened with particular care at the places he had tapped so long. Then he stuck the stethoscope under his arm, put his hands on his back, and looked at the floor between himself and Hans Castorp.

'Yes, Castorp,' he said—this was the first time he had called the young man simply by his surname—'the thing works out *praeter propter* as I thought it would. I had my suspicions—I can tell you now—from the first day I had the undeserved honour of making your acquaintance; I made a pretty shrewd guess that you were one of us and that you would find it out, like many another who has come up here on a lark and gone about with his nose in the air, only to discover, one fine day, that it would be as well for him—and not only *as* well, mark that—to make a more extended stay, quite without reference to the beauties of the scenery.'

Hans Castorp had flushed; Joachim, in act to button his braces, paused as he stood, and listened.

'You have such a kind, sympathetic cousin over there,' went on the Hofrat, motioning with his head in Joachim's direction and balancing himself on his heels. 'Very soon, we hope, we will be able to say that he *has been* ill; but even when he gets that far, it will still be true that he *has been* ill—and the fact—*a priori*, as the philosophers say—casts a certain light upon yourself, my dear Castorp.'

'But he is only my step-cousin, Herr Hofrat.'

'Tut! You won't disown him, will you? Even a step-cousin is a blood relation. On which side?'

'The mother's, Herr Hofrat. He is the son of a step——'

'And your mother—she's pretty jolly?'

'No, she is dead. She died when I was little.'

'And of what?'

'Of a blood-clot, Herr Hofrat.'

'A blood-clot, eh? Well, that's a long time ago. And your father?'

'He died of pneumonia,' Hans Castorp said; 'and my grandfather too,' he added.

'Both of them, eh? Good. So much for your ancestors. Now about yourself—you have always been rather chlorotic, haven't you? But you didn't tire easily at physical or mental work. Or did you—what? A good deal of palpitation? Only of late? Good. And a strong inclination to catarrhal and bronchial trouble? Did you know you have been infected before now?'

'I?'

'Yes, you—I have you personally in mind. Can you hear any difference?' The Hofrat tapped by turns on Hans Castorp's left side, first above and then lower down.

'It sounds rather duller there,' said Hans Castorp.

'Capital. You ought to be a specialist. Well, that is a dullness, and such dullnesses are caused by the old places, where fibrosis has supervened. Scars, you know. You are an old patient, Castorp, but we won't lay it up against anybody that you weren't found out. The early diagnosis is very difficult—particularly for my colleagues down below; I won't say we have better ears—though the regular practice does do something. But the air helps us, helps us to hear, if you understand what I mean, this thin, dry air up here.'

'Certainly, of course,' Hans Castorp said.

'Very good, Castorp. And now listen, young man, to my words of wisdom. If that were all the trouble with you, if it was a case of nothing but the dullness and the scars on your bagpipe in there, I should send you back to your lares and penates and not trouble my head further

about you.   But as things stand, and according to what
we find, and since you are already up here—well, there is
no use in your going down, for you 'd only have to come
up again.'

Hans Castorp felt the blood rush back to his heart; it
hammered violently; and Joachim still stood with his
hands on his back buttons, his eyes on the floor.

'For besides the dullness,' said the Hofrat, 'you have
on the upper left side a rough breathing that is almost
bronchial and undoubtedly comes from a fresh place.   I
won't call it a focus of softening, but it is certainly a moist
spot, and if you go down below and begin to carry on,
why, you 'll have the whole lobe at the devil before you
can say Jack Robinson.'

Hans Castorp stood motionless.   His mouth twitched
fearfully, and the hammering of his heart against his
ribs was plain to see.   He looked across at Joachim,
but could not meet his cousin's eye; then again in the
Hofrat's face, with its blue cheeks, blue, goggling eyes,
and little, crooked moustache.

'For independent confirmation,' Behrens continued,
'we have your temperature of 99·6° at ten o'clock in the
morning, which corresponds pretty well to the indications
given by the auscultation.'

'I thought,' Hans Castorp said, 'that the fever came
from my cold.'

'And the cold,' rejoined the Hofrat, 'where does that
come from?   Listen, Castorp, let me tell you something,
and mark my words—for so far as I can tell you, you 've
all the cerebral convolutions a body needs.   Now: our
air up here is good for the disease—I mean good *against*
the disease, you understand—you think so, don't you?
Well, it is true.   But also it is good *for* the disease; it
begins by speeding it up, in that it revolutionizes the
whole body; it brings the latent weakness to the surface

and makes it break out. Your catarrh, fortunately for you, is a breaking-out of that kind. I can't tell you if you were febrile down below; but it is certainly my opinion that you have been from your first day up here, and not merely since you had your catarrh.'

'Yes,' Hans Castorp said, 'I think so too.'

'You were probably fuddled right from the start, in my opinion,' the Hofrat confirmed him. 'Those were the soluble toxins thrown off by the bacteria; they act like an intoxicant upon the central nervous system and give you a hectic flush. Now, Castorp, we'll stick you into bed and see if a couple of weeks' rest will sober you up. What follows will follow. We'll take a handsome X-ray of you—you'll enjoy seeing what goes on in your own inside. But I tell you straight away, a case like yours doesn't get well from one day to the next; it isn't a question of the miracle cures you read about in advertisements. I thought when I first clapped eyes on you that you would be a better patient than your cousin, with more talent for illness than our brigadier-general here, who wants to clear out directly he has a couple of points less fever. As if "Lie down" wasn't just as good a word of command as "Stand up"! It is the citizen's first duty to be calm, and impatience never did any good to any one. Now, Castorp, take care you don't disappoint me and give the lie to my knowledge of human nature! Get along now, into the caboose with you—march!'

With that Hofrat Behrens closed the interview and sat down at the writing-table; this man of many occupations began to fill in his time with writing until the advent of the next patient. But Dr Krokowski arose from his place and strode up to Hans Castorp. With his head tipped back sideways, and one hand on the young man's shoulder, smiling so heartily that the yellowish teeth showed in his beard, he shook him warmly by the hand.

SNOW

Daily, five times a day, the guests expressed unanimous dissatisfaction with the kind of winter they were having. They felt it was not what they had a right to expect of these altitudes. It failed to deliver the renowned meteorological specific in anything like the quantity indicated by the prospectus, quoted by old inhabitants, or anticipated by new. There was a very great failure in the supply of sunshine, an element so important in the cures achieved up here that without it they were distinctly retarded. And whatever Herr Settembrini might think of the sincerity of the patients' desire to finish their cure, leave 'home,' and return to the flat land, at any rate they insisted on their just dues. They wanted what they were entitled to, what their parents or husbands had paid for, and they grumbled unceasingly, at table, in lift, and in hall. The management showed a consciousness of what it owed them by installing a new apparatus for heliotherapy. They had two already, but these did not suffice for the demands of those who wished to get sunburnt by electricity — it was so becoming to the ladies, young and old, and made all the men, though confirmed horizontallers, look irresistibly athletic. And the ladies, even though aware of the mechanico-cosmetical origin of this conquering-hero air, were foolish enough to be carried away by it. There was Frau Schönfeld, a red-haired, red-eyed patient from Berlin. In the salon she looked thirstily at a long-legged, sunken-chested gallant, who described himself on his visiting-card as 'Aviateur diplomé et Enseigne de la Marine allemande.' He was

fitted out with the pneumothorax and wore 'smoking'
at the midday meal but not in the evening, saying this
was their custom in the navy. 'My God,' breathed
Frau Schönfeld at him, 'what a tan this demon has—he
gets it from the helio—it makes him look like a hunter
of eagles!' 'Just wait, nixie!' he whispered in her ear, in
the lift, 'I 'll make you pay for looking at me like that!'
It made goose-flesh and shivers run over her. And along
the balconies, past the glass partitions, the demon eagle
hunter found his way to the nixie.

But the artificial sun was far from making up for the
lack of the real one. Two or three days of full sunshine
in the month—it was not good enough, gorgeous though
these were, with deep, deep velvety blue sky behind the
white mountain summits, a glitter as of diamonds and a
fine hot glow on the face and the back of the neck, when
they dawned resplendent from the prevailing thick
mantle of grey mist. Two or three such days in the
course of weeks could not satisfy people whose lot might
be said to justify extraordinary demands from the external
world. They had made an inward compact, by the
terms of which they resigned the common joys and sorrows
proper to flat-land humanity, and in exchange were made
free of a life that was, to be sure, inactive, but on the other
hand very lively and diverting, and carefree to the point
of making one forget altogether the flight of time. Thus
it was not much good for the Hofrat to tell them how
favourably the Berghof compared with a Siberian mine
or a penal settlement, nor to sing the praises of the atmosphere, so thin and light, well-nigh as rare as the empty
universal ether, free of earthly admixture whether good
or bad, and even without actual sunshine to be preferred
to the rank vapours of the plain. Despite all he could
say, the gloomy disaffection gained ground, threats of
unlicensed departure were the order of the day, were

even put into execution, without regard for the warning afforded by the melancholy return of Frau Solomon to the fold, now a 'life member,' her tedious but not serious case having taken that turn by reason of her self-willed visit to her wet and windy Amsterdam.

But if they had no sun, they had snow. Such masses of snow as Hans Castorp had never till now in all his life beheld. The previous winter had done fairly well in this respect, but it had been as nothing compared to this. The snowfall was monstrous and immeasurable, it made one realize the extravagant, outlandish nature of the place. It snowed day in, day out, and all through the night. The few roads kept open were like tunnels, with towering walls of snow on either side, crystal and alabaster surfaces that were pleasant to look at, and on which the guests scribbled all sorts of messages, jokes, and personalities. But even this path between walls was above the level of the pavement, and made of hard-packed snow, as one could tell by certain places where it gave way, and let one suddenly sink in up to the knee. One might, unless one were careful, break a leg. The benches had disappeared, except for the high back of one emerging here and there. In the town, the street level was so raised that the shops had become cellars, into which one descended by steps cut in the snow.

And on all these lying masses more snow fell, day in, day out. It fell silently, through air that was moderately cold, perhaps twenty to thirty degrees of frost. One did not feel the cold, it might have been much less, for the dryness and absence of wind deprived it of sting. The mornings were very dark, breakfast was taken by the light of the artificial moon that hung from the vaulted ceiling of the dining-room, above the gay stencilled border. Outside was the reeking void, the world enwrapped in grey-white cotton wool, packed to the window panes in snow and mist. No sight of the mountains; of the nearest evergreens now and again a glimpse through the fog, standing laden, and from time to time shaking free a bough of their heavy load, that flew into the air, and sent a cloud of white against the grey. At ten o'clock the sun, a wan wisp of light, came up behind its mountain, and gave the indistinguishable scene some shadowy hint of life, some sallow glimmer of reality; yet even so, it retained its delicate ghostliness, its lack of any definite line for the eye to follow. The contours of the peaks dissolved, disappeared, were dissipated in the mist, while the vision, led on from one pallidly gleaming slope of snow to another, lost itself in the void. Then a single cloud, like smoke, lighted up by the sun, might spread out before a wall of rock and hang there for long, motionless.

At midday the sun would half break through, and show signs of banishing the mist. In vain—yet a shred of blue would be visible, and suffice to make the scene, in its strangely falsified contours, sparkle marvellously far and wide. Usually, at this hour, the snowfall stopped, as though to have a look at what it had done; a like effect was produced by the rare days when the storm ceased, and the uninterrupted power of the sun sought to thaw away the pure and lovely surface from the new-fallen masses. The sight was at once fairylike and comic, an infan-tine fantasy. The thick light cushions plumped up on the boughs of trees, the humps and mounds of snow-covered outcrop or undergrowth, the droll, dwarfish, crouching disguise all ordinary objects wore, made of the scene a landscape in gnome-land, an illustration for a fairy tale. Such was the immediate view—wearisome to move in, quaintly, roguishly stimulating to the fancy. But when one looked across the intervening space, at the towering marble statuary of the high Alps in full snow, one felt a quite different emotion, and that was awe of their majestic sublimity.

Afternoons, between three and four, Hans Castorp lay in his balcony box, well wrapped, his head against the cushion, not too high or too low, of his excellent chair, and looked out at forest and mountain over his thick-upholstered balustrade. The snow-laden firs, dark green to blackness, went marching up the sides of the valley, and beneath them the snow lay soft like down pillows. Above the tree line, the mountain walls reared themselves into the grey-white air: huge surfaces of snow, with softly veiled crests, and here and there a black jut of rock. The snow came silently down. The scene blurred more and more, it inclined the eye, gazing thus into woolly vacuity, to slumber. At the moment of slipping off one might give a start—yet what sleep could be purer than this in the icy air? It was dreamless. It was as free from the burden—even the unconscious burden—of organic life, as little aware of an effort to breathe this contentless, weightless, imperceptible air, as is the breath-less sleep of the dead. When Hans Castorp stirred again, the mountains would be wholly lost in a cloud of snow; only a pinnacle, a jutting rock, might show one instant, to be rapt away the next. It was absorbing to watch these ghostly pranks; one needed to keep alert to follow the transmutations, the veiling and unveiling. One moment a great space of snow-covered rock would reveal itself standing out bold and free, though of base or peak naught was to be seen. But if one ceased to fix one's gaze upon it, it was gone, in a breath.

Then there were storms so violent as to prevent one's sitting on the balcony for the driven snow which blew in, in such quantity as to cover floor and chair with a thick mantle. Yes, even in this sheltered valley it knew how to storm. The thin air would be in a hurly-burly, so whirling full of snow one could not see a hand's breadth before one's face. Gusts strong enough to take one's breath away flung the snow about, drew it up cyclone fashion from the valley floor to the upper air, whisked it about in the maddest dance; no longer a snowstorm, it was a blinding chaos, a white dark, a monstrous dereliction on the part of this inordinate and violent region; no living creature save the snow bunting—which suddenly appeared in troops—could flourish in it.

And yet Hans Castorp loved this snowy world. He found it not unlike life beside the sea. The monotony of the scene was in both cases profound. The snow, so deep, so light, so dry and spotless, was the sand of down below. One was as clean as the other: you could shake the snow from boots and clothing, just as you could the fine-ground, dustless stone and shell, product of the sea's depth—neither left trace behind. And walking in the snow was as toilsome as on the dunes; unless, indeed, a crust had come upon it, by dint of thawing and freezing, when the going became easy and pleasant, like marching along the smooth, hard, wet, and resilient strip of sand close to the edge of the sea.

But the storms and high-piled drifts of this year gave pedestrians small chance. They were favourable only for ski-ing. The snow plough, labouring its best, barely kept free the main street of the settlement and the most indispensable paths. Thus the few short feasible stretches were always crowded with other walkers, ill and well: the native, the permanent guest, and the hotel population; and these in their turn were bumped by the sleighs as they swung and swerved down the slopes, steered by men and women who leaned far back as they came on, and shouted importunely, being obsessed by the importance of their occupation. Once at the bottom they would turn and trundle their toy sleighs uphill again.

Hans Castorp was thoroughly sick of all the walks. He had two desires: one of them, the stronger, was to be alone with his thoughts and his stock-taking projects; and this his balcony assured to him. But the other, allied to it, was a lively craving to come into close and freer touch with the mountains, the mountains in their snowy desolation; towards them he was irresistibly drawn. Yet how could he, all unprovided and footbound as he was, hope to gratify such a desire? He had only to step beyond the end of the shovelled paths—an end soon reached upon any of them—to plunge breast high in the snowy element.

Thus it was Hans Castorp, on a day in his second winter with those up here, resolved to buy himself skis and learn to walk on them, enough, that is, for his purposes. He was no sportsman, had never been physically inclined to sport; and did not behave as though he were, as did many guests of the cure, dressing up to suit the mode and the spirit of the place. Hermine Kleefeld, for instance, among other females, though she was constantly blue in the face from lack of breath, loved to appear at luncheon in tweed knickers, and loll about after the meal in a basket chair in the hall, with her legs sprawled out. Hans Castorp knew that he would meet with a refusal were he to ask the Hofrat to countenance his plan. Sports activities were unconditionally forbidden at the Berghof as in all other establishments of the kind. This atmosphere, which one seemed to breathe in so effortlessly, was a severe strain on the heart, and as for Hans Castorp personally, his lively comment on his own state, that 'getting used to being up here consisted in getting used to not getting used,' had continued in force. His fever, which Rhadamanthus ascribed to a moist spot, remained obstinate. Why else indeed should he be here? His desire, his present purpose, was then clearly inconsistent

and inadmissible. Yet we must be at the pains to understand him aright. He had no wish to imitate the fresh-
air faddists and smart pseudo-sportsmen, who would have
been equally eager to sit all day and play cards in a stuffy
room, if only that had been interdicted by authority. He
felt himself a member of another and closer community
than this small tourist world; a new and a broader point
of view, a dignity and restraint set him apart and made him
conscious that it would be unfitting for him to emulate
their rough-and-tumble antics in the snow. He had no
escapade in view, his plans were so moderate that Rhadamanthus himself, had he known, might well have ap-
proved them. But the rules stood in the way, and Hans
Castorp resolved to act behind his back.

He took occasion to speak of his plan to Herr Settembrini—who for sheer joy could have embraced him. 'Si,
si, si! Do so, do so, engineer, do so with the blessing
of God! Ask for nobody's leave, but simply do it! Ah,
your good angel must have whispered the thought to
you! Do it straightway, before the impulse leaves you.
I'll go along. I'll go to the shop with you, and together we will acquire the instruments of this happy
inspiration. I would go with you even into the mountains, I would be by your side, on winged feet, like
Mercury's—but that I may not. May not! If that
were all, how soon would I do it! That I cannot is the
truth, I am a broken man. But you—it will do you no
harm, none at all, if you are sensible and do nothing rash.
Even—even if it does you harm—just a little harm—it
will still have been your good angel who roused you to it.
I say no more. Ah, what an unsurpassable plan! Two
years up here, and still capable of such projects—ah, yes,
your heart is sound, no need to despair of you. Bravo,
bravo! By all means pull the wool over the eyes of your
Prince of Shadows! Buy the snow shoes, have them

sent to me or Lukaçek, or the grocer downstairs. You fetch them from here to go and practise, you go off on them——'

So it befell. Under Herr Settembrini's critical eye— he played the connoisseur, though innocent of sports— Hans Castorp acquired a pair of oaken skis, finished a light brown, with tapering, pointed ends and the best quality of straps. He bought the iron-shod staff with the little wheel as well, and was not content to have his purchases sent, but carried them on his shoulder to Settembrini's quarters, where he arranged with the grocer to take care of them for him. He had looked on enough at the sport to know the use of his tools; and choosing for his practice ground an almost treeless slope not far behind the sanatorium, remote from the hubbub of the spot where other beginners learned the art, he began daily to make his first blundering attempts, watched by Herr Settembrini, who would stand at a little distance, leaning on his cane, with legs gracefully crossed, and greet his nursling's progress with applause. One day Hans Castorp, steering down the cleared drive towards the Dorf, in the act of taking the skis back to the grocer's, ran into the Hofrat. Behrens never recognized him, though it was broad day, and our beginner had well-nigh collided with him. Shrouded in a haze of tobacco smoke, he stalked past unheeding.

Hans Castorp found that one quickly gets readiness in an art where strong desire comes in play. He was not ambitious of expert skill, and all he needed he acquired in a few days, without undue strain on wind or muscles. He learned to keep his feet tidily together and make parallel tracks; to avail himself of his stick in getting off; he learned how to take obstacles, such as small elevations of the ground, with a slight soaring motion, arms outspread, rising and falling like a ship on a billowy sea; learned, after the twentieth trial, not to trip and roll

over when he braked at full speed, with the right telemark
turn, one leg forward, the other bent at the knee. Gradually he widened the sphere of his activities. One day it
came to pass that Herr Settembrini saw him vanish in the
far white mist; the Italian shouted a warning through
cupped hands, and turned homewards, his pedagogic soul
well pleased.

It was beautiful here on these wintry heights; not mildly
and ingratiatingly beautiful, more as the North Sea is
beautiful in a westerly gale. There was no thunder of
surf, a deathly stillness reigned, but roused similar feelings
of awe. Hans Castorp's long, pliant soles carried him in
all directions; along the left slope to Clavadel, on the
right to Frauenkirch and Glarus, when he could see the
shadowy massif of the Amselfluh, ghostlike in the mist;
into the Dischma valley, or up behind the Berghof in the
direction of the wooded Seehorn, only the top of which,
snow-covered, rose above the tree line, or the Drusatscha
forest, with the pale outline of the Rhätikon looming
behind it, smothered in snow. He took his skis and
went up on the funicular to the Schatzalp; there, rapt six
thousand feet above the sea, he revelled at will on the
gleaming slopes of powdery snow—whence, in good
weather, there was a view of majestic extent over all the
surrounding territory.

He rejoiced in his new resource, before which all
difficulties and hindrances to movement fell away. It
gave him the utter solitude he craved, and filled his soul
with impressions of the wild inhumanity, the precarious-
ness of this region into which he had ventured. On his
one hand he might have a precipitous, pine-clad declivity,
falling away into the mists; on the other sheer rock might
rise, with masses of snow, in monstrous, Cyclopean forms,
all domed and vaulted, swelling or cavernous. He
would halt for a moment, to quench the sound of his

own movement, when the silence about him would be absolute, complete, a wadded soundlessness, as it were, elsewhere all unknown. There was no stir of air, not so much as might even lightly sway the tree boughs; there was not a rustle, nor the voice of a bird. It was primeval silence to which Hans Castorp hearkened, when he leaned thus on his staff, his head on one side, his mouth open. And always it snowed, snowed without pause, endlessly, gently, soundlessly falling.

No, this world of limitless silences had nothing hospitable; it received the visitor at his own risk, or rather it scarcely even received him, it tolerated his penetration into its fastnesses, in a manner that boded no good; it made him aware of the menace of the elemental, a menace not even hostile, but impersonally deadly. The child of civilization, remote from birth from wild nature and all her ways, is more susceptible to her grandeur than is her untutored son who has looked at her and lived close to her from childhood up, on terms of prosaic familiarity. The latter scarcely knows the religious awe with which the other regards her, that awe which conditions all his feeling for her, and is present, a constant, solemn thrill, in the profoundest depth of his soul. Hans Castorp, standing there in his puttees and long-sleeved camel's-hair waistcoat, on his skis *de luxe*, suddenly seemed to himself exceedingly presumptuous, to be thus listening to the primeval hush, the deathlike silence of these wintry fastnesses. He felt his breast lightened when, on his way home, the first chalets, the first abodes of human beings, loomed visible through the fog. Only then did he become aware that he had been for hours possessed by a secret awe and terror. On the island of Sylt he had stood by the edge of the thundering surf. In his white flannels, elegant, self-assured, but most respectful, he had stood there as one stands before a lion's cage, and looks deep into the yawning maw of the beast, lined with murderous fangs. He had bathed in the surf, and heeded the blast of the coastguard's horn, warning all and sundry not to venture rashly beyond the first line of billows, not to approach too nearly the oncoming tempest—the very last impulse of whose cataract, indeed, struck upon him like a blow from a lion's paw. From that experience our young man had learned the fearful pleasure of toying with forces so great that to approach them nearly is destruction. What he had not then felt was the temptation to come closer, to carry the thrilling contact with these deadly natural forces up to a point where the full embrace was imminent. Weak human being that he was—though tolerably well equipped with the weapons of civilization—what he at this moment knew was the fascination of venturing just so far into the monstrous unknown, or at least abstaining just so long from flight before it, that the adventure grazed the perilous, that it was just barely possible to put limits to it, before it became no longer a matter of toying with the foam and playfully dodging the ruthless paw—but the ultimate adventure, the billow, the lion's maw, and the sea.

In a word, Hans Castorp was valorous up here—if by valour we mean not mere dull matter-of-factness in the face of nature, but conscious submission to her, the fear of death cast out by irresistible oneness. Yes, in his narrow, hypercivilized breast, Hans Castorp cherished a feeling of kinship with the elements, connected with the new sense of superiority he had lately felt at sight of the silly people on their little sleighs; it had made him feel that a profounder, more spacious, less luxurious solitude than that afforded by his balcony chair would be beyond all price. He had sat there and looked abroad, at those mist-wreathed summits, at the carnival of snow, and blushed to be gaping thus from the breastwork of material well-being. This motive, and no momentary fad—no, nor yet any native love of bodily exertion—was what impelled him to learn the use of skis. If it was uncanny up there in the magnificence of the mountains, in the deathly silence of the snows—and uncanny it assuredly was, to our son of civilization—this was equally true, that in these months and years he had already drunk deep of the uncanny, in spirit and in sense. Even a colloquy with Naphta and Settembrini was not precisely the canniest thing in the world; it, too, led one on into uncharted and perilous regions. So if we can speak of Hans Castorp's feeling of kinship with the wild powers of the winter heights, it is in this sense, that despite his pious awe he felt these scenes to be a fitting theatre for the issue of his involved thoughts, a fitting stage for one who, scarcely knowing how, found it had devolved upon him to take stock of himself, in reference to the rank and status of the *homo Dei*.

No one was here to blow a warning to the rash one— unless, indeed, Herr Settembrini, with his farewell shout at Hans Castorp's disappearing back, had been that man. But possessed by valorous desire, our youth had given the call no heed—as little as he had the steps behind him on a certain carnival night. 'Eh, ingegnere, un po' di ragione, sa!' 'Yes, yes, pedagogic Satana, with your *ragione* and your *ribellione*,' he thought. 'But I 'm rather fond of you. You are a windbag and an organ grinder, to be sure. But you mean well, you mean much better, and more to my mind, than that knife-edged little Jesuit and Terrorist, apologist of the Inquisition and the knout, with his round eye-glasses—though he is nearly always right when you and he come to grips over my paltry soul, like God and the devil in the medieval legends.'

He struggled one day, powdered in snow to the waist, up a succession of snow-shrouded terraces, up and up,

he knew not whither.   Nowhither, perhaps; these upper
regions blended with a sky no less misty-white than they,
and where the two came together, it was hard to tell.
No summit, no ridge was visible, it was a haze and a
nothing, toward which Hans Castorp strove; while
behind him the world, the inhabited valley, fell away
swiftly from view, and no sound mounted to his ears.
In a twinkling he was as solitary, he was as lost, as heart
could wish, his loneliness was profound enough to awake
the fear which is the first stage of valour.   'Praeterit
figura huius mundi,' he said to himself, quoting Naphta,
in a Latin hardly humanistic in spirit.   He stopped and
looked about.   On all sides there was nothing to see,
beyond small single flakes of snow, which came out of a
white sky and sank to rest on the white earth.   The
silence about him refused to say aught to his spirit.   His
gaze was lost in the blind white void, he felt his heart
pulse from the effort of the climb—that muscular organ
whose animal-like shape and contractile motion he had
watched with a feeling of sacrilege, in the X-ray labora-
tory.   A naïve reverence filled him for that organ of his,
for the pulsating human heart, up here alone in the icy
void, alone with its question and its riddle.

On he pressed; higher and higher towards the sky.
Walking, he thrust the end of his stick in the snow and
watched the blue light follow it out of the hole it made.
That he liked; and stood for long at a time to test the
little optical phenomenon.   It was a strange, a subtle
colour, this greenish-blue; colour of the heights and
deeps, ice-clear, yet holding shadow in its depths, mysteriously exquisite.   It reminded him of the colour of
certain eyes, whose shape and glance had spelled his
destiny; eyes to which Herr Settembrini, from his
humanistic height, had referred with contempt as 'Tartar
slits' and 'wolf's eyes'—eyes seen long ago and then

found again, the eyes of Pribislav Hippe and Clavdia Chauchat. 'With pleasure,' he said aloud, in the profound stillness. 'But don't break it—c'est à visser, tu sais.' And his spirit heard behind him words of warning in a mellifluous tongue.

A wood loomed, misty, far off to the right. He turned that way, in order to have some goal before his eyes, instead of sheer white transcendence; and made towards it with a dash, not remarking an intervening depression of the ground. He could not have seen it, in fact; everything swam before his eyes in the white mist, obliterating all contours. When he perceived it, he gave himself to the decline, unable to measure its steepness with his eye.

The grove that had attracted him lay the other side of the gully into which he had unintentionally steered. The trough, covered with fluffy snow, fell away on the side next the mountains, as he observed when he pursued it a little distance. It went downhill, the steep sides grew higher, this fold of the earth's surface seemed like a narrow passage leading into the mountain. Then the points of his skis turned up again, there began an incline, soon there were no more side walls; Hans Castorp's trackless course ran once more uphill along the mountain side.

He saw the pine grove behind and below him, on his right, turned again towards it, and with a quick descent reached the laden trees; they stood in a wedge-shaped group, a vanguard thrust out from the mist-screened forests above. He rested beneath their boughs, and smoked a cigarette. The unnatural stillness, the monstrous solitude, still oppressed his spirit; yet he felt proud to have conquered them, brave in the pride of having attained to the height of surroundings such as these.

It was three in the afternoon. He had set out soon

after luncheon, with the idea of cutting part of the long rest cure, and tea as well, in order to be back before dark. He had brought some chocolate in his breeches pocket, and a small flask of wine; and told himself exultantly that he had still several hours to revel in all this grandeur.

The position of the sun was hard to recognize, veiled as it was in haze. Behind him, at the mouth of the valley, above that part of the mountains that was shut off from view, the clouds and mist seemed to thicken and move forward. They looked like snow — more snow — as though there were pressing demand for it! Like a good hard storm. Indeed, the little soundless flakes were coming down more quickly as he stood.

Hans Castorp put out his arm and let some of them come to rest on his sleeve; he viewed them with the knowing eye of the nature lover. They looked mere shapeless morsels; but he had more than once had their like under his good lens, and was aware of the exquisite precision of form displayed by these little jewels, insignia, orders, agraffes—no jeweller, however skilled, could do finer, more minute work. Yes, he thought, there was a difference, after all, between this light, soft, white powder he trod with his skis, that weighted down the trees, and covered the open spaces, a difference between it and the sand on the beaches at home, to which he had likened it. for this powder was not made of tiny grains of stone; but of myriads of tiniest drops of water, which in freezing had darted together in symmetrical variation—parts, then, of the same inorganic substance which was the source of protoplasm, of plant life, of the human body. And among these myriads of enchanting little stars, in their hidden splendour that was too small for man's naked eye to see, there was not one like another; an endless inventiveness governed the development and unthinkable differentiation of one and the same basic scheme, the

equilateral, equiangular hexagon. Yet each, in itself—
this was the uncanny, the anti-organic, the life-denying
character of them all—each of them was absolutely
symmetrical, icily regular in form. They were too regular, as substance adapted to life never was to this degree—
the living principle shuddered at this perfect precision,
found it deathly, the very marrow of death—Hans Castorp
felt he understood now the reason why the builders of
antiquity purposely and secretly introduced minute
variation from absolute symmetry in their columnar
structures.

He pushed off again, shuffling through the deep snow
on his flexible runners, along the edge of the wood, down
the slope, up again, at random, to his heart's content,
about and into this lifeless land. Its empty, rolling
spaces, its dried vegetation of single dwarf firs sticking
up through the snow, bore a striking resemblance to a
scene on the dunes. Hans Castorp nodded as he stood
and fixed the likeness in his mind. Even his burning
face, his trembling limbs, the peculiar and half-intoxicated
mingled sensations of excitement and fatigue, were pleasur-
able, reminding him as they did of that familiar feeling
induced by the sea air, which could sting one like whips,
and yet was so laden with sleepy essences. He rejoiced
in his freedom of motion, his feet were like wings. He
was bound to no path, none lay behind him to take him
back whence he had come. At first there had been posts,
staves set up as guides through the snow—but he had
soon cut free from their tutelage, which recalled the
coastguard with his horn, and seemed inconsistent with
the attitude he had taken up towards the wild.

He pressed on, turning right and left among rocky,
snow-clad elevations, and came behind them on an incline,
then a level spot, then on the mountains themselves—
how alluring and accessible seemed their softly covered

gorges and defiles! His blood leaped at the strong allure-
ment of the distance and the height, the ever profounder
solitude. At risk of a late return he pressed on, deeper
into the wild silence, the monstrous and the menacing,
despite the gathering darkness that was sinking down over
the region like a veil, and heightening his inner apprehension until it presently passed into actual fear. It was
this fear which first made him conscious that he had
deliberately set out to lose his way and the direction in
which valley and settlement lay—and had been as successful as heart could wish. Yet he knew that if he were to
turn in his tracks and go downhill, he would reach the
valley bottom — even if at some distance from the Berghof
—and that sooner than he had planned. He would
come home too early, not have made full use of his time.
On the other hand, if he were overtaken unawares by the
storm, he would probably in any case not find his way
home. But however genuine his fear of the elements,
he refused to take premature flight; his being scarcely
the sportsman's attitude, who only meddles with the
elements so long as he knows himself their master, takes
all precautions, and prudently yields when he must—
whereas what went on in Hans Castorp's soul can only
be described by the one word challenge. It was perhaps
a blameworthy, presumptuous attitude, even united to
such genuine awe. Yet this much is clear to any human
understanding: that when a young man has lived for
years in the way this one had, something may gather—
may accumulate, as our engineer might put it—in the
depths of his soul, until one day it suddenly discharges
itself, with a primitive exclamation of disgust, a mental
'Oh, go to the devil!' a repudiation of all caution what-
soever, in short, with a challenge. So on he went, in his
seven-league slippers, glided down this slope too and
pressed up the incline beyond, where stood a wooden hut

that might be a hay shed or shepherd's shelter, its roof weighted with flat stones. On past this to the nearest mountain ridge, bristling with forest, behind whose back the giant peaks towered upward in the mist. The wall before him, studded with single groups of trees, was steep, but looked as though one might wind to the right and get round it by climbing a little way up the slope. Once on the other side, he could see what lay beyond. Accordingly Hans Castorp set out on this tour of investigation, which began by descending from the meadow with the hut into another and rather deep gully that dropped off from right to left.

He had just begun to mount again when the expected happened, and the storm burst, the storm that had threatened so long, if one can say 'threatened' of the action of blind, insentient forces, which have no purpose to destroy us—that would be comforting by comparison—but are merely horribly indifferent to our fate should we become involved with them? 'Hallo!' Hans Castorp thought, and stood still, as the first blast whirled through the densely falling snow and caught him. 'That's a gentle zephyr—tells you what's coming.' And truly this wind was savage. The air was in reality frightfully cold, probably some degrees below zero; but so long as it remained dry and still one almost found it balmy. It was when a wind came up that the cold began to cut into the flesh; and in a wind like the one that blew now, of which that first gust had been a forerunner, the furs were not bought that could protect the limbs from its icy rigours. And Hans Castorp wore no fur, only a woollen waistcoat, which he had found quite enough, or even, with the faintest gleam of sunshine, a burden. But the wind was at his back, a little sidewise; there was small inducement to turn and receive it in the face; so the mad youth, letting that fact reinforce the fundamental challenge of his attitude, pressed on among the single tree trunks, and tried to outflank the mountain he had attacked.

It was no joke. There was almost nothing to be seen for swimming snow flakes, that seemed without falling to fill the air to suffocation by their whirling dance. The icy gusts made his ears burn painfully, his limbs felt half paralysed, his hands were so numb he hardly knew if they held the staff. The snow blew inside his collar and melted down his back. It drifted on his shoulders and right side; he thought he should freeze as he stood into a snow man, with his staff stiff in his hands. And all this under relatively favouring circumstances; for let him turn his face to the storm and his situation would be still worse. Getting home would be no easy task—the harder, the longer he put it off.

At last he stopped, gave an angry shrug, and turned his skis the other way. Then the wind he faced took his breath away on the spot, so that he was forced to go through the awkward process of turning round again to get it back, and collect his resolution to advance in the teeth of his ruthless foe. With bent head and cautious breathing he managed to get under way; but even thus forewarned, the slowness of his progress and the difficulty of seeing and breathing dismayed him. Every few minutes he had to stop, first to get his breath in the lee of the wind, and then because he saw next to nothing in the blinding whiteness, and moving as he did with head down, had to take care not to run against trees, or be flung headlong by unevennesses in the ground. Hosts of flakes flew into his face, melted there, and he anguished with the cold of them. They flew into his mouth, and died away with a weak, watery taste; flew against his eyelids so that he winked, overflowed his eyes and made seeing as difficult as it was now almost impossible for other reasons: namely, the dazzling effect of all that whiteness, and the veiling of his field of vision, so that his sense of sight was almost put out of action.   It was nothingness, white, whirling nothingness, into which he looked when he forced himself to do so.   Only at intervals did ghostly seeming forms from the world of reality loom up before him: a stunted fir, a group of pines, even the pale silhouette of the hay shed he had lately passed.

He left it behind, and sought his way back over the slope on which it stood.   But there was no path.   To keep direction, relatively speaking, into his own valley would be a question far more of luck than management; for while he could see his hand before his face, he could not see the ends of his skis.   And even with better visibility, the host of difficulties must have combined to hinder his progress: the snow in his face, his adversary the storm, which hampered his breathing, made him fight both to take a breath and to exhale it, and constantly forced him to turn his head away to gasp.   How could any one—either Hans Castorp or another and much stronger than he—make head?   He stopped, he blinked his lashes free of water drops, knocked off the snow that like a coat of mail was sheathing his body in front—and it struck him that progress, under the circumstances, was more than any one could expect.

And yet Hans Castorp did progress.   That is to say, he moved on.   But whether in the right direction, whether it might not have been better to stand still, remained to be seen.   Theoretically the chances were against it; and in practice he soon began to suspect something was wrong.   This was not familar ground beneath his feet, not the easy slope he had gained on mounting with such difficulty from the ravine, which had of course to be retraversed.   The level distance was too short, he was already mounting again.   It was plain that the storm, which came from the south-west, from the mouth

of the valley, had with its violence driven him from his
course.   He had been exhausting himself, all this time,
with a false start.   Blindly, enveloped in white, whirling
night, he laboured deeper and deeper into this grim and
callous sphere.

'No, you don't,' said he, suddenly, between his teeth,
and halted.   The words were not emotional, yet he felt
for a second as though his heart had been clutched by an
icy hand; it winced, and then knocked rapidly against
his ribs, as it had the time Rhadamanthus found the moist
cavity.   Pathos in the grand manner was not in place,
he knew, in one who had chosen defiance as his role, and
was indebted to himself alone for all his present plight.
'Not bad,' he said, and discovered that his facial muscles
were not his to command, that he could not express in his
face any of his soul's emotions, because it was stiff with
cold.   'What next?   Down this slope; follow your nose
home, I suppose, and keep your face to the wind—
though that is a good deal easier said than done,' he went
on, panting with his efforts, yet actually speaking half
aloud, as he tried to move on again: 'but something has
to happen, I can't sit down and wait, I should simply be
buried in six-sided crystalline symmetricality, and Settembrini, when he came with his little horn to find me,
would see me squatting here with a snow cap over one
ear.'   He realized that he was talking to himself, and not
too sensibly—for which he took himself to task, and then
continued on purpose, though his lips were so stiff he
could not shape the labials, and so did without them,
as he had on certain other occasions that came to his mind.
'Keep quiet, and get along with you out of here,' he
admonished himself, adding: 'You seem to be wool-
gathering, not quite right in your head, and that looks
bad for you.'

But this he only said with his reason—to some extent

detached from the rest of him, though after all nearly concerned. As for his natural part, it felt only too much inclined to yield to the confusion which laid hold upon him with his growing fatigue. He even remarked this tendency and took thought to comment upon it. 'Here,' said he, 'we have the typical reaction of a man who loses himself in the mountains in a snowstorm and never finds his way home.' He gasped out other fragments of the same thought as he went, though he avoided giving it more specific expression. 'Whoever hears about it afterwards, imagines it as horrible; but he forgets that disease—and the state I am in is, in a way of speaking, disease—so adjusts its man that it and he can come to terms; there are sensory appeasements, short circuits, a merciful narcosis—yes, oh, yes, yes. But one must fight against them, after all, for they are two-faced, they are in the highest degree equivocal, everything depends upon the point of view. If you are not meant to get home, they are a benefaction, they are merciful; but if you mean to get home, they become sinister. I believe I still do. Certainly I don't intend—in this heart of mine so stormily beating it doesn't appeal to me in the least—to let myself be snowed under by this idiotically symmetrical crystallometry.'

In truth, he was already affected, and his struggle against oncoming sensory confusion was feverish and abnormal. He should have been more alarmed on discovering that he had already declined from the level course—this time apparently on the other slope. For he had pushed off with the wind coming slantwise at him, which was ill-advised, though more convenient for the moment. 'Never mind,' he thought, 'I'll get my direction again down below.' Which he did, or thought he did—or, truth to tell, scarcely even thought so; worst of all, began to be indifferent whether he had done or no.

Such was the effect of an insidious double attack, which he but weakly combated. Fatigue and excitement combined were a familiar state to our young man— whose acclimatization, as we know, still consisted in getting used to not getting used; and both fatigue and excitement were now present in such strength as to make impossible any thought of asserting his reason against them. He felt as often after a colloquy with Settembrini and Naphta, only to a far greater degree; dazed and tipsy, giddy, a-tremble with excitement. This was probably why he began to colour his lack of resistance to the stealing narcosis with half-maudlin references to the latest-aired complex of theories. Despite his scornful repudiation of the idea that he might lie down and be covered up with hexagonal symmetricality, something within him maundered on, sense or no sense; told him that the feeling of duty which bade him fight against insidious sensory appeasements was a purely ethical reaction, representing the sordid bourgeois view of life, irreligion, Philistinism; while the desire, nay, craving, to lie down and rest whispered him in the guise of a comparison between this storm and a sand storm in the desert, before which the Arab flings himself down and draws his burnous over his head. Only his lack of a burnous, the unfeasibility of drawing his woollen waistcoat over his head, prevented him from following suit—this although he was no longer a child, and pretty well aware of the conditions under which a man freezes to death.

There had been a rather steep declivity, then level ground, then again an ascent, a stiff one. This was not necessarily wrong; one must of course, on the way to the valley, traverse rising ground at times. The wind had turned capriciously round, for it was now at Hans Castorp's back, and that, taken by itself, was a blessing. Owing, perhaps, to the storm, or the soft whiteness of the incline before him, dim in the whirling air, drawing him towards it, he bent as he walked.   Only a little farther—supposing one were to give way to the temptation, and his temptation was great; it was so strong that it quite lived up to the many descriptions he had read of the 'typical danger state.'   It asserted itself, it refused to be classified with the general order of things, it insisted on being an exception, its very exigence challenged comparison—yet at the same time it never disguised its origin or aura, never denied that it was, so to speak, garbed in Spanish black, with snow-white, fluted ruff, and stood for ideas and fundamental conceptions that were characteristically gloomy, strongly Jesuitical, and anti-human, for the rack-and-knout discipline which was the particular horror of Herr Settembrini, though he never opposed it without making himself ridiculous, like an organ grinder for ever grinding out *ragione* to the same old tune.

And yet Hans Castorp did hold himself upright and resist his craving to lie down.   He could see nothing, but he struggled, he went forward.   Whether to the purpose or not, he could not tell; but he did his part, and moved on despite the weight the cold more and more laid upon his limbs.   The present slope was too steep to ascend directly, so he slanted a little, and went on thus awhile without much heed whither.   Even to lift his stiffened lids to peer before him was so great and so nearly useless an effort as to offer him small incentive.   He merely caught glimpses: here clumps of pines that merged together; there a ditch or stream, a black line marked out between overhanging banks of snow.   Now, for a change, he was going downhill, with the wind in his face, when, at some distance before him, and seeming to hang in the driving wind and mist, he saw the faint outline of a human habitation.

Ah, sweet and blessed sight!   Verily he had done well,

to march stoutly on despite all obstacles, until now
human dwellings appeared, a sign that the inhabited
valley was at hand. Perhaps there were even human
beings, perhaps he might enter and abide the end of the
storm under shelter, then get directions, or a guide if the
dark should have fallen. He held towards this chimerical
goal, that often quite vanished in mist, and had an
exhausting climb against the wind before it was reached;
finally drew near it—to discover, with what staggering
astonishment and horror may be imagined, that it was
only the hay shed with the weighted roof, to which, after
all his striving, by all his devious paths, he had come back.

That was the very devil. Hans Castorp gave vent to
several heartfelt curses—of which his lips were too stiff
to pronounce the labials. He examined the hut, to get
his bearings, and came to the conclusion that he had
approached it from the same direction as before—namely
from the rear; and therefore, what he had accomplished
for the past hour—as he reckoned it—had been sheer
waste of time and effort. But there it was, just as the
books said. You went in a circle, gave yourself endless
trouble under the delusion that you were accomplishing
something, and all the time you were simply describing
some great silly arc that would turn back to where it had
its beginning, like the riddling year itself. You wandered
about, without getting home. Hans Castorp recognized
the traditional phenomenon with a certain grim satisfaction—and even slapped his thigh in astonishment at this
punctual general law fulfilling itself in his particular case.

The lonely hut was barred, the door locked fast, no
entrance possible. But Hans Castorp decided to stop
for the present. The projecting roof gave the illusion
of shelter, and the hut itself, on the side turned towards
the mountains, afforded, he found, some little protection
against the storm. He leaned his shoulder against the

rough-hewn timber, since his long skis prevented him from leaning his back. And so he stood, obliquely to the wall, having thrust his staff in the snow; hands in pockets, his collar turned up as high as it would go, bracing himself on his outside leg, and leaning his dizzy head against the wood, his eyes closed, but opening them every now and then to look down his shoulder and across the gully to where the high mountain wall palely appeared and disappeared in mist.

His situation was comparatively comfortable. 'I can stick it like this all night, if I have to,' he thought, 'if I change legs from time to time, lie on the other side, so to speak, and move about a bit between whiles, as of course I must. I 'm rather stiff, naturally, but the effort I made has accumulated some inner warmth, so after all it is not quite in vain that I have come round all this way. Come round—not coming round—that 's the regular expression they use, of people drowned or frozen to death. I suppose I used it because I am not quite so clear in the head as I might be. But it is a good thing I can stick it out here; for this frantic nuisance of a snow storm can carry on until morning without a qualm, and if it only keeps up until dark it will be quite bad enough, for in the dark the danger of going round and round and *not* coming round is as great as in a storm. It must be towards evening already, about six o'clock, I should say, after all the time I wasted on my circular tour. Let 's see, how late is it?' He felt for his watch; his numbed fingers could scarcely find and draw it from his pocket. Here it was, his gold hunting watch, with his monogram on the lid, ticking faithfully away in this lonely waste, like Hans Castorp's own heart, that touching human heart that beat in the organic warmth of his interior man.

It was half-past four. But deuce take it, it had been nearly as much before the storm burst. Was it possible his whole bewildered circuit had lasted scarcely a quarter of an hour? '"Coming round" makes time seem long,' he noted. 'And when you *don't* "come round"—does it seem longer? But the fact remains that at five or half-past it will be really dark. Will the storm hold up in time for me to start running in circles again? Suppose I take a sip of port—it might strengthen me.'

He had brought with him a bottle of that amateurish drink, simply because it was always kept ready in flat bottles at the Berghof, for excursions—though not, of course, excursions like this unlawful escapade. It was not meant for people who went out in the snow and got lost and night-bound in the mountains. Had his senses been less befogged, he would have said to himself that if he were bent on getting home, it was almost the worst thing he could have done. He did say so, after he had drunk several mouthfuls, for they took effect at once, and it was an effect much like that of the Kulmbacher beer on the evening of his arrival at the Berghof, when he had angered Settembrini by his ungoverned prattle anent fish sauces and the like—Herr Ludovico, the pedagogue, the same who held madmen to their senses when they would give themselves rein. Hans Castorp heard through thin air the mellifluous sound of his horn; the orator and schoolmaster was nearing by forced marches, to rescue his troublesome nursling, life's delicate child, from his present desperate pass and lead him home. All of which was of course sheer rubbish, due to the Kulmbacher he had so foolishly drunk. For of course Herr Settembrini had no horn, how could he have? He had a hand-organ, propped by a sort of wooden leg against the pavement, and as he played a sprightly air, he flung his humanistic eyes up to the people in the houses. And furthermore he knew nothing whatever of what had happened, as he no longer lived at the Berghof, but with Lukaçek the tailor, in his little attic room with the water bottle, above Naphta's silken cell. Moreover, he would have neither right nor reason to interfere—no more than upon that carnival night on which Hans Castorp had found himself in a position quite as mad and bad as this one, when he gave the ailing Clavdia Chauchat back *son crayon*—his, Pribislav Hippe's, pencil. What position was that? What position could it be but the horizontal, literally and not metaphorically the position of all long-termers up here? Was he himself not used to lie long hours out of doors, in snow and frost, by night as well as day? And he was making ready to sink down when the idea seized him, took him as it were by the collar and fetched him up standing, that all this nonsense he was uttering was still inspired by the Kulmbacher beer and the impersonal, quite typical, and traditional longing to lie down and sleep, of which he had always heard, and which would by quibbling and sophistry now betray him.

'That was the wrong way to go to work,' he acknow-ledged to himself. 'The port was not at all the right thing; just the few sips of it have made my head so heavy I cannot hold it up, and my thoughts are all just confused, stupid quibbling with words. I can't depend on them— not only the first thought that comes into my head, but even the second one, the correction which my reason tries to make upon the first—more's the pity. "Son crayon!" That means her pencil, not his pencil, in this case; you only say *son* because *crayon* is masculine. The rest is just a pretty feeble play on words. Imagine stopping to talk about that when there is a much more important fact; namely, that my left leg, which I am using as a support, reminds me of the wooden leg on Settembrini's hand-organ, that he keeps jolting over the pavement with his knee, to get up close to the window and hold out his velvet hat for the girl up there to throw something into. And at the same time I seem to be drawn, as though with hands, to lie down in the snow. The only thing to do is to move about. I must pay for the Kulmbacher, and limber up my wooden leg.'

He pushed himself away from the wall with his shoulder. But one single pace forward, and the wind sliced at him like a scythe, and drove him back to the shelter of the wall. It was unquestionably the position indicated for the time; he might change it by turning his left shoulder to the wall and propping himself on the right leg, with sundry shakings of the left, to restore the circulation as much as might be. 'Who leaves the house in weather like this?' he said. 'Moderate activity is all right; but not too much craving for adventure, no flirting with the bride of the storm. Quiet, quiet—if the head be heavy, let it droop. The wall is good, a certain warmth seems to come from the logs—probably the feeling is entirely subjective. Ah, the trees, the trees! Oh, living climate of the living— how sweet it smells!'

It was a park. It lay beneath the terrace on which he seemed to stand—a spreading park of luxuriant green shade trees, elms, planes, beeches, oaks, birches, all in the dappled light and shade of their fresh, full, shimmering foliage, and gently rustling tips. They breathed a deliciously moist, balsamic breath into the air. A warm shower passed over them, but the rain was sunlit. One could see high up in the sky the whole air filled with the bright ripple of raindrops. How lovely it was! Oh, breath of the homeland, oh, fragrance and abundance of the plain, so long forgone! The air was full of bird song—dainty, sweet, blithe, fluting, piping, twittering, cooing, trilling, warbling, though not a single little creature could be seen. Hans Castorp smiled, breathing gratitude. But still more beauties were preparing. A rainbow flung its arc slanting across the scene, most bright and perfect, a sheer delight, all its rich, glossy, banded colours moistly shimmering down into the thick, lustrous green. It was like music, like the sound of harps commingled with flutes and violins. The blue and the violet were transcendent. And they descended and magically blended, were transmuted and re-unfolded more lovely than at first.   Once, some years before, our young Hans Castorp had been privileged to hear a world-famous Italian tenor, from whose throat had gushed a glorious stream to witch the world with gracious art.   The singer took a high note exquisitely; then held it, while the passionate harmony swelled, unfolded, glowed from moment to moment with new radiance.   Unsuspected veils dropped from before it one by one; the last one sank away, revealing what must surely be the ultimate tonal purity—yet no, for still another fell, and then a well-nigh incredible third and last, shaking into the air such an extravagance of tear-glistening splendour, that confused murmurs of protest rose from the audience, as though it could bear no more; and our young friend found that he was sobbing. So now with the scene before him, constantly transformed and transfigured as it was before his eyes.   The bright, rainy veil fell away; behind it stretched the sea, a southern sea of deep, deepest blue shot with silver lights, and a beautiful bay, on one side mistily open, on the other enclosed by mountains whose outline paled away into blue space.   In the middle distance lay islands, where palms rose tall and small white houses gleamed among cypress groves.   Ah, it was all too much, too blessed for sinful mortals, that glory of light, that deep purity of the sky, that sunny freshness on the water!   Such a scene Hans Castorp had never beheld, nor anything like it. On his holidays he had barely sipped at the south, the sea for him meant the colourless, tempestuous northern tides, to which he clung with inarticulate, childish love.   Of the Mediterranean, Naples, Sicily, he knew nothing. And yet—he *remembered*. Yes, strangely enough, that was recognition which so moved him. 'Yes, yes, its very image,' he was crying out, as though in his heart he had always cherished a picture of this spacious, sunny bliss.   Always—and that always went far, far, unthinkably far back, as far as the open sea there on the left where it ran out to the violet sky bent down to meet it.

The sky line was high, the distance seemed to mount to Hans Castorp's view, looking down as he did from his elevation on the spreading gulf beneath.   The mountains held it embraced, their tree-clad foot-hills running down to the sea; they reached in half-circle from the middle distance to the point where he sat, and beyond.   This was a mountainous littoral, at one point of which he was crouching upon a sun-warmed stone terrace, while before him the ground, descending among undergrowth, by moss-covered rocky steps, ran down to a level shore, where the reedy shingle formed little blue-dyed bays, minute archipelagos and harbours.   And all the sunny region, these open coastal heights and laughing rocky basins, even the sea itself out to the islands, where boats plied to and fro, was peopled far and wide.   On every hand human beings, children of sun and sea, were stirring or sitting.   Beautiful young human creatures, so blithe, so good and gay, so pleasing to see—at sight of them Hans Castorp's whole heart opened in a responsive love, keen almost to pain.

Youths were at work with horses, running hand on halter alongside their whinnying, head-tossing charges; pulling the refractory ones on a long rein, or else, seated bareback, striking the flanks of their mounts with naked heels, to drive them into the sea.   The muscles of the riders' backs played beneath the sun-bronzed skin, and their voices were enchanting beyond words as they shouted

to each other or to their animals.   A little bay ran deep
into the coast line, mirroring the shore as does a mountain
lake; about it girls were dancing.   One of them sat with
her back towards him, so that her neck, and the hair
drawn to a knot above it, smote him with loveliness.   She
sat with her feet in a depression of the rock, and played
on a shepherd's pipe, her eyes roving above the stops to
her companions, as in long, wide garments, smiling, with
outstretched arms, alone, or in pairs, swaying gently
towards each other, they moved in the paces of the dance.
Behind the flute player—she too was white-clad, and her
back was long and slender, laterally rounded by the movement of her arms—other maidens were sitting, or standing
entwined to watch the dance, and quietly talking.   Beyond them still, young men were practising archery.
Lovely and pleasant it was to see the older ones show the
younger, curly-locked novices, how to bend the bow and
take aim; draw with them, and laughing support them
staggering back from the thrust of the arrow as it leaped
from the bow.   Others were fishing, lying prone on a
jut of rock, swinging one leg in the air, holding the line
out over the water, approaching their heads in talk.
Others sat straining forward to fling the bait far out.
A ship, with mast and yards, lying high out of the tide,
was being eased, shoved, and steadied into the sea.   Children played and exulted among the breaking waves.   A
young female, lying outstretched, drawing with one hand
her flowered robe high between her breasts, reached with
the other in the air after a twig bearing fruit and leaves,
which a second, a slender-hipped creature, erect at her
head, was playfully withholding.   Young folk were
sitting in nooks of the rocks, or hesitating at the water's
edge, with crossed arms clutching either shoulder, as they
tested the chill with their toes.   Pairs strolled along the
beach, close and confiding, the lips of the youth at the

maiden's ear. Shaggy-haired goats leaped from ledge to ledge of the rocks, while the young goatherd, wearing perched on his brown curls a little hat with the brim turned up behind, stood watching them from a height, one hand on his hip, the other holding the long staff on which he leaned.

'Oh, lovely, lovely!' Hans Castorp breathed. 'How joyous and winning they are, how fresh and healthy, happy and clever they look! It is not alone the outward form, they seem to be wise and gentle through and through. That is what makes me in love with them, the spirit that speaks out of them, the sense, I might almost say, in which they live and play together.' By which he meant the friendliness, the mutual courteous regard these children of the sun showed to each other, a calm, reciprocal reverence veiled in smiles, manifested almost imperceptibly, and yet possessing them all by the power of sense association and ingrained idea. A dignity, even a gravity, was held, as it were, in solution in their lightest mood, perceptible only as an ineffable spiritual influence, a high seriousness without austerity, a reasoned goodness conditioning every act. All this, indeed, was not without its ceremonial side. A young mother, in a brown robe loose at the shoulder, sat on a rounded mossy stone and suckled her child, saluted by all who passed with a characteristic gesture which seemed to comprehend all that lay implicit in their general bearing. The young men, as they approached, lightly and formally crossed their arms on their breasts, and smilingly bowed; the maidens shaped the suggestion of a curtsy, as the worshipper does when he passes the high altar, at the same time nodding repeatedly, blithely and heartily. This mixture of formal homage with lively friendliness, and the slow, mild mien of the mother as well, where she sat pressing her breast with her forefinger to ease the flow of milk to her babe, glancing

up from it to acknowledge with a smile the reverence paid
her—this sight thrilled Hans Castorp's heart with something very close akin to ecstasy. He could not get his
fill of looking, yet asked himself in concern whether he
had a right, whether it was not perhaps punishable, for
him, an outsider, to be a party to the sunshine and gracious
loveliness of all these happy folk. He felt common,
clumsy-booted. It seemed unscrupulous.

A lovely boy, with full hair drawn sideways across his
brow and falling on his temples, sat directly beneath him,
apart from his companions, with arms folded on his breast
—not sadly, not ill-naturedly, quite tranquilly on one
side. This lad looked up, turned his gaze upward and
looked at him, Hans Castorp, and his eyes went between
the watcher and the scenes upon the strand, watching
his watching, to and fro. But suddenly he looked past
Hans Castorp into space, and that smile, common to
them all, of polite and brotherly regard, disappeared in a
moment from his lovely, purely cut, half-childish face.
His brows did not darken, but in his gaze there came a
solemnity that looked as though carved out of stone,
inexpressive, unfathomable, a deathlike reserve, which
gave the scarcely reassured Hans Castorp a thorough
fright, not unaccompanied by a vague apprehension of its
meaning.

He too looked in the same direction. Behind him rose
towering columns, built of cylindrical blocks without
bases, in the joinings of which moss had grown. They
formed the façade of a temple gate, on whose foundations
he was sitting, at the top of a double flight of steps with
space between. Heavy of heart he rose, and, descending
the stair on one side, passed through the high gate below,
and along a flagged street, which soon brought him before
other propylaea. He passed through these as well, and
now stood facing the temple that lay before him, massy,

weathered to a grey-green tone, on a foundation reached
by a steep flight of steps. The broad brow of the temple
rested on the capitals of powerful, almost stunted columns,
tapering towards the top—sometimes a fluted block had
been shoved out of line and projected a little in profile.
Painfully, helping himself on with his hands, and sighing
for the growing oppression of his heart, Hans Castorp
mounted the high steps and gained the grove of columns.
It was very deep, he moved in it as among the trunks
in a forest of beeches by the pale northern sea. He
purposely avoided the centre, yet for all that slanted back
again, and presently stood before a group of statuary, two
female figures carved in stone, on a high base; mother and
daughter, it seemed; one of them sitting, older than the
other, more dignified, right goddess-like and mild, yet
with mourning brows above the lightless empty eye
sockets; clad in a flowing tunic and a mantle of many folds,
her matronly brow with its waves of hair covered with a
veil. The other figure stood in the protecting embrace
of the first, with round, youthful face, and arms and hands
wound and hidden in the folds of the mantle.

Hans Castorp stood looking at the group, and from
some dark cause his laden heart grew heavier still, and
more oppressed with its weight of dread and anguish.
Scarcely daring to venture, but following an inner compulsion, he passed behind the statuary, and through the
double row of columns beyond. The bronze door of
the sanctuary stood open, and the poor soul's knees all
but gave way beneath him at the sight within. Two
grey old women, witchlike, with hanging breasts and
dugs of finger length, were busy there, between flaming
braziers, most horribly. They were dismembering a
child. In dreadful silence they tore it apart with their
bare hands—Hans Castorp saw the bright hair blood-
smeared—and cracked the tender bones between their

jaws, their dreadful lips dripped blood. An icy coldness held him. He would have covered his eyes and fled, but could not. They at their gory business had already seen him, they shook their reeking fists and uttered curses—soundlessly, most vilely, with the last obscenity, and in the dialect of Hans Castorp's native Hamburg. It made him sick, sick as never before. He tried desperately to escape; knocked into a column with his shoulder—and found himself, with the sound of that dreadful brawling still in his ears, still wrapped in the cold horror of it, lying by his hut in the snow, leaning against one arm, with his head upon it, his legs in their skis stretched out before him.

It was no true awakening. He blinked his relief at being free from those execrable hags, but was not very clear, nor even greatly concerned, whether this was a hay hut, or the column of a temple, against which he lay; and after a fashion continued to dream, no longer in pictures, but in thoughts hardly less involved and fantastic.

'I felt it was a dream, all along,' he rambled. 'A lovely and horrible dream. I knew all the time that I was making it myself—the park with the trees, the delicious moisture in the air, and all the rest, both dreadful and dear. In a way, I knew it all beforehand. But how is it a man can know all that and call it up to bring him bliss and terror both at once? Where did I get the beautiful bay with the islands, where the temple precincts, whither the eyes of that charming boy pointed me, as he stood there alone? Now I know that it is not out of our single souls we dream. We dream anonymously and communally, if each after his fashion. The great soul of which we are a part may dream through us, in our manner of dreaming, its own secret dreams, of its youth, its hope, its joy and peace—and its blood sacrifice. Here I lie at my column and still feel in my body the actual

remnant of my dream—the icy horror of the human
sacrifice, but also the joy that had filled my heart to its
very depths, born of the happiness and brave bearing of
those human creatures in white.   It is meet and proper,
I hereby declare that I have a prescriptive right to lie
here and dream these dreams.   For in my life up here
I have known reason and recklessness.   I have wandered
lost with Settembrini and Naphta in high and mortal
places.   I know all of man.   I have known mankind's
flesh and blood.   I gave back to the ailing Clavdia
Chauchat Pribislav Hippe's lead pencil.   But he who
knows the body, life, knows death.   And that is not all;
it is, pedagogically speaking, only the beginning.   One
must have the other half of the story, the other side.
For all interest in disease and death is only another
expression of interest in life, as is proven by the humanistic faculty of medicine, that addresses life and its ails
always so politely in Latin, and is only a division of the
great and pressing concern which, in all sympathy, I now
name by its name: the human being, the delicate child
of life, man, his state and standing in the universe.   I
understand no little about him, I have learned much from
'those up here,' I have been driven up from the valley,
so that the breath almost left my poor body.   Yet now
from the base of my column I have no meagre view.   I
have dreamed of man's state, of his courteous and enlightened social state; behind which, in the temple, the
horrible blood sacrifice was consummated.   Were they,
those children of the sun, so sweetly courteous to each
other, in silent recognition of that horror?   It would
be a fine and right conclusion they drew.   I will hold
to them, in my soul, I will hold with them and not
with Naphta, neither with Settembrini.   They are both
talkers; the one luxurious and spiteful, the other for ever
blowing on his penny pipe of reason, even vainly imagining

he can bring the mad to their senses.   It is all Philistinism
and morality, most certainly it is irreligious.   Nor am I
for little Naphta either, or his religion, that is only a
guazzabuglio of God and the devil, good and evil, to the
end that the individual soul may plump into it head
first, for the sake of mystic immersion in the universal.
Pedagogues both!   Their quarrels and counter-positions
are just a *guazzabuglio* too, and a confused noise of battle,
which need trouble nobody who keeps a little clear in his
head and pious in his heart.   Their aristocratic question!
Disease, health!   Spirit, nature!   Are those contra-
dictions?   I ask, are they problems?   No, they are no
problems, neither is their aristocracy a problem.   The
recklessness of death is in life, it would not be life
without it—and in the centre is the position of the *homo
Dei*, between recklessness and reason, as his state is
between mystic community and windy individualism.   I,
from my column, perceive all this.   In this state he must
live gallantly, associate in friendly reverence with himself,
for only he is aristocratic, and the counter-positions are
not at all.   Man is the lord of counter-positions, they can
be only through him, and thus he is more aristocratic
than they.   More so than death, too aristocratic for
death—that is the freedom of his mind.   More aristocratic than life, too aristocratic for life, and that is the
piety in his heart.   There is both rhyme and reason in
what I say, I have made a dream poem of humanity.   I
will cling to it.   I will be good.   I will let death have
no mastery over my thoughts.   For therein lies goodness
and love of humankind, and in nothing else.   Death is
a great power.   One takes off one's hat before him, and
goes weavingly on tiptoe.   He wears the stately ruff
of the departed and we do him honour in solemn black.
Reason stands simple before him, for reason is only virtue,
while death is release, immensity, abandon, desire.

Desire, says my dream. Lust, not love. Death and love—no, I cannot make a poem of them, they don't go together. Love stands opposed to death. It is love, not reason, that is stronger than death. Only love, not reason, gives sweet thoughts. And from love and sweetness alone can form come: form and civilization, friendly, enlightened, beautiful human intercourse — always in silent recognition of the blood-sacrifice. Ah, yes, it is well and truly dreamed. I have taken stock. I will remember. I will keep faith with death in my heart, yet well remember that faith with death and the dead is evil, is hostile to humankind, so soon as we give it power over thought and action. *For the sake of goodness and love, man shall let death have no sovereignty over his thoughts.* And with this — I awake. For I have dreamed it out to the end, I have come to my goal. Long, long have I sought after this word, in the place where Hippe appeared to me, in my loggia, everywhere. Deep into the snow mountains my search has led me. Now I have it fast. My dream has given it me, in utter clearness, that I may know it for ever. Yes, I am in simple raptures, my body is warm, my heart beats high and knows why. It beats not solely on physical grounds, as fingernails grow on a corpse; but humanly, on grounds of my joyful spirits. My dream word was a draught, better than port or ale, it streams through my veins like love and life, I tear myself from my dream and sleep, knowing as I do, perfectly well, that they are highly dangerous to my young life. Up, up! Open your eyes! These are your limbs, your legs here in the snow! Pull yourself together, and up! Look—fair weather!'

The bonds held fast that kept his limbs involved. He had a hard struggle to free himself—but the inner compulsion proved stronger. With a jerk he raised himself on his elbows, briskly drew up his knees, shoved, rolled,

wrestled to his feet; stamped with his skis in the snow,
flung his arms about his ribs and worked his shoulders
violently, all the while casting strained, alert glances
about him and above, where now a pale blue sky showed
itself between greyish-blue clouds, and these presently drew
away to discover a thin sickle of a moon.   Early twilight
reigned: no snowfall, no storm.   The wall of the opposite
mountain, with its shaggy, tree-clad ridge, stretched out
before him, plain and peaceful.   Shadow lay on half its
height, but the upper half was bathed in palest rosy light.
How were things in the world? Was it morning?
Had he, despite what the books said, lain all night in the
snow and not frozen?   Not a member was frost-bitten,
nothing snapped when he stamped, shook, and struck
himself, as he did vigorously, all the time seeking to
establish the facts of his situation.   Ears, toes, finger tips,
were of course numb, but not more so than they had often
been at night in his loggia.   He could take his watch
from his pocket—it was still going, it had not stopped, as
it did if he forgot to wind it.   It said not yet five—was
in fact considerably earlier, twelve, thirteen minutes.
Preposterous!   Could it be he had lain here in the snow
only ten minutes or so, while all those scenes of horror
and delight and those presumptuous thoughts had spun
themselves in his brain, and the hexagonal hurly vanished
as it came?   If that were true, then he must be grateful
for his good fortune; that is, from the point of view of a
safe home-coming.   For twice such a turn had come, in
his dream and fantasy, as had made him start up—once
from horror, and again for rapture.   It seemed, indeed,
that life meant well by her lone-wandering delicate child.

Be all that as it might, and whether it was morning
or afternoon—there could in fact be no doubt that it was
still late afternoon—in any case, there was nothing in the
circumstances or in his own condition to prevent his going

home, which he accordingly did: descending in a fine sweep, as the crow flies, to the valley, where, as he reached it, lights were showing, though his way had been well enough lighted by reflection from the snow. He came down the Brehmenbühl, along the edge of the forest, and was in the Dorf by half-past five. He left his skis at the grocer's, rested a little in Herr Settembrini's attic cell, and told him how the storm had overtaken him in the mountains. The horrified humanist scolded him roundly, and straightway lighted his spirit kettle to brew coffee for the exhausted one—the strength of which did not prevent Hans Castorp from falling asleep as he sat.

An hour later the highly civilized atmosphere of the Berghof caressed him. He ate enormously at dinner. What he had dreamed was already fading from his mind. What he had thought—even that selfsame evening it was no longer so clear as it had been at first.

MARIO AND THE MAGICIAN

THE atmosphere of Torre di Venere remains unpleasant in the memory. From the first moment the air of the place made us uneasy, we felt irritable, on edge; then at the end came the shocking business of Cipolla, that dreadful being who seemed to incorporate, in so fateful and so humanly impressive a way, all the peculiar evilness of the situation as a whole. Looking back, we had the feeling that the horrible end of the affair had been preordained and lay in the nature of things; that the children had to be present at it was an added impropriety, due to the false colours in which the weird creature presented himself. Luckily for them, they did not know where the comedy left off and the tragedy began; and we let them remain in their happy belief that the whole thing had been a play up till the end.

Torre di Venere lies some fifteen kilometres from Portoclemente, one of the most popular summer resorts on the Tyrrhenian Sea. Portoclemente is urban and elegant and full to overflowing for months on end. Its gay and busy main street of shops and hotels runs down to a wide sandy beach covered with tents and pennanted sand castles and sunburnt humanity, where at all times a lively social bustle reigns, and much noise. But this same spacious and inviting fine-sanded beach, this same border of pine grove and near, presiding mountains, continues all the way along the coast. No wonder then that some competition of a quiet kind should have sprung up further on. Torre di Venere—the tower that gave the town its name is gone long since, one looks for it in vain—is an offshoot of the larger resort, and for some years remained an idyll for the few, a refuge for more unworldly spirits.   But the usual history of such places repeated itself: peace has had to retire further along the coast, to Marina Petriera and dear knows where else.   We all know how the world at once seeks peace and puts her to flight—rushing upon her in the fond idea that they two will wed, and where she is, there it can be at home.   It will even set up its Vanity Fair in a spot and be capable of thinking that peace is still by its side.   Thus Torre—though its atmosphere so far is more modest and contemplative than that of Portoclemente —has been quite taken up, by both Italians and foreigners. It is no longer the thing to go to Portoclemente—though still so much the thing that it is as noisy and crowded as ever.   One goes next door, so to speak: to Torre.   So much more refined, even, and cheaper to boot.   And the attractiveness of these qualities persists, though the qualities themselves long ago ceased to be evident.   Torre has got a Grand Hotel.   Numerous pensions have sprung up, some modest, some pretentious.   The people who own or rent the villas and pinetas overlooking the sea no longer have it all their own way on the beach.   In July and August it looks just like the beach at Portoclemente: it swarms with a screaming, squabbling, merrymaking crowd, and the sun, blazing down like mad, peels the skin off their necks.   Garish little flat-bottomed boats rock on the glittering blue, manned by children, whose mothers hover afar and fill the air with anxious cries of Nino! and Sandro! and Bice! and Maria!   Pedlars step across the legs of recumbent sun bathers, selling flowers and corals, oysters, lemonade, and *cornetti al burro*, and crying their wares in the breathy, full-throated southern voice.

Such was the scene that greeted our arrival in Torre: pleasant enough, but after all, we thought, we had come too soon.   It was the middle of August, the Italian season was still at its height, scarcely the moment for strangers to learn to love the special charms of the place. What an afternoon crowd in the cafés on the front! For instance, in the Esquisito, where we sometimes sat and were served by Mario, that very Mario of whom I shall have presently to tell. It is well-nigh impossible to find a table; and the various orchestras contend together in the midst of one's conversation with bewildering effect. Of course, it is in the afternoon that people come over from Portoclemente. The excursion is a favourite one for the restless denizens of that pleasure resort, and a Fiat motor bus plies to and fro, coating inch-thick with dust the oleander and laurel hedges along the high road—a notable if repulsive sight.

Yes, decidedly one should go to Torre in September, when the great public has left. Or else in May, before the water is warm enough to tempt the southerner to bathe. Even in the before and after seasons Torre is not empty, but life is less national and more subdued. English, French, and German prevail under the tent awnings and in the pension dining-rooms; whereas in August—in the Grand Hotel, at least, where, in default of private addresses, we had engaged rooms—the stranger finds the field so occupied by Florentine and Roman society that he feels quite isolated and even temporarily *déclassé*.

We had, rather to our annoyance, this experience on the evening we arrived, when we went in to dinner and were shown to our table by the waiter in charge. As a table it had nothing against it, save that we had already fixed our eyes upon those on the veranda beyond, built out over the water, where little red-shaded lamps glowed—and there were still some tables empty, though it was as full as the dining-room within. The children went into raptures at the festive sight, and without more ado we announced our intention to take our meals by preference in the veranda. Our words, it appeared, were prompted by ignorance; for we were informed, with somewhat embarrassed politeness, that the cosy nook outside was reserved for the clients of the hotel: 'ai nostri clienti.' Their clients? But we were their clients. We were not tourists or trippers, but boarders for a stay of some three or four weeks. However, we forbore to press for an explanation of the difference between the likes of us and that clientele to whom it was vouchsafed to eat out there in the glow of the red lamps, and took our dinner by the prosaic common light of the dining-room chandelier—a thoroughly ordinary and monotonous hotel bill of fare, be it said. In Pensione Eleonora, a few steps landward, the table, as we were to discover, was much better.

And thither it was that we moved, three or four days later, before we had had time to settle in properly at the Grand Hotel. Not on account of the veranda and the lamps. The children, straightway on the best of terms with waiters and pages, absorbed in the joys of life on the beach, promptly forgot those colourful seductions. But now there arose, between ourselves and the veranda clientele—or perhaps more correctly with the compliant management—one of those little unpleasantnesses which can quite spoil the pleasure of a holiday. Among the guests were some high Roman aristocracy, a Principe X and his family. These grand folk occupied rooms close to our own, and the principessa, a great and a passionately maternal lady, was thrown into a panic by the vestiges of a whooping cough which our little ones had lately got over, but which now and then still faintly troubled the unshatterable slumbers of our youngest born. The nature of this illness is not clear, leaving some play for the imagination. So we took no offence at our elegant neighbour for clinging to the widely held view that whooping cough is acoustically contagious and quite simply fearing lest her children should yield to the bad example set by ours. In the

fullness of her feminine self-confidence she protested to the
management, which then, in the person of the proverbial
frock-coated manager, hastened to represent to us, with
many expressions of regret, that under the circumstances
they were obliged to transfer us to the annexe. We did our
best to assure him that the disease was in its very last stages,
that it was actually over, and presented no danger of infection to anybody. All that we gained was permission to bring
the case before the hotel physician—not one chosen by us
—by whose verdict we must then abide. We agreed,
convinced that thus we should at once pacify the princess
and escape the trouble of moving. The doctor appeared,
and behaved like a faithful and honest servant of science.
He examined the child and gave his opinion: the disease
was quite over, no danger of contagion was present. We
drew a long breath and considered the incident closed—
until the manager announced that despite the doctor's
verdict it would still be necessary for us to give up our
rooms and retire to the *dépendance*. Byzantinism like
this outraged us. It is not likely that the principessa was
responsible for the wilful breach of faith. Very likely the
fawning management had not even dared to tell her what
the physician said. Anyhow, we made it clear to his
understanding that we preferred to leave the hotel
altogether and at once—and packed our trunks. We
could do so with a light heart, having already set up casual
friendly relations with Casa Eleonora. We had noticed
its pleasant exterior and formed the acquaintance of its
proprietor, Signora Angiolieri, and her husband: she
slender and black-haired, Tuscan in type, probably at the
beginning of the thirties, with the dead ivory complexion
of the southern woman, he quiet and bald and carefully
dressed. They owned a larger establishment in Florence
and presided only in summer and early autumn over the
branch in Torre di Venere. But earlier, before her mar-

riage, our new landlady had been companion, fellow traveller, wardrobe mistress, yes, friend of Eleonora Duse and manifestly regarded that period as the crown of her career. Even at our first visit she spoke of it with animation. Numerous photographs of the great actress, with affectionate inscriptions, were displayed about the drawing-room, and other souvenirs of their life together adorned the little tables and *étagères*. This cult of a so interesting past was calculated, of course, to heighten the advantages of the signora's present business. Nevertheless our pleasure and interest were quite genuine as we were conducted through the house by its owner and listened to her sonorous and staccato Tuscan voice relating anecdotes of that immortal mistress, depicting her suffering saintliness, her genius, her profound delicacy of feeling.

Thither, then, we moved our effects, to the dismay of the staff of the Grand Hotel, who, like all Italians, were very good to children. Our new quarters were retired and pleasant, we were within easy reach of the sea through the avenue of young plane trees that ran down to the esplanade. In the clean, cool dining-room Signora Angiolieri daily served the soup with her own hands, the service was attentive and good, the table capital. We even discovered some Viennese acquaintances, and enjoyed chatting with them after luncheon, in front of the house. They, in their turn, were the means of our finding others—in short, all seemed for the best, and we were heartily glad of the change we had made. Nothing was now wanting to a holiday of the most gratifying kind.

And yet no proper gratification ensued. Perhaps the stupid occasion of our change of quarters pursued us to the new ones we had found. Personally, I admit that I do not easily forget these collisions with ordinary humanity, the naïve misuse of power, the injustice, the sycophantic corruption. I dwelt upon the incident too much, it irritated me in retrospect—quite futilely, of course, since such phenomena are only all too natural and all too much the rule. And we had not broken off relations with the Grand Hotel. The children were as friendly as ever there, the porter mended their toys, and we sometimes took tea in the garden. We even saw the principessa. She would come out, with her firm and delicate tread, her lips emphatically corallined, to look after her children, playing under the supervision of their English governess. She did not dream that we were anywhere near, for so soon as she appeared in the offing we sternly forbade our little one even to clear his throat.

The heat—if I may bring it in evidence—was extreme. It was African. The power of the sun, directly one left the border of the indigo-blue wave, was so frightful, so relentless, that the mere thought of the few steps between the beach and luncheon was a burden, clad though one might be only in pyjamas. Do you care for that sort of thing? Weeks on end? Yes, of course, it is proper to the south, it is classic weather, the sun of Homer, the climate wherein human culture came to flower—and all the rest of it. But after a while it is too much for me, I reach a point where I begin to find it dull. The burning void of the sky, day after day, weighs one down; the high coloration, the enormous *naïveté* of the unrefracted light —they do, I dare say, induce lightheartedness, a carefree mood born of immunity from downpours and other meteorological caprices. But slowly, slowly, there makes itself felt a lack: the deeper, more complex needs of the northern soul remain unsatisfied. You are left barren— even, it may be, in time, a little contemptuous. True, without that stupid business of the whooping cough I might not have been feeling these things. I was annoyed, very likely I wanted to feel them and so half unconsciously seized upon an idea lying ready to hand to induce, or if not to induce, at least to justify and strengthen, my attitude. Up to this point, then, if you like, let us grant some ill will on our part. But the sea; and the mornings spent extended upon the fine sand in face of its eternal splendours —no, the sea could not conceivably induce such feelings. Yet it was none the less true that, despite all previous experience, we were not at home on the beach, we were not happy.

It was too soon, too soon. The beach, as I have said, was still in the hands of the middle-class native. It is a pleasing breed to look at, and among the young we saw much shapeliness and charm. Still, we were necessarily surrounded by a great deal of very average humanity—a middle-class mob, which, you will admit, is not more charming under this sun than under one's own native sky. The voices these women have! It was sometimes hard to believe that we were in the land which is the western cradle of the art of song. 'Fuggièro!' I can still hear that cry, as for twenty mornings long I heard it close behind me, breathy, full-throated, hideously stressed, with a harsh open *e*, uttered in accents of mechanical despair. 'Fuggièro! Rispondi almeno!' Answer when I call you! The *sp* in *rispondi* was pronounced like *shp*, as Germans pronounce it; and this, on top of what I felt already, vexed my sensitive soul. The cry was addressed to a repulsive youngster whose sunburn had made disgusting raw sores on his shoulders. He outdid anything I have ever seen for ill-breeding, refractoriness, and temper, and was a great coward to boot, putting the whole beach in an uproar, one day, because of his outrageous sensitiveness to the slightest pain. A sand crab had pinched his toe in the water, and the minute injury made him set up a cry of heroic proportions—the shout of an antique hero in his agony—that pierced one to the marrow and called up visions of some frightful tragedy. Evidently he

considered himself not only wounded, but poisoned as well;
he crawled out on the sand and lay in apparently intolerable
anguish, groaning 'Ohi!' and 'Ohimè!' and thrashing
about with arms and legs to ward off his mother's tragic
appeals and the questions of the bystanders.   An audience
gathered round.   A doctor was fetched—the same who
had pronounced objective judgment on our whooping
cough—and here again acquitted himself like a man of
science.   Good-naturedly he reassured the boy, telling
him that he was not hurt at all, he should simply go into
the water again to relieve the smart.   Instead of which,
Fuggièro was borne off the beach, followed by a concourse
of people.   But he did not fail to appear next morning,
nor did he leave off spoiling our children's sand castles.
Of course, always by accident.   In short, a perfect terror.

And this twelve-year-old lad was prominent among the
influences that, imperceptibly at first, combined to spoil our
holiday and render it unwholesome.   Somehow or other,
there was a stiffness, a lack of innocent enjoyment.   These
people stood on their dignity—just why, and in what spirit,
it was not easy at first to tell.   They displayed much
self-respectingness; towards each other and towards the
foreigner their bearing was that of a person newly conscious of a sense of honour.   And wherefore?   Gradually
we realized the political implications and understood that
we were in the presence of a national ideal.   The beach,
in fact, was alive with patriotic children—a phenomenon
as unnatural as it was depressing.   Children are a human
species and a society apart, a nation of their own, so to
speak.   On the basis of their common form of life, they
find each other out with the greatest ease, no matter how
different their small vocabularies.   Ours soon played with
natives and foreigners alike.   Yet they were plainly both
puzzled and disappointed at times.   There were wounded
sensibilities, displays of assertiveness—or rather hardly

assertiveness, for it was too self-conscious and too didactic to deserve the name. There were quarrels over flags, disputes about authority and precedence. Grown-ups joined in, not so much to pacify as to render judgment and enunciate principles. Phrases were dropped about the greatness and dignity of Italy, solemn phrases that spoilt the fun. We saw our two little ones retreat, puzzled and hurt, and were put to it to explain the situation. These people, we told them, were just passing through a certain stage, something rather like an illness, perhaps; not very pleasant, but probably unavoidable.

We had only our own carelessness to thank that we came to blows in the end with this 'stage'—which, after all, we had seen and sized up long before now. Yes, it came to another 'cross-purposes,' so evidently the earlier ones had not been sheer accident. In a word, we became an offence to the public morals. Our small daughter— eight years old, but in physical development a good year younger and thin as a chicken—had had a good long bathe and gone playing in the warm sun in her wet costume. We told her that she might take off her bathing suit, which was stiff with sand, rinse it in the sea, and put it on again, after which she must take care to keep it cleaner. Off goes the costume and she runs down naked to the sea, rinses her little jersey, and comes back. Ought we to have foreseen the outburst of anger and resentment which her conduct, and thus our conduct, called forth? With- out delivering a homily on the subject, I may say that in the last decade our attitude towards the nude body and our feelings regarding it have undergone, all over the world, a fundamental change. There are things we 'never think about' any more, and among them is the freedom we had permitted to this by no means provocative little childish body. But in these parts it was taken as a challenge. The patriotic children hooted. Fuggièro whistled on his fingers. The sudden buzz of conversation among the grown people in our neighbourhood boded no good. A gentleman in city togs, with a not very apropos bowler hat on the back of his head, was assuring his outraged women-folk that he proposed to take punitive measures; he stepped up to us, and a philippic descended on our unworthy heads, in which all the emotionalism of the sense-loving south spoke in the service of morality and discipline. The offence against decency of which we had been guilty was, he said, the more to be condemned because it was also a gross ingratitude and an insulting breach of his country's hospitality. We had criminally injured not only the letter and spirit of the public bathing regulations, but also the honour of Italy; he, the gentleman in the city togs, knew how to defend that honour and proposed to see to it that our offence against the national dignity should not go unpunished.

We did our best, bowing respectfully, to give ear to this eloquence. To contradict the man, overheated as he was, would probably be to fall from one error into another. On the tips of our tongues we had various answers: as, that the word 'hospitality,' in its strictest sense, was not quite the right one, taking all the circumstances into consideration. We were not literally the guests of Italy, but of Signora Angiolieri, who had assumed the role of dispenser of hospitality some years ago on laying down that of familiar friend to Eleonora Duse. We longed to say that surely this beautiful country had not sunk so low as to be reduced to a state of hypersensitive prudishness. But we confined ourselves to assuring the gentleman that any lack of respect, any provocation on our parts, had been the furthest from our thoughts. And as a mitigating circumstance we pointed out the tender age and physical slightness of the little culprit. In vain. Our protests were waved away, he did not believe in them; our defence would not

hold water. We must be made an example of. The
authorities were notified, by telephone, I believe, and
their representative appeared on the beach. He said the
case was 'molto grave.' We had to go with him to the
Municipio up in the Piazza, where a higher official confirmed the previous verdict of 'molto grave,' launched into
a stream of the usual didactic phrases—the selfsame tune
and words of the man in the bowler hat—and levied a fine
and ransom of fifty lire. We felt that the adventure must
willy-nilly be worth to us this much of a contribution to
the economy of the Italian Government; paid, and left.
Ought we not at this point to have left Torre as well?

If we only had! We should thus have escaped that
fatal Cipolla. But circumstances combined to prevent us
from making up our minds to a change. A certain poet
says that it is indolence that makes us endure uncomfortable situations. The *aperçu* may serve as an explanation
for our inaction. Anyhow, one dislikes voiding the field
immediately upon such an event. Especially if sympathy
from other quarters encourages one to defy it. And in the
Villa Eleonora they pronounced as with one voice upon
the injustice of our punishment. Some Italian after-
dinner acquaintances found that the episode put their
country in a very bad light, and proposed taking the man
in the bowler hat to task, as one fellow citizen to another.
But the next day he and his party had vanished from the
beach. Not on our account, of course. Though it
might be that the consciousness of his impending departure
had added energy to his rebuke; in any case his going was
a relief. And, furthermore, we stayed because our stay
had by now become remarkable in our own eyes, which is
worth something in itself, quite apart from the comfort or
discomfort involved. Shall we strike sail, avoid a certain
experience so soon as it seems not expressly calculated to
increase our enjoyment or our self-esteem? Shall we go

away whenever life looks like turning in the slightest uncanny, or not quite normal, or even rather painful and
mortifying? No, surely not. Rather stay and look
matters in the face, brave them out; perhaps precisely in
so doing lies a lesson for us to learn. We stayed on and
reaped as the awful reward of our constancy the unholy
and staggering experience with Cipolla.

I have not mentioned that the after season had begun,
almost on the very day we were disciplined by the city
authorities. The worshipful gentleman in the bowler
hat, our denouncer, was not the only person to leave the
resort. There was a regular exodus, on every hand you
saw luggage carts on their way to the station. The
beach denationalized itself. Life in Torre, in the cafés
and the pinetas, became more homelike and more
European. Very likely we might even have eaten at a
table in the glass veranda, but we refrained, being content
at Signora Angiolieri's—as content, that is, as our evil star
would let us be. But at the same time with this turn for
the better came a change in the weather: almost to an hour
it showed itself in harmony with the holiday calendar of
the general public. The sky was overcast; not that it
grew any cooler, but the unclouded heat of the entire
eighteen days since our arrival, and probably long before
that, gave place to a stifling sirocco air, while from time
to time a little ineffectual rain sprinkled the velvety surface
of the beach. Add to which, that two-thirds of our intended stay at Torre had passed. The colourless, lazy
sea, with sluggish jelly-fish floating in its shallows, was at
least a change. And it would have been silly to feel
retrospective longings after a sun that had caused us so
many sighs when it burned down in all its arrogant power.

At this juncture, then, it was that Cipolla announced
himself. Cavaliere Cipolla he was called on the posters
that appeared one day stuck up everywhere, even in the

dining-room of Pensione Eleonora. A travelling virtuoso, an entertainer, 'forzatore, illusionista, prestigiatore,' as he called himself, who proposed to wait upon the highly respectable population of Torre di Venere with a display of extraordinary phenomena of a mysterious and staggering kind. A conjuror! The bare announcement was enough to turn our children's heads. They had never seen anything of the sort, and now our present holiday was to afford them this new excitement. From that moment on they besieged us with prayers to take tickets for the performance. We had doubts, from the first, on the score of the lateness of the hour, nine o'clock; but gave way, in the idea that we might see a little of what Cipolla had to offer, probably no great matter, and then go home. Besides, of course, the children could sleep late next day. We bought four tickets of Signora Angiolieri herself, she having taken a number of the stalls on commission to sell them to her guests. She could not vouch for the man's performance, and we had no great expectations. But we were conscious of a need for diversion, and the children's violent curiosity proved catching.

The cavaliere's performance was to take place in a hall where during the season there had been a cinema with a weekly programme. We had never been there. You reached it by following the main street under the wall of the *palazzo*, a ruin with a 'For sale' sign, that suggested a castle and had obviously been built in lordlier days. In the same street were the chemist, the hairdresser, and all the better shops; it led, so to speak, from the feudal past the bourgeois into the proletarian, for it ended off between two rows of poor fishing huts, where old women sat mending nets before the doors. And here, among the proletariat, was the hall, not much more, actually, than a wooden shed, though a large one, with a turreted entrance, plastered on either side with layers of gay placards. Some while after dinner, then, on the appointed evening, we wended our way thither in the dark, the children dressed in their best and blissful with the sense of so much irregularity.   It was sultry, as it had been for days; there was heat lightning now and then, and a little rain; we proceeded under umbrellas.   It took us a quarter of an hour.

Our tickets were collected at the entrance, our places we had to find ourselves.   They were in the third row left, and as we sat down we saw that, late though the hour was for the performance, it was to be interpreted with even more laxity.   Only very slowly did an audience—who seemed to be relied upon to come late—begin to fill the stalls.   These comprised the whole auditorium; there were no boxes.   This tardiness gave us some concern. The children's cheeks were already flushed as much with fatigue as with excitement.   But even when we entered, the standing room at the back and in the side aisles was already well occupied.   There stood the manhood of Torre di Venere, all and sundry, fisherfolk, rough-and-ready youths with bare forearms crossed over their striped jerseys.   We were well pleased with the presence of this native assemblage, which always adds colour and animation to occasions like the present; and the children were frankly delighted.   For they had friends among these people— acquaintances picked up on afternoon strolls to the further ends of the beach.   We would be turning homeward, at the hour when the sun dropped into the sea, spent with the huge effort it had made and gilding with reddish gold the oncoming surf; and we would come upon bare-legged fisherfolk standing in rows, bracing and hauling with long-drawn cries as they drew in the nets and harvested in dripping baskets their catch, often so scanty, of *frutta di mare*. The children looked on, helped to pull, brought out their little stock of Italian words, made friends.   So now they exchanged nods with the 'standing room' clientele; there

was Guiscardo, there Antonio, they knew them by name
and waved and called across in half-whispers, getting
answering nods and smiles that displayed rows of healthy
white teeth.   Look, there is even Mario, Mario from the
Esquisito, who brings us the chocolate.   He wants to see
the conjuror, too, and he must have come early, for he is
almost in front; but he does not see us, he is not paying
attention; that is a way he has, even though he is a waiter.
So we wave instead to the man who lets out the little boats
on the beach; he is there too, standing at the back.

It had got to a quarter-past nine, it got to almost half-
past.   It was natural that we should be nervous.   When
would the children get to bed?   It had been a mistake to
bring them, for now it would be very hard to suggest
breaking off their enjoyment before it had got well under
way.   The stalls had filled in time; all Torre, apparently,
was there: the guests of the Grand Hotel, the guests
of Villa Eleonora, familiar faces from the beach.   We
heard English and German and the sort of French that
Rumanians speak with Italians.   Madame Angiolieri herself sat two rows behind us, with her quiet, bald-headed
spouse, who kept stroking his moustache with the two
middle fingers of his right hand.   Everybody had come
late, but nobody too late.   Cipolla made us wait for him.

He made us wait.   That is probably the way to put it.
He heightened the suspense by his delay in appearing.
And we could see the point of this, too—only not when it
was carried to extremes.   Towards half-past nine the
audience began to clap—an amiable way of expressing
justifiable impatience, evincing as it does an eagerness to
applaud.   For the little ones, this was a joy in itself—all
children love to clap.   From the popular sphere came
loud cries of 'Pronti!' 'Cominciamo!'   And lo, it
seemed now as easy to begin as before it had been hard.
A gong sounded, greeted by the standing rows with a

many-voiced 'Ah-h!' and the curtains parted. They revealed a platform furnished more like a schoolroom than like the theatre of a conjuring performance—largely because of the blackboard in the left foreground. There was a common yellow hat stand, a few ordinary straw-bottomed chairs, and further back a little round table holding a water carafe and glass, also a tray with a liqueur glass and a flask of pale yellow liquid. We had still a few seconds of time to let these things sink in. Then, with no darkening of the house, Cavaliere Cipolla made his entry.

He came forward with a rapid step that expressed his eagerness to appear before his public and gave rise to the illusion that he had already come a long way to put himself at their service—whereas, of course, he had only been standing in the wings. His costume supported the fiction. A man of an age hard to determine, but by no means young; with a sharp, ravaged face, piercing eyes, compressed lips, small black waxed moustache, and a so-called imperial in the curve between mouth and chin. He was dressed for the street with a sort of complicated evening elegance, in a wide black pelerine with velvet collar and satin lining; which, in the hampered state of his arms, he held together in front with his white-gloved hands. He had a white scarf round his neck; a top hat with a curving brim sat far back on his head. Perhaps more than anywhere else the eighteenth century is still alive in Italy, and with it the charlatan and mountebank type so characteristic of the period. Only there, at any rate, does one still encounter really well-preserved specimens. Cipolla had in his whole appearance much of the historic type; his very clothes helped to conjure up the traditional figure with its blatantly, fantastically foppish air. His pretentious costume sat upon him, or rather hung upon him, most curiously, being in one place drawn too tight, in another a

mass of awkward folds.   There was something not quite
in order about his figure, both front and back—that was
plain later on.   But I must emphasize the fact that there
was not a trace of personal jocularity or clownishness in
his pose, manner, or behaviour.   On the contrary, there
was complete seriousness, an absence of any humorous
appeal; occasionally even a cross-grained pride, along with
that curious, self-satisfied air so characteristic of the deformed.   None of all this, however, prevented his appearance from being greeted with laughter from more than one
quarter of the hall.

All the eagerness had left his manner.   The swift entry
had been merely an expression of energy, not of zeal.
Standing at the footlights he negligently drew off his
gloves, to display long yellow hands, one of them adorned
with a seal ring with a lapis lazuli in a high setting.   As
he stood there, his small hard eyes, with flabby pouches
beneath them, roved appraisingly about the hall, not
quickly, rather in a considered examination, pausing here
and there upon a face with his lips clipped together, not
speaking a word.   Then with a display of skill as surprising as it was casual, he rolled his gloves into a ball and
tossed them across a considerable distance into the glass on
the table.   Next from an inner pocket he drew forth a
packet of cigarettes; you could see by the wrapper that they
were the cheapest sort the Government sells.   With his
finger tips he pulled out a cigarette and lighted it, without
looking, from a quick-firing benzine lighter.   He drew
the smoke deep into his lungs and let it out again, tapping
his foot, with both lips drawn in an arrogant grimace and
the grey smoke streaming out between broken and saw-
edged teeth.

With a keenness equal to his own his audience eyed
him.   The youths at the rear scowled as they peered at
this cocksure creature to search out his secret weaknesses.

He betrayed none.   In fetching out and putting back the cigarettes his clothes got in his way.   He had to turn back his pelerine, and in so doing revealed a riding-whip with a silver claw-handle that hung by a leather thong from his left forearm and looked decidedly out of place.   You could see that he had on not evening clothes but a frock coat, and under this, as he lifted it to get at his pocket, could be seen a striped sash worn about the body.   Some-body behind me whispered that this sash went with his title of cavaliere.   I give the information for what it may be worth—personally, I never heard that the title carried such insignia with it.   Perhaps the sash was sheer pose, like the way he stood there, without a word, casually and arrogantly puffing smoke into his audience's face.

People laughed, as I said.   The merriment had become almost general when somebody in the 'standing seats,' in a loud, dry voice, remarked: 'Buona sera.'

Cipolla cocked his head.   'Who was that?' asked he, as though he had been dared.   'Who was that just spoke? Well?   First so bold and now so modest?   *Paura*, eh?' He spoke with a rather high, asthmatic voice, which yet had a metallic quality.   He waited.

'That was me,' a youth at the rear broke into the still-ness, seeing himself thus challenged.   He was not far from us, a handsome fellow in a woollen shirt, with his coat hanging over one shoulder.   He wore his curly, wiry hair in a high, dishevelled mop, the style affected by the youth of the awakened Fatherland; it gave him an African appearance that rather spoiled his looks.   'Bé! That was me.   It was your business to say it first, but I was trying to be friendly.'

More laughter.   The chap had a tongue in his head.

'Ha sciolto la scilinguágnolo,' I heard near me.   After all, the retort was deserved.

'Ah, bravo!' answered Cipolla.   'I like you, *gio-*

vanotto. Trust me, I 've had my eye on you for some time. People like you are just in my line. I can use them. And you are the pick of the lot, that 's plain to see. You do what you like. Or is it possible you have ever not done what you liked—or even, maybe, what you didn't like? What somebody else liked, in short? Hark ye, my friend, that might be a pleasant change for you, to divide up the willing and the doing and stop tackling both jobs at once. Division of labour, sistema americano, sa'! For instance, suppose you were to show your tongue to this select and honourable audience here—your whole tongue, right down to the roots?'

'No, I won't,' said the youth, hostilely. 'Sticking out your tongue shows a bad bringing up.'

'Nothing of the sort,' retorted Cipolla. 'You would only be *doing* it. With all due respect to your bringing up, I suggest that before I count ten, you will perform a right turn and stick out your tongue at the company here further than you knew yourself that you could stick it out.'

He gazed at the youth, and his piercing eyes seemed to sink deeper into their sockets. 'Uno!' said he. He had let his riding-whip slide down his arm and made it whistle once through the air. The boy faced about and put out his tongue, so long, so extendedly, that you could see it was the very uttermost in tongue which he had to offer. Then turned back, stony-faced, to his former position.

'That was me,' mocked Cipolla, with a jerk of his head towards the youth. 'Bé! That was me.' Leaving the audience to enjoy its sensations, he turned towards the little round table, lifted the bottle, poured out a small glass of what was obviously cognac, and tipped it up with a practised hand.

The children laughed with all their hearts. They had understood practically nothing of what had been said, but it pleased them hugely that something so funny should happen, straightway, between that queer man up there and somebody out of the audience. They had no pre-conception of what an 'evening' would be like and were quite ready to find this a priceless beginning. As for us, we exchanged a glance and I remember that involuntarily I made with my lips the sound that Cipolla's whip had made when it cut the air. For the rest, it was plain that people did not know what to make of a preposterous begin-ning like this to a sleight-of-hand performance. They could not see why the *giovanotto*, who after all in a way had been their spokesman, should suddenly have turned on them to vent his incivility. They felt that he had be-haved like a silly ass and withdrew their countenances from him in favour of the artist, who now came back from his refreshment table and addressed them as follows:

'Ladies and gentlemen,' said he, in his wheezing, metallic voice, 'you saw just now that I was rather sensi-tive on the score of the rebuke this hopeful young linguist saw fit to give me'—'questo linguista di belle speranze' was what he said, and we all laughed at the pun. 'I am a man who sets some store by himself, you may take it from me. And I see no point in being wished a good evening unless it is done courteously and in all seriousness. For anything else there is no occasion. When a man wishes me a good evening he wishes himself one, for the audience will have one only if I do. So this lady-killer of Torre di Venere' (another thrust) 'did well to testify that I have one to-night and that I can dispense with any wishes of his in the matter. I can boast of having good evenings almost without exception. One not so good does come my way now and again, but very seldom. My calling is hard and my health not of the best. I have a little physical defect which prevented me from doing my bit in the War for the greater glory of the Fatherland. It is perforce with my mental and spiritual parts that I conquer life—which after all only means conquering oneself. And I flatter myself that my achievements have aroused interest and respect among the educated public. The leading newspapers have lauded me, the *Corriere della Sera* did me the courtesy of calling me a phenomenon, and in Rome the brother of the Duce honoured me by his presence at one of my evenings. I should not have thought that in a relatively less important place' (laughter here, at the expense of poor little Torre) 'I should have to give up the small personal habits which brilliant and elevated audiences had been ready to overlook. Nor did I think I had to stand being heckled by a person who seems to have been rather spoilt by the favours of the fair sex.' All this of course at the expense of the youth whom Cipolla never tired of presenting in the guise of *donnaiuolo* and rustic Don Juan. His persistent thin-skinnedness and animosity were in striking contrast to the self-confidence and the worldly success he boasted of. One might have assumed that the *giovanotto* was merely the chosen butt of Cipolla's customary professional sallies, had not the very pointed witticisms betrayed a genuine antagonism. No one looking at the physical parts of the two men need have been at a loss for the explanation, even if the deformed man had not constantly played on the other's supposed success with the fair sex. 'Well,' Cipolla went on, 'before beginning our entertainment this evening, perhaps you will permit me to make myself comfortable.'

And he went towards the hat stand to take off his things.

'Parla benissimo,' asserted somebody in our neighbourhood. So far, the man had done nothing; but what he had said was accepted as an achievement, by means of that he had made an impression. Among southern peoples speech is a constituent part of the pleasure of living, it enjoys far livelier social esteem than in the north. That national cement, the mother tongue, is paid symbolic

honours down here, and there is something blithely symbolical in the pleasure people take in their respect for its
forms and phonetics.   They enjoy speaking, they enjoy
listening; and they listen with discrimination.   For the
way a man speaks serves as a measure of his personal rank;
carelessness and clumsiness are greeted with scorn,
elegance and mastery are rewarded with social éclat.
Wherefore the small man too, where it is a question of
getting his effect, chooses his phrase nicely and turns it
with care.   On this count, then, at least, Cipolla had won
his audience; though he by no means belonged to the class
of men which the Italian, in a singular mixture of moral
and aesthetic judgments, labels 'simpatico.'

After removing his hat, scarf, and mantle he came to
the front of the stage, settling his coat, pulling down his
cuffs with their large cuff buttons, adjusting his absurd
sash.   He had very ugly hair; the top of his head, that is,
was almost bald, while a narrow, black-varnished frizz of
curls ran from front to back as though stuck on; the side
hair, likewise blackened, was brushed forward to the corners of the eyes—it was, in short, the hairdressing of an
old-fashioned circus director, fantastic, but entirely suited
to his outmoded personal type and worn with so much
assurance as to take the edge off the public's sense of
humour.   The little physical defect of which he had
warned us was now all too visible, though the nature of it
was even now not very clear: the chest was too high, as
is usual in such cases; but the corresponding malformation
of the back did not sit between the shoulders, it took the
form of a sort of hips or buttocks hump, which did not
indeed hinder his movements but gave him a grotesque
and dipping stride at every step he took.   However, by
mentioning his deformity beforehand he had broken the
shock of it, and a delicate propriety of feeling appeared to
reign throughout the hall.

'At your service,' said Cipolla. 'With your kind permission, we will begin the evening with some arithmetical tests.'

Arithmetic? That did not sound much like sleight-of-hand. We began to have our suspicions that the man was sailing under a false flag, only we did not yet know which was the right one. I felt sorry on the children's account; but for the moment they were content simply to be there.

The numerical test which Cipolla now introduced was as simple as it was baffling. He began by fastening a piece of paper to the upper right-hand corner of the blackboard; then lifting it up, he wrote something underneath. He talked all the while, relieving the dryness of his offering by a constant flow of words, and showed himself a practised speaker, never at a loss for conversational turns of phrase. It was in keeping with the nature of his performance, and at the same time vastly entertained the children, that he went on to eliminate the gap between stage and audience, which had already been bridged over by the curious skirmish with the fisher lad: he had representatives from the audience mount the stage, and himself descended the wooden steps to seek personal contact with his public. And again, with individuals, he fell into his former taunting tone. I do not know how far that was a deliberate feature of his system; he preserved a serious, even a peevish air, but his audience, at least the more popular section, seemed convinced that that was all part of the game. So then, after he had written something and covered the writing by the paper, he desired that two persons should come up on the platform and help to perform the calculations. They would not be difficult, even for people not clever at figures. As usual, nobody volunteered, and Cipolla took care not to molest the more select portion of his audience. He kept to the populace. Turning to two sturdy young louts standing behind us, he beckoned them to the front, encouraging and scolding by turns. They should not stand there gaping, he said, unwilling to oblige the company. Actually, he got them in motion; with clumsy tread they came down the middle aisle, climbed the steps, and stood in front of the blackboard, grinning sheepishly at their comrades' shouts and applause. Cipolla joked with them for a few minutes, praised their heroic firmness of limb and the size of their hands, so well calculated to do this service for the public. Then he handed one of them the chalk and told him to write down the numbers as they were called out. But now the creature declared that he could not write! 'Non so scrivere,' said he in his gruff voice, and his companion added that neither did he.

God knows whether they told the truth or whether they wanted to make game of Cipolla. Anyhow, the latter was far from sharing the general merriment which their confession aroused. He was insulted and disgusted. He sat there on a straw-bottomed chair in the centre of the stage with his legs crossed, smoking a fresh cigarette out of his cheap packet; obviously it tasted the better for the cognac he had indulged in while the yokels were stumping up the steps. Again he inhaled the smoke and let it stream out between curling lips. Swinging his leg, with his gaze sternly averted from the two shamelessly chuckling creatures and from the audience as well, he stared into space as one who withdraws himself and his dignity from the contemplation of an utterly despicable phenomenon.

'Scandalous,' said he, in a sort of icy snarl. 'Go back to your places! In Italy everybody can write—in all her greatness there is no room for ignorance and unenlightenment. To accuse her of them, in the hearing of this international company, is a cheap joke, in which you yourselves cut a very poor figure and humiliate the Government and the whole country as well. If it is true that

Torre di Venere is indeed the last refuge of such ignorance, then I must blush to have visited the place—being, as I already was, aware of its inferiority to Rome in more than one respect——'

Here Cipolla was interrupted by the youth with the Nubian coiffure and his jacket across his shoulder. His fighting spirit, as we now saw, had only abdicated temporarily, and he now flung himself into the breach in defence of his native heath. 'That will do,' said he loudly. 'That's enough jokes about Torre. We all come from the place and we won't stand strangers making fun of it. These two chaps are our friends. Maybe they are no scholars, but even so they may be straighter than some folks in the room who are so free with their boasts about Rome, though they did not build it either.'

That was capital. The young man had certainly cut his eye teeth. And this sort of spectacle was good fun, even though it still further delayed the regular performance. It is always fascinating to listen to an altercation. Some people it simply amuses, they take a sort of kill-joy pleasure in not being principals. Others feel upset and uneasy, and my sympathies are with these latter, although on the present occasion I was under the impression that all this was part of the show—the analphabetic yokels no less than the *giovanotto* with the jacket. The children listened well pleased. They understood not at all, but the sound of the voices made them hold their breath. So this was a 'magic evening'—at least it was the kind they have in Italy. They expressly found it 'lovely.'

Cipolla had stood up and with two of his scooping strides was at the footlights.

'Well, well, see who's here!' said he with grim cordiality. 'An old acquaintance! A young man with his heart at the end of his tongue' (he used the word *linguaccia*, which means a coated tongue, and gave rise to much hilarity). 'That will do, my friends,' he turned to the yokels. 'I do not need you now, I have business with this deserving young man here, con questo torreggiano di Venere, this tower of Venus, who no doubt expects the gratitude of the fair as a reward for his prowess——'

'Ah, non scherziamo! We're talking earnest,' cried out the youth. His eyes flashed, and he actually made as though to pull off his jacket and proceed to direct methods of settlement.

Cipolla did not take him too seriously. We had exchanged apprehensive glances; but he was dealing with a fellow countryman and had his native soil beneath his feet. He kept quite cool and showed complete mastery of the situation. He looked at his audience, smiled, and made a sideways motion of the head towards the young cockerel as though calling the public to witness how the man's bumptiousness only served to betray the simplicity of his mind. And then, for the second time, something strange happened, which set Cipolla's calm superiority in an uncanny light, and in some mysterious and irritating way turned all the explosiveness latent in the air into matter for laughter.

Cipolla drew still nearer to the fellow, looking him in the eye with a peculiar gaze. He even came half-way down the steps that led into the auditorium on our left, so that he stood directly in front of the trouble maker, on slightly higher ground. The riding-whip hung from his arm.

'My son, you do not feel much like joking,' he said. 'It is only too natural, for any one can see that you are not feeling too well. Even your tongue, which leaves something to be desired on the score of cleanliness, indicates acute disorder of the gastric system. An evening entertainment is no place for people in your state; you yourself,

I can tell, were of several minds whether you would not do better to put on a flannel bandage and go to bed.   It was not good judgment to drink so much of that very sour white wine this afternoon.   Now you have such a colic you would like to double up with the pain.   Go ahead, don't be embarrassed.   There is a distinct relief that comes from bending over, in cases of intestinal cramp.'

He spoke thus, word for word, with quiet impressiveness and a kind of stern sympathy, and his eyes, plunged the while deep in the young man's, seemed to grow very tired and at the same time burning above their enlarged tear ducts—they were the strangest eyes, you could tell that not manly pride alone was preventing the young adversary from withdrawing his gaze.   And presently, indeed, all trace of its former arrogance was gone from the bronzed young face.   He looked open-mouthed at the cavaliere and the open mouth was drawn in a rueful smile.

'Double over,' repeated Cipolla.   'What else can you do?   With a colic like that you *must* bend.   Surely you will not struggle against the performance of a perfectly natural action just because somebody suggests it to you?'

Slowly the youth lifted his forearms, folded and squeezed them across his body; it turned a little sideways, then bent, lower and lower, the feet shifted, the knees turned inward, until he had become a picture of writhing pain, until he all but grovelled upon the ground.   Cipolla let him stand for some seconds thus, then made a short cut through the air with his whip and went with his scooping stride back to the little table, where he poured himself out a cognac.

'Il boit beaucoup,' asserted a lady behind us.   Was that the only thing that struck her?   We could not tell how far the audience grasped the situation.   The fellow was standing upright again, with a sheepish grin—he looked as though he scarcely knew how it had all happened.   The scene had been followed with tense interest and applauded at the end; there were shouts of 'Bravo, Cipolla!' and 'Bravo, giovanotto!' Apparently the issue of the duel was not looked upon as a personal defeat for the young man. Rather the audience encouraged him as one does an actor who succeeds in an unsympathetic role. Certainly his way of screwing himself up with cramp had been highly picturesque, its appeal was directly calculated to impress the gallery—in short, a fine dramatic performance. But I am not sure how far the audience were moved by that natural tactfulness in which the south excels, or how far it penetrated into the nature of what was going on.

The cavaliere, refreshed, had lighted another cigarette. The numerical tests might now proceed. A young man was easily found in the back row who was willing to write down on the blackboard the numbers as they were dictated to him. Him too we knew; the whole entertainment had taken on an intimate character through our acquaintance with so many of the actors. This was the man who worked at the greengrocer's in the main street; he had served us several times, with neatness and dispatch. He wielded the chalk with clerkly confidence, while Cipolla descended to our level and walked with his deformed gait through the audience, collecting numbers as they were given, in two, three, and four places, and calling them out to the grocer's assistant, who wrote them down in a column. In all this, everything on both sides was calculated to amuse, with its jokes and its oratorical asides. The artist could not fail to hit on foreigners, who were not ready with their figures, and with them he was elaborately patient and chivalrous, to the great amusement of the natives, whom he reduced to confusion in their turn, by making them translate numbers that were given in English or French. Some people gave dates concerned with great events in Italian history. Cipolla took them up at once and made patriotic comments. Somebody shouted: 'Number one!' The cavaliere, incensed at this as at every attempt to make game of him, retorted over his shoulder that he could not take less than two-place figures. Whereupon another joker cried out 'Number two!' and was greeted with the applause and laughter which every reference to natural functions is sure to win among southerners.

When fifteen numbers stood in a long straggling row on the board, Cipolla called for a general adding match. Ready reckoners might add in their heads, but pencil and paper were not forbidden. Cipolla, while the work went on, sat on his chair near the blackboard, smoked and grimaced, with the complacent, pompous air cripples so often have. The five-place addition was soon done. Somebody announced the answer, somebody else confirmed it, a third had arrived at a slightly different result, but the fourth agreed with the first and second. Cipolla got up, tapped some ash from his coat, and lifted the paper at the upper right-hand corner of the board to display the writing. The correct answer, a sum close on a million, stood there; he had written it down beforehand.

Astonishment, and loud applause. The children were overwhelmed. How had he done that? they wanted to know. We told them it was a trick, not easily explainable offhand. In short, the man was a conjuror. This was what a sleight-of-hand evening was like, so now they knew. First the fisherman had cramp, and then the right answer was written down beforehand—it was all simply glorious, and we saw with dismay that despite the hot eyes and the hand of the clock at almost half-past ten, it would be very hard to get them away. There would be tears. And yet it was plain that this magician did not 'magick'— at least not in the accepted sense, of manual dexterity— and that the entertainment was not at all suitable for children. Again, I do not know, either, what the

audience really thought. Obviously there was grave
doubt whether its answers had been given of 'free choice';
here and there an individual might have answered of his
own motion, but on the whole Cipolla certainly selected
his people and thus kept the whole procedure in his own
hands and directed it towards the given result.   Even so,
one had to admire the quickness of his calculations, however much one felt disinclined to admire anything else about
the performance.   Then his patriotism, his irritable sense
of dignity—the cavaliere's own countrymen might feel in
their element with all that and continue in a laughing
mood; but the combination certainly gave us outsiders food
for thought.

Cipolla himself saw to it—though without giving them
a name—that the nature of his powers should be clear
beyond a doubt to even the least instructed person.   He
alluded to them, of course, in his talk—and he talked without stopping—but only in vague, boastful, self-advertising
phrases.   He went on awhile with experiments on the
same lines as the first, merely making them more complicated by introducing operations in multiplying, sub-
tracting, and dividing; then he simplified them to the last
degree in order to bring out the method.   He simply
had numbers 'guessed' which were previously written
under the paper; and the guess was nearly always right.
One guesser admitted that he had had in mind to give a
certain number, when Cipolla's whip went whistling
through the air, and a quite different one slipped out,
which proved to be the 'right' one.   Cipolla's shoulders
shook.   He pretended admiration for the powers of the
people he questioned.   But in all his compliments there
was something fleering and derogatory; the victims could
scarcely have relished them much, although they smiled,
and although they might easily have set down some part
of the applause to their own credit.   Moreover, I had not

the impression that the artist was popular with his public. A certain ill will and reluctance were in the air, but courtesy kept such feelings in check, as did Cipolla's competency and his stern self-confidence. Even the riding-whip, I think, did much to keep rebellion from becoming overt.

From tricks with numbers he passed to tricks with cards. There were two packs, which he drew out of his pockets, and so much I still remember, that the basis of the tricks he played with them was as follows: From the first pack he drew three cards and thrust them without looking at them inside his coat. Another person then drew three out of the second pack, and these turned out to be the same as the first three—not invariably all the three, for it did happen that only two were the same. But in the majority of cases Cipolla triumphed, showing his three cards with a little bow in acknowledgment of the applause with which his audience conceded his possession of strange powers—strange whether for good or evil. A young man in the front row, to our right, an Italian, with proud, finely chiselled features, rose up and said that he intended to assert his own will in his choice and consciously to resist any influence, of whatever sort. Under these circumstances, what did Cipolla think would be the result? 'You will,' answered the cavaliere, 'make my task somewhat more difficult thereby. As for the result, your resistance will not alter it in the least. Freedom exists, and also the will exists; but freedom of the will does not exist, for a will that aims at its own freedom aims at the unknown. You are free to draw or not to draw. But if you draw, you will draw the right cards—the more certainly, the more wilfully obstinate your behaviour.'

One must admit that he could not have chosen his words better, to trouble the waters and confuse the mind. The refractory youth hesitated before drawing. Then he pulled out a card and at once demanded to see if it was among the chosen three. 'But why?' queried Cipolla. 'Why do thing by halves?' Then, as the other defiantly insisted, 'È servito,' said the juggler, with a gesture of exaggerated servility; and held out three cards fanwise, without looking at them himself. The left-hand card was the one drawn.

Amid general applause, the apostle of freedom sat down. How far Cipolla employed small tricks and manual dexterity to help out his natural talents, the deuce only knew. But even without them the result would have been the same: the curiosity of the entire audience was unbounded and universal, everybody both enjoyed the amazing character of the entertainment and unanimously conceded the professional skill of the performer. 'Lavora bene,' we heard, here and there in our neighbourhood; it signified the triumph of objective judgment over antipathy and repressed resentment.

After his last, incomplete, yet so much the more telling success, Cipolla had at once fortified himself with another cognac. Truly he did 'drink a lot,' and the fact made a bad impression. But obviously he needed the liquor and the cigarettes for the replenishment of his energy, upon which, as he himself said, heavy demands were made in all directions. Certainly in the intervals he looked very ill, exhausted, and hollow-eyed. Then the little glassful would redress the balance, and the flow of lively, self-confident chatter run on, while the smoke he inhaled gushed out grey from his lungs. I clearly recall that he passed from the card tricks to parlour games—the kind based on certain powers which in human nature are higher or else lower than human reason: on intuition and 'magnetic' transmission; in short, upon a low type of manifestation. What I do not remember is the precise order things came in. And I will not bore you with a description of these experiments; everybody knows them, everybody has at one time or another taken part in this finding of hidden articles, this blind carrying out of a series of acts, directed by a force that proceeds from organism to organism by unexplored paths. Everybody has had his little glimpse into the equivocal, impure, inexplicable nature of the occult, has been conscious of both curiosity and contempt, has shaken his head over the human tendency of those who deal in it to help themselves out with humbuggery, though, after all, the humbuggery is no disproof whatever of the genuineness of the other elements in the dubious amalgam. I can only say here that each single circumstance gains in weight and the whole greatly in impressiveness when it is a man like Cipolla who is the chief actor and guiding spirit in the sinister business. He sat smoking at the rear of the stage, his back to the audience while they conferred. The object passed from hand to hand which it was his task to find, with which he was to perform some action agreed upon beforehand. Then he would start to move zigzag through the hall, with his head thrown back and one hand outstretched, the other clasped in that of a guide who was in the secret but enjoined to keep himself perfectly passive, with thoughts directed upon the agreed goal. Cipolla moved with the bearing typical in these experiments: now groping upon a false start, now with a quick forward thrust, now pausing as though to listen and by sudden inspiration correcting his course. The roles seemed reversed, the stream of influence was moving in the contrary direction, as the artist himself pointed out, in his ceaseless flow of discourse. The suffering, receptive, performing part was now his, the will he had before imposed on others was shut out, he acted in obedience to a voiceless common will which was in the air. But he made it perfectly clear that it all came to the same thing. The capacity for self-surrender, he said, for becoming a tool, for the most unconditional and utter self-abnegation, was but the reverse side of that other power to will and to command. Commanding and obeying formed together one single principle, one indissoluble unity; he who knew how to obey knew also how to command, and conversely; the one idea was comprehended in the other, as people and leader were comprehended in one another. But that which was *done*, the highly exacting and exhausting performance, was in every case his, the leader's and mover's, in whom the will became obedience, the obedience will, whose person was the cradle and womb of both, and who thus suffered enormous hardship. Repeatedly he emphasized the fact that his lot was a hard one—presumably to account for his need of stimulant and his frequent recourse to the little glass.

Thus he groped his way forward, like a blind seer, led and sustained by the mysterious common will. He drew a pin set with a stone out of its hiding-place in an English-woman's shoe, carried it, halting and pressing on by turns, to another lady—Signora Angiolieri—and handed it to her on bended knee, with the words it had been agreed he was to utter. 'I present you with this in token of my respect,' was the sentence. Their sense was obvious, but the words themselves not easy to hit upon, for the reason that they had been agreed on in French; the language complication seemed to us a little malicious, implying as it did a conflict between the audience's natural interest in the success of the miracle, and their desire to witness the humiliation of this presumptuous man. It was a strange sight: Cipolla on his knees before the signora, wrestling, amid efforts at speech, after knowledge of the preordained words. 'I must say something,' he said, 'and I feel clearly what it is I must say. But I also feel that if it passed my lips it would be wrong. Be careful not to help me unintentionally!' he cried out, though very likely that was precisely what he was hoping for.   'Pensez très fort,' he cried all at once, in bad French, and then burst out with the required words—in Italian, indeed, but with the final substantive pronounced in the sister tongue, in which he was probably far from fluent: he said *vénération* instead of *venerazione*, with an impossible nasal.   And this partial success, after the complete success before it, the finding of the pin, the presentation of it on his knees to the right person—was almost more impressive than if he had got the sentence exactly right, and evoked bursts of admiring applause.

Cipolla got up from his knees and wiped the perspiration from his brow.   You understand that this experiment with the pin was a single case, which I describe because it sticks in my memory.   But he changed his method several times and improvised a number of variations suggested by his contact with his audience; a good deal of time thus went by.   He seemed to get particular inspiration from the person of our landlady; she drew him on to the most extraordinary displays of clairvoyance.   'It does not escape me, madame,' he said to her, 'that there is something unusual about you, some special and honourable distinction.   He who has eyes to see descries about your lovely brow an aureola—if I mistake not, it once was stronger than now—a slowly paling radiance . . . hush, not a word!   Don't help me.   Beside you sits your husband—yes?'   He turned towards the silent Signor Angiolieri.   'You are the husband of this lady, and your happiness is complete.   But in the midst of this happiness memories rise . . . the past, signora, so it seems to me, plays an important part in your present.   You knew a king . . . has not a king crossed your path in bygone days?'

'No,' breathed the dispenser of our midday soup, her golden-brown eyes gleaming in the noble pallor of her

'No? No, not a king; I meant that generally, I did not mean literally a king. Not a king, not a prince, and a prince after all, a king of a loftier realm; it was a great artist, at whose side you once—you would contradict me, and yet I am not wholly wrong. Well, then! It was a woman, a great, a world-renowned woman artist, whose friendship you enjoyed in your tender years, whose sacred memory overshadows and transfigures your whole existence. Her name? Need I utter it, whose fame has long been bound up with the Fatherland's, immortal as its own? Eleonora Duse,' he finished, softly and with much solemnity.

The little woman bowed her head, overcome. The applause was like a patriotic demonstration. Nearly every one there knew about Signora Angiolieri's wonderful past; they were all able to confirm the cavaliere's intuition—not least the present guests of Casa Eleonora. But we wondered how much of the truth he had learned as the result of professional inquiries made on his arrival. Yet I see no reason at all to cast doubt, on rational grounds, upon powers which, before our very eyes, became fatal to their possessor.

At this point there was an intermission. Our lord and master withdrew. Now I confess that almost ever since the beginning of my tale I have looked forward with dread to this moment in it. The thoughts of men are mostly not hard to read; in this case they are very easy. You are sure to ask why we did not choose this moment to go away —and I must continue to owe you an answer. I do not know why. I cannot defend myself. By this time it was certainly eleven, probably later. The children were asleep. The last series of tests had been too long, nature had had her way. They were sleeping in our laps, the little one on mine, the boy on his mother's. That was, in a way, a consolation; but at the same time it was also ground for compassion and a clear leading to take them home to bed. And I give you my word that we wanted to obey this touching admonition, we seriously wanted to. We roused the poor things and told them it was now high time to go. But they were no sooner conscious than they began to resist and implore—you know how horrified children are at the thought of leaving before the end of a thing. No cajoling has any effect, you have to use force. It was so lovely, they wailed. How did we know what was coming next? Surely we could not leave until after the intermission; they liked a little nap now and again— only not go home, only not go to bed, while the beautiful evening was still going on!

We yielded, but only for the moment, of course—so far as we knew—only for a little while, just a few minutes longer. I cannot excuse our staying, scarcely can I even understand it. Did we think, having once said A, we had to say B—having once brought the children hither we had to let them stay? No, it is not good enough. Were we ourselves so highly entertained? Yes, and no. Our feelings for Cavaliere Cipolla were of a very mixed kind, but so were the feelings of the whole audience, if I mistake not, and nobody left. Were we under the sway of a fascination which emanated from this man who took so strange a way to earn his bread; a fascination which he gave out independently of the programme and even between the tricks and which paralysed our resolve? Again, sheer curiosity may account for something. One was curious to know how such an evening turned out; Cipolla in his remarks having all along hinted that he had tricks in his bag stranger than any he had yet produced.

But all that is not it—or at least it is not all of it. More correct it would be to answer the first question with another. Why had we not left Torre di Venere itself before now? To me the two questions are one and the

same, and in order to get out of the impasse I might simply
say that I had answered it already. For, as things had
been in Torre in general: queer, uncomfortable, troublesome, tense, oppressive, so precisely they were here in this
hall to-night. Yes, more than precisely. For it seemed
to be the fountain head of all the uncanniness and all the
strained feelings which had oppressed the atmosphere of
our holiday. This man whose return to the stage we
were awaiting was the personification of all that; and, as
we had not gone away in general, so to speak, it would
have been inconsistent to do it in the particular case. You
may call this an explanation, you may call it inertia, as you
see fit. Any argument more to the purpose I simply do
not know how to adduce.

Well, there was an interval of ten minutes, which grew
into nearly twenty. The children remained awake.
They were enchanted by our compliance, and filled the
break to their own satisfaction by renewing relations with
the proper sphere, with Antonio, Guiscardo, and the
canoe man. They put their hands to their mouths and
called messages across, appealing to us for the Italian
words. 'Hope you have a good catch to-morrow, a
whole netful!' They called to Mario, Esquisito Mario:
'Mario, una cioccolata e biscotti!' And this time he
heeded and answered with a smile: 'Subito, signorini!'
Later we had reason to recall this kindly, if rather absent
and pensive smile.

Thus the interval passed, the gong sounded. The
audience, which had scattered in conversation, took their
places again, the children sat up straight in their chairs
with their hands in their laps. The curtain had not been
dropped. Cipolla came forward again, with his dipping
stride, and began to introduce the second half of the programme with a lecture.

Let me state once for all that this self-confident cripple

was the most powerful hypnotist I have ever seen in my life. It was pretty plain now that he threw dust in the public eye and advertised himself as a prestidigitator on account of police regulations which would have prevented him from making his living by the exercise of his powers. Perhaps this eye-wash is the usual thing in Italy; it may be permitted or even connived at by the authorities. Certainly the man had from the beginning made little concealment of the actual nature of his operations; and this second half of the programme was quite frankly and exclusively devoted to one sort of experiment. While he still practised some rhetorical circumlocutions, the tests themselves were one long series of attacks upon the will power, the loss or compulsion of volition. Comic, exciting, amazing by turns, by midnight they were still in full swing; we ran the gamut of all the phenomena this natural-unnatural field has to show, from the unimpressive at one end of the scale to the monstrous at the other. The audience laughed and applauded as they followed the grotesque details; shook their heads, slapped their knees, fell very frankly under the spell of this stern, self-assured personality. At the same time I saw signs that they were not quite complacent, not quite unconscious of the peculiar ignominy which lay, for the individual and for the general, in Cipolla's triumphs.

Two main features were constant in all the experiments: the liquor glass and the claw-handled riding-whip. The first was always invoked to add fuel to his demoniac fires; without it, apparently, they might have burned out. On this score we might even have felt pity for the man; but the whistle of his scourge, the insulting symbol of his domination, before which we all cowered, drowned out every sensation save a dazed and outbraved submission to his power. Did he then lay claim to our sympathy to boot? I was struck by a remark he made—it suggested no less. At the climax of his experiments, by stroking and breathing upon a certain young man who had offered himself as a subject and already proved himself a particularly susceptible one, he had not only put him into the condition known as deep trance and extended his insensible body by neck and feet across the backs of two chairs, but had actually sat down on the rigid form as on a bench, without making it yield. The sight of this unholy figure in a frock coat squatted on the stiff body was horrible and incredible; the audience, convinced that the victim of this scientific diversion must be suffering, expressed its sympathy: 'Ah, poveretto!' Poor soul, poor soul! 'Poor soul!' Cipolla mocked them, with some bitterness. 'Ladies and gentlemen, you are barking up the wrong tree. Sono io il poveretto. I am the person who is suffering, I am the one to be pitied.' We pocketed the information. Very good. Maybe the experiment was at his expense, maybe it was he who had suffered the cramp when the *giovanotto* over there had made the faces. But appearances were all against it; and one does not feel like saying *poveretto* to a man who is suffering to bring about the humiliation of others.

I have got ahead of my story and lost sight of the sequence of events. To this day my mind is full of the cavaliere's feats of endurance; only I do not recall them in their order—which does not matter. So much I do know: that the longer and more circumstantial tests, which got the most applause, impressed me less than some of the small ones which passed quickly over. I remember the young man whose body Cipolla converted into a board, only because of the accompanying remarks which I have quoted. An elderly lady in a cane-seated chair was lulled by Cipolla in the delusion that she was on a voyage to India and gave a voluble account of her adventures by land and sea. But I found this phenomenon less impres-

sive than one which followed immediately after the intermission. A tall, well-built, soldierly man was unable to
lift his arm, after the hunchback had told him that he
could not and given a cut through the air with his whip.
I can still see the face of that stately, mustachioed colonel
smiling and clenching his teeth as he struggled to regain
his lost freedom of action. A staggering performance!
He seemed to be exerting his will, and in vain; the trouble,
however, was probably simply that he could not will.
There was involved here that recoil of the will upon itself
which paralyses choice—as our tyrant had previously
explained to the Roman gentleman.

Still less can I forget the touching scene, at once comic
and horrible, with Signora Angiolieri. The cavaliere,
probably in his first bold survey of the room, had spied out
her ethereal lack of resistance to his power. For actually
he bewitched her, literally drew her out of her seat, out of
her row, and away with him whither he willed. And in
order to enhance his effect, he bade Signor Angiolieri call
upon his wife by her name, to throw, as it were, all the
weight of his existence and his rights in her into the scale,
to rouse by the voice of her husband everything in his
spouse's soul which could shield her virtue against the evil
assaults of magic. And how vain it all was! Cipolla was
standing at some distance from the couple, when he made
a single cut with his whip through the air. It caused our
landlady to shudder violently and turn her face towards
him. 'Sofronia!' cried Signor Angiolieri—we had not
known that Signora Angiolieri's name was Sofronia. And
he did well to call, everybody saw that there was no time
to lose. His wife kept her face turned in the direction of
the diabolical cavaliere, who with his ten long yellow
fingers was making passes at his victim, moving backwards
as he did so, step by step. Then Signora Angiolieri, her
pale face gleaming, rose up from her seat, turned right

round, and began to glide after him.   Fatal and forbidding
sight!   Her face as though moonstruck, stiff-armed, her
lovely hands lifted a little at the wrists, the feet as it were
together, she seemed to float slowly out of her row
and after the tempter.   'Call her, sir, keep on calling,'
prompted the redoubtable man.   And Signor Angiolieri,
in a weak voice, called: 'Sofronia!'   Ah, again and again
he called; as his wife went further off he even curved one
hand round his lips and beckoned with the other as he
called.   But the poor voice of love and duty echoed un-
heard, in vain, behind the lost one's back; the signora
swayed along, moonstruck, deaf, enslaved; she glided into
the middle aisle and down it towards the fingering hunchback, towards the door.   We were convinced, we were
driven to the conviction, that she would have followed her
master, had he so willed it, to the ends of the earth.

'Accidente!' cried out Signor Angiolieri, in genuine
affright, springing up as the exit was reached.   But at the
same moment the cavaliere put aside, as it were, the
triumphal crown and broke off.   'Enough, signora, I
thank you,' he said, and offered his arm to lead her back
to her husband.   'Signor,' he greeted the latter, 'here is
your wife.   Unharmed, with my compliments, I give her
into your hands.   Cherish with all the strength of your
manhood a treasure which is so wholly yours, and let your
zeal be quickened by knowing that there are powers
stronger than reason or virtue, and not always so mag-
nanimously ready to relinquish their prey!'

Poor Signor Angiolieri, so quiet, so bald!   He did not
look as though he would know how to defend his happiness, even against powers much less demoniac than
these which were now adding mockery to frightfulness.
Solemnly and pompously the cavaliere retired to the stage,
amid ap lause to which his eloquence gave double strength.
It was this particular episode, I feel sure, that set the seal

upon his ascendancy.   For now he made them dance, yes,
literally; and the dancing lent a dissolute, abandoned,
topsy-turvy air to the scene, a drunken abdication of the
critical spirit which had so long resisted the spell of this
man.   Yes, he had had to fight to get the upper hand—
for instance against the animosity of the young Roman
gentleman, whose rebellious spirit threatened to serve
others as a rallying point.   But it was precisely upon the
importance of example that the cavaliere was so strong.
He had the wit to make his attack at the weakest point
and to choose as his first victim that feeble, ecstatic youth
whom he had previously made into a board.   The master
had but to look at him, when this young man would fling
himself back as though struck by lightning, place his
hands rigidly at his sides, and fall into a state of military
somnambulism, in which it was plain to any eye that he
was open to the most absurd suggestion that might be
made to him.   He seemed quite content in his abject state,
quite pleased to be relieved of the burden of voluntary
choice.   Again and again he offered himself as a subject
and gloried in the model facility he had in losing consciousness.   So now he mounted the platform, and a single cut
of the whip was enough to make him dance to the cavaliere's orders, in a kind of complacent ecstasy, eyes closed,
head nodding, lank limbs flying in all directions.

It looked unmistakably like enjoyment, and other
recruits were not long in coming forward: two other
young men, one humbly and one well dressed, were soon
jigging alongside the first.   But now the gentleman from
Rome bobbed up again, asking defiantly if the cavaliere
would engage to make him dance too, even against his
will.

'Even against your will,' answered Cipolla, in unfor-
gettable accents.   That frightful 'anche se non vuole'
still rings in my ears.   The struggle began.   After

Cipolla had taken another little glass and lighted a fresh cigarette he stationed the Roman at a point in the middle aisle and himself took up a position some distance behind him, making his whip whistle through the air as he gave the order: 'Balla!' His opponent did not stir. 'Balla!' repeated the cavaliere incisively, and snapped his whip. You saw the young man move his neck round in his collar; at the same time one hand lifted slightly at the wrist, one ankle turned outward. But that was all, for the time at least; merely a tendency to twitch, now sternly repressed, now seeming about to get the upper hand. It escaped nobody that here a heroic obstinacy, a fixed resolve to resist, must needs be conquered; we were beholding a gallant effort to strike out and save the honour of the human race. He twitched but danced not; and the struggle was so prolonged that the cavaliere had to divide his attention between it and the stage, turning now and then to make his riding-whip whistle in the direction of the dancers, as it were to keep them in leash. At the same time he advised the audience that no fatigue was involved in such activities, however long they went on, since it was not the automatons up there who danced, but himself. Then once more his eye would bore itself into the back of the Roman's neck and lay siege to the strength of purpose which defied him.

One saw it waver, that strength of purpose, beneath the repeated summons and whip-crackings. Saw with an objective interest which yet was not quite free from traces of sympathetic emotion—from pity, even from a cruel kind of pleasure. If I understand what was going on, it was the negative character of the young man's fighting position which was his undoing. It is likely that *not* willing is not a practicable state of mind; *not* to want to do something may be in the long run a mental content impossible to subsist on. Between not willing a certain thing and not willing at all—in other words, yielding to another person's will—there may lie too small a space for the idea of freedom to squeeze into.   Again, there were the cavaliere's persuasive words, woven in among the whip-crackings and commands, as he mingled effects that were his own secret with others of a bewilderingly psychological kind.   'Balla!' said he.   'Who wants to torture himself like that?   Is forcing yourself your idea of freedom?   Una ballatina!   Why, your arms and legs are aching for it.   What a relief to give way to them—there, you are dancing already!   That is no struggle any more, it is a pleasure!'   And so it was.   The jerking and twitching of the refractory youth's limbs had at last got the upper hand; he lifted his arms, then his knees, his joints quite suddenly relaxed, he flung his legs and danced, and amid bursts of applause the cavaliere led him to join the row of puppets on the stage.   Up there we could see his face as he 'enjoyed' himself; it was clothed in a broad grin and the eyes were half-shut.   In a way, it was consoling to see that he was having a better time than he had had in the hour of his pride.

His 'fall' was, I may say, an epoch.   The ice was completely broken, Cipolla's triumph had reached its height. The Circe's wand, that whistling leather whip with the claw handle, held absolute sway.   At one time—it must have been well after midnight—not only were there eight or ten persons dancing on the little stage, but in the hall below a varied animation reigned, and a long-toothed Anglo-Saxoness in a pince-nez left her seat of her own motion to perform a tarantella in the centre aisle.   Cipolla was lounging in a cane-seated chair at the left of the stage, gulping down the smoke of a cigarette and breathing it impudently out through his bad teeth.   He tapped his foot and shrugged his shoulders, looking down upon the abandoned scene in the hall; now and then he snapped his whip backwards at a laggard upon the stage. The children were awake at the moment. With shame I speak of them. For it was not good to be here, least of all for them; that we had not taken them away can only be explained by saying that we had caught the general devil-may-careness of the hour. By that time it was all one. Anyhow, thank goodness, they lacked understanding for the disreputable side of the entertainment, and in their innocence were perpetually charmed by the unheard-of indulgence which permitted them to be present at such a thing as a magician's 'evening.' Whole quarter-hours at a time they drowsed on our laps, waking refreshed and rosy-cheeked, with sleep-drunken eyes, to laugh to bursting at the leaps and jumps the magician made those people up there make. They had not thought it would be so jolly; they joined with their clumsy little hands in every round of applause. And jumped for joy upon their chairs, as was their wont, when Cipolla beckoned to their friend Mario from the Esquisito, beckoned to him just like a picture in a book, holding his hand in front of his nose and bending and straightening the forefinger by turns.

Mario obeyed. I can see him now going up the stairs to Cipolla, who continued to beckon him, in that droll, picture-book sort of way. He hesitated for a moment at first; that, too, I recall quite clearly. During the whole evening he had lounged against a wooden pillar at the side entrance, with his arms folded, or else with his hands thrust into his jacket pockets. He was on our left, near the youth with the militant hair, and had followed the performance attentively, so far as we had seen, if with no particular animation and God knows how much comprehension. He could not much relish being summoned thus, at the end of the evening. But it was only too easy to see why he obeyed. After all, obedience was his calling in life; and then, how should a simple lad like him find it within his human capacity to refuse compliance to a man so throned and crowned as Cipolla at that hour? Willy-nilly he left his column and with a word of thanks to those making way for him he mounted the steps with a doubtful smile on his full lips.

Picture a thickset youth of twenty years, with clipped hair, a low forehead, and heavy-lidded eyes of an indefinite grey, shot with green and yellow. These things I knew from having spoken with him, as we often had. There was a saddle of freckles on the flat nose, the whole upper half of the face retreated behind the lower, and that again was dominated by thick lips that parted to show the salivated teeth. These thick lips and the veiled look of the eyes lent the whole face a primitive melancholy—it was that which had drawn us to him from the first. In it was not the faintest trace of brutality—indeed, his hands would have given the lie to such an idea, being unusually slender and delicate even for a southerner. They were hands by which one liked being served.

We knew him humanly without knowing him per-sonally, if I may make that distinction. We saw him nearly every day, and felt a certain kindness for his dreamy ways, which might at times be actual inattentiveness, sud-denly transformed into a redeeming zeal to serve. His mien was serious, only the children could bring a smile to his face. It was not sulky, but uningratiating, without intentional effort to please—or, rather, it seemed to give up being pleasant in the conviction that it could not suc-ceed. We should have remembered Mario in any case, as one of those homely recollections of travel which often stick in the mind better than more important ones. But of his circumstances we knew no more than that his father was a petty clerk in the Municipio and his mother took in washing.

His white waiter's coat became him better than the faded striped suit he wore, with a gay-coloured scarf instead of a collar, the ends tucked into his jacket. He neared Cipolla, who, however, did not leave off that motion of his finger before his nose, so that Mario had to come still closer, right up to the chair seat and the master's legs. Whereupon the latter spread out his elbows and seized the lad, turning him so that we had a view of his face. Then gazed him briskly up and down, with a careless, commanding eye.

'Well, *ragazzo mio*, how comes it we make acquaintance so late in the day? But believe me, I made yours long ago. Yes, yes, I 've had you in my eye this long while and known what good stuff you were made of. How could I go and forget you again? Well, I 've had a good deal to think about. . . . Now tell me, what is your name? The first name, that 's all I want.'

'My name is Mario,' the young man answered, in a low voice.

'Ah, Mario. Very good. Yes, yes, there is such a name, quite a common name, a classic name too, one of those which preserve the heroic traditions of the Fatherland. Bravo! Salve!' And he flung up his arm slantingly above his crooked shoulder, palm outward, in the Roman salute. He may have been slightly tipsy by now, and no wonder; but he spoke as before, clearly, fluently, and with emphasis. Though about this time there had crept into his voice a gross, autocratic note, and a kind of arrogance was in his sprawl.

'Well, now, Mario *mio*,' he went on, 'it 's a good thing you came this evening, and that 's a pretty scarf you 've got on; it is becoming to your style of beauty. It must stand you in good stead with the girls, the pretty, pretty girls of Torre——'

From the row of youths, close by the place where Mario

had been standing, sounded a laugh.   It came from the youth with the militant hair.   He stood there, his jacket over his shoulder, and laughed outright, rudely and scornfully.

Mario gave a start.   I think it was a shrug, but he may have started and then hastened to cover the movement by shrugging his shoulders, as much as to say that the neckerchief and the fair sex were matters of equal indifference to him.

The cavaliere gave a downward glance.

'We needn't trouble about him,' he said.   'He is jealous, because your scarf is so popular with the girls, maybe partly because you and I are so friendly up here. Perhaps he 'd like me to put him in mind of his colic—I could do it free of charge.   Tell me, Mario.   You 've come here this evening for a bit of fun—and in the daytime you work in an ironmonger's shop?'

'In a café,' corrected the youth.

'Oh, in a café.   That 's where Cipolla nearly came a cropper!   What you are is a cup-bearer, a Ganymede—I like that, it is another classical allusion—*Salvietta!*' Again the cavaliere saluted, to the huge gratification of his audience.

Mario smiled too.   'But before that,' he interpolated, in the interest of accuracy, 'I worked for a while in a shop in Portoclemente.'   He seemed visited by a natural desire to assist the prophecy by dredging out its essential features.

'There, didn't I say so?   In an ironmonger's shop?'

'They kept combs and brushes,' Mario got round it.

'Didn't I say that you were not always a Ganymede? Not always at the sign of the serviette?   Even when Cipolla makes a mistake, it is a kind that makes you believe in him.   Now tell me: Do you believe in me?'

An indefinite gesture.

'A half-way answer,' commented the cavaliere.

'Probably it is not easy to win your confidence.   Even for me, I can see, it is not so easy.   I see in your features a reserve, a sadness, un tratto di malinconia . . . tell me' (he seized Mario's hand persuasively), 'have you troubles?'

'Nossignore,' answered Mario, promptly and decidedly.

'You *have* troubles,' insisted the cavaliere, bearing down the denial by the weight of his authority.   'Can't I see? Trying to pull the wool over Cipolla's eyes, are you?   Of course, about the girls—it is a girl, isn't it?   You have love troubles?'

Mario gave a vigorous head-shake.   And again the *giovanotto's* brutal laugh rang out.   The cavaliere gave heed.   His eyes were roving about somewhere in the air; but he cocked an ear to the sound, then swung his whip backwards, as he had once or twice before in his conversation with Mario, that none of his puppets might flag in their zeal.   The gesture had nearly cost him his new prey: Mario gave a sudden start in the direction of the steps. But Cipolla had him in his clutch.

'Not so fast,' said he.   'That would be fine, wouldn't it?   So you want to skip, do you, Ganymede, right in the middle of the fun, or, rather, when it is just beginning? Stay with me, I'll show you something nice.   I'll convince you.   You have no reason to worry, I promise you. This girl—you know her and others know her too— what's her name?   Wait!   I read the name in your eyes, it is on the tip of my tongue and yours too——'

'Silvestra!' shouted the *giovanotto* from below.

The cavaliere's face did not change.

'Aren't there the forward people?' he asked, not looking down, more as in undisturbed converse with Mario. 'Aren't there the young fighting cocks that crow in season and out?   Takes the word out of your mouth, the conceited fool, and seems to think he has some special right to it.   Let him be.   But Silvestra, your Silvestra—ah, what

a girl that is!   What a prize!   Brings your heart into your
mouth to see her walk or laugh or breathe, she is so lovely.
And her round arms when she washes, and tosses her head
back to get the hair out of her eyes!   An angel from
paradise!'

Mario stared at him, his head thrust forward.   He
seemed to have forgotten the audience, forgotten where
he was.   The red rings round his eyes had got larger,
they looked as though they were painted on.   His thick
lips parted.

'And she makes you suffer, this angel,' went on Cipolla,
'or, rather, you make yourself suffer for her—there is a
difference, my lad, a most important difference, let me
tell you.   There are misunderstandings in love, maybe
nowhere else in the world are there so many.   I know
what you are thinking: What does this Cipolla, with his
little physical defect, know about love?   Wrong, all
wrong, he knows a lot.   He has a wide and powerful
understanding of its workings, and it pays to listen to
his advice.   But let's leave Cipolla out, cut him out
altogether, and think only of Silvestra, your peerless
Silvestra!   What!   Is she to give any young gamecock
the preference, so that he can laugh while you cry?   To
prefer him to a chap like you, so full of feeling and so
sympathetic?   Not very likely, is it?   It is impossible—
we know better, Cipolla and she.   If I were to put myself
in her place and choose between the two of you, a tarry
lout like that—a codfish, a sea urchin—and a Mario, a
knight of the serviette, who moves among gentlefolk and
hands round refreshments with an air—my word, but my
heart would speak in no uncertain tones—it knows to
whom I gave it long ago.   It is time that he should see
and understand, my chosen one!   It is time that you see
me and recognize me, Mario, my beloved!   Tell me,
who am I?'

It was grisly, the way the betrayer made himself irresistible, wreathed and coquetted with his crooked shoulder, languished with the puffy eyes, and showed his splintered teeth in a sickly smile. And alas, at his beguiling words, what was come of our Mario? It is hard for me to tell, hard as it was for me to see; for here was nothing less than an utter abandonment of the inmost soul, a public exposure of timid and deluded passion and rapture. He put his hands across his mouth, his shoulders rose and fell with his pantings. He could not, it was plain, trust his eyes and ears for joy, and the one thing he forgot was precisely that he could not trust them. 'Silvestra!' he breathed, from the very depths of his vanquished heart.

'Kiss me!' said the hunchback. 'Trust me, I love thee. Kiss me here.' And with the tip of his index finger, hand, arm, and little finger outspread, he pointed to his cheek, near the mouth. And Mario bent and kissed him.

It had grown very still in the room. That was a monstrous moment, grotesque and thrilling, the moment of Mario's bliss. In that evil span of time, crowded with a sense of the illusiveness of all joy, one sound became audible, and that not quite at once, but on the instant of the melancholy and ribald meeting between Mario's lips and the repulsive flesh which thrust itself forward for his caress. It was the sound of a laugh, from the *giovanotto* on our left. It broke into the dramatic suspense of the moment, coarse, mocking, and yet—or I must have been grossly mistaken—with an undertone of compassion for the poor bewildered, victimized creature. It had a faint ring of that 'Poveretto' which Cipolla had declared was wasted on the wrong person, when he claimed the pity for his own.

The laugh still rang in the air when the recipient of the caress gave his whip a little swish, low down, close to his

chair-leg, and Mario started up and flung himself back.
He stood in that posture staring, his hands one over the
other on those desecrated lips.   Then he beat his temples
with his clenched fists, over and over; turned and staggered down the steps, while the audience applauded, and
Cipolla sat there with his hands in his lap, his shoulders
shaking.   Once below, and even while in full retreat,
Mario hurled himself round with legs flung wide apart;
one arm flew up, and two flat shattering detonations
crashed through applause and laughter.

There was instant silence.   Even the dancers came to a
full stop and stared about, struck dumb.   Cipolla bounded
from his seat.   He stood with his arms spread out, slanting
as though to ward everybody off, as though next moment
he would cry out: 'Stop!   Keep back!   Silence!   What
was that?'   Then, in that instant, he sank back in his
seat, his head rolling on his chest; in the next he had fallen
sideways to the floor, where he lay motionless, a huddled
heap of clothing, with limbs awry.

The commotion was indescribable.   Ladies hid their
faces, shuddering, on the breasts of their escorts.   There
were shouts for a doctor, for the police.   People flung
themselves on Mario in a mob, to disarm him, to take
away the weapon that hung from his fingers—that small,
dull-metal, scarcely pistol-shaped tool with hardly any
barrel—in how strange and unexpected a direction had fate
levelled it!

And now—now finally, at last—we took the children
and led them towards the exit, past the pair of *carabinieri*
just entering.   Was that the end, they wanted to know,
that they might go in peace?   Yes, we assured them, that
was the end.   An end of horror, a fatal end.   And yet a
liberation—for I could not, and I cannot, but find it so!

LEAH AND RACHEL

As the seven years drew on to their end, and the time approached when Jacob should know Rachel, he found he scarcely realized the truth, yet rejoiced beyond measure, and his heart beat mightily when he thought upon the hour. For Rachel was now nineteen years old and had waited for him in the purity of her blood, invulnerable through it to evil spirits and sickness which might have snatched her from her bridegroom; so that she was indeed, in respect to her bloom and beauty, all that Jacob had so tenderly prophesied: lovely to look at beyond all the daughters of the land, with her full and yet delicate forms, the soft braids of her hair, the thick nostrils of her little nose, the sweet, short-sighted gaze of her slanting eyes and the friendly night that rested in their depths; lovely above all in the smiling way the upper lip lay upon the lower, and shaped the inexpressible charm of the corner of her mouth. Yes, lovely was she beyond all others; but if I say, as Jacob always said to himself, that she was lovely most of all before Leah, that does not mean that Leah was uglier than any other maiden, but merely that she was the nearest object of comparison, and suffered most of all next to Rachel. For it is quite possible to imagine a man less enslaved than Jacob to that single point of view, who might have preferred the elder daughter, despite the stupid gaze and the 'tenderness' of her blue eyes, and the trick she had, both proud and bitter, of dropping the lids over their squinting stare. For Leah's rich blond hair hung knotted on her neck, and she had the figure of a fruitful woman, ripe for motherhood. Much might be said in praise of Rachel, that she did not vaunt her own charms above her sister's, or take undue advantage of her lovely little face, the image and likeness of the full moon, as Leah's might be of the waning one. Rachel was not so untaught as not to reverence the latter in right of its condition, and indeed at the bottom of her heart she disapproved of Jacob, that he so utterly rejected the thought of her sister and turned the brightness of his sole regard upon her—even though she could not quite put out of her heart all feminine satisfaction in his preference.

The nuptial feast was set for the full moon of the summer solstice; and Rachel too confessed that she longed for the coming of the festal day. Yet in the weeks just before she had been sad, weeping silently on Jacob's shoulder and against his cheek, answering his anxious query only by a painful smile and a quick head-shake that dashed the tears from her eyes. What weighed upon her heart? Jacob did not know—yet often he himself felt sad as well. Was she mourning over her maidenhead, since now the time of her blossoming drew to an end, when she should become a fruit-bearing tree? Such is the sadness inseparable from life yet not from joy, and Jacob knew it too. For the day of high marriage is the day of death and a feast of the solstice: the moon climbs to her height and from then on turns her face again to the sun, into which she will sink. Jacob was to know her whom he loved, and begin to die. For from then on he would not stand alone, living for himself and as lord of the world; he would be dissolved into his sons and in their persons belong to death. Yet he would love them, them who became the bearers of his divided and diverse lives, because it was himself that consciously he had poured into Rachel's womb.

At this time he had a dream, which he remembered long on account of its strange mood of peaceful sadness. He dreamed it on a warm night of Tammuz, in the meadows by his flocks, when the moon's sickle stood facing left in the sky, which at its fullness should usher in the marriage feast. But in the dream he was still upon his flight from home, or another flight, driven once more to ride into the red waste; and as before a jackal trotted before him, prick-eared, dog-headed, with tail held stiffly out behind him, looked round and laughed. It was a repetition of reality, yet the same reality; recurring to work itself out, since the first time it had been left incomplete.

He was riding among loose boulders and dry scrub —naught else grew. The evil one wound among rock and bushes, appearing, disappearing, looking round. Once, when he had vanished, Jacob blinked; when he looked again, the creature sat in front of him on a stone, and was an animal still as to the head, the usual dog's head with sharp upstanding ears and a projecting snout whose mouth ran right round to them; but his body was human down to the slightly dusty toes, and pleasant to look on, like the body of a slender youth. He sat on the piece of rock in a careless posture; one leg was drawn up, and he leaned with his elbow upon that thigh so that a fold came across his abdomen; the other was stretched out before him sidewise, the ankle on the ground. This limb, the delicate knee, the long, fine-sinewed, slightly curving leg, was a most pleasant sight. But a fell, the colour of yellow clay, began on the slender shoulders, the upper back and breast of the god, merging into the dog's head with the wide jaws and crafty little eyes, which suited the body so ill, was so painful a humiliation of it, that one could only say how lovely, without it, that body might have been. As Jacob rode up he got a strong whiff of the pungent odour which, sad to say, the boy-jackal exhaled. And how sad and strange at once it was to see the figure open its wide jaws and address itself to speech in a labouring, throaty voice:

'Ap-uat, Ap-uat.'

'There is no need, son of Osiris, that thou shouldst trouble thyself,' Jacob said. 'Thou art Anubis, guide and opener of the way, as well I know. And I had marvelled not to meet thee here.'

'It was a blunder,' said the god.

'What meanest thou?' asked Jacob.

'They were in error,' the other said, in his difficult speech, 'they who begot me, the lord of the west and my mother, Nephthys.'

'I am sad to hear it,' said Jacob, 'but relate to me how it fell out.'

'She should not have been my mother,' responded the youth, gradually learning to manage his jaws in speech. 'She was the wrong one. The darkness was to blame. She is a cow, it is all one to her. She wears the disk of the sun between her horns, in sign that now and again the sun goes in unto her to beget with her the young day; but the bearing of so many radiant sons has made no abatement in her dull indifference.'

'I seem to understand,' Jacob said, 'that that might be a danger.'

'Very dangerous,' agreed the other, nodding. 'Blindly, in all the good-natured warmth of her cowishness she embraces all that comes to her, and dully passive lets it come to pass, though it happen only on account of the dark.'

'That is an evil,' said Jacob. 'But which had been the right one, then, if Nephthys were not she?'

'Dost thou not know?' asked the jackal youth.

'I cannot precisely distinguish,' Jacob answered, 'between that which thou tellest me and that which I know of myself.'

'If thou knewest it not,' the other responded, 'then I could not tell thee. In the beginning—not quite in the beginning, but nearly so, there were Geb and Nut. The earth god and the heaven goddess. They had four

children: Osiris, Set, Isis, and Nephthys.   But Isis was
the sister-bride of Osiris and Nephthys of Set the red.

'So much is clear,' said Jacob.   'And then these four
did not keep the arrangement clearly enough in mind?'

'Alas, no,' responded Anubis, 'two of them did not.
What wouldst thou, for we are feckless beings, heedless
and distracted from birth onwards.   Carefulness and fore-
sight are base earthly characteristics, whereas what has
not carefreeness been the cause of in this life?'

'It is but too true,' Jacob confirmed.   'One must take
care.   For to speak openly, it dependeth on the fact that
ye are all idols.   God knoweth always what He willeth
and doth.   He promiseth and keepeth to His word.   He
setteth up a bond and is true unto eternity.'

'What god?' asked Anubis.   But Jacob answered
him:

'Thou feignest.   When earth and heaven mingle, then
indeed come forth heroes and great kings, but no god,
neither four nor one.   Geb and Nut, thou hast thyself
said it, were not quite the beginning.   Whence came
they?'

'Out of Tefnut, the Great Mother,' came the prompt
reply from the stone.

'Good, thou sayest it because I know it,' Jacob went on
in his dream.   'But was Tefnut the beginning?   Whence
came Tefnut?'

'The secret, the unbegotten one, whose name is Nun,
he called her,' responded Anubis.

'I asked thee not his name,' said Jacob.   'But now
thou beginnest to speak sensibly, boy-dog.   I had no
intent to reason with thee.   After all, thou art an idol.
Relate to me of thy parents' error.'

'The darkness was to blame,' repeated the evil-smelling
one.   'And he that carrieth the scourge and the shepherd's
crook, he was carefree and distraught.   And in his majesty

he sought for Isis, his sister-bride, and by mistake he came in the night upon Nephthys, sister of the red one. Thus she received that great god, thinking he was her bridegroom, and they were both enfolded in the utter unconcern of the night of love.'

'Can such things come to pass?' cried Jacob.

'With ease,' answered the other. 'For in its unconcern night knoweth the truth, and in her eyes the lively prepossessions of the daylight are as naught. For one woman's body is like another's, good to love, good to beget upon. Only the countenance distinguishes one from another and is the cause of our choosing one and not another. For the countenance is of the day, full of living fancies, but before the night, that knows the truth, it is as nothing.'

'Thou speakest crudely and without feeling,' said Jacob, greatly disquiet. 'One may have ground to speak thus when one hath an head like to thine and a face which one must cover up only to be able to say that thy leg is pretty and well-favoured as it lies stretched out before thee.'

Anubis looked down, drew his leg in beside the other one, and put his hands between his knees.

'Leave me out,' said he. 'I shall one day be rid of my head too. Wouldst thou hear the rest of the tale?'

'What happened?' asked Jacob.

'In that night,' went on the other, 'the lord Osiris was for Nephthys like Set the red her lord, and she for Osiris like to the lady Isis. For he was on begetting bent and she on conceiving, and to the night naught else was of importance. And they delighted one another in begetting and conceiving, for thinking to love each other they could but beget. Then was that goddess pregnant with me, whereas it should have been Isis the true wife.'

'Sad,' Jacob said.

'When morning came, they parted in great haste; yet might all have been well, had not the god left behind with Nephthys the lotus garland that he wears; Set the red found it and roared aloud. Since that time he seeketh Osiris's life.'

'As thou tellest it, so I know it,' said Jacob. 'Then came the affair with the chest, into which the red one lured his brother, and slew him by its means, so that Osiris, the dead lord, swam downstream into the sea in the sealed-up chest.'

'And Set became king of all his lands and sat upon the throne of Geb,' concluded Anubis. 'But it is not that upon which I would dwell, or which gives this dream of thine its point. For the red one was not for long king of the lands, for Isis gave birth to the youth Horus, who slew him. And lo, as Isis went searching and bewailing through the world, after her lost and murdered lord, and cried unceasingly: "Come into thy house, come into thy house, beloved, O beautiful child, come into thy house!" there stood beside her Nephthys, wife of his murderer, whom the slain god had in his error embraced, and went beside her whither she went, and they agreed together in their grief and mourned together: "O thou, whose heart beats no more, O lord of beauty, thee I would fain behold!"'

'That was sad and friendly,' said Jacob.

'And that,' responded the other from his stone, 'is the meaning of the dream. For who else was with her and aided her in her search, her roving, and her wailing, then as well as later, when Set found the discovered and re-hidden corpse and cut it up into fourteen pieces, which then Isis must seek anew? Who but I, Anubis, son of the unlawful wife, fruit of the murdered one, who was ever at Isis's side in her erring and seeking, and as she wandered she laid her arm about my neck that she might lean upon me, and we lamented together: "Where art thou, thou left arm of my beautiful god, where shoulder-blade and foot of his right side, where art thou, lovely head, and holy sex, which it seemeth is irreparably lost so that we are fain to replace it with an image made of sycamore wood?'''

'Thou speakest obscenely,' said Jacob, 'and like to the death-god of the two countries.'   But Anubis replied:

'And thou, where thou standest, shouldst have more understanding for such matters, for thou art a bridegroom, and shalt beget and die.   For in sex is death and in death sex, that is the miracle of the grave chamber, and sex teareth the bonds of death and standeth up against death, as it happened to the lord, Osiris, above whom Anubis hovered as a female vulture and made his seed flow out of the dead and cohabited with him even as she mourned.'

'It is best now that I should awake,' thought Jacob. And even as he still thought to see the god swing himself up from the stone and vanish, so that movement and vanishing were the same, he found himself lying under the starry night beside the sheep pens.   His dream of Anubis the jackal soon faded, it returned into his simple recollection of the experience of his journey and he remembered it, after a while, only thus.   But a faint melancholy, pleasant to feel, lingered still awhile in his soul, in that Nephthys, wrongfully embraced, had yet sought and mourned with Isis, and the bereaved one been cherished and supported by the wrongly begot.

At this time Laban and Jacob often took counsel together over the approaching event and the nuptial cele-brations, and how Laban in general thought to hold the feast; and Jacob learned that his father-in-law had ambi-tious plans and meant to celebrate regardless of expense.

'It will cost me,' Laban said, 'a pretty penny, for there are now many more mouths and I must feed them.   But I shall not rue it, for lo, trade is not at all bad, rather fairly favourable in these times, thanks to many circumstances among which we should mention the blessing of Isaac. Therefore it is I can pay for more labour in the court, and have bought two maids in addition to that lazy Iltani, and they are quite seemly wenches, named Zilpah and Bilhah. And on the wedding days I will give these to my two daughters, Zilpah to Leah my eldest and to the second Bilhah.   And at the marriage will the maid be thine, and I will give her thee as dowry and her price shall be reckoned as two-thirds of the mina of silver, according to our contract.'

'I embrace thee in thanks,' said Jacob, shrugging his shoulders.

'But that is the least of it,' went on Laban.   'For all the feast will be at my sole charge, and I will invite people on the sabbath from far and near and have musicians who shall play and dance, and I will lay two bullocks and four sheep upon their backs, and comfort the guests with drink until they see all things double.   All that will be a heavy charge, but I will bear it and not pull a long face, for is it not my daughter's wedding?   And besides I have in mind to make the bride a gift, that she may wear it and it will rejoice her heart.   I bought it long ago of a traveller, and it cost much money, and I have kept it in the chest: a veil, for the bride to shroud herself in, that she may be holy unto Ishtar and a consecrated one, whose veil also thou shalt lift.   It may have belonged to a king's daughter in times past, being the maiden garment of a daughter of princes, so artfully is it embroidered throughout with manifold symbols of Ishtar and Tammuz, but she, the spotless one, shall veil her head in it.   For immaculate is she and shall be like one of the *enitu*, like to the bride of heaven, whom each year at the feast of Ishtar the priests at Babel lead up to God before all the people, up the steps of the stairs and through the seven gates, and take from her some piece of her garment and her ornaments at every gate, and at the last gate her shame, and they lead the holy maid naked into the uppermost bedchamber of the tower E-temenanki. There she receives the god upon the bed in the darkness of the night and exceedingly great is the mystery.'

'H'm,' said Jacob. For Laban opened his eyes and spread out his fingers at the sides of his head and put on an air of sanctimoniousness that in his nephew's view suited him not at all. Laban continued:

'Of course, it is very fine and lovely when the bride-groom hath a house and court of his own, or is held in great esteem in the house of his parents, whence he cometh in great pomp to fetch the bride and to lead her in procession by land or by water to his own place, and his inheritance. But thou as thou knowest art but a fugitive and homeless man, fallen out with thine own, and sittest with me as my son-in-law, and I make no complaint. There will be no bridal procession by land or water, and you will sojourn here after the feast and the nuptial night; but when I have come between you and touched your fore-heads, then we shall do as is the custom of our land in these cases and lead you with singing round the court and into the bridal chamber. Thou shalt sit there upon the bed with a flower in thy hand, and await the bride. For her too, the spotless one, shall we lead round about the court with torches and singing, and at the door of the chamber we put out the torches, and I lead the devoted one in unto thee, and leave you, that thou mayest hand her the flower in the darkness.'

'Is that the custom and lawful?' asked Jacob.

'Far and wide, thou sayest it,' replied Laban.

'Then will I also approve it,' responded Jacob.   'And

I assume that there will likewise be a torch burning, or a little lamp with a wick, that I may see my bride when I hand her the flower and also afterwards.'

'Be silent,' cried Laban. 'Would I might know what thou hast in thy mind, with thy unchaste speaking, to speak so before the father, to whom it is moreover painful and bitter to lead his child in unto a man that he may uncover her and sleep with her. At least in my presence hold thy lewd tongue and restrain within thyself thy overgreat lustfulness. For hast thou not hands to see, and must thou also swallow up the spotless one with thine eyes to sharpen thy lust upon her shame and her maiden trembling? Have respect before the mystery of the high tower!'

'Pardon!' said Jacob, 'and forgive me. I have not meant it so unchastely in my thoughts as it soundeth in thy mouth. Gladly would I have looked upon my bride with my eyes. But since it is far and wide the custom to do as thou sayest, I will be satisfied for the time.'

Thus the day of the fullness of splendour came on, and the nuptial feast, and in the house of Laban, the prosperous breeder of sheep, and in his court, there was a slaughtering and a seething and roasting and brewing, so that everything steamed and all was bustle and noise, and all eyes watered from the smoke of the fires that burned under pots and ovens. For Laban was saving of charcoal and heated almost altogether with thorns and dung. And the master and mistress and all that were in the house, including Jacob, hurried on the work and the servants, to make hospitality for so many and to prepare the banquet; for the wedding would last seven days and for all that time the supplies must be inexhaustible, of cakes and buns and fish bread, of thick soups and plantains and milk dishes, of beer and fruit juices and strong waters, not to mention the roasted mutton and joints of beef — else shame and mockery would be the portion of the household.   And as they worked they sang songs to Uduntamku the fat, the god of the belly, the presiding deity of feasting, they all sang and composed them, Laban, Adina, Jacob, and Leah, Iltani the idle and Bilhah and Zilpah the daughters' maids, Abdcheba the twenty-shekel man, and the latest-acquired slaves.   Laban's sons in their little shirts ran boisterously among the press, slipped on the blood from the slaughtering and befouled themselves, so that their father wrung their ears and they howled like jackals.   Only Rachel sat still and idle in the house—for she might not see the bride-groom now nor he his bride—and examined the costly veil, her father's present, which she should wear at the feast.   It was splendid to see, a magnificent specimen of the arts of weaving and embroidering: it seemed an un-merited piece of good fortune that such a thing should have found its way into Laban's house and his chest; the man who let it go so cheap must have been greatly pressed by circumstances.

It was large and broad, a garment and over-garment, with wide sleeves to put one's arms in at will; so cut that a piece of it could either be drawn over the head to cover it or else wound about the head and shoulders, or else left to hang down the back.   And the maiden garment weighed uncertainly in the hand, for it was heavy and light at once, and of unequal weight in different places.   The back-ground was of the palest blue, woven thin and fine as a breath of air, a misty nothing, to be squeezed together in one hand, and yet weighted heavily everywhere by the embroidered pictures which covered it with brilliant, glittering colours, carried out in close, fine work, in gold and silver and bronze, and every imaginable shade: white, purple, rose, and olive, likewise black and white, all blended together like paintings in bright enamel.   And such clever pictures and designs!   Here was Ishtar-Mami, in various shapes, a tiny nude figure, pressing milk out of her breast with both hands, the sun and moon on either side. Everywhere the five-pointed star was repeated in varying colours, signifying god; the dove, the bird of the mother-goddess of love, was woven most often in silver thread. Gilgamesh, the hero, two-thirds god and one-third man, was displayed strangling a lion in the bend of his arm. One recognized the human scorpion pair who at the ends of the earth guarded the gate through which the sun goes down to the lower world. One distinguished various animals, sometime paramours of Ishtar and transformed by her—a wolf, a bat, the same who had once been Isullanu, the gardener. But Tammuz, the shepherd, was represented by a brilliant bird, the first partner of her lust, to whom she had decreed weeping year for year; and there was not lacking the fire-breathing bull of heaven, whom Anubis sent against Gilgamesh because of Ishtar's baffled longing and perfervid plaints. The garment slipped through Rachel's hands: she saw a man and woman sitting at both sides of a tree, stretching up their hands to the fruit, while a snake rose up behind the woman's back. And again there was embroidered a sacred tree, with two bearded angels on either side, touching it with scaly masculine cones to make it bear; while above the tree of life the female emblem hovered surrounded by sun, moon, and stars. And likewise there were sayings woven into the veil, in broad-pointed signs, lying down or standing straight or slanting. Rachel made out: 'I have put off my coat, how shall I put it on?'

She sat and played with the bright-coloured weave, the splendid garment and veil; she wrapped it round her and turned herself about in it, she found new ways to drape its picture-book transparency. Thus she beguiled the time while she waited and the others prepared the feast. Sometimes she had visits from Leah, her sister, who also tried

the beauties of the veil upon her own person and afterwards they sat together, and caressed each other, with
tears. Why did they weep? They alone knew—though
I might go so far as to say that they had different reasons.

When Jacob sat and mused, with swimming gaze, and
all the tales that had written themselves in the lines of his
face and weighed down his life with their dignified burden,
came back and were present in his mind, as they had been
on the day when he and his red-haired twin had buried
their father; then there was one day, and one story, which
possessed beyond all others this power of presentness,
having inflicted upon him a defeat so devastating to his
senses and so humiliating to his feeling that his soul for
long could not shake it off, and only regained faith in itself
with the advent of a feeling that was like a rebirth and
resurrection of those shamed and shattered ones.   Present,
I say, before all, was the story of his wedding day.

They had all, the people of Laban, washed their heads
and limbs in the water of the blessed pond, had anointed
and curled themselves to their taste, put on their festal
garments, and burned much fragrant oil, to receive the
incoming guests with a sweet savour.   And they came,
on foot, on the backs of asses, in carts drawn by bullocks
and mules, men alone, men with women, even with
children, if they could not be left at home: the peasants
and cattle breeders of the neighbourhood, likewise
anointed and curled and clad in festal garments; people
like Laban, of the same heavy-handed tribe, with the
same prosaic habits of thought.   They saluted, hand to
forehead, made inquiry into the health of all and sundry,
and then settled down in house and court, round cook
pots and shaded tables.   Water having been poured over
their hands and feet, they smacked their lips and fell to
upon the lengthy meal, amid loud invocations in praise of
Shamash and of Laban, father of the bride and giver of the

feast. The banquet was laid in the outer court of the
steading, between the storehouses, as well as in the inner
court round the altar, on the roof of the house and in the
wooden galleries; and round the altar were grouped the
musicians hired from Harran—they played on harps,
drums, and cymbals and likewise danced. The day was
windy, the evening still more so. Clouds glided across
the moon, hiding her altogether from time to time, a bad
omen to many of those present though they did not
expressly say so. They were simple folk, and made no
distinction between complete darkening and a cloud passing over her face. A sultry wind went sighing through
the steading, got caught in the chimney of the storehouses,
made the tall poplars creak and groan, and whirling among
the savours of the feast, the odours of the anointed guests,
and the fumes of the cookery, mingled them all together
in gusts of vapour, and seemed to try to snatch the flames
from the tripods where nard grass and *budulhu* gum were
burning. Jacob, when he recalled his wedding day,
always recognized in his nostrils that wind-driven mingling
of spices and sweat and roasted meats.

He sat with the family among the feasting guests in the
upper room, where seven years before he had first broken
bread with his stranger kin; sat with the master, his fruitful wife and their daughters at a table heaped up with
dessert and dainties of various sorts, sweet breads and
dates, cucumbers and garlic, and pledged the guests who
lifted their glasses to him and Laban. Rachel, his bride,
whom soon he should receive for his own, sat beside him,
and he kissed from time to time the seam of her veil that
enveloped her in its heavy picture-folds. She did not lift
it to eat or drink; it seemed the consecrated one's hunger
had been satisfied earlier. She sat quiet and silent, only
bending meekly her shrouded head when he kissed her
veil. Jacob too sat silent and dreamy, with a flower in his

hand, a blossoming twig of myrtle from Laban's well-watered garden. He had drunk beer and date wine and his senses were somewhat clouded; his soul could neither free itself for thought nor rouse itself to observation, but was heavy within his anointed body, and his body was his soul. Gladly would he have thought, gladly comprehended how his God had brought all this to pass; how He had brought the beloved in the way of the fugitive, the human creature whom he had but needed to behold for his heart to elect her and love her for all time and eternity —beyond itself, and in the children whom his love would beget. He tried to rejoice in his victory over time, that hard time of waiting, laid upon him, it seemed in penance for Esau's undoing and his bitter weeping; to lay it at the feet of God the Lord, in thanks and praise, this triumph, for that it was His; God through him and his not un-achieving patience having enforced time, that seven-headed monster, as once the dragon of chaos, so that what had been but inward wish and waiting was now the present, and Rachel sat beside him in the veil, which in a little while he would be permitted to lift. He tried to partake of this joy in his soul. But with joy it is as with the waiting for it; the longer one waits, the less it is pure joy, the more it is filled with practical activities and living needs. And when it comes, that joy so actively awaited, it is not of the stuff of the divine, but has become bodily present and has material weight, like all life. For the life of the body is never pure bliss, but a mixture, in part un-pleasant, and if joy becomes the life of the body the soul does also, and is no longer anything else but the body, with the oil-soaked pores, whose affair that once distant bliss has now become.

Jacob sat, and stretched his thighs, and thought of his sex, whose property this joy had now become, and which very soon might and must approve itself mightily in the holy darkness of the nuptial chamber. For his joy was marriage joy and a feast of Ishtar; it was celebrated with overeating and drunkenness, wreathed about with the odours of spices—whereas once it had been God's affair and rested in his hand. And as once Jacob had been pained over the waiting, and forced to forget it in life and action, so now he was pained for the sake of God, who was the Lord of life and all the longed-for future, yet, when the hour came to pass, must yield His dominion to the special idols of the physical, in whose sign it stood. And therefore Jacob kissed the little nude figure of Ishtar, lifting the hem of Rachel's veil as she sat beside him, immaculate sacrifice to procreation.

Laban sat opposite, leaning forward with his heavy arm on the table and looking steadfastly at his son-in-law.

'Rejoice, my son and my sister's son, for thy hour is at hand and the day of rewarding, and thou shalt be paid the reward according to law and contract for the seven years that thou hast laboured for my house and my business to the reasonable satisfaction of its head. And the reward is neither goods nor gold but a tender maiden, my daughter, whom thy heart desireth, and thou shalt have her after thy heart's desire, and she shall be submissive to thee in thy arms. I marvel how thy heart may be beating, for the hour is big for thee, truly an hour of life like to be thy greatest hour, great as the hour when in thy father's tent thou wonnest the blessing, as thou hast told me, thou crafty one and son of a crafty woman!'

Jacob did not hear.

But Laban mocked at him with gross words before the guests:

'Tell me, then, son-in-law, hear me and answer how dost feel? Dost thou quake before the bliss of embracing thy bride? Hast thou not fear as once in that matter of the blessing, when thou wentest in to thy father with thy

knees shaking? Didst thou not say the sweat ran down
thy thighs for dread and thy voice stuck in thy throat even
when thou wouldst win the blessing away from Esau the
accursed? Thou happy man, pray that joy take not
away thy manliness in the moment when thou needest it
most—else the bride might take it ill!'

They all roared with laughter in the upper room, and
once more Jacob smiled and kissed the picture of Ishtar to
whom God had given the hour. But Laban got heavily
to his feet, swaying somewhat, and said:

'Come then, for it is midnight, come up to me and I will
put you together.'

The crowd pressed close to see Jacob and Rachel kneel
down on the paved floor before the bride's father, and to
hear how Jacob answered to the questions according to
custom. For Laban asked him whether this woman
should be his wedded wife and he her husband, and if he
willed to give her the flower—to which he answered yes.
Asked whether he was well-born, whether he would make
rich this woman and fruitful her womb; Jacob answered
that he was the son of the great and would fill her lap with
silver and gold and make fruitful this woman like the fruit
of the garden. Then Laban touched both their foreheads,
and stepped between them and laid his hands upon them.
Then he told them to stand up and embrace each other
and that then they were wed. And he led the dedicated
one back to her mother, but the nephew he took by the
hand and led him in front of the guests, who crowded after,
beginning to sing. They passed down the brick staircase
into the paved court and the musicians left their stand and
walked before them. Next came boys with torches and
after them children in short smocks with censers hanging
between chains. Jacob, led by Laban, walked in the
sweet-smelling cloud, with the white blossoming myrtle
twig in his right hand. He did not join in the traditional

songs that swelled up as they marched, and only hummed a
little when Laban nudged him and told him to open his
mouth.   But Laban sang in a heavy bass and knew all the
songs by heart; they were sentimental and amorous ditties
about loving couples in general, on the verge of their nup-
tials, and how on both sides they can scarcely wait.   They
told of the procession, coming out of the wilderness like
pillars of smoke, perfumed with myrrh and frankincense;
and of the bridegroom walking, with the crown where-
with his mother crowned him on the day of his espousals.
All this was about the procession in which they were
actually moving, but the allusions did not fit Jacob; his
mother was far away, he was a fugitive, and he was not
leading his beloved into his mother's house and into the
chamber of her who had borne him.   Just for that reason,
it seemed, Laban sang the more lustily, honouring the
pattern in the face of all present lacks, that Jacob might
feel how different it was.   And then the bridegroom
spoke, in the song, and the bride gave ardent answer and
they sang in turn long rapturous speeches of mutual praise
and longing.   Their bed was freshly prepared in the
panelled chamber; they pointed one another the way
thither, promising the greatest pleasure in the union of
their nard-scented loveliness.   For his left hand would be
under her head and his right hand embrace her, and
sweeter than wine from the hills would be their mutual
love.   Thus they told one another in song, each painting
in intoxicated language the other's loveliness.   And
finally they charged the company to stir not up nor awake
from voluptuous slumber either bride or bridegroom until
they pleased.   They implored the people in song, by the
roes and by the hinds of the field, and the company took
up the words as they paced and sang them with great
heartiness; even the incense-bearing boys sang lustily if
without precise understanding.   And so they marched,

in the windy, moon-darkened night, round Laban's
steading, once and twice, and came before the house and
before the house door of palm wood, and Laban pressed
through, with the musicians in the lead, and came to the
bedchamber on the ground floor, that likewise had a door,
and Laban led in Jacob by the hand. He made light with
the torches, that Jacob might see into the room and make
out the position of table and bed. Then he wished him
blessings on his manhood and turned back to the company
that crowded about the doorway. They went away,
singing as they went, and Jacob was alone.

After long decades, and in his old age, and even on his
dying bed, where he still spoke solemnly of it, Jacob
remembered naught more clearly than how he had stood
alone in the darkness of the bridal chamber, where it blew,
and was draughty, for the night wind burst through the
window openings under the roof and out again through
the openings on the side toward the court, getting caught
in the carpets and hangings with which, as Jacob had seen
by the torchlight, they had adorned the walls, and making
a great flapping and clapping. It was the room above the
archive and grave chamber, with the teraphim and the
receipts. Jacob could feel through the thin carpet they
had put down the ring of the little trapdoor by which one
went down. And he had seen the bed and he went
towards it with his hands out. It was the best bed in the
house, one of three; Laban and Adina had sat on it at that
first meal seven years ago: a sofa on metal-covered feet,
with a round headrest of polished bronze. They had put
covers on the wooden frame, with linen over them, Jacob
could feel it, and there were pillows against the headrest.
But it was a narrow bed. On the table beside it stood
beer and a little food. There were two tabourets in the
room, also covered with stuff, and lamp stands at the bed's
head, but there was no oil in the lamps.

Jacob tried the lamps and discovered their emptiness, as he stood in the wind and the darkness while the train was fetching the bride and filling house and court with the noise of their singing and the trampling of their feet. He sat down on the bed and listened, the flower in his hand. The procession was leaving the house again, with the harps and cymbals at its head, bringing Rachel, his beloved, to whom all his heart belonged, and she walked there in her veil. Laban led her by the hand as he had done Jacob; perhaps Adina was there too, and the music of the wedding songs rose and died away. At last he heard the words:

My beloved is mine, he is altogether mine;
I am a garden enclosed, full of pleasant fruits and full of the
    odours of the finest spices.
Come, O beloved, into thy garden!
Eat of thy pleasant fruits, take unto thee the refreshment of their
    juices!

The feet of those who sang were before the door, and the door opened a little so that snatches of the song and the music came through, and then the veiled one was in the room, ushered by Laban, who closed the door quickly and they were alone in the darkness.

'Is it thou, Rachel?' Jacob asked after a little while, during which he had waited for those outside to move away from the door. He asks as one says: 'Have you returned from your journey?' when the traveller stands there in the flesh and it cannot be otherwise than that he has returned, so that the question is nonsense, only asked that the voice may be heard and the traveller does not answer but can only laugh. But Jacob heard that she bent her head, he knew it from the faint rustling and rattling of the light-heavy veil.

'Thou beloved, little one, my dove, and apple of my eye, heart of my heart,' he said fervently. 'It is so dark

. . . and bloweth. . . . I am sitting here upon the bed,
if thou hast not seen it, straight into the room and
then somewhat to the right.   Come, then, but strike not
against the table, else a bruise will come upon thy tender
skin and also thou wouldst knock over the beer.   I am
not thirsty for beer, I am only thirsty for thee, my pomegranate.   How good that they have brought thee to me
and that I sit here no longer alone in the wind.   Comest
thou now?   Gladly would I come to meet thee, but that
probably I may not, for it is by law and custom that I hand
thee the flower while sitting, and though no one seeth us,
yet we will hold to that which is prescribed, that we may
be well and truly wedded as we have steadfastly desired
so many years of waiting.'

The thought overcame him, his voice broke.   Memories
of the time when in patience and in impatience he had
arisen for the sake of this hour, laid hold on him mightily
and moved him to the depths; and the thought that she
had waited with him and now on her side saw herself at
the goal of her desires stirred the tenderest emotions of his
heart.   Such is love, when it is complete: feeling and lust
together, tenderness and desire; and while feeling made
the tears gush out of Jacob's eyes, at the same time he felt
the tension of his manhood.

'Here art thou,' he said, 'thou hast found me in the
darkness, as I found thee after more than seventeen days'
journey and thou camest on among the sheep and spoke:
"Behold, a stranger!"   Then we chose each other among
men and I have served for thee seven years and the time
lies at our feet.   My doe and my dove, here is the flower.
Thou seest it and findest it not, and therefore I will guide
thy hand to the twig that thou mayest take it, and I give it
to thee and thus we are one.   But thy hand I keep, since
I so love it, and I love the bones of thy wrist, so well
known unto me that I know it again in the darkness, and

thy hand is to me like thyself, and like thy whole body, but that is like to a sheaf of wheat garlanded with roses. My sister, my love, let thyself down to me and sit by my side and I will move that there may be space for two and would be for three if needful.   Yet how good is God, that He lets us be two alone together, thee by me and me by thee!   For I love only thee, for the sake of thy face that I cannot now see but saw a thousand times and kissed for very love, for it is thy loveliness that crowns thy body as with roses, and when I think that thou art Rachel, with whom I have often been, yet never thus, and who waited for me and likewise now waiteth for me, and upon my tenderness, then a bliss cometh upon me stronger than I am, so that it overcometh me.   A darkness enfoldeth us, thicker than thy veil which enfoldeth thee, thou purest one, and darkness is bound upon our eyes so that they see naught beyond themselves and are blind.   But it is only they, thanks be to God, and not one of our other senses. For we hear each other when we speak, and the darkness cannot part us more.   Tell me, my soul, thou too art enraptured by the greatness of this hour?'

'I am thine in bliss, dear lord,' she softly said.

'That might have been Leah who spoke, thy older sister,' he answered.   'Not according to the sense, of course, but in the way of speaking.   The voices of sisters are alike, indeed, and words come from their mouths with the same sound.   For the same father begot them, upon the same mother, and they are a little distinguished in time and move with separate movement, yet are one in the womb of their origin.   Lo, I am afraid, a little, at my own blind words, for I had lightly said that the darkness hath no power over our speech, yet I feel after all that it presseth hard upon my words and sinketh into them so that I fear somewhat before them.   Let us be glad of the distinction, that thou art Rachel and I Jacob, and not for instance

Esau, my red brother! My forefathers and I, at night
beside the flocks, have pondered much upon the person of
God, who He is, and our children and our children's
children will follow us in our musings. But I at this
hour will say and make clear my words, that the darkness
may roll back away from them: "God is the distinction!"
And therefore now I lift thy veil, beloved, that I may see
thee with seeing hands; and I lay it carefully upon this
chair that is here, for it is priceless with pictures and shall
be handed down through generations, and be worn by
beloved ones without number. Lo, here is thy hair,
black but comely, I know it so well, I know the fragrance
of it, I carry it to my lips and what power hath darkness
over it? It cannot come between my lips and thy hair.
Here are thy eyes, smiling night in the night, and their
tender sockets and the soft places beneath them where so
many a time I have kissed away the impatient tears, and
my lips were wet from them. Here are thy cheeks, soft
as down and the costliest wool of goats from strange lands.
Here thy shoulders, which feel to mine hands larger than
I see them in the day, and here thine arms, and here——'

He ceased. As his seeing hands left her face and found
her body and the skin of her body, Ishtar pierced them
both to the marrow, the bull of heaven breathed and its
breath was as the breath of both that mingled. And all
that windy night did Jacob find the child of Laban a
glorious mate, great in delights and mighty to conceive,
and she received him many times and again and again, so
that they counted no more, but the shepherds answered
one another that it was nine times.

Later he slept on the ground beside her, for the bed was
narrow and he gave her room and comfort for her rest,
sleeping himself crouching beside the bed, with his cheek
against her hand that hung over the edge. The morning
dawned. Dim red and hushed it stood before the windows,

and slowly filled with light the bridal chamber.   It was Jacob who first awakened, from the daylight between his lids, and from the stillness; for until deep into the night the feasting had continued, with much laughter and noise in house and court, and only toward morning, when the bridal pair already slept, had quiet descended.   And also he was uncomfortable—though how joyfully—and waked the easier.   He stirred and felt her hand, remembered everything and turned his mouth to kiss it.   Then raised his head to see his dear one in her slumbers.   With eyes heavy and sticky from sleep, still unwilling to focus, he looked at her.   And it was Leah.

He dropped his eyes and shook his head with a smile. 'Ah,' thought he, while even then a chill crept round his heart and into the pit of his stomach, 'what madness, what a "morning-after" mockery!   Darkness was hung before mine eyes, and now that they are unblinded they see false things.   Are then sisters so mysteriously alike, and show it in their sleep, though no likeness shows itself in their features?   Let me look again!'

But he did not look, because he feared to, and what he said to himself was only a panic-struck gabbling.   He had seen that she was blonde, and her nose somewhat red.   He rubbed his eyes with his knuckles and forced himself to look.   It was Leah who lay and slept.

The thoughts tumbled over each other in his head. How came Leah here, and where was Rachel, whom they had brought in unto him and whom he had known this night?   He staggered backwards away from the bed into the middle of the room and stood there in his shirt, his fists to his cheeks.   'Leah!' he screamed, in a strangled voice.   She sat up at once.   She blinked, smiled, and dropped her eyelids as he had so often seen her do.   One shoulder and breast were bare; they were white and beautiful.

'Jacob, my husband,' she said, 'let it be so, according to the father's will. For he would have it so and so arranged it, and the gods shall give me that to make thee thank both him and them.'

'Leah,' he stammered, and he pointed to his throat, his breast, and his brow, 'since when is it thou?'

'Always it was I,' she answered, 'and I was thine this night ever since I entered in the veil. And always I was tender towards thee and ready as Rachel, since I saw thee from the roof; and have I not proved it to thee the whole of this night? For say thyself if I have not served thee as well as any woman could, and been strong in desire! And certain am I in my inwards that I have conceived from thee, and it shall be a son, strong and brave and we shall call his name Reuben.'

Then Jacob cast back and bethought himself how he had taken her for Rachel this night, and he went to the wall and laid his arm along it and his forehead on his arm and wept bitterly.

Thus for some while he stood, torn by his emotions, and each time the thought returned, how he had believed and had known her, how all his joy had been delusion and the hour of fulfilment turned to shame, for which he had served and conquered the time, it was with him as though his stomach and his brain turned over within him, and he despaired with his whole soul. But Leah knew no more to say, and only wept likewise, from time to time, as she had done the day before with Rachel. For she saw how little it had been she who had again and again received him, and only the thought that she would now in all probability have a fine son named Reuben came to strengthen her heart.

Then he left her and rushed out of the chamber. He had almost stumbled over the sleepers that lay everywhere outside in house and court, in the disorder from the feast,

on covers and mats or on the bare ground, sleeping off their
debauch. 'Laban!' he cried, and stepped over forms that
emitted surly grunts, stretched out and snored again.
'Laban!' he repeated more quietly, for torment and bitterness and the fierce demand for a reckoning did not slay in
him all consideration for these sleepers in the early morning after the heavy feasting. 'Laban! where art thou?'
And came before the master's chamber, where he lay
with Adina his wife, knocked and cried: 'Laban, come
forth!'

'What, what!' answered Laban from within. 'Who
is it calleth me in the early dawn, after I have been
sleeping?'

'It is I. Thou must come out!' Jacob cried.

'Oh, indeed,' said Laban. 'So it is my son-in-law that
calleth, and sayeth I, like a child, as though one could tell
from that alone who he is, but I know the voice and will
come forth to hear what he hath to tell to me in the dawning, though just then I was enjoying my best sleep.' And
came forth in his shift, with rumpled hair, and blinking.

'I was asleep,' he repeated. 'Such a deep sleep and
doing me so much good. How comes it thou thyself
sleepest not or dost according to thy new state?'

'It is Leah,' said Jacob, with trembling lips.

'Of a surety,' replied Laban, 'and callest thou me in the
grey dawn out of beneficent slumber after heavy drinking
to tell me what I know as well as thou?'

'Thou monster, thou tiger, thou devilish man!' cried
Jacob beside himself. 'I tell thee not that thou mayest
know it, but to show thee that I know it and to bring thee
to accounting in my torment.'

'Take care of thy voice above all, then,' said Laban,
'tnat thou lowerest it considerably: that I counsel thee, if
thou lettest not thyself be counselled by the plain circumstances. For not enough that I am thy uncle and father-

in-law, and thy master to boot, whom it beseemeth not to
breathe upon with cries of murder, but also house and
court lie full of sleeping guests, as thou seest, who in a few
hours will go out with me to the hunt and take their
pleasure in the wild and in the reedy places of the swamps,
where we will set snares for birds, the partridge and the
bustard, or slay a wild boar, that we may pour out a tribute
of liquor to him.   Thereto my guests strengthen themselves in slumber, and I mar it not, and in the evening the
drinking bout shall go on.   But thou, when on the fifth
day thou issuest out of the bride's chamber, shalt join with
us in the pleasures of the chase.'

'No pleasures can there be for me in the chase,'
answered Jacob, 'and my poor senses do not set that way,
which thou hast confused and brought to shame so that
they cry out from earth to heaven.   For thou hast
deceived me beyond all bounds, with cruelty and shame-
lessness, and hast privily brought in Leah to me, thy
elder daughter, in the place of Rachel for whom I
have served thee.   How shall I then deal with thee and
with me?'

'Hearken now,' said Laban, 'there are words which
thou hadst best not take upon thy tongue and shouldst
shame thyself to utter them aloud; for in Amurruland
there sits as I know a shaggy-haired man who weeps and
tears his fleece and seeks after thy life, and he is it might
well speak of deception.   It is unpleasant when a man
must blush for another man because he blusheth not for
himself, and thus standeth it at the moment between thee
and me because of thy ill-chosen words.   Sayst thou I
have betrayed thee?   In what respect?   Have I brought
in unto thee a bride who was no longer unspotted and unworthy to mount the seven stairs into the arms of the god?
Or have I brought thee one deformed and incapable in
body or who cried out at the hurt thou gavest her, and was

not willing and serviceable to thee in thy lust? Is it after this fashion I have betrayed thee?'

'No,' Jacob said, 'not after such a fashion. Leah is great in conceiving. But thou hast gone behind me and duped me, and made it so that I did not see and took Leah for Rachel throughout the night, and I have given to the wrong one my soul and all the best of my strength, so that it repenteth me beyond my power to utter. This, thou wolf-man, hast thou done unto me.'

'And thou callest it betraying and shamelessly likenest me to wild beasts and evil spirits because I held with the custom and as a righteous man did not presume to reject that which is sacred and traditional? I know not how such things are in Amurruland or in the country of King Gog, but in our land we give not the younger before the elder; that would be to smite tradition in the face, and I am a respectable man and law-abiding. Thus did I what I did, and dealt wisely against thy unreason and like a father who knoweth what is owing to his children. For thou hast bluntly affronted my love to my eldest born, saying to me, "Leah speaketh not unto my manly desires." And therefore hast thou not deserved a correction and called down upon thee an admonishment? For now thou hast seen whether she speaketh to thy manly desires or no!'

'I have seen nothing at all,' Jacob cried. 'It was Rachel whom I embraced.'

'Yes, so the dawning hath proven,' answered Laban mockingly; 'but the truth is that Rachel, my little one, hath nothing whereover to complain. For the reality was Leah's but the intent was Rachel's. And now have I also taught thee the intent for Leah, and whichsoever thou embracest in the future there will be the reality as well as the intent.'

'Wilt thou then give me Rachel?' Jacob asked.

'Of a surety,' answered Laban. 'If thou wilt have her and pay me the legal price, thou shalt have her.'

But Jacob cried:

'I have served thee for Rachel seven years!'

'Thou hast,' responded Laban with dignity and solemnity, 'served me for a child. Wilt thou now have the second, as would be agreeable unto me, then must thou pay again.'

Jacob was silent.

After a little he said: 'I will obtain the buying price and see to it that I contribute the dowry. I will borrow a mina of silver from people with whom I deal in trade, and I will likewise pay for presents to hang on the bride's girdle; for some possessions have, naturally and without my will, cleaved unto me in this long time, and I am of more substance than when I first wooed for Rachel.'

'Again thou speakest without any delicacy,' answered Laban, with a smug shake of the head, 'and foolishly bringest things to speech which it were better to bury in thy bosom; thou shouldst rather be glad if others also keep silent and dwell not upon them to rebuke thee for them, instead of shouting them aloud and making it so that a man must be ashamed for thee since thou art not for thyself. I will hear nothing of unexpected possessions and inducements of that sort. I will have no silver of thee as dowry and no gear, from whomever it be, as presents for the bride, but rather shalt thou serve me for the second child as long as for the first.'

'Wolf-man!' cried Jacob, hardly restraining himself. 'And thou wilt give me Rachel only after another seven years?'

'Who hath said so?' countered Laban, superiorly. 'Who hath even so much as suggested such a thing? Thou alone pratest without any reason and in thy haste comparest me to a werewolf; for I am a father and I will

not that my child pine after the man until he is old. Go
thou now to thy right place and keep thy week and thine
honour. Then shall the second be given thee in all stillness,
and thou shalt serve me as her husband other seven years.'

Jacob hung his head and was silent.

'Thou art silent,' Laban said, 'and canst not bring
thyself to fall at my feet. Truly I am curious, whether
I shall yet succeed in awakening thy heart to thankful-
ness. That I stand here in the dawning in my shift,
disturbed out of my most needful slumber, and deal with
thee, it seems is not enough to engender in thee such a
feeling. I have not mentioned yet that with the second
child thou receivest likewise the second maid whom I
bought. For to Leah I give Zilpah as dowry, and to
Rachel Bilhah, and two-thirds of the mina of silver that
I give thee shall be reckoned in. Thus thou hast four
wives overnight and a women's house like the king of
Babel, thou that sattest so lately barren and forlorn.'

Jacob still kept silence.

'Thou cruel man,' he said at last, with a sigh. 'Thou
knowest not what thou hast done unto me; thou knowest
and thinkest not on it, I must believe, nor can have any
imagining of it in thy iron heart. I have squandered my
soul and all the best of me upon the wrong woman this
night, and that crusheth my heart together at thought of
the right one for whom it was meant, and I shall have to
do with Leah all the week, and when my flesh is weary, for
I am only human, and it is sated and my soul all too
drowsy for high feelings, then shall I be given the right
one, Rachel, my treasure. And thou thinkest it is good
so. But that can never be made good, which thou hast
done to me and to Rachel thy child, and even unto Leah,
who sitteth there upon her bed in tears because I had her
not in my mind.'

'Dost thou mean,' Laban asked, 'that after the marriage

week with Leah thou wilt have no more manhood left to
make fruitful the second?'

'Not that, may God forbid,' answered Jacob.

'All the rest is whimsies and moonshine,' concluded
Laban. 'Art satisfied with our new contract, and shall it
be so or no between me and thee?'

'Yea, it shall be so,' said Jacob, and went back to Leah.

But Reuben was Leah's and not Rachel's; Leah bore to
Jacob his first son, who later trifled away his birthright,
being like water for instability, it was not Rachel who conceived and bore him, the bride of Jacob's affection did not
present to her lord this child, nor, according to the will of
God, Simeon, Levi, Dan, or Judah, or any of the ten end-
ing with Zebulon; although at the end of the wedding
feast, after Jacob had left Leah on the fifth day and somewhat refreshed himself by going bird-shooting with the
company, Rachel was brought in unto him—upon which
event I will not further dwell. For I have already told
how Jacob received Rachel; as the result of Laban's
chicanery he first received her in Leah, and it was in fact
a double wedding that was held, the marriage with two
sisters, one of whom he actually married but the other in
intent—and in this sense what do we mean by actually?
For from this point of view Reuben was after all Rachel's
son, conceived by union with her. And yet she that was
so ready and willing went empty away, and Leah rounded
apace, and folded her hands in contentment over her burden, with her head meekly on one side and her lids dropped
to hide her squint.

She was delivered on the bricks, and displayed great
talent; it was a matter of a couple of hours, mere child's

play.   Reuben shot out like a stream of water, and when Jacob, being hastily summoned, came in from the field, for it was the time of the sesame harvest, the infant was already bathed, rubbed with salt, and wrapped up in swaddling bands.   He put his hand upon him, and in the presence of all the household he said: 'My son.'   Laban made a congratulatory speech.   He adjured Jacob to be as untiring as himself, to add a new name to his credit three years running —and the newly delivered cried out joyfully from her bed across the court: twelve years running, without pause, she would be fruitful.   Rachel heard it.

Rachel could not be got to leave the cradle; it hung from the ceiling by cords, so that Leah could guide it with her hand.   Rachel sat at the other side and looked at the child. When it cried she got up and gave it to her sister, who put it to her swelling, milk-veined breast; looked on greedily as it suckled, growing red and steamy with satisfaction; and watching pressed her hands against her own delicate bosom.

'Poor little one,' Leah would say to her.   'Fret not thyself, thy turn will come.   And thy prospects are far better than mine, for it is thou upon whom the master's eyes are turned, and for once that he cometh to me there are four or six times that he is with thee, then how canst thou fail?'

But whatever the prospects for Rachel, it was Leah, by God's will, in whom they were fulfilled; for scarcely was she about than she was again expectant, and went carrying Reuben upon her back and Simeon in her belly; and felt hardly sick as he began to wax, and found it no matter for sighing that he made her greatly mis-shapen; but was sturdy and of good cheer up till the end, and worked in Laban's fruit garden until her hour came and her face changed and she gave orders for the bricks to be set up.   Then came forth Simeon with the greatest ease, and sneezed.   He was admired of all, and most by Rachel, and what anguish it gave her to admire him! For the matter stood a little differently this time, indeed: consciously and undeceived Jacob had begot him upon Leah, he was hers entirely and beyond a doubt.

And Rachel—how was it with the little one? How blithely and earnestly she had looked in her cousin's eyes, with what courage and loving readiness for life! How confidently she had hoped and felt that she would bring forth to him children in both their likenesses, even sometimes twins! And now she went empty away, while Leah rocked her second born. How came this about?

The letter of the tradition is all we have, when we seek to explain this melancholy fact. Briefly it says: 'And when the Lord saw that Leah was hated He opened her womb, but Rachel was barren.' Just for that reason. It is an attempt at explanation, as good as another, a hypothesis, for we have no direct and authentic utterance of El Shaddai as to the meaning of his decree and doubtless none ever existed. It would be proper, however, to reject the interpretation if I knew a better one; but since I do not, I prefer to consider this one as essentially correct.

The kernel of it is that God's dispensation was not primarily directed against Rachel, nor in Leah's favour. Rather it constituted a discipline and an admonishment for Jacob himself, who, that is, was therein instructed that the soft and sentimental sovereignty he permitted to his feelings, the arrogance with which he cherished and promulgated them, were looked upon by Elohim with much disfavour—although this very tendency to selection, and unbridled indulgence in arbitrary favouritism, this pride of feeling which would not submit itself to judgment but rather required all the world to take it at its own valuation, might be referred back to a higher prototype, of which it was in fact the mortal counterpart. Do I say although? Precisely because Jacob's glorification of his feelings was a duplicate of the other, it was punished. Any one undertaking to speak on this point must take heed to his words; but even after the most scrupulous examination of the words I have quoted, there is no doubt that the motive power of the measure was God's jealousy of a privilege which, as He sought to make clear by this humiliation of Jacob's feelings, He regarded as His sole prerogative. I may be blamed for this interpretation, and it will hardly escape the objection that so petty and passionate a motive as jealousy is inapplicable as an explanation of divine decrees. But those who feel the offensiveness of the interpretation are free to regard the decree as a relic, spiritually unabsorbed, of earlier and less disciplined stages in the development of the divine essence—primitive manifestations, upon which I have earlier sought to cast some light: I mentioned, for instance, the facial type of Yahu, warrior and weather controller, lord of a swarthy troop of sons of the desert who called themselves his soldiers, which displayed harsh and violent traits as distinct from holy ones as can be imagined.

The bond of God with the human spirit active in Abraham was a bond for the purpose of mutual sanctification, a bond in which human and divine necessity were so mingled that one can scarcely say from which side, human or divine, the original impulse went out; but a bond, in any case, the existence of which betrays that the sanctification of God and that of man represent a dual process in which both are most intimately 'bound up.' Else, one might ask, why a bond? God's command to men: 'Be holy, even as I am holy,' already assumes the sanctification of God in man; it really means: 'Let me become sanctified in thee and be thou also sanctified.' In other words, the purification of God from the gloomy and violent deity into the sanctified one includes, if we work it backwards, that of man too, in whom it is consummated by God's urgent wish. This inward link, however, between the two situations, and the facts that God only attains His true dignity by the aid of the human spirit, and that man, on the other hand, only becomes worthy by contemplation of the actuality of God and its reference to himself— precisely this highly connubial combination and reciprocity of relations, sealed in the flesh, and vouched for by the ring of circumcision, makes it understandable that jealousy, as a survival of God's passionate and unsanctified stage, has remained longest with Him, either as jealousy of idols or perhaps of His prior right and prerogative of extravagant feeling—which is at bottom the same thing.

For what was that uncontrolled feeling of one human being for another, which Jacob permitted himself for Rachel, and later, perhaps even more intensely, for her first-born, but idolatry? Jacob's experiences with Laban may still, in part, be rightly understood as a just retribution for Esau's sufferings and fate, as a squaring of accounts with him in whose favour the balance had inequitably been weighed down. But on the other hand when one considers Rachel's sad destiny, and after that remembers all that young Joseph had to bear, so that it was only by exceeding shrewdness and adroitness in his dealings with God and man that he managed to give things a turn to the good at last, one feels convinced beyond the shadow of a doubt that what we are dealing with is jealousy of the purest water and in the most literal sense; not merely general and with respect to a prerogative, but highly personal jealousy of the objects of the idolatrous feeling by which it was roused to an avenging rage—in a word, with passion. We may call it a primitive survival, if we will; the fact remains that only in passion does the turbulent word of 'the living God' rightly test and fulfil itself. After we have heard the whole story we shall realize that Joseph, however much his weaknesses injured him, possessed more understanding for this livingness of God, and knew better how to take skilful cognizance of it than his father who begot him.

In the twelfth year of marriage, the nineteenth of Jacob's sojourn, no child was born. But in the thirteenth and twentieth, Rachel became expectant.

What a turn that was, what a new beginning! We may fancy the anxious, incredulous rejoicing, and Jacob's trembling exaltation. She was then thirty-one years old; no one still thought that God meant thus at last to smile upon her. In Jacob's eyes she was Sarai, to whom the threefold man announced a son against all the laws of probability; he called her by the name of that early mother, as he sat at her feet and gazed through adoring tears into her pale and twitching face which to him seemed lovelier than ever. But their fruit, the long withheld, at length conceived, the child which had by inscrutable providence so many years been denied to their hopeful longings, it he called, while she was carrying it, by the primitive, archaic name of a youthful god scarcely any longer officially recognized, though beloved among the people: Dumuzi, the true son. Leah heard it. She had borne him six true sons and an equally true daughter.

It was summer; the month of Tammuz, master of the herds, the mangled one, was already advanced some days. Since the great moment when he knew that his true and most beloved wife was expectant, Jacob had never stirred

from her side; he had shared with his own hands in her
care and treatment, renewing the bandages and ointments,
and even once smashing and burying the image of
Lamashtu: treatments and practices which were not commanded by the God of his fathers, but notwithstanding
the idols and soothsayers might come from Him after all,
and in any case were the only ones there were to follow.
Rachel—pale and wasted, heavy only in the body, where
her fruit, insensate and pitiless, sucked up all her strength
and her juices to its own advantage—would often carry
his hand to where he might feel the muffled movements,
and he would speak to Dumuzi through the fleshly veil
and tell him to take heart and come forth into the daylight,
but in so doing to take care how he climbed over the hills
that the dear shepherdess might anguish as little as possible.
And now, when she gave a wry little smile and said breath-
lessly that she felt it near, he fell into great excitement,
called her parents and the maids, told them to make ready
the bricks, and bustled aimlessly to and fro, his heart great
with supplications.

No praise could be too great for the readiness and
courage which Rachel displayed. Valiantly, joyously,
resolved to bear and to endure greatly, she entered upon
the work of nature. And this not for the sake of increased
outward respect nor because she would now no longer be
the childless and unloved wife of the popular phrase; but
out of a much deeper, a more physical sense of honour—
for not only human society has its sense of honour, the
flesh knows one too and a better one, as Rachel learned
when scatheless and for honour's sake she became a mother
through Bilhah. The smile she wore when her trial
began was other than that bewildered one which the painful conscience of her flesh had then painted upon her face.
The lovely short-sighted eyes alight with happiness rested
on Jacob's eyes, to whom she should now bear a child

in honour; this was the hour to which in open-eyed readiness for life she had looked forward when the stranger, the cousin from afar, had first stood before her in the fields.

Poor Rachel! So glad she was, so full of goodwill for the work of nature—and nature showed her so little goodwill in turn, made it so hard for the brave sufferer! Impatient for motherhood as she had been, sincerely convinced of her gift and aptitude, Rachel was probably in the flesh much less made for maternity than Leah the unloved; so that the sword of death hovered over her when she was brought to bed, and even at the second time it fell upon her and slew her.   Can nature so strive against herself, so mock the confidence and proud desire which she herself has implanted in the heart?   It seems so.   For Rachel's joyousness was not acceptable, her trust was given the lie—such was the lot that fell to her ready and willing heart.   Seven years had she and Jacob waited in hope, and then for thirteen more been incomprehensibly disappointed.   And now, when nature had at last granted the longed-for boon, she asked a harsher price than Leah, Zilpah, and Bilhah together had paid for all their maternal honours.   Thirty-six hours, from midnight to midday and again through a whole night to the following noon the frightful labour went on, and had it lasted even an hour or a half-hour more it would have left her lifeless.   Even at the beginning Jacob grieved to see her disappointment, for she had dreamed of a swift, triumphant finish, and now nothing stirred.   The first indications proved deceptive; long pauses supervened after the early pains, empty, silent, and fruitless hours, in which she did not suffer, but felt weary and ashamed.   Often she said to Leah: 'With thee, sister, it was another matter,' and Leah had to admit, with a quick glance at her husband, that this was so.   Then anguish would seize upon the sufferer, crueller and longer each time, yet when it passed, seemed to have been all in vain.   She went from bricks to bed and from bed to bricks; the hours, the night watches, the times of the day came and went; she blushed and groaned for her unableness.   Rachel shrieked not when her pains took her and would not let her go; she bit her teeth together and obstinately did her part; she would not frighten her lord, whose soft heart she well knew, and who in the pauses of exhaustion kissed her hands and feet in the distraction of his soul.   Her fortitude helped her not at all, it was rejected.   And after it was exhausted she shrieked indeed, wild and frenziedly, so that one would not have known her for the little Rachel.   For at this time—the second morning had then come—she was no longer in her senses, one could tell it by the hideous howling, for the voice was no longer hers, it was the demons yelling, and the sucking pig's heart had had no power to lure them away from her body into the puppet.

They were unavailing pangs, that merely held the precious sufferer in a gripe of relentless torture, so that the shrieking mask that was her face went blue and her fingers clutched the air.   Jacob ran through house and court, knocking against everything, since he had his thumbs in his ears and his eight other fingers before his eyes.   He called on God—no longer for a son, he had no longer any thought of him, but only that Rachel might have a peaceful death and lie quiet and released from these hellish torments. Laban and Adina, whose draughts and anointings and strokings had borne no fruit, in deep dejection muttered invocations and amid the shrieks chanted prayers to Sin the moon god, reminding him how once he had sustained a cow in labour, and might now so untie the knots of this woman's body and aid the pangs of the sufferer.   Leah stood bolt upright in a corner of the room, her arms at her sides, hands lifted at the wrists, and gazed silently with her squinting blue eyes at this life-and-death struggle of Jacob's beloved.

And then came forth out of a Rachel a final shriek, the last furious demonic yell, such as one cannot twice shriek without dying and not twice hear without losing one's mind—and then Laban's wife had something else to do than chant about Sin's cow, for Jacob's son had issued forth, his eleventh and his first, issued out of the dark and bleeding womb of life—Dumuzi-absu, true son of the abyss.   It was Bilhah, mother of Dan and Naphtali, who came running, white-faced and laughing, out to the court whither Jacob had rushed, and with flattering tongue announced to the master that 'unto us a child is born,' and 'unto us a son is given,' and that Rachel liveth; and trembling in every limb, he dragged himself to the bed, fell down beside it, and wept.   She was covered with sweat transfigured as by the hand of death, and she was singing in breathless exhaustion.   The gateway of her body was torn, she had bitten through her tongue, and she was weary unto death.   Such was the reward of her joyful readiness.

She had no strength to turn her head, nor to smile, but she stroked his brow as he knelt beside her, and her eyes went towards the hanging cradle in sign that he should see the child was alive and lay his hand upon his son.   The infant had been bathed, it had stopped screaming, it was swaddled and slept.   It had smooth black hair upon its little head that in issuing had torn the mother; long lashes and tiny hands with well-shaped nails.   It was not then beautiful—one cannot speak of beauty in so young a child. And yet Jacob saw as he had not seen in Leah's children nor observed in the sons of the maids, saw at first glance, what filled his heart, the longer he looked, full to overflowing, with reverent rapture.   There was about this newborn babe something ineffable, a clear-shining loveliness, equability, sympathy, divine charm, of which Jacob thought, if not to understand, yet to recognize the essence. He laid his hand on the child and said: 'My son.' But as he touched it, it opened its eyes, which then were blue and reflected the radiance of its birthday sun shining high in the heavens; with its tiny, strangely complete little hand it laid hold on Jacob's finger, holding it in a gentle clasp as it fell asleep. Rachel, the mother, slept too, a profound slumber. But Jacob stood there bent, a prisoner to his tender feelings, and gazed upon the brightness of his little son, perhaps an hour, until it nestled and whimpered for its food, and Jacob lifted it over.

They called the boy Joseph, which being interpreted means increase—as when we name our sons Augustus. His whole name, with God, was Joseph-el, or Josiph-ya; but liking to think that the first syllable also had reference to the Most High, they spoke to him as Jehosiph.

JOSEPH IN THE PIT

WE have been told how Jacob bowed his head when he heard the embittered brethren announce their departure from his hearth. From then on he lifted it but seldom. It was now the season of parching heat; at no other time in the year did the sun's rays so cruelly scorch the land, for the moment of its waning was at hand. This was the solstice, the season in which the true wife had presented Joseph to Jacob, in the month of Tammuz. Yet even so Jacob's spirit was wont to suffer beneath the blackened desolation of this quarter of the circle; that he suffered now might be explained in the same way. But no. The true ground of his depression was the unanimous departure of his sons. I should be saying too much if I asserted that this had given Jacob great pain. In his heart he truly did 'give ten for one'; yet it was quite another matter to reckon with the objective fact, to realize that the brothers' notice to quit was decisive; and that he, Jacob, would be left with two sons instead of twelve, a tree lopped of its branches. It was a blow to his dignity, first of all; but also it put him in an embarrassing position before his God, and he inquired of himself how much these actions of his went counter to the plans of the Lord of the Promise, and how great was the accounting he had invited upon his own head. For He that ruled future things, had He not taken care that not all matters should go after Jacob's heart and he be fruitful in Rachel alone? Yes, He had made him fruitful against his own will, and even those unwanted sons from the unloved wife were themselves the fruit of the blessing and bearers of destinies unknown. Jacob was

well aware that his elevation of Joseph was a piece of arbitrary self-indulgence, which might easily come to clash
with the vast designs of God and so reveal itself as culpable
presumption.   Indeed, it seemed already to have done so;
for though Joseph's folly may have been the immediate
occasion of the catastrophe, and though Jacob had suffered
in chiding him, yet the father well knew who it was who
must pay for this folly, before God and man.   In con-
tending with Joseph he contended with himself.   The
boy had been only the medium of whatever mischief had
been done; the real culprit was Jacob's own loving heart.
It had not availed to hide it from himself; for God knew it,
and one hid not oneself before God.   For the truth was,
therein lay the inheritance of Abraham: it meant no more
than that one did not give false evidence in matters known
to God.

Such were the mental struggles, in the time after the
grain harvest, which slowly shaped Jacob's decisions.   He
had conceived evil in his heart; now that heart must conquer its weakness by seeing to it that the spoilt darling
who had been the medium of the harm should also be the
medium of the healing.   He would treat the lad with a
little severity, would lay a responsibility upon him by way
of doing penance himself.

Seeing him at a distance he summoned him rather
peremptorily:

'Joseph!'

'Here am I,' answered the boy, and was beside him at
once.   He was glad to be called, for since the departure of
the brothers his father had spoken to him but little.   Besides, that last meeting with the brethren had left him,
even in his folly, with a feeling of discomfortable anxiety.

'Hearken,' said Jacob.   Some obscure motive made
him feign absent-mindedness; he blinked repeatedly and
drew his beard through his hand.   'Tell me if I am right

in thinking that thy elder brothers are grazing the sheep together in the vale of Shechem.'

'Yes, of a surety,' responded Joseph; 'for it seemeth to me too, if my memory erreth not, they desired to go together to Shechem to tend thy flocks, on account of the fat meadows there and because this valley will not hold all of thine.'

'So it is,' confirmed Jacob, 'and it is for this reason that I called thee.   For I hear naught of the sons of Leah, and of the sons of the maids all knowledge is hidden from me. It is not known to me how it standeth in the meadows of Shechem; whether Yitzchak's blessing was upon the summer lambing or whether my herds are afflicted with swelling and with liver fluke.   For my children thy brothers, I know naught of them nor hear whether they exercise our pasture rights in peace, in that district where, as I mind me, serious things once came to pass.   It giveth me to think; and in such thoughts I resolved to send thee to them to greet them from me.'

'Here am I,' cried Joseph again.   He flashed his white teeth at his father, hopped up and down, and stamped with his heels, on fire to be off.

'When I consider,' went on Jacob, 'that thou enterest into the eighteenth year of thy age, methinks it is time to put thy manhood to some sterner test than thou hast known.   And therefore I am resolved to stir thee up to this mission; that thou leave me for thy brothers, for some short space; to inquire of them concerning all that of which I am ignorant, and to return to me, with God's help, after ten or nine days and tell me what thou hast learned.'

'Verily, here am I,' cried Joseph again, enraptured with the idea.   'My father's words are golden and silver.   I will make a journey across the land, I will visit the brethren and look after things in the vale of Shechem, and all that will be the greatest pleasure. Could I have wished for my heart's desire it would not have been other than this.'

Jacob said: 'Thou dost not go to look after things. Thy brethren, they are men enough to do that themselves and need not a child. Moreover, that is not the sense in which I send thee. Rather shalt thou bow before them with all seemliness and the forms of courtesy and speak thus: "I am come some days' journey to greet you and ask after your well-being, from my own desire as well as at my father's bidding, for our wishes in this matter are one."'

'Give me Parosh to ride; he is long-legged and hard, very strong-boned and like to my brother Issachar.'

'It speaketh for thy manliness,' answered Jacob after a pause, 'that thou rejoicest over thy mission, and regardest it not as strange to go away from me for a number of days, so that the moon shall change from a sickle to a half-round before I see thee again. But say to thy brethren: "The father willed it."'

'Shall I have Parosh?'

'I am indeed minded not to deal with thee softly, but according to thy age. Yet the ass Parosh I will not give thee for he is balky, and his intelligence doth not keep pace with his fire. A much better choice is white Hulda, a friendly and careful beast, also trim to look at; when thou journeyest abroad thou shalt ride her. But that thou mayest know that I expect somewhat of thee, and that the brothers may know it too, it is my command that thou make the journey alone, from here to the meadows of Shechem. For I will give thee no servant along with thee nor let Eliezer ride at thy side. Thou shalt travel independently, and shalt tell the brethren: "Alone I come, upon a white ass, to visit you, according to our father's will." Then may it be, that thou needest not to ride back alone but that the brethren may journey with thee, some or all. At least such is my second purpose in this order.'

'That I will contrive,' promised Joseph; 'I make myself bail to bring them back to thee, indeed I will be guarantee therefor, and say to thee I come not again unless to bring them to thee.'

Thus Joseph pranced about his father, prattling away heedlessly and giving praise to Yah that he was to travel by himself and see the world. He ran off to Benjamin and to Eliezer the old man, to tell them all. Jacob, looking after him, nodded his head. For he perceived that if one could speak of a challenge, it was directed towards himself and nobody else. But was he not doing rightly, and acting as his inward responsibility for Joseph bade him act? He would not see the lad for several days; it seemed to him sufficient penance; and he refused to speculate as to what the upper spheres would have considered due severity. He reckoned with a failure of Joseph's mission; that is, he realized that the latter might return without the brethren. That they might return without him was so frightful a thought that his conscious mind did not even deal with the possibility. But since things always turn out otherwise than as one had thought, we might forestall destiny by our fears and apprehensions as with an exorcism; and therefore fate paralyses our imagination, that it may deal its crushing blows unhampered by our preventive spells.

The needful preparations for Joseph's journey put Jacob in mind of his own past and of that fateful day when Rebecca got him ready and he left, after the transfer of the blessing which she had conceived and carried through. And his soul was full of the solemn emotions of recurrence. Certainly the comparison was far-fetched enough. For his was by no means the heroic part which

Rebecca had played, when she deliberately sacrificed her own heart, assumed responsibility for the rectifying deceit, and then, fully conscious that she would probably never see him again, sent away the beloved son into a strange land. The theme admitted of some variations. True, Joseph too was leaving home on account of his outraged brethren's wrath; yet he was not flying from the wrath; Joseph was sending him as it were into Esau's arms. It was the scene by Jabbok ford which Jacob had in mind and whose recurrence he was so eager to bring about: the outward humiliation, the outward reconciliation which was inwardly so full of reservations; the smoothing over of obvious discords, the achievement of apparent harmony. How different from all that was Rebecca's resolute assumption of the guilt! Jacob's aim in sending Joseph was the impossible one of putting things back where they were; but since it was already plain that that could not be done, the result would simply be a resumption of the game, in which the pieces were Jacob's weakness, Joseph's blind conceit, and the brothers' deadly grudge, and which would have led, in all probability, to the same result.

But it held so far good, that the favourite was being sent a journey on account of fraternal discord; and Jacob conformed to the pattern by fixing the time of Joseph's departure for the earliest dawn, before sunrise; it having been so in his own case. But when the parting took place, Jacob—or rather Rebecca, for he was playing the mother's role—held the traveller in long embrace, murmuring blessings against his cheek; took an amulet from his own neck and hung it round the boy's, pressed him to his heart again and again, and all in all behaved as though Joseph were to be gone for years or for ever, seventeen days or more distant Naharainwards, into the unknown, whereas instead, amply supplied with provisions, he was setting out, to his own great joy, on safe roads and to travel no farther than to Shechem. Which shows that a man can behave out of all proportion, as measured by his own knowledge; while from the point of view of the still unknown destiny his conduct may turn out to have been only too suitable. There may even lie some consolation therein, when we learn the real state of the case. Thus men should never take leave of each other lightly; for then should the worst happen they can say to themselves: 'At least I did press him to my heart!'

Father and son took leave in the dawning, standing at the stirrup of white Hulda, who was laden down with good things and adorned with glass beads and bright worsted flowers. The leave taking, of course, was only the last of the many counsels, admonitions, warnings which had gone before. Jacob had instructed the boy in his route and the well-known stages on it, just in his mother's way; had warned him of the dangers of overheating and sudden cold; given him the names of folk and brethren in the faith, in the various villages at which the traveller might spend the night; and sternly forbade him, when he touched at the city of Urusalim and saw at Baal's temple the dwellings of those consecrate to Ashera, who lived and moved and had their being in her, to permit himself the smallest speech with them. Above all he enjoined him to behave with particular courtesy towards the brethren. It could do no harm, he remarked, were Joseph to fling himself down seven times before them, addressing them frequently as lords; when they would in all likelihood resolve to dip their hands at once in the bowl with him and not to go from his side for the rest of their lives.

Much of all this Rebecca-Jacob repeated afresh in the grey morning, before he allowed the youth to fling his leg over his ass, chirrup to it, and ride off northwards.

Jacob even went a piece alongside the lively Hulda, as she curvetted in the high spirits of the dawn. But he could not keep it up long; and stopped with an absurdly heavy heart. One last gleam of Joseph's teeth as the lad looked laughing back and waved his hand; then his son's figure was hidden by a turn in the road. Joseph had ridden away, he saw him no more.

Now it happened that Asher, Zilpah's son, with curiosity unquenched even by affliction, peered out over his knees so that his eyes roved across the plain. And afar off in the morning light he saw something glitter like a flash of silver, which disappeared and came again, sometimes in a single flash, sometimes two or more close together.

Asher jogged his brother Gad as they sat next each other, pointed out the will-o'-the-wisp, and asked him what it meant. They shaded their eyes to look and gestured their surprise; the others saw and heard, and those who sat with their backs to the plain turned round to gaze, following the direction of Asher's eyes; until at last all the brothers had lifted their heads and peered out together at a shimmering figure which was moving towards them.

'A man cometh, all shining,' said Judah. But after they had waited awhile for the figure to come nearer, Dan answered:

'It is not a man, it is a boy.'

And with one accord their sunburnt faces all went ashen as Reuben's had done a little time before, and their hearts beat with a wild and rapid rhythm, like drums, so that a hollow concerted drumming arose in the breathless stillness.

Joseph came on across the plain, directly towards them, in his coat of many colours, and his garland resting on his veiled head.

They did not believe it. They sat with their thumbs in their cheeks, fingers before their mouths, elbows on their knees, and stared out over their fists with starting eyes at the approaching illusion. They hoped they were dreaming, yet feared to find it so. Some of them, even, in a confusion of fear and hope, refused to believe their eyes when the oncoming figure smiled and spoke, and there was no more doubt.

'Yea, verily, and greetings to you all,' he said in his very voice and came close up to them. 'It is indeed I. I am come for our father's sake on Hulda, the she-ass, to look after things with you and to——' He stopped, disconcerted. They sat without word or stir and stared, a sinister group, like men bewitched. But as they so sat, although there was no sunrise and no sunset which might have painted their faces, yet these grew red as the writhen trunks of the trees at their backs, red as the desert, dark red as the star in the sky, and their eyes looked as though blood would spurt out. He stepped back. There arose and swelled a thunderous roar, that bull's roar of the twins, which made one's inwards to quake; and with a long-drawn shriek as from tortured gullets, a furiously exultant yell of rage and hate and sudden release, they all ten sprang up as one man and flung themselves savagely upon him.

They fell upon him as the pack of hungry wolves falls upon the prey; their blood-blinded lust knew no pause or consideration, it was as though they would tear him into fourteen pieces at least. Rending, tearing apart, tearing off—upon that they were bent, to their very marrow. 'Down, down, down!' they panted with one voice; it was the *ketonet* they meant, the picture robe, the veil. It must come off, and that was not so easy, for it was wound about him and fastened at head and shoulder; and they were too many for the deed. They got in each other's way; one thrust another away from the victim as he flew and fell and bounded among them. The blows meant for him showered upon themselves—though he received plenty as well. His nose bled almost at once, and one eye was closed with a great blue weal.

But the confusion served Reuben's ends, as he towered among them shrieking 'Down, down,' with the rest. He used the immemorial tactics of those who wish to control a savage mob and keep a grip upon the course of events; he took part with apparent zeal in the fray, in order to prevent the worst from coming to pass. He dealt out blows while feigning to receive them, all the while cuffing and pushing those nearest Joseph, protecting him as best he might when they were about to strike him and tear off his robe. He aimed particularly at Levi on account of the crook in his hands; blundering against it as often as he could. But despite all Reuben's manœuvres, Joseph was served worse than the petted youth could ever have dreamed possible. He reeled, half-dazed, with his head drawn down between his shoulders, and his elbows spread against the hailstorm of brutality descending out of a blue sky, which horribly seemed not to care where it struck, but beat down upon him, utterly demolishing his trust, his whole notion of the world, his conviction that everybody must love him more than themselves, as though it were a law of nature.

'Brothers,' he stammered, with the blood streaming down his chin from his nose and his bruised lips. 'What are you——' A rude blow, which Reuben failed to fend off, knocked the words from his mouth. Another, landing in the pit of the stomach, between the ribs, made him collapse and disappear beneath the pack. I cannot deny, rather I must emphatically say, that this uprising

of the sons of Jacob, however much justice they had on
their side, was a most shameful relapse into savagery.
They sank below the level of the human, and availed
themselves of their teeth, being otherwise busy with their
hands, to tear his mother's garment from the body of the
bleeding, reeling lad. They were not dumb at the work,
they said other things besides 'Down, down, down!'
They were like labourers pulling and heaving and with
monotonous cries subduing themselves to the common
task: bringing up broken words out of the depths of their
hate, to feed their rage and stave off thought. 'Bow
down, bow down, thou sayest?' 'Look after things,
wilt thou, thou thorn in the flesh, thou lingering sickness!
Take that for thy dreams.' And their unhappy victim?

To him, the most horrible and incredible thing of all
was what happened to the *ketonet*. That was worse,
crueller, even, than all this howling horror about him.
Desperately he tried to protect the garment, and keep
the remnants and ruins of it still upon him. Several
times he cried out: 'My coat! my coat!' and even after
he stood naked still begged them like a girl to spare it.
Yes, he was naked, for not only had the violence of the
brothers' onslaught torn off the veil, but shift, loin cloth,
and myrtle wreath lay in tatters beside it on the moss;
while blows rained down upon his naked flesh and he
sought as best he could to ward them off with his arms.
'Bow down, bow down! Take that for thy dreams!'
Big Reuben did what he could to keep them off by behav-
ing as though the others prevented him from coming at
the victim and dealing his blows. 'Thou thorn in the
flesh, thou lingering sickness!' he cried out with the rest.
But also he cried out something else, which occurred
to him on the spur of the moment; cried it loud and
repeatedly, in order that they might all hear it and be
guided in their blind rage: 'Bind him, bind him! Tie

his hands and feet!' It was a new suggestion, invented in haste to a good end: namely, to set a definite goal to this otherwise incalculable business and introduce a breathing space, in which big Reuben, as he feverishly prayed, might avert the worst. They would not strike Joseph while they were busy binding him; and when he lay bound that would be a temporary gratification, a stage at which they might stand off and consider what next. Such was Reuben's hasty calculation. And thus with desperate zeal he proposed his expedient, as though he were indicating the one and only useful and reasonable plan and as though any one was a fool who did not hearken to it. 'There—that for thy dreams!' he shrieked. 'Bind him —bind him! You fools! What a senseless revenge! Instead of hitting me bind him. Is there no rope?' he cried once more with all his strength.

Yes, Gaddiel for one wore a length round his waist; and he took it off. As their heads were empty there was room in them for Reuben's words. They bound the naked lad, bound his arms and legs with one long piece of cord, trussed him up properly while he moaned and groaned; and Reuben assisted zealously at the work. When it was done, he stepped back and wiped off his sweat with a gasp, as if he had worked harder than any.

The others stood there, their lust for battle slaked for the present; panting, inactive, dazed. Before them lay Rachel's son, in grievous state. He lay on his bound arms, with the back of his head buried in the grass, his knees drawn up stiffly, his ribs going in and out, all bludgeoned. Moss and dirt clung to his body, it was slobbered with the foam of his brothers' fury, and across it ran in winding streams the red juice which gushes out of beauty when its surface is marred. His undamaged eye now gazed terror-struck at his murderers, now closed spasmodically in a reflex action against fresh violence.

The evil-doers stood getting their wind; they exaggerated their breathlessness in order to cover the lack of counsel, of which, as reason returned, they were slowly aware. They, like Reuben, wiped off their sweat with the backs of their hands; they puffed out their lips and made faces expressive of justified revenge, as who should say: 'Whatever we have done, can any reproach us for it?' They said the same in words. They panted out words justifying themselves in each other's eyes or before any court in the world: 'Cuckoo! Thorn in the flesh! But we have shown him, we have cast him out!' 'Could one credit it? Cometh here—here before us, in his coat —before our eyes—to look after things—but we 've looked after them—so he 'll not forget it!' and all the while there was stirring within them a horror and shuddering, which all their words were meant to quiet. And if the horror and shuddering were looked at nearly, it would turn out to be—the thought of Jacob.

Great God, what had they done with the father's lamb —to what state had they brought the youthful heir of the departed Rachel? How would the master of words behave when he knew or learned it, how would they stand before him and what would happen to them? Reuben thought of Bilhah. Simeon and Levi thought of Shechem and of Jacob's wrath and how he had come down upon them when they returned from their heroic deeds. Naphtali, Naphtali especially, found it a present consolation that Jacob was five days away and entirely unsuspecting. Yes, for the first time, Naphtali realized as a blessing the power of space, which separates and spares. But they all realized that the blessing could not be preserved. Jacob must presently hear all. When Joseph came again before his eyes, the storm of emotion, the rolling thunder of his words, the flashing lightning of his curses—the brethren could not escape nor yet

endure them.   Grown up as they were, they were fright-
ened like children, possessed with the fear of the curse, in
itself, and in all its meaning and consequence.   Cursed
they would be, one and all, because they had raised their
hand against the lamb; and now the young hypocrite
would definitely be exalted above them as the chosen heir.
They would actually have themselves to thank for the
fulfilment of those shameful dreams; precisely that which
God willed would have been brought about by this accomplished fact.   They perceived that big Reuben had made
fools of them with his advice.   Here they stood, and
there lay the thief of the blessing; pretty well punished
indeed, and bound—but was that really an accomplished
fact?   It would be different if Joseph never did come
before his father's eyes again: if something final and
conclusive happened to him.   The calamity and the
lamentation would be even greater, of course—too great
to think on.   But—somehow or other—it would pass.
Stopping half-way, even so they were guilty.   If they
went on they needed not to be.   All this went through
their heads as they stood—through Reuben's too.   He
could not help recognizing the situation.   He had
brought the brawl to a halt with a shrewdness which
came from his heart.   But his reason told him that too
much had happened for it to stop there.   That more had
to happen, and yet on no account and at no price must
happen—this it was which made him giddy.   Big
Reuben's sinewy features had never before worn that
baffled, sullen look.

Each moment he feared they would voice the inevitable
—and he had no answer.   Then they voiced it, and he
heard.   One of them said it—no matter who, since they
must all be thinking the same thing: 'He must away.'

'Away,' nodded Reuben with grim confirmation.
'Thou sayest it.   But thou sayest not where.'

'Away altogether,' answered the voice. 'He must go down into the pit, and be no more. Long time he ought not to have been; now certainly he must be no more.'

'I agree,' responded Reuben with bitter scorn. 'And then come we before Jacob, his father, without him. "Where is the boy?" he will ask. "He is no more," we answer. But if he ask: "Why is he no more," then we answer: "We have killed him."'

They were silent.

'No,' said Dan, 'not so. Brothers, hear me, I am called serpent and otter and a certain subtlety is not to be denied me. Thus will we do. We will put him in the pit, down in the dry well here, half choked, in which is no water. There lieth he in safety and put away; and will see what his dreams bring him to. But before Jacob we must lie and speak with assurance: "We have not seen him and know not whether he still is or is not. If not, then in any case a ravening beast hath devoured him, oh, woe, alas!" We must add "Oh, woe" for the sake of the lie.'

'Be quiet,' said Naphtali, 'he lieth close at hand and heareth us.'

'No matter,' answered Dan. 'He will tell no one. That he heareth it is one reason more that he may not go from here; even before that he could not, but now everything goeth together. We can speak as we like before him, for he is already as good as dead.'

A cry came from Joseph, he wailed out of his breast, stretched taut under his bonds, on which the tender red nipples stood out. He wept.

'Can you hear it and not pity?' Reuben asked.

'Of what avail is that, Reuben?' Judah answered him, 'and what talkest thou of pity, when the rest of us may feel it as well as thou? Doth his weeping in this hour blot it out that he hath been a shameless toad all his days and stunk to heaven, and hath supplanted us with the father with most shameless guile? Doth pity avail against necessity, and is it a good reason why he should go from hence and tell all? What good to talk of pity, even if it be felt? Hath he not already heard how we shall lie before Jacob? That is enough to end his life, that he hath heard it; and whether with or without pity Dan spoke the truth: he is as good as dead.'

'Thou art right,' said Reuben then. 'Let us throw him in the pit.'

Again Joseph wailed piteously.

'But he still weepeth,' one of them reminded them.

'Must he then not even weep?' cried Reuben. 'Let him go weeping into the pit; what more can you ask?'

I would fain pass over what was said next, for it would shock our modern taste and even glancingly put would place the brothers, or some of them, in an exceedingly bad light. The truth is that Simeon and Levi, as well as the downright Gad, offered to make an end of the lad without more ado. The twins wanted to do it with their staves, hitting out with the full strength of their arms, as Cain had done, until he was no more. But Gad asked to be given the job of cutting his throat quickly with the knife, as Jacob had once done with the kid whose skin he needed for the blessing-barter. That these suggestions were made is undeniable; but I am not anxious that the reader should be finally disgusted with the sons of Jacob, therefore I will not put their thoughts into precise words. They uttered them because those things had to be said; because, so to speak, they lay in the nature of the business. Besides, it was only natural that those best suited to the role were they who expressed their readiness and so conformed to their myth on earth, namely, the savage twins and the stout Gad.

But Reuben opposed. It is known that he opposed,

and would not have it happen to Joseph as it had to Abel or to the kid. 'To that I will not agree,' he said, protesting in his character as Leah's eldest, which despite fall and curse entitled him to a voice. The boy was as good as dead, they had said so themselves. He was only sobbing a little still, it would suffice to throw him in the pit. Let them look at him and say whether that was still Joseph the dreamer. He was already unrecognizable from the punishment, in which he, Reuben, had taken part, and would have done more had he not been struck from all sides. But what had happened had been just a happening, it was not an act, not a deed, you could not call it so. It had come about, indeed, through them, but they had not done it, it had simply happened to them. Now, however, they were deliberately proposing, of set purpose, to commit a crime and raise their hands against the boy; they were about to spill their father's blood, whereas up to now it had only flowed. And that was a world-wide difference, it was all the difference between an act and an occurrence; and if they did not see that, then they were short in their understanding. Were they, he asked, appointed judges of life and death, to judge in their own matter and then carry out the blood decree as well? No, there should be no shedding of blood, he would not endure it. What remained to them to do, after what had occurred, was to put the boy into the pit and leave the rest to happen.

Thus big Reuben, but nobody believed that he was deceiving himself or that he was so stoutly convinced of the hard and fast difference between happening and doing. Or that he did not see that putting Joseph in the pit would be the same as killing him. After a while Jehudah asked him what it would avail to kill the boy and conceal his blood; the question told Reuben nothing new. For all along we have looked into Reuben's heart and seen that his great desire was to gain time. He could not have said for what: simply time to feed the hope that he might save Joseph out of the brethren's hands and somehow bring him back to his father. It was his fear of Jacob which actuated him, as well as his crabbed and shamefaced love of the culprit; they drove him to conceal his thoughts and meditate treason against the clan—for it could be called nothing else. Moreover, Reuben the unstable had manifold sins to atone for in Jacob's eyes, on account of Bilhah. What if he brought Joseph safe home? Would not then the ancient wrong be more than made good, the curse lifted, and his primogeniture be restored? I do not profess to understand all Reuben's thoughts and actions, nor would I minimize the motives of his deeds. But need it belittle them to guess that in his secret heart he hoped both to save and to vanquish Rachel's son?

In any case his words met with scarcely any opposition from the brothers. They were willing to refrain and to let events decide. Probably they would have preferred that the 'happenings' should have continued and led in one blind thrust to the goal they sought. But to continue deliberately and to shed blood, to 'act' now that a pause for reflection had intervened—nobody wanted to do that, not even the twins, however savage, nor yet Gaddiel, no matter how stoutly he spoke. They were all glad, indeed, that their offer about bludgeons and knives had not been taken up, but that Reuben's authority should prevail again; first the tying up, now the pit.

'Into the pit,' was the word. They seized the cord which bound Joseph, caught hold here and there, and dragged the poor wretch across the field towards the pit at the edge of the pasture land. Some dragged in front, some tugged at the sides, the rest ran behind. Reuben did not run but moved with a long stride at the tail of the convoy; when a stone lay in the way, a gnarled root or stump or a prickly shrub, he lifted the poor soul that he might not suffer needless pain.

So it was off with Joseph to the pit, with a hey and a ho, for as they went a fury of merriment seized upon the brethren, the animal spirits of men working in unison. They laughed and joked and shouted nonsense to each other; as that this was a sheaf, which had been well bound, and now should bow itself into the pit, into the well, into the depths. In all this they were venting the relief they felt at not being impelled to follow the pattern represented by Abel and the kid. Besides, it drowned the sound of Joseph's prayers and lamentations: 'Brothers! Have pity!' he mumbled with his bruised mouth. 'What is it you do? Stop, stop! Woe, alas, what will befall me?'

His moans helped him not at all; on they went at a trot, through bush and grass, a long way across country to a mossy slope. Here some steep, broken steps led down to a walled-in bottom, paved with cracked flags. The air was cool, and oak scrub and fig-trees grew out of the ruined walls. They dragged Joseph down the steps, he struggling desperately in their arms and against his bonds, for he shuddered at the thought of the well that was there and from the hole of the well, but even more at the broken, mossy well stone that lay on the flags and was meant to lay over the top. But let him struggle and weep as he might, his unclosed eye directed in horror into the blackness of the well, they hoisted him to the brink with a heave ho, and tipped him in, to fall who knew how far!

It was far enough, though not an abyss, not a bottomless pit. Such wells often reach a hundred feet and more down, but this one had been long out of use and choked with earth and broken stone—perhaps on account of old quarrels about the place. It was no more than five or six fathoms deep, if that. Certainly too much to climb out of with bound limbs. But he fell with as much care

for life and limb as he could, braking here and there with
feet and elbows against the wall, and moderating his fall
to a slipping which landed him fairly sound among the
rubbish at the bottom, to the discomfiture of all sorts of
beetles, wood lice, and other crawling things. While
he was collecting himself, the brethren did the rest,
shouting as they lifted the stone at the top and heaved it
into place. It was heavy—not one man's work to roll it
on top of the pit; so they all laid hold and shared in the
task. For the ancient stone, all green with moss and full
five feet across, was split into two halves; and when they
had rolled each into place the two did not meet but
gaped; and through the uneven gap some light fell into
the hole. Joseph looked up at it with his one eye as he
lay huddled anyhow, naked and exposed, in the depths.

Their task being done, the brothers sat down on the
steps of the well chamber to rest; some drew bread and
cheese out of their girdles and ate. Levi, religious in all
his savagery, bade them remember indeed that one should
not eat at the shedding of blood, but they answered him
that what they had done was to avoid bloodshed. Upon
which, Levi ate too.

They ruminated as they chewed. For the moment
their thoughts were occupied with sensations which,
though of little importance, yet altogether possessed them:
their hands and arms, that is, bore the memory of the
contact with Joseph's bare skin, as they dragged him to
his doom. No matter how ungentle the contact had
been, now that it was all over it gave them a retrospective
feeling of tenderness which was very strong, however
little they understood what it meant.

Nobody gave expression to it by so much as a syllable; and what they said concerned only the fact that Joseph was now safely out of the way, together with his dreams; and that they were greatly lightened thereby.

'Now he is no more,' said they.   That was done; now they could sleep; they could sleep in peace, they repeated, the more emphatically the more uncertain they felt about it.   It might be true with regard to the dreamer who was gone and could tell the father nothing.   But the thought failed to soothe, or it reminded them of the father waiting in vain for Joseph's home-coming—eternally in vain. Such a picture, however much security it afforded, in no way invited to slumber.   For all the ten, including the savage twins, it was a picture full of horror.   Their childish fear of Jacob and of the tenderness and power of his soul was clear and lively.   True, Joseph would never be able to accuse them.   But they had bought their security by means of an offence against their father's emotions which it terrified them to realize.   What they had done to Joseph had its cause in jealousy; but we all know what feeling it is which suffers this distortion.   It seems hardly convincing, looking at the slick brutality of the twins, to ascribe any such feeling to them; and it is precisely on this ground that I do not make any positive statements.   There are cases where only half-words will serve.

So they mused and blinked as they chewed, feeling on hands and arms the memory of the softness of Joseph's flesh.   Their reflections were not light, and they were further weighted by the wails and entreaties that rose faintly out of the pit.   After the fall he had so far gathered himself together as to realize the need of crying out, and he implored them from below:

'Brothers, where are you?   Ah, go not away, leave me not alone in the pit.   It is so earthy and so horrible. Brothers, have pity and save me out of the night of this pit where I perish. I am your brother Joseph. Brothers, hide not your ears from my sighs and cryings, for you do falsely to me. Reuben, where art thou? Reuben, I cry thy name from below in the pit. You have all misunderstood, you have misunderstood, dear brothers, so help me, please, and save my life. I came to you on our father's account five days' journey on Hulda the white ass, to bring you presents, ears of corn and fruit cakes, ah, how it hath all gone wrong! The man is to blame that it went wrong, the man who led me. Brothers in Jacob, hearken and understand me, I came not to you to see how things were, for I am but a child. I came to bow before you with decorum and the forms of courtesy and to ask after your welfare, that you should return home to our father. Brothers! the dreams . . . was I so unmannerly as to relate my dreams? Believe me, I have only told quite modest dreams in comparison with what I could have, but it was not this I wanted to say. Oh, oh, my bones, my sinews right and left, and all my limbs! I thirst, brothers, the child thirsteth, for he has lost much blood and all through a mistake. Are ye yet there? Am I already quite forsaken? Reuben, let me hear thy voice. Tell them that I will say nothing if they will but spare my life. Brothers, I know you think you must leave me in the pit, otherwise I would tell. But by the God of Abraham, God of Isaac, God of Jacob, by the heads of your mothers and by Rachel's head, my little mother's, I swear that I will not tell for ever and ever, if you let me out of the pit but this one time.'

'He would tell, of a certainty, if not to-day, then to-morrow,' muttered Judah between his teeth; and there was none who did not share this view, Reuben not excepted, however much it might conflict with his wavering hopes and plans. But so much the more must he keep these secret and assert the contrary; therefore he hollowed his hands about his mouth and called:

'If thou art not quiet we will throw down stones upon thee that shall kill thee entirely, for we will hear no more of thee, thou art sped.'

When Joseph heard this and recognized Reuben's voice, he was terrified and ceased to speak, and they might sit undisturbed and taste their fear of Jacob. Of course, if they had meant to prolong their self-imposed exile and live in lasting discord with their father, then they need not have troubled themselves over the agony of waiting and long despair which was hovering over Jacob's head. But the truth was exactly the opposite. The casting away of Joseph could serve only one purpose: that of removing the obstacle between them and the father's heart. Upon that they were childishly bent. The trouble was that they had been driven to extremes in order to win this soft but mighty heart for their own. This was the point of view from which at all times they saw the affair. Not punishment of Joseph's presumption, they were of one mind in thinking, nor yet revenge, nor even, in the first instance, the obliteration of the dreams, was their main concern. What they thought of was how to smooth their path to their father's heart. This now was done, and they would return—without Joseph, as they had set out. Where was he? He had been sent after them. And thus sent, to those who by their departure had demonstrated that they could not endure him, and their return without him would look very suspicious. Certainly Jacob would have an awful right to question them. They might shrug their shoulders in reply. Were they their brother's keepers? Of course not; but the answer would not satisfy Jacob's piercing, mistrustful gaze which he would direct upon them relentlessly, while they continued to be witnesses of his

tortured expectancy and of the prolonged despair which
in the nature of things must be its only issue.   It was a
penance before which they quailed.   On the other hand,
were they to stop away until all hope had died and waiting
had given way to the knowledge that Joseph would never
return?   That would last long, for the stout-hearted
can bear long suspense, and besides, in the meantime, the
question might easily answer itself and become a curse
for them all.   No, it was clear that they must once and
for all establish the fact that Joseph would not come back;
that alone could clear their skirts.   Their minds were
all busy with these thoughts, but the snake-and-otter
Dan formulated a proposal.   He combined his own earlier
idea of telling the old man that a wild beast had killed
Joseph with Gad's reminder of the kid which Jacob had
killed to obtain the blessing; and he said:

'Hear me, brothers, for I have power to judge and I
know what we should do.   For we shall take a beast
of the flock and cut its throat and let the blood run out.
But in the blood of the beast we shall dip the accursed
thing, the coat of many colours, Rachel's bridal garment
that lieth all in rags.   Let us bring it before Jacob and say
to him: "This have we found on the ground, torn and
covered with blood.   Is it not thy son's garment?"
Then may he draw his conclusion from the state of the
garment and it will be as when a shepherd showeth to
the master the remains of the sheep that a lion hath slain;
thus is he cleansed and needeth not to swear himself free
from guilt.'

'Hush,' muttered Judah, shuddering.   'For he can
hear what you say under the stone and can understand
what we shall do.'

'What harm in that?' Dan retorted.   'Shall I whisper
and mutter for his sake?   It has naught to do with his
life; it is our affair but no longer his.   Thou forgettest

that he is as good as dead and done for. When he hath understood that and also this, that I now say with my natural voice, then everything is settled. Never have we been able to speak freely and without caution when he was amongst us, for we well knew that he would tell the father and then we had to pay. But now at last we have him amongst us as our brother, whom we trust and who may hear everything we say—it maketh me to feel that I should like to throw a kiss to him there in the pit. But what think you all of my idea?'

They were about to speak; but Joseph lifted up his voice once more, imploring them from the pit not to do it.

'Brothers,' he cried, 'do not that with the beast and the robe, treat not the father so, for he will not survive it. Ah, I beg you not for myself, for body and soul are broken in me and I lie in the grave. But spare our father and bring him not the bloody garment—it would kill him. Ah, had you heard how he warned me in his anxiousness about the lion, when he found me alone by night, and now it will be that a lion hath eaten me! Had you seen the care with which he prepared me for the journey while I indifferently endured his concern! Woe is me, it is most likely unwise that I speak to you of his love of me, but what shall I do, dear brothers, and how counsel myself that I do not vex you? Why, after all, is my life involved with his, that I cannot adjure you to spare his without begging for my own? Ah, dear brothers, hear my weeping and do no violence to his suffering by showing him the bloody robe, for his gentle soul will bear it not and he will be stricken to the earth.'

'Nay,' Reuben said, 'that is more than I can stand, it is unbearable.' He stood up. 'Let us move further away, if you like; one cannot talk with him wailing, nor think for his crying out of the depths. Come to the

huts.' He said it angrily, they might think he had gone
pale with rage. But actually his pallor was due to his
having agreed in his heart with what the boy had said.
He too realized that Jacob, at sight of the robe, would
literally be struck to the earth. But more than that,
Joseph's words had impressed it upon Reuben that the
lad, in his hour of need, was mindful of their father and
pleaded with the brethren in his behalf and for himself
only for the father's sake. But was he perhaps pretending
as of old? No, no, this time it was different. This was
another Joseph, who cried out from beneath the stone,
from the one whom he once had shaken by the shoulder
to awaken him from vanity and folly. What the shaking
had not achieved the fall into the pit had done; Joseph was
aroused, he pleaded for the father-heart, he mocked
no more but felt distress and remorse. The discovery
strengthened big Reuben's vacillating purpose, while at
the same time it made him more acutely sensitive of its
helpless and hopeless character.

Thence his pallor, as he got up and suggested to them
all to go with him away from the place where Joseph was
buried. They followed him, they went from thence, to
gather up the rags of the veil on the spot of the beating,
to bring them to the tents and there to take counsel over
Dan's idea. So Joseph was left alone.

His soul was anguished to remain alone in the grave;
for some time he wailed after the brothers and implored
them not to leave him. Yet he scarcely knew what
he cried out; his actual thoughts were not with these
mechanical and superficial prayers and lamentations but far
below them, while lower down again were others yet more

real, like their undertones and ground basses, so that the whole was like a moving music, perpendicularly composed, which his spirit was occupied in conducting on all three levels. This preoccupation was what caused him to commit the blunder of saying to the brethren that he had only told them comparatively modest dreams, considering those others which he had also dreamed. No one in his right senses could even for a moment think that the remark was calculated to soften their hearts; but an absent and preoccupied mind might have done so, and thus it was with Joseph.

Much had gone on within him, even since that astonishing and horrible moment when the brethren fell upon him like wolves and he had looked into their faces distorted by fury and hate, out of the eye which they had not closed at once with their fists. Their faces had been very near to him while with nails and teeth they tore the picture robe from his body—frightfully near; and the hatred which he had read therein had been the greatest torture and the main cause of the horror he felt at the onslaught. Certainly he had quaked with fear and wept for pain under their blows; but fear and pain were quite permeated with the pity he felt for the torturing hatred which he read in the mask-like faces, dripping with sweat, that rose and fell and were thrust into his own. But pity for a pain, the source of which we must recognize to be ourselves, comes close to being remorse. Reuben's intuition had been quite right: this time Joseph had been so rudely shaken that his eyes were opened and he saw what he had done—and that he had done it. While he was flung hither and thither among their raging fists; while his robe was torn off; while he lay bound, and during his penitential journey to the well house, amid all his daze of horror his thoughts had never once stood still. They had not paused upon the frightful present, but

sped back over a past in which all this, hidden from his
blissful self-conceit though partly and shamelessly known
to it, had the while been preparing itself.

My God, the brothers! To what had he brought
them? For he did understand that he had brought them
to this: through manifold and great mistakes which he
had committed in assuming that everybody loved him more
than themselves—this assumption, which he believed and
yet did not actually quite believe, but according to which
he had always acted and which had brought him, as he
now clearly and distinctly recognized, to the pit. In the
brothers' distorted and sweating masks he had read clearly
with his one eye, that this assumption had become un-
endurable, and over a long period had strained their souls
and given them great suffering, until now at last the final
issue had been reached in this end, so frightful for him
and doubtless for them too.

Alas, poor brothers! What must they have borne
before in desperation they laid hold on the father's lamb
and actually threw it into the pit! Into what a state
had they thereby brought themselves—to say nothing of
his own, which was hopeless, as he shudderingly confessed to himself. It was not credible that he would hold
his tongue if he were restored to his father. He could
never make them believe it, he could not believe it. And
so they must leave him in the grave, to perish there, there
was nothing else for it. This he saw; yet wonderful to
say, horror at his own impending fate left room in his
soul for pity for his murderers. We know this to be true.
Joseph was quite aware, he admitted it to himself openly
and honourably as he sat at the bottom of the well, that
the unashamed presumption which had been the guiding
principle of his life had been a game in which he himself
had not seriously believed nor could have done; that, for
one thing, he ought never to have told his brothers his

dreams. It had been impossibly and incredibly tactless. He even realized that he had actually known this all the time—and yet he had done it. Why? That he did not know. Apparently, that he might be destroyed. But at the bottom of his heart Joseph did not believe it. Privately he was convinced that God looked further than the pit, that He bore far-reaching things in mind as usual and had His eye upon some distant purpose, in the service of which he, Joseph, had been made to drive the brethren to extremities. They were being sacrificed to the future, and he suffered for them, however badly things went with himself. They would send their father the robe, unhappy man, after they had dipped it in the blood of the kid in lieu of his own; and Jacob would be struck to the earth. At the thought Joseph was moved to start up, to protect his father from the sight—with the only result, of course, that torn with pain as if by wild beasts he sank back in his bonds against the stones of the well, and began once more to weep.

He had an agony of leisure in which to weep, to feel remorse and pity; and, despairing of his life, yet in his inmost being to believe in the wise and healing future purposes of God. For, frightful as it is to think of it, he was to remain three days in the pit, three days and nights in his bonds, naked and exposed, in mud and dirt, among crawling worms, without bite or sup, without consolation or any reasonable hope of ever reaching the light again. I, who tell it, must take care to paint it as it was, to make clear what it meant for Jacob's little son, who had never imagined that fate could be so harsh: how dismally the hours passed, till his scrap of daylight died in the crack between the stones and a pitying star sent down its diamond ray into the grave; how the pale dawn twice came, abode, and went again; how he constantly peered up in the twilight at the round

walls of his house to see whether there were footholds
in the broken wall, or crevices made by pushing roots—
but his bonds, and the stone well cover, each by itself
and certainly together, nipped every hope in the bud;
how he twisted himself about in the cords to find an easier
posture, which quickly became even worse than the
other; how thirst and hunger tortured him and the
emptiness of his stomach gave him burning sensations in
his back; how, like the sheep, he soiled himself with his
own filth and therein nestled and shivered till his teeth
chattered. I am greatly concerned to give a lively and
exact picture of this all-embracing unpleasantness; at
the same time I must be careful to cling to reality and
not let my imagination get the upper hand and lose itself
in empty emotion. Reality is sober—precisely in its
character as reality. At grips with the actual and undeniable, driven to an understanding with it, reality
insists upon our suiting ourselves to the circumstances
and adapting us without loss of time. We are easily
persuaded to call a situation unbearable. Our easily
roused humanity protests indignantly, and that probably
does the sufferer good; but it becomes a little absurd
in the face of the *really* intolerable. The sympathetic
friend's relation to this reality, which is, of course, not his
own, is an unreal and sentimental one. He commits
an error of the imagination, for the sufferer, thanks to his
suffering, is in a different category. What do we really
mean by the unbearable, when there is nothing to be done
but bear it so long as we are in our senses?

But young Joseph had not been entirely and clearly in
his senses for a long time; not since the moment when
the brethren had turned into wolves before his eyes.
The storm which then broke over him had numbed him
very much, effecting those palliations which the unbearable needs in order to be borne. The beatings he had

received had dulled his feelings, as had that unbelievable conveyance into the well. His situation was certainly desperate, but at least it had put a period to those frightful shocks, and produced a sort of equilibrium. However objectionable his present state, it had the advantage of security. Buried in the womb of the earth, he needed not to fear further violence and had time to pursue his labouring thoughts—for these at times almost made him forget his physical sufferings and dangers. And his security (if we may use the word with reference to almost certain death—but why not, since death is at all times certain and yet we feel secure?), his feeling of security, then, inclined him to sleep. His exhaustion was so great that it outweighed all else. He fell asleep, and through long stretches of time knew little or nothing of himself. When he roused, his astonishment at the refreshment which the sleep had brought (for food and sleep can for a while replace each other) mingled with a fresh sense of horror that he was still in the pit and still in misery. Even in sleep he did not entirely lose the sense of misery: but its worst rigours did as it were manage to relax a little. The bonds were hard, the cramped position still endured; but even they began to relax, on the second and third days the cords had given way a little and yielded to the needs of the poor tortured limbs. I say all this, once more, to confront our sympathy with the solid reality of facts. But on the other hand, if I add that Joseph was, of course, growing weaker all the time, it will serve to keep our pity from quite dying out, even though I must add that his very weakness was an amelioration of his sufferings. From this point of view one might almost say that the longer his stay in the pit lasted the more tolerable it was; so that by the end he was scarcely aware of his own misery.

But his thoughts worked on and on, the body almost

forgotten. It was as though, in the piece of music which
we have imagined them to represent, those undertones
and basses at the bottom came out stronger and stronger,
thanks to that dreamy weakness of his, until at last they
almost drowned out the overtones. So long as the
brethren were near, the fear of death had been apparent,
as expressed in his urgent entreaties and wailings. But
now they were gone, the cries had died away, why was it
that Joseph did not shout in hopes of a chance rescue?
Because he quite forgot to, absorbed as he was in far
other trains of thought, having to do with his abrupt
downfall, with the past and its errors, perhaps ordained
by God but not on that account less heavy and grievous.

The garment which the brothers had torn off his body
—partly with their teeth, shocking to say—played a
prominent role in his reflections. That he ought not
to have spread himself in it before them, nor made his
ownership visible to their eyes; above all things, that he
ought not to have appeared before them in it here and
now, came over him so forcibly that he could have beat
himself on the head but for his bonds. He did so in
spirit; but even so he had to confess to himself the futility
and curious hypocrisy of the gesture; for now he saw
that he had always understood the whole thing and
yet had so behaved. With amazement he contemplated
the riddle of self-destructive arrogance presented to him
by his own extraordinary behaviour. His wits could not
cope with the riddle successfully—nor can any one's.
Perhaps because so much of the incalculable is implicit
therein, so much that is contrary to reason and even perhaps
holy. How he had trembled lest Jacob should discover
the *ketonet* in the bag—trembled, that is, before his own
salvation! He had deceived his father, taken advantage
of the old man's failing memory, and packed the *ketonet*;
but not because he had disagreed with the father as to the

effect which the sight of the veil would have upon the brothers. He had understood perfectly, and had packed it none the less. How could he have done so? Again, since he had not forgotten to provide for his own destruction—why had Jacob forgotten to prevent it? Another puzzle. Joseph's desire to smuggle the coat could not have been stronger than the father's loving concern that he should leave it at home. Why had not love and anxiety been strong enough to remind the old man and so to foil Joseph's plan? Joseph had succeeded in beguiling away the rich garment from Jacob's tent; it was partly because they were playing a game with each other, partly because Jacob wanted the child to have the robe quite as much as the latter desired it. The consequences followed promptly. Together they had brought the lamb to the pit and now Jacob would be struck to earth.

But after that, he might well bethink him of the mistakes of the past, common to them all — just as Joseph was now doing. The boy was honest with himself: he admitted that he had forsworn himself when he said he would say nothing to Jacob if the brothers released him. The promise had been born of fear; Joseph knew that if the old state of things were restored— which with some part of his being he ardently desired— he must unavoidably tell all, and the brethren would suffer the consequences. Restoration was out of the question; but even if it were not, he was in a way at one with the brethren in not wishing for it. He could almost have returned the kiss which Dan had wanted to throw to him in the pit, so much did he feel that for the first time he was really among them as their brother and might hear all that they said: might even hear that about the blood of the kid which should pass for his blood; it did not matter, since he was as good as dead and buried already.

A strong impression had been made upon Joseph by what Dan had said: that every word uttered was like a nail in his coffin, and that it was good to utter them, since each one bound him more firmly to the lower world, and made of him more and more a ghost before whom one shudders. Joseph saw in such words the reversal and negation of the role which he had played so far in life, that of needing to heed nobody because all the world loved him more than they did themselves. For it was come to this, that no one heeded him at all! The thought conditioned those undertones and basses of his composition, and the weaker he became the more did they sonorously predominate over the upper tones.

But they had begun to play, even earlier; at the moment when the undreamed-of became reality; when his provocative conduct had called down punishment and he was tossed to and fro like a toy amongst the brethren and they had torn the picture robe with their nails and teeth. From that moment on, then, they had been vocal; in the midst of that hail of horrifying blows his ear had in good part hearkened to them. It would be wrong to suppose that under such deadly serious circumstances Joseph had stopped playing and dreaming—if one may still speak of his activity as playing and dreaming in this connection. He was a true son of Jacob, the man of thoughts and dreams and mystical lore, who always understood what happened to him, who in all earthly events looked up to the stars and always linked his life to God's. Granted that Joseph's way of dignifying his life by attaching it to the higher law and reality was not the same as Jacob's, less spiritual, more shrewdly calculating; yet he seriously held that a life and activity without the hall mark of higher reality, which does not base upon the traditionally sacred and support itself thereupon, nor is able to mirror itself in anything heavenly and recognize itself therein, is no life or activity at all. He was convinced that nothing in the lower world would know how to happen or be thought of, without its starry prototype and counterpart; and the great certainty guiding his life was belief in the unity of the dual, in the fact of the revolving sphere, the exchangeability of above and below, one turning into the other and gods becoming men and men gods. Not for nothing was he the pupil of old Eliezer, who knew how to say 'I' in such an ample way that Joseph's eyes grew dim with musing as he beheld him. The transparency of being, the characteristic recurrence of the prototype—this fundamental creed was in his flesh and blood too, and all spiritual dignity and significance seemed to him bound up with awareness of it. That was as it should be. What was after all not quite as it should be, but seemed more like a degenerate deviation from the significant and admirable type, was Joseph's inclination to draw advantage from the general prepossession in his favour and consciously to impose himself upon those about him.

From the first moment on he was aware of all this. Incredible as it may seem, in the thick of the turmoil, in the acutest moment of fear and danger of death, he had kept his mental eye open to realities. Not that fear and danger grew less thereby; but he actually experienced a sort of joy as well; the pleasure of enlightenment, almost like the relief which laughter brings, had illuminated the dark terror in his soul.

'My coat!' he had cried out in the anguish of his concern, 'tear it not, I pray you.' Yes, they had rent it in pieces and torn it off him, that was his mother's robe and that belonged also to her son, so that they wore it by turns and became one, and god and goddess by its means. Mercilessly had the brethren unveiled him. As love unveils the bride in the bedchamber, thus had their fury done to him, and they had known him naked, so that his frame

quivered with the deathly shame. In his mind thoughts
of unveiling and of death dwelt close together—how
could he then have helped holding the rags of the garment
round him in his fright, begging them to tear it not?
Yet no more could he have helped being filled with the
joy of understanding, coming to him through association
of thought, through the conviction of repetition and
realization. No danger of the flesh and the soul could
prevent the concentration of his spirit upon the wealth
of allusion by which the event proclaimed itself as higher
reality, as a transparency of the ancient pattern, as the
uppermost turning undermost, in short, as written in
the stars. And his concentration was very natural, as the
allusions all had to do with being and selfhood, with the
vista of his ego which he had opened to Reuben a little
time ago to the latter's amaze, and which now was growing
brighter and brighter. He had wept and wailed when
big Reuben had given his voice that they should throw
him in the pit; yet at the same time his reason had laughed
as at a joke, the word used was so laden with allusions:
'Bôr' the brothers had said. And the monosyllable was
capable of various interpretations. It meant not only
well but prison, not only prison but the underworld, the
kingdom of the dead; so that prison and the underworld
were one and the same thought, one being only a word for
the other. Again, the well, in its property as entrance
to the underworld, likewise the round stone which covered
it, signified death; for the stone covered the round opening
as the shadow covers the dark moon. In Joseph's mind
the primeval prototype of the death of the planet peered
through the present event: the dead moon, which is
invisible for three days until its new birth, means the
death of the gods of light, who must for a time descend to
the underworld. When the horror happened, and the
brothers hoisted him on to the edge of the well and on to

the margin of the pit, so that he must descend below the daylight with all the caution he could muster—then his quick mind had clearly understood the allegory of the star which in the evening is a woman and in the morning a man and which sinks into the well of the abyss as evening star.

It was the abyss into which the true son descends, he who is one with the mother and wears the robe by turns with her. It was the subterranean sheepfold, Etura, the kingdom of the dead, where the son becomes the lord, the shepherd, the sacrifice, the mangled god. Mangled? They had torn not only his lips and his skin here and there, but the robe they had torn off and rent it with nails and teeth, those red murderers and conspirators, his brothers, and they would dip it in the blood of a kid, which should pass for his blood, and they would bring it before the father. God demanded from the father the sacrifice of the son, from the soft-hearted one who, shuddering, had confessed that he 'could not do it.' Poor man, he would have to do it, and it was like God that He paid little heed to what man thinks he can do.

Here Joseph wept in his transparent misery, presided over by his understanding. He wept over poor Jacob, who would have to summon his endurance, and over the brethren's confidence in his death. He wept for weakness and giddiness from the exhalations of the well; but the more lamentable his situation became in the course of the seventy-two hours which he spent here below, the more clearly the undertones of his thoughts came out, the more deceptively his present mirrored itself in its heavenly prototype; so that by the end he no longer distinguished the heavenly from the earthly at all and in the dreamy self-satisfaction of death saw only the unity of the double. We may with justice regard that as a device of nature to tide him over the unbearable. For the natural hope, to which life clings up to the last, needs a reasonable justification; and Joseph found it in this identification.   Indeed it extended beyond his life, his hope that he would finally not perish, but somehow be saved out of the pit.   For literally speaking he gave himself up for dead.   There was the brothers' evidence, there was the bloody robe, which Jacob would receive.   The pit was deep; and return to his former life was inconceivable—a thought as monstrous as that the evening star might return out of the abyss wherein it was sunk, and the shadow be withdrawn from the dark moon, that it should again be full.   But the conception of the death of the planet, the darkening and setting of the sun, whose habitation becomes the lower world, included likewise the idea of reappearance, new light, resurrection.   And therein Joseph's natural hope that he might live justified itself by faith.   It was not a hope that he might return out of the grave into his former life; yet by its means the grave was defeated.   Joseph cherished it not only for itself and for its own sake, but for the poor old man at home, whom he had brought down into the pit together with himself and who would be stricken to the earth. It would probably be after the son's death that Jacob would receive the bloody robe.   But if only the father could have faith beyond death according to the ancient hope, then, thought Joseph entombed, the blood of the beast would be taken, as once it had been, for the blood of the son.

EVERYMAN'S LIBRARY

A Selected List, arranged under Authors

Anthologies, composite works, etc., are given at the end of the list.

January 1959